The Van Gogh Woman

DEBBY BEECE

ARCHWAY PUBLISHING

Archway Publishing books may be ordered through booksellers or by contacting:

Archway Publishing
1663 Liberty Drive
Bloomington, IN 47403
www.archwaypublishing.com
844-669-3957

ISBN: 978-1-6657-2036-6 (sc)
ISBN: 978-1-6657-2035-9 (hc)
ISBN: 978-1-6657-2034-2 (e)

Library of Congress Control Number: 2022904862

Print information available on the last page.

Archway Publishing rev. date: 03/23/2022

*To my husband Larry May in thanks for his invaluable help,
and to Elizabeth, Sarah and Patrick May*

AMSTERDAM 1971

"Think what shuts you up, imagine what sets you free." I had been mulling over one of Uncle Vincent's more poignant self-reflections. Today I will be set free.

I pry from the wall a letter my mother had hung there, against my wishes, decades ago. I hated this news article, and I'd begged her to throw it in the fire.

> "Mrs. Van Gogh is charming enough, but it irritates me when someone gushes fanatically on a subject she understands nothing about, and although blinded by sentimentality still thinks she is adopting a strictly critical attitude. It is girlish twaddle, nothing more. The work that Mrs. Van Gogh would like best is the one that was the most bombastic and sentimental, the one that made her shed the most tears. She forgets that her sorrow is turning Vincent into a god."

"Shame is a wasted emotion," my mother would say. When I think of my family, I gasp with a flushing warmth. I've become an emotional old man. In this ancient office I see them all sitting in the bay window, young. I see myself as a child stepping between the most beautiful women in the world: my mother and Aunt Fleur. They both reach out to me and pet and coddle me until I squirm away, pretending. They loved me. This is what I remember from over six decades ago.

But my pair of guests are here, wearing eager but strained smiles to mask their confusion at this incongruous scene. A once-professional office, now neglected, broken down into storage spaces loaded with packed four-foot wooden crates. It is filthy with dust, dim too, with windows boarded up. These rooms hold treasure. And my guests have figured it out. The decades-old rumors in Amsterdam about hidden art, worth millions, are true and they are enthralled.

"I am Willem van Gogh, the nephew of Vincent van Gogh, and the son of Johanna Bonger and Theo van Gogh, Vincent's younger brother." They smile and nod in excitement at Vincent's name, Theo's too. Nothing but curious faces, raised eyebrows, at Johanna's name. They look to each other and nod out of politeness. This is part of what I need to change to be free.

"What an honor!" They are effusive, which is lovely. They are young, modern, but still tasteful.

They walk around the old offices, where Vincent's personal belongings, memorabilia, drawings, and unsold treasured paintings are now stored.

"You are looking at hundreds of paintings, drawings, sketches, letters, and Vincent's own collection of prints and paintings. And there is more in the basement, as well as my own personal collection. Here is the inventory. This is what I will gift to create the Van Gogh Museum." I want to be tantalizing but feel more like a circus barker. It isn't necessary. I see their eyes sparkle with excitement as I hand them the inventory list.

Elizabeth, the young woman, keeps her head tilted toward me, her eyes prying at the containers as she tries to read the lettering sideways and upside-down. Her hands instinctively reach for the tops as she walks by. The young man, Patrick, is more aggressive, to the point.

"Mr. Van Gogh, this storefront is housing millions of dollars' worth of art and history of Vincent van Gogh," Patrick says after looking at the inventory list. "Incredible," he says, his hands searching for a way to pry open an already-ajar crate, one I had prepared for this visit. "May I…"

"Here, let me," I say as I tug open the lid, as I had done countess times for my mother, decades ago.

"She had all these crates especially made by a local carpenter. She was very particular in storing." I stop speaking as my guests crowd around me, desperate for a peak in. "Too bad the light isn't—"

The young man reaches into the crate.

"No, don't!" she says, tugging on a pair of white cotton museum gloves used to protect art objects from hand oils. "We can't have any damage."

I know the crate well—still after so many years. I pull out the painting by the edge of the support without touching the image. They are both breathing heavily, and they bend down to stare closely at the painting. "Outstanding," breathes Elizabeth.

"I picked this one to show you," I say. It's one of his finest. "My mother saved this sunflower for the museum." In the light the thick impasto of yellow golds sparkles. It is most impressive.

"I heard rumors there was a family collection of van Goghs, but I could only dream this," says Elizabeth.

"It is a museum's worth, right here in this old horse of a building," I say proudly.

'Yes, Mr. Van Gogh, it certainly is. If you don't mind my asking, how did this all come to be?" asks Elizabeth.

"My mother, Johanna. This building used to be her family offices."

Johanna van Gogh-Bonger, again. I can see the young woman making a mental note. She will investigate Johanna. They might now hunt for her, but they won't find much.

Elizabeth walks behind the greeting desk, her hand lingering on the old wood. "Even the furnishings are lovely," she says, looking at the large desk with admiration.

She picks up a box of diaries my mother left me, still unopened, unread, in the same spot I left them, covered in decades of dust. "Ah, what is this treasure? *The Journals of Johanna van Gogh-Bonger.* Wow, may I look at these?"

An old memory is trying to shake loose. Was Johanna the final blow pushing Vincent to his dismal end? The woman who won Theo's heart and forever changed the history of the two brothers?

I extend my hand for the package of diaries, and she swallows and turns them over like a cache of stolen diamonds. I motion for them both to move to the sitting area in the front. She wants those journals.

"Would you prefer for us to take you out for tea or lunch?" asks the young man.

I wave my hand at the offer. After a moment of silence, I am ready.

"Did you ever wonder how Vincent, selling only one painting in his lifetime, dying in obscurity, could rise posthumously and within twenty years become a household name?"

They look at each other, and then smile back at me.

"My mother, Johanna."

PART 1

Amsterdam

1887

1

"I am chained to misfortune and failure and the more unfavorable outward circumstances become, the more inner resources are required ...the love of work increases. Life is not long for anybody, and the problem is only to make something of it."
    Vincent

Johanna

Inside the office Jo double checked her savings ledger. Eight years of teaching, six years of part-time translations into the six different languages she spoke, and the meager salary her father paid her for managing his back office at Bonger Insurance. She was proud, it was a good amount. The turn of the century was coming slowly here in Amsterdam, but culture was changing a decade faster in Paris, and she had to be there. Women lived on their own in Paris and pursued their choice of careers. Every woman with aspirations needed to move to Paris. She had enough money to get to Paris, sightsee and educate herself on the possibilities of life there.

In one ear she heard her brother Andries trying to get her attention. She threw him a quick smile and held up her pointer finger hoping he would give her a moment.

"Johanna?" Her brother sounded annoyed.

"What?" She looked up from her ledger. The numbers still repeated in front of her eyes as Andries's face came into focus.

"I have spoken to you about my good friend, Theo van Gogh. You remember?" She did remember because he was a fellow Dutchman who had moved to Paris and was involved with the arts.

"Yes, I remember. He's helping you begin an art collection. New art. You promised to show me the paintings."

"Theo wants to meet you. This afternoon if possible. He is here visiting his brother, but he'll be heading back to Paris in a few days."

"Mr. Van Gogh wants to meet me?" Jo was surprised. "Why?"

Her brother answered too fast. "I have no idea why." He sat with his legs crossed, weary. Andries was very handsome and smart, which he seemed to think entitled him to feel superior.

"Do you mean he wants a *personal* introduction…today?"

"Yes, Jo, like that."

"One day I hope you grow up," she said, and meant it.

"I know, I am working on it."

He was sarcastic again. She could just say no and end this inane conversation. "This is the man who convinced you to invest in modern art…you probably spent more shipping it here than acquiring it."

"Very funny."

Her family was worried about her, unmarried, still living at home, past twenty-five, with no regular man in her life. But she wasn't worried and wouldn't be made to feel guilty or inadequate because she hadn't met the right man. That was yesterday's sorry thinking.

She stood up behind the tall, carved-walnut counter at the Bonger Insurance Company, closed her ledger and placed it out of sight in her bag. Andries sat at the desk behind her. The clerks threw them glances, wondering what the future owner of Bonger Insurance was discussing with his sister. Women were still not allowed to inherit in this backward world.

"How does Mr. Van Gogh know of me?" Jo asked, this time

in Italian to confuse the workers. She was entitled to information despite Andries's stingy introduction.

"He saw your picture at my apartment in Paris. Last year's family portrait. He said you looked pretty and asked about your hair and eyes. I told him both were brown. You always look beautiful, Jo."

"Thank you, you do too," she said. "Do you have his photo?" She held out her hand.

With a flourish, he handed her a small pocket photo. She scanned it, careful not to let her face betray anything. Theo van Gogh seemed wooden in the photo, no smile, but that was common for photo portraits. "Why me? Why not a Parisian exotic?"

"I tried to warn him."

"Ha ha. Let's go out back and talk in private."

They stepped into the spacious alley where, on a nice day, the office workers gathered for breaks, lunch and fresh air. Late morning sun cut an angle into the alley as they stepped into the brightness. Andries stuffed a hand in his pocket and withdrew a hand-rolled cigarette. He rolled back and forth on his feet, heels to toes, which was his habit when annoyance was getting the better of him. He lit the cigarette –he was going to wait her out. She hated interference in her life.

She wondered if he was entirely comfortable with this arrangement, either. Sometimes he pursed his lips and drawing them back to a thin line of anger. Like when they were children and she and her best friend Fleur got into a schoolyard brawl, shouting at bullying boys and caught in a shoving match. She hated bullies and so did Fleur. It was almost always Andries who would break up the mess.

Jo cleared her throat and smiled at him, waiting for him to say something.

"I believe you will like him. His background is interesting. He is not the usual bourgeois type you avoid. He might even tolerate your obsession with right, wrong, fair, unfair," Andries threw a smug challenge.

Jo pointed a finger at him, "You're a spoiled brat," she snapped.

"So, I will tell him yes or no?" This was all part of the fabulous world Andries lived in that she hungered to hear about. His life in Paris, new art, new anything was a thrill she couldn't get enough of. Out of dreary Amsterdam to Paris, the capital of the world.

"This meeting was your idea?" she asked.

"Absolutely not, I know better."

She breathed a sigh of relief.

"What do you think he wants to do? I need to dress accordingly."

"Try wearing a smile."

She smiled, baring her teeth and bulging her eyes. He threw his cigarette down.

"Theo's family has a good history, famous galleries in Paris and London."

"How avant-garde!"

"Yes, right up your alley. Just try not to embarrass me. Go have fun. Remember fun, Jo? It's not like he's proposing marriage."

Johanna twirled her small white parasol as she walked alongside Andries at the Amsterdam Zoo where they would meet Theo van Gogh. She had changed into her light-blue cotton summer dress. They moved slowly around the entrance. She thought she must look very plain compared to the fashionable women of Paris. She was surprised this man would really want to meet her from seeing her in a photograph. She never considered her looks noteworthy. Her best friend Fleur was a beautiful woman. Just walking down the street with Fleur and watching men of all ages unabashedly stare was entertaining. Fleur never paid any notice.

She grabbed her handkerchief and dabbed at her face discreetly. "Pungent here at the zoo today."

The musky zoo smell reminded her of both her childhood and

her teaching. So many school trips to the zoo with squealing children. Outings were hard work for a teacher, but she loved seeing the children so happy and engaged. When she was a child, the zoo smell seemed exotic. Now she felt queasy—maybe the smell, or from the awkwardness of meeting a man in front of her brother. She didn't get nervous or even anxious meeting men anymore. Usually, she knew the moment she laid eyes on a man. Always the meeting turned boring for both and ended pleasantly and quickly. But she was intrigued by Theo. He looked handsome enough in the photo. An art dealer—that was interesting, unusual, and better than talking to another teacher, banker or boring broker selling everyday nothings. Or the worst, a man whose living depended on Dutch colonialism, or selling sugar harvested by exploited workers. Jo was proud to be among the new thinkers who found these old ways of profiting at the expense of others to be immoral and cruel.

Theo and Andries had become fast friends. Theo recommended paintings for Andries to buy as investments. Either way this went with Mr. Van Gogh, good or bad, it would make for fun chatter with Fleur, who always loved hearing about Andries's schemes.

"I'll light up a smoke ring around us. Keep the bugs away and hide the smell for you." Andries reminded her to smile by pointing at her mouth.

Right, smile, she thought.

Suddenly a man stood next to Andries, clapping him on the back. The man came right up to her and bowed, smiling.

"Where did you come from?" Andries asked.

Theo ignored him. "My pleasure to meet you, Miss Bonger." He offered his hand, and Johanna took it. "Thank you for meeting me on such short notice."

"Jo, this is Theo van Gogh, my good friend. Theo, my sister Johanna."

"How do you do?" asked Theo.

"Very well, thank you," replied Johanna.

Theo didn't take his eyes off her and unexpectedly she felt quite comfortable with him staring. "Thank you, Andries, for making the introduction."

He was more attractive than the grim man in the photo. This man smiled with his entire face, and even his eyes laughed. She'd imagined an avant-garde showman, trolling the streets of Paris with her too-handsome brother, freely hobnobbing with all the internationals who lived in the home of modern art. She hadn't expected this tall, lean figure in an understated suit. His jacket was short, and he wore no waistcoat. It was not at all the way Dutch men dressed, but he did maintain the familiar bowler hat.

They strolled through the zoo, Andries behind them, tipping his hat to all the lovelies, young and old alike.

"Your photograph doesn't do you justice," Theo said. "What do you think of my photo? Accurate?"

"No, you appear younger and happier in person," she said, smiling and excited by his openness in asking such a bold question.

"You teach school and sell insurance?" They were standing in front of a large Gothic-style wrought-iron cage filled with lethargic monkeys dangling from tree branches.

"I teach and work in the family business." *I sound like a parrot,* she thought. "I suppose Andries told you everything."

"Yes, Andries said you are very good at managing the office. Two jobs—impressive."

Two jobs weren't unusual for a Dutch woman. Two boring jobs. But he was complimenting her.

"Do you like the insurance business?"

"It's very routine, but sometimes we save the day! Fix what is broken, replace what is stolen, restore order. There is power and purpose in that. But really there is no way to make insurance interesting to me."

Theo smiled at her in a way that told her he liked her answer, his eyes, a deep hypnotic brown color, crinkling at the corners. She felt it in the back of her head, making her lighter. *This is already a good meeting*, she thought. He offered her his arm and she asked him about his art dealing.

"Every day is new. The art world constantly changes, and my mission is the change. New painters, new collectors, a new way of doing business. Bigger bets, planning the future, rather than simple transactions. Now the new trick is to identify an artist, assess his long-term potential, get exclusivity from him. Pay him money up front, house the work carefully, encourage critics to review the work. And it also helps to have a network of galleries, across Europe and America. Then a solo show, a whole room—one artist only. Then again, sometimes it is simple matchmaking between those who desire beautiful works and artists who live to create. Too long an answer?"

"No, it's fascinating—so much to think about—I never imagined. What if you choose a painter who doesn't sell?"

"Why he or she doesn't sell would be the question. Financial challenges are part of the business, though we try to avoid bankruptcy." Theo laughed, a low, rolling rumble, unexpected.

"Your love of art, this is why you live in Paris?" she asked.

"Paris is the center of the art world now. Some say the capital of the world. I plan to open my own gallery, specializing in modern art."

"I am planning to spend my summer break from teaching in Paris, hopefully longer. With my good friend Fleur Dutcher."

"What excellent timing, Johanna. I could introduce you to the art world personally."

Andries broke in. She'd forgotten he was still with them. "Really Jo, Paris with Fleur? I didn't know. Anyway, I need to leave. Theo, I trust you will return Johanna home?" He gave her a peck on the cheek and whispered in her ear, "Au revoir, Jo."

Theo acknowledged him with a bow. "Yes, I will make sure Jo gets home safely. Thank you. See you in Paris."

She and Theo walked farther into the zoo. He asked which way she would like to go, what she was interested in seeing. She had seen everything there a thousand times. She walked quietly, wishing she could study his handsome face and voice more. His voice was a deep baritone, and he emphasized each word as if he were on stage, making everything he said feel loaded with meaning. She wanted to make him laugh and hear that low rumble again.

Theo led her to a bench shaded beneath a lush tree. Bright white flowers bloomed against the dark green leaves. For a moment there, under the flowering tree, the smell was sweet.

She asked him questions about his work. There were no modern art dealers in Amsterdam so far as she knew. Modern art wasn't known, much less popular. She hadn't yet seen the paintings Andries had collected as investments and stored at Bonger Insurance. She would find a way to open them, to study them. She had read periodicals that were disparaging of the new artists and what was called the "impressionist" approach. But Theo made it sound interesting and elegant. His passion was infectious.

"Each painter develops his own, or maybe her own, uniqueness—a new way, a total break from the past. And with the impressionists, they are exploring light and its effects for maximum chromatic impact. But so critical to the new movement is the artist's selection of subjects. Real life, real people, working life, a celebration of the everyday."

"I love that idea," Jo said. "Celebration of the everyday…so powerful." She paused a moment. What is chromatic impact?"

"The new artists aim to use the science of colors and color theory. Their goal is to make the colors vibrate to the eye."

From his breast pocket he pulled out a few chromolithographs, postcard reproductions of paintings, and handed them to her. They were colorful landscapes, mostly of France.

"The smaller scale doesn't do them justice," she said. "I've read some critics think the color is a vulgarity. They think the work is ludicrous and make fun of the painters in cartoons. Anarchy, some say." She loved that word *anarchy*, so provocative.

"Yes, and some think the word 'impression' means unfinished. They are afraid of change, but change is our only sure thing."

His voice hummed in her head.

His deep tones vibrated like music. Was he staring at her?

"Johanna, will you trust me for a moment? Close your eyes."

"Yes." He made yes easy.

"Turn your face to the sun."

She collapsed her parasol and turned toward the sun.

"Keep your eyes closed, but not too tight. What do you see?"

"I see dancing dots."

"What colors are they?"

"Bright…purple, blue, red, pink, yellow, orange…Have I left any color out?"

She could feel Theo staring, examining her face. His shadow on her skin felt larger as he moved in closer. The brightness of the dots diminished to purple and blue.

She was amazed at how bold he was. She felt herself smile, couldn't stop it from taking over her face. She struggled to control her breathing as she felt his shadow grow bigger, the dots dimmer. She had to bite her lips to keep from laughing. She felt him inches from her face, so close.

Heaven. She felt Theo lean back. Opening her eyes, she realized he was more handsome up close—only his modest lips kept him from being overwhelmingly so, and his smile was unselfconscious and inviting.

"That is what the new painting is, Johanna—pure color. Mostly, I wanted to study your face."

She felt herself flush with happiness and laughed. She had never had such an intimate moment with a man she had just met. She liked it.

"I wonder what you're thinking?" Theo asked.

"I am thinking art is your passion."

"My purpose." Theo responded.

"Your life?" She looked into his brown eyes rimmed with gold and held his gaze for a delicious moment.

"Yes, you understand. Of course, I am leaving room in my life for family, Johanna." He said the words softly, sweetly, not in his theatrical baritone.

She felt a flush again. He was so bold, but not inappropriate, just daring and exciting. She was feeling excited by this man in a way she hadn't ever felt.

"You're turning pink."

"The sun, I suppose. Should we walk some more?" *Yes, move, get my wits back.*

Afterward, euphoria still lifted her as she and Theo sat close and easy by the canal, talking and laughing until the sun dimmed. They walked back to the Bonger family home.

"What a perfect day," Theo said.

And it was, her most perfect day ever.

"May I kiss you good night?"

"In public, how scandalous!" she said and laughed, but hoped he would go ahead and kiss her.

"Yes, I suppose you are right, Jo."

"Sadly, Amsterdam is not Paris."

"Then may I see you tomorrow?"

"Yes."

"…and then in Paris?"

"Yes, Paris." Inches away from kissing, and they held each other's eyes for a very long moment. So close, the world disappeared around her.

"Tomorrow," she agreed.

Theo held Jo's hand and helped her down the narrow dock along the canal to the rowboat he had arranged for them.

Blue ripples and foamy gray waves brushed against the rowboat as he gracefully pulled on the oars. He made it look effortless, but soon sweat was forming a nice glow on his skin.

Did he notice her staring? He looked at her between his scans of the water, always with a smile. Last night, she'd thought perhaps she had overestimated his appeal—sometimes memories were bigger than reality. But no, he was the most interesting and romantic man she had ever met.

He had a way of moving that was uniquely his—his gestures were strong but slow, always calm. Johanna knew from her years teaching children that bodies betray minds. Nervous, compulsive minds produced twitching, restless bodies. Theo had a serene, confident quality that made her feel as though she was being pulled toward him. And she wanted to get closer.

Now, with his jacket off, she could see his shoulders—square and strong, not bulky or bunchy. His skin was clear, no childhood scars, not puffy from drink He was nicely groomed. He was thoughtful, sincere. She felt his magnetism slowly drawing her in. Light sparkled off the water and bounced around him.

He rowed them out from the canal into open water, away from the other boats. Jo looked. "You're taking us out?"

"Why do you look nervous? Every Dutch girl knows how to swim," Theo teased. She didn't feel nervous, in fact she felt completely at ease and excited to be with Theo again.

"Swimming will be demanding in this dress. And if the boat hits my head on the way over, I might fall unconscious. Then I will die." She teased back.

"Perish the thought. You can count on me." He winked at her.

"What if you are hit on the head too? Or you strangle in your clothes?"

"Do you always worry so much, Johanna? Fortunately, there are many people around. You will be saved, even if I sink." He continued to row a few more strokes.

"Do you go out this far a lot?"

"No. In fact I haven't rowed since I was a boy."

"Then why are we leaving the canal?"

"It is such an amazingly blue, beautiful day. And the water is so tempting. I am happy to be with you."

"I'm glad you're happy. I'm happy too, Theo."

She *was* happy. Everything about Theo was a wonderful surprise. He had passion, purpose. He was a step ahead of her in his thinking, and he had found a path for his life with meaning and value to others.

Her parents often told her she was too picky about men. She always found something that bothered her so enormously she couldn't see beyond it—a man's work, his politics, or trivial matters such as his hair or his smell. You felt something when you looked at someone or you didn't.

Once they were in the tributary, he put the oars down and the boat rocked with the waves.

"What a surprise. I've never been out this far," she said.

"What do you think?"

"I think the city looks smaller and far away. 'Perspective' in painting—smaller the farther away, correct?"

"Oui, mademoiselle," Theo said.

He looked at her for a long time, not saying anything, just smiling. She smiled back, relishing their serene silence. She stretched out her legs and leaned back against the boat, enjoying the soothing rocking of the small waves.

Theo reached into his coat. The boat shimmied with his movements, and she let herself jog with the movement too.

Theo inched up, sitting on the very edge of the bench.

He reached across the space and held her hand.

"I should have rented a smaller boat. We could be closer," Theo said, chuckling.

He released her hand and then reached into his jacket pocket. He pulled out a small red velvet jewelry box, opened it, and handed it to her. A shining gold ring sat inside.

"Don't drop it in the water," he joked.

"It's beautiful." She heard her voice quiver. Her throat was dry. She'd been holding her breath.

"Will you marry me?"

"What?"

"Will you marry me?"

"Are you serious?"

"Yes, very serious. I'm deeply in love with you."

"After two meetings? Really? Theo, I'm shocked." She had not seen this coming. She was at a loss for words. Confusion reigned. He looked so confident, smiling brilliantly at her.

"You've turned red," Theo said. "Are you alright? Too much sun?"

She handed the ring back to him. "Please take it." She leaned forward and forced herself to put it on his lap, surprised that this was hard to do. She couldn't marry a man after two days, could she?

"For now, for safety, you hold it." Jo said and looked out across the water. Maybe she was making a mistake. Instead of leaping for joy she felt herself withdraw.

He took back the ring and she slid away on the bench, her body suddenly rigid against the rocking.

"Jo, may I presume to guess what you are thinking?" She nodded.

"You are surprised, naturally, this is so sudden. And now wondering...maybe this man is crazy?" Theo said.

"No, I don't think you're crazy. I wonder why the rush to marriage?"

"You don't believe in love at first sight?"

She thought and watched the sun bounce around the boat.

"I do believe in love at first sight," she said. "But I never considered marriage at first sight. Why do you want to marry me? You don't even know me. I wonder how much I know you after two days."

His eyes, so intense and sincere. "I know enough."

To that she was speechless again. Didn't they meet just yesterday? She hadn't even talked about herself much. "Name three things you know about me," she said.

He very quickly responded.

"I know you enough. I love you because you are smart and, even better, an independent thinker. You have big ideas going around up there"—he touched her forehead. "You don't know them yourself yet." He held his finger on her head and paused there. The he slowly traced his finger down the side of her cheek. "I believe you will accomplish all you set out to. That is two."

"How do you know all that?"

"And the last reason," he took a breath and gestured a sweeping waving hand before her. "You're not afraid to be unmarried. You are choosy, and many men have thrown themselves before you. I admire that."

She half laughed, half gasped. What an astonishing thing to say! Theo was the first man who somehow understood and approved of her independence and her desire to live a different life. "Well, what about you? Have you ever proposed before?"

"No. You are the one and only."

I am the first and only! "I don't know you enough to...trust you."

"You said you believed in love at first sight. Knowing and trusting don't have to go together. You can just believe in me, trust your instincts."

"My instincts?" She was intrigued. He was challenging her, another complete surprise. "Please don't take offense—things often go wrong, as you know."

"None taken. Tell me your concerns, I will debate them with you."

She paused, thinking. "You won't make a living selling art."

At this, his eyebrows rose. "You surprise me with this bourgeois fear. There are challenges, but generally art is very profitable. Modern art, now bought for pennies, will soon be worth thousands. Within our lifetime. No, Johanna, I will be a great success. What else?"

She frowned. "You really want me to come up with things that can go wrong?"

"Yes"

"What if I say yes even though I don't really know you. And then…discover I am not really in love with you, that we aren't suited to be together?" She felt a huge relief just saying it. She could be as bold as he was. "Then what?"

"Jo, in your heart you know I am true. And you instinctively understand that with me, you will not live the ordinary, meaningless life you dread."

Theo knew her already—how? He was unlike anyone she was ever likely to meet again. "Let's get to shore," she said. "This rocking is making me ill. I need the ground to think straight." Theo nodded. He began rowing and labored against the current.

They walked down the quiet street in a well-to-do part of residential Amsterdam. Rich, vibrantly colored flowerpots decorated all the windows and delivered a sweet calming effect as the dusk settled in around them. *Marry me…Theo wants to marry me.* Her brain kept repeating the proposal—no other thoughts, only the same echoing refrain.

"This has been perfect, Johanna—the weekend I fell in love with a wonderful Dutch girl. May I kiss you tonight?"

She smiled her answer. Theo took off his hat and embraced her.

She felt his kiss warm and soft, igniting slowly. She surrendered to the floating, drifting, dreaming into a dark sweet place she never knew existed. Her insides were watery, her thighs trembling. The kiss didn't end.

After a long time, Theo broke off the kiss. He rested his forehead against her forehead, and they stood like that, so close, so wonderful.

"I think that was a perfect kiss. What do you think?" His deep voice, almost as arousing as the kiss.

Johanna felt as if her brain had walls and she was up against them, and she couldn't think of a single word to say. She could only parrot what Theo had said.

"Yes, a perfect kiss," she whispered, out of breath. She heard her heart pound fast and loud.

"I love you, Johanna."

She still couldn't speak.

"I see you need more time to consider."

"Yes, more time is what I was thinking."

"I will convince you and ask again. In the meantime, shall we write? Until Paris?"

"Yes. Write, and Paris," she said.

"Paris with Jo, my dream. Your hand, please?"

She gave him her hand. He kissed it and tried to put the ring on her finger, but she pulled away. Theo placed the ring back in his pocket, took her hand again, and laid it over his heart.

"We will be together. Good night, Johanna."

She watched him walk away, and when he was gone her heart pumped an unfamiliar jolt. He disappeared so fast, and she instantly wondered when she would see him again.

She paused at her door trying to hold on to her herself and her vision for her future. Anxiety was clawing its way through her happiness. She bit her lip and slowly pulled the door open, holding her breath. But the minute she closed the door behind her she heard the creaking from her parent's bedroom. She knew what would follow: the crack of her father's step on the stairs and his breathless immediate confrontation. Before he moved to Paris, Andries could stay out all night, come in sloppy from too much drink with friends, and their mother would run down the stairs and wait on him hand and foot. But me, get ready for a diatribe of one hundred hostile, judgmental questions.

Her parents lived by society's most backward social conventions of the day. She was constantly at odds with them over what they considered her most recent odious actions. Joining women's causes, not marrying, next it would be Theo—an art dealer—on top of Paris, young women living independently and unchaperoned in Paris! She wouldn't tell them about Theo van Gogh. It would just be another bone for them to bludgeon her with.

Just get to Paris. How could they stop her anyway?

2

Vincent

"Vincent, get your nose out of the dirt!" I remember my mother scolding me.

To understand man, I study the blade of grass. The green fills my eyes and takes up all space. The green at one edge tinged yellow, the other blue. Up close, the black stays gone, and I see only the fuzzy, blurry green shimmering of the blades.

You can't always say what shuts you up. Black floats over me. I see my days as though I were a prisoner, buried alive in my failures. I swim in this darkness like a child in the womb. I try to reject this as my natural state, and I study the blade of grass.

When I feel my hand work, and I see the line, the color, I can fight for another chance at destiny. And I know also I can make the prison disappear with deep affection.

There are no blades of grass here, only Clasina's lines filling my eyes while she snores in her pose. And I have chosen lines in such a way, they speak for themselves.

There is a knock on the door, the child nudges me. Clasina doesn't hear. That would be my beloved brother, Theo, coming to kill me.

Theo

Theo knew when he looked at his brother, he saw a man the rest of the world could not see.

He hadn't met with Vincent in months, yet their reunion would not be a happy one. Still, he had a duty to do, and he would not let Vincent's usual theatrics deter him. He walked down the narrow streets of Amsterdam, away from the canals, past the elegantly colored houses with pots of tulips, and into a dank alley, stepping carefully over refuse until he reached the shabby building where Vincent resided.

Theo stood at the door, closed his eyes, and said his silent prayer. Their father had demanded Theo be the one to tell Vincent. Or else. He put his ear to the door and knocked. "Vincent?"

A moment later his brother opened the door, and they embraced. Theo pounded Vincent's back and held him tight. He felt little arms thrown around his thighs and looked down to see a boy about four years old smiling up at them. Dust floated in the air and swirled around them as they embraced.

Over Vincent's shoulder he saw the woman—Clasina Maria Hoornik was her name—posing on a stool in a pool of light by the only window, naked. Her head was buried in her crossed arms. She didn't look up but greeted him warmly, "Hello, brother."

The child prattled away at the small table in center of the room. Vincent let Theo out of his embrace. Theo smoothed his clothes and discreetly wiped charcoal from his jacket. Vincent's deep blue eyes darted around the room, never meeting Theo's. *He must know why I am here.* Theo kept an easy smile on his face as he tried not to focus on the desperate squalor in the small room. Debris was simply pushed against the barren cracked walls, some in the cold dark fireplace.

"Theo, look at the picture and compare it to me," Clasina called. "It's first-class, isn't it?"

Vincent handed Theo the drawing and he checked it against Clasina, still holding her pose. Theo wished she would cover up—she was obviously suffering from an infectious skin ailment with large red patches on her neck and arms. He didn't want to look at her and didn't want to be seen avoiding her.

The sketch was good—no, it was great, intuitively modern. Vincent had captured the essence of the model's melancholy pose, yet he had wrought it in his own uncanny way. Vincent had titled the drawing "Sorrow."

"Vincent, it's excellent. Very strong composition." The academic drawing lessons hadn't killed his brother's unique hand.

Theo knew his praise had an instant effect on Vincent. His eyes finally held still, his tense muscular body relaxed as he sat down, the small rickety chair squeaking. Vincent threw his arm around the back of the chair and smiled at Theo. All in all, he looked good, Theo thought. His complexion slightly ruddy, his reddish-blond hair nicely combed, his weight solid. Something here, perhaps the poverty, was agreeing with him.

"I want the lines to speak for themselves. To say what the subject alone never can," Vincent said with a wave of his hand.

"You've succeeded." Theo handed the picture back to him.

"I think it shows precise intention," Vincent said. "Perfect for a lithograph. I want to find work as a commercial lithographer. Do you know anyone?"

Theo was about to say he didn't when Clasina slowly broke her pose, first letting her arms drop, then sitting upright and swiveling her head on her neck.

When she stood, Theo saw she was pregnant, perhaps midway through her term. A chill ran through him. Vincent gave her a faded blue robe and helped her to bed, tenderly pulling the grayed bedsheet over her. He fluffed a pillow and held it for her. She smiled and became pretty.

"Vincent, are you still able to lunch with me?" Theo asked.

Vincent looked at Clasina, checking for her approval.

The child ran behind Vincent and hugged legs. "Papa, me go too, me go too, please?" he pleaded over and over, stopping only when Vincent placed his large, freckled hand, still covered in charcoal, on the boy's head.

"Yes, you all go," Clasina said and relit a half-smoked cigar, closing her eyes.

At the café, they sat along one of the canals that veined the city. The child on Vincent's lap quietly ate a plate of meat and potatoes. Vincent was drinking too much wine and only picked at his food.

"You look decent for an old man." Theo joked.

"Ha. I am optimistic. I feel well, despite this filthy air. And what about you, still good for an almost-old man? How is Paris? Blazing trails of artistic innovation?"

Theo slowly sipped a coffee. "Monet sells. You should come to Paris, study the impressionists, Vincent."

Vincent's face closed. "No. My family is here. And I know the reason for this visit now."

I am here to keep the peace, Vincent, Theo thought. *The family cannot tolerate this relationship. I am here to prevent drastic measures on their part.*

But he said none of that. "Then you know your duty, Vincent." He watched his brother drain his glass. "Is it your child?" he asked gently in French.

"Why does it matter to you? Do you have another wife for me?" Vincent's voice rose, attracting attention from the other diners. He held his glass to the waiter for more wine.

His brother's loneliness was a crippling disease. Vincent had always been unhappy alone. Why was this tragic woman the only one in Amsterdam who would have him?

"She isn't your wife Vincent, she's a prostitute. And I know you haven't married her."

Vincent's eyes blazed, instantly furious. "You used to love me. I have come down in the world, while you are rising. I have lost sympathy, and you have gained it. But I am the eldest, Theo. I won't accept this betrayal from you." He pointed, jabbing into Theo's chest.

Theo felt his heart slice in half, and he struggled to meet Vincent's glare.

The child stopped eating and raised his hand to Vincent's face. Vincent kissed his hand and smiled, and the child returned to his plate.

"When you are finished, let's take a walk," Theo said. "Let's go to the park. It will be good for the boy."

At the park, Vincent inhaled deeply on his pipe and pushed the child on a swing, waiting. Each time the child swung to Vincent, his face broke into a big smile and squealing laugh. Vincent returned the smile with a *zoom* noise and higher push.

Unseemly to bring up the topic now, but Theo was out of time. He plunged in bluntly, flatly stating fact. "You must end the relationship with Clasina. Father is preparing legal action, ridiculous as it may be, if you marry her."

"Father, really, he knows nothing. Let me ask you, isn't it better to help someone with love?"

"I think what you're doing is noble. But you have to consider your dream of becoming an artist. Why not go home and sort out your future?"

"My *dream*—I am an artist. Home is failure. What will happen to Clasina then?"

"What will happen to you without funds? Father will cut you off if you continue with that woman." It was the truth he hated to speak. Vincent had been unable, unwilling, to support himself in any profession. He had followed his father into the ministry, he'd tried teaching.

Their uncle Cent had given him work in his Paris gallery selling reproductions. But Vincent had taken no pleasure in making deals. The subjectivity of art—whose opinions were valued, whose were ignored—it all agitated him beyond reason. He was brilliant but couldn't accept the hypocrisy, the unfairness of life. As a child, the death of a pet, or farm animal, had led to days of spiritual misery. His ideals were right, but he took everything too far.

After Vincent had left their uncle's gallery, Theo was thrilled to be asked to join. Knowing Vincent's frustrations, he expected a tense life catering to grating clients with awful taste and endless demands. But he found the opposite—a world of people interested in new ideas, and far from the provincial thoughts of their childhood in Holland.

"You are cruel in your worldly wisdom," Vincent snapped. "And legal action against me is preposterous, but it does betray everyone's evil nature."

They stood together, silent, the child swinging back and forth, yelling "Higher, higher!"

"I reasoned with father," Theo said, "but I lost the argument."

He felt Vincent's piercing glare. "Make them understand."

"Vincent, we all have our duty—"

"Shut up, Theo! You are killing me! Forcing me to betray my wife!" Vincent gently pulled the boy off the swing and onto his hip. "Give me everything you have."

Theo sighed but knew he had won. He pulled out his wallet, fuller than usual for this very purpose, and emptied it into Vincent's hand.

"I foresee, Theo, you will soon be sorry for this." Vincent didn't hug him good-bye.

3

Johanna

Jo was feeling the euphoric—new possibilities, change, Theo. It was tickling her, she was moving faster, getting through the busy work. Her cheeks felt stuck in a smile. From across the office floor, her father caught her with his habitually disapproving eye, snapping her mind back to the present. He squinted questioningly at her, and she nodded to appease him, but she was determined to hold her mood. Feeling charitable, she thought that in a certain light her father looked almost like Andries, still handsome.

Last night and every night at dinner it was the same tense quiet, her mother looking only at her food or her lap, and her father's disapproval—only because they loved her so much and cared so much.

She silently endured the barrage of parental questions at the dinner table. She dared not move, almost holding her breath not to give them anymore to disapprove of, when what she really wanted to do was roll her eyes and debate her parents' backward thinking. She examined every stitch on the white cloth her grandmother had crocheted, which covered the table. It was perfect, every stitch identical, each circular window a small hole that obscured the scarred wooden table it covered. Johanna traced her finger around its tight edge stitches. The thought of the hours it took to create -- she would die if she had to spend her days creating floral patterns in cotton after cooking and cleaning: all the dreary, dreadful work of a housewife. Didn't her mother, or her grandmother, once feel ambition and think of life beyond crafting with a crochet hook or knitting needles? How did they bear such a life? They couldn't understand why she longed for a different existence. But she needed more. She longed for a life rich with purpose and intellectual challenges.

And then there were her parents' opinions about her. They knew she didn't really like teaching, but what could a woman do in Amsterdam? Why waste all that time and energy to learn five foreign languages? Ambition only opens a woman to humiliation, her parents thought. And then her age—she wasn't a young girl. Did she have time to be choosy? Her mother had married her father at eighteen, an arranged marriage. A fate worse than death, Jo thought.

Jo, dear, what are you thinking?

She was thinking, "I want to live in the future. I won't bear another summer wasting my life suffocating in this dreary office." They couldn't understand this, but finally they knew she couldn't be stopped from getting on a train. They would demand she stay with Andries but would not underwrite a penny of her expenses.

Fleur blew into the office then, with her excessively polite, "Hello, Mr. Bonger," stopping her father in midsentence. Fleur had a secret that made her dazzling. She was as smart and quick as any man, and beautiful blonde hair and blue eyes. She led Jo back to the storage room.

"Does Tall-and-Handsome know about our Paris plans yet?" Fleur asked as she poked around Andries's paintings. Jo burst out laughing at Fleur's latest nickname for her brother.

"Stop, you will make me spill our lash line concoction." Jo carefully stirred her mixture of ash, charcoal, and petroleum jelly. She needed just the right color for a natural look and a good consistency for spreading, not flaking or, worse, dripping into her eyes. "He knows and he is not thrilled to have me come to his new city."

Fleur lifted the sheet off one of the paintings Andries had

acquired. She whistled—a nude. "Well, well, *well*, me oh my! Just what is Mr. Too-Blond-and-Blue doing in Paris?" Jo had snuck a look through the paintings herself, and she thought the nude subject might be a prostitute. "I say we'll find out, won't we?" Fleur said, carefully drawing back a few more sheets, exposing the colorful paintings. They were paintings of real people, manual laborers, the celebration of the everyday. Theo's thoughts echoed to Johanna and filled her mind with a new, fearless energy.

Her father hated the paintings, no surprise. He described them as "bohemian scratches," indecent, with anarchist messages. Not at all in the rich history of Dutch art. He demanded they be moved to the cellar.

The paintings looked beautiful to Jo, as though she were seeing them through Theo's eyes. Everything he did and said impressed her. The way he began a conversation with a sincere "Why?" *Why does that appeal to you?* he would ask, leaning in, smiling.

"That's right," Jo said, "we will find out—I must get a job in Paris."

"We will, nobody's better than us," said Fleur. Then she carefully replaced the sheet over the paintings. "Hurry up, Jo. The early bird gets the worm, and we need two."

Jo handed her a tiny bowl filled with the black charcoal concoction and held up a hand mirror.

"Oh, Jo, you are so clever." Fleur swiped the mixture with the tip of a large bone darning needle and gently dabbed a very thin line just above her eyelashes. "Well? It is perfect, isn't it?"

"Yes," said Jo, looking very closely. "Not noticeable, your lashes just look thicker than ever. Does it stay put?"

Fleur batted her eyes and tossed her head, then tilted her face up for Jo to examine. She held the mirror for Jo to take her turn.

The formula felt a little heavy, and she reached for a handkerchief to wipe it.

"No, leave it, you look pretty. So, Andries doesn't like you staying with him in Paris?"

"He will, if you come over every day!" In her mind, she and Fleur should have their own apartment, but that was unacceptable to both sets of parents. Women could never live alone. She knew Andries would sulk about his baby sister infringing on his life, but when Fleur was around, he was almost pleasant.

Fleur put her hat back on and cocked her head toward the door. "Well maybe I will come around every day. Let's run."

"Wait," Jo said. "Let's go out the back, so Father won't see my eyes."

Jo and Fleur entered a dark hotel lobby, walking past a large sign "Exposition Universelle—The Dutch Pavilion, Hostess Applications," with a directional arrow. This job was very competitive, judging by the long line that wound through the opulent lobby and into the dining room. Not a prestigious job, nor the beginnings of a career, but it would pay their expenses and they would be in Paris, Jo thought.

There was little talking, only a low hum of voices, the rustle of swishing fabric, and the occasional *ting* from the reception desk.

Clerks with clipboards roamed the line, taking names and interviewing candidates. They all wore the same dark-blue Dutch suit with its annoyingly high collar. The line moved at a brisk pace, the clerks directing applicants to the appropriate sections. Johanna and Fleur joined the end of their assigned line.

"I didn't expect so many. Now I'm nervous, you?" Fleur asked quietly, taking a deep breath.

"No, we're the best," Jo said, stepping half out of line to see the front. There were a lot of applicants.

"You promised to tell me more about Mr. Theo van Gogh."

"Not now."

"Just whisper."

"He is very unusual. I liked him immediately."

"Aren't we leaving something very important out?" Fleur stared at her, waiting. When she said nothing, Fleur continued the quizzing. "*The kiss?* A man doesn't ask for your hand unless he has kissed you. Especially after just two meetings. Why don't you tell? You always tell *me*."

"In fact, he asked me before the kiss, for your information."

"Really? Astonishing! You know, Jo, I can tell everything about a man by the way he kisses." She gave Jo a gentle elbow nudge.

"It was very…" Jo paused, looking to see if anyone was listening.

"Very what?"

"Great." Proud she didn't sound dreamy.

"How?" Fleur was quick.

"I can't describe it. It was wonderful, that's all." Johanna felt herself flush, annoyed with herself.

"Remember I always said you just needed the right man. More please."

"Fleur, not now."

"Come on."

"It was a kiss felt in all right places, I think I read that someplace, but there is truth in it," Jo said hoping to quiet Fleur down.

"I wonder if Theo has had too much practice. Now, how will you live without it?" Fleur teased. "Ha! Please, Lord, give Paris to me." She clasped her elegant hands to her perfectly round chest, raised her almond-shaped blue eyes to the heavens, and said, "I promise I will do good work, especially when I'm old"

A woman with a clipboard began interviewing the candidate ahead of them. Johanna studied her. She had an easygoing manner, confident, natural. She is so smartly dressed, Jo thought.

Fleur nudged Jo and whispered. "Look around. See what I am seeing?"

"A hundred girls standing in line?" Jo whispered back.

"Yes...*girls*!" Fleur said, her eyes wide. "*Girls*. We must have ten years on most of them. We need to appear younger immediately. Of course, they would only want to hire little girls!"

Jo glanced around. Fleur was right, the others were younger. Jo felt her jaw tense, her teeth clamp down.

"Paris is really expensive," Fleur said as the woman with the clipboard moved down the line. "My baking class alone is a fortune!"

"Shush... I can tell what she is saying." Jo did her best to read the lips of the woman with the clipboard. She was always able to lip-read the whispers in the back of her class.

Fleur dug into her bag and pulled out a rouge pot and dotted her cheeks and lips. Then she touched some to Jo's cheeks.

"You aren't smiling—stop frowning." Fleur grabbed a little of Jo's hair and loosened her bun, pulling a few tendrils down to the side.

"Fleur, it doesn't matter how young we are. She is asking about languages! This is fantastic! I have six languages. No one in this town has as many languages as I do. And you are the most beautiful woman in Amsterdam. They will pick you right off. Let's switch places, you go first."

"Jo, stand still and please don't be difficult. I am going to tell them I have three languages, then you will have to tutor me pronto."

"*Sì.*"

Johanna froze her smile and Fleur struck a splendid pose, head held upright and shoulders back.

"Your name, please?" The woman had an open face, friendly, but no chitchat.

"Johanna Bonger—I'm fluent in six languages: French, Italian, Spanish, English, German, and Dutch. I have a teaching degree, am a trained public speaker, and I have studied all of French history, including architecture and music. And I did translations for the British Museum."

"Very good," the woman said, impressed. "How old are you, dear? It's only a formality, dear, for the application. Shall I say twenty-five? All those skills will be very helpful, especially the languages. What is your dress size?"

"I am average size."

"I'll say petite for now, they will measure you in the next line for your costume. Which native Dutch crafts are you proficient in? For the demonstrations at the pavilion?"

"You mean do I carve shoes or something?" Jo asked. Was she serious? No one did this anymore.

"Yes. Sew dolls? Braid cheese?"

"Yes, we are excellent cheese braiders," Fleur interjected. Then added proudly, "Fleur Dutcher."

The woman with the clipboard looked Fleur up and down and smiled. "You two are together?"

"Yes, we are," they said.

"You are twenty-five also and petite. And any languages?"

"Three languages. In addition to Dutch." Fleur looked to the lady for confirmation.

"Excellent. Take these tags, write your full names. Congratulations, ladies.

This way, please." She pointed to the small line snaking into the dining room at the far end of the lush lobby.

"They are going to measure us," Fleur whispered.

"We are moving to Paris!" *Now nothing will stop us*, Jo thought as a burst of joy flooded her.

"My cravings await! French food and French lovers!"

Jo laughed, thinking about Theo's perfect kiss, and they walked gracefully down to the end of the lobby.

4

Theo

Theo clasped his hands behind his back in the wide storefront window of the Goupil Gallery, looking up and down the Parisian boulevard, watching his appointment approach.

He held open the door. "Paul, a pleasure to see you again! Thank you for making the time to visit us here at Goupil. May I take your hat and cape?" Theo believed one day Gauguin would be an important painter, even though now he was a challenge to sell. Still undiscovered, this was a great opportunity. Theo needed new artists to cultivate, to place his bets on.

"Mr. Gauguin!" Mr. Goupil came forward and gestured for him to take a seat on the puffy, padded red and green velvet couch by the window.

Paul Gauguin towered over Theo and Mr. Goupil, and he didn't sit. He cut a dramatic figure in the well-appointed and carefully designed gallery. He was tall, dark, and exceptionally handsome, with a self-satisfied swagger. His clothes were a creation of his own, full of symbolic meaning. Instead of the typical bowler, a woolen beret slanted down his face. He wore a flowing black cape on his oversized shoulders and a vest designed with boldly colored flower embroidery, from the countryside. On his feet, he wore wooden clogs, hand painted in a traditional floral design.

To emphasize his impressive height, he had a habit of tilting his head back so that he perpetually looked down his face to those below him.

"Let's go upstairs," Goupil said. "This way, Mr. Gauguin."

Theo gestured to the staircase. Which way would this go, he wondered? Paul was a difficult person: bristly, arrogant, unable to hear any suggestion.

If Theo's uncle Cent were still here at Goupil Gallery, things might be different. They had success with some of the new painters, Monet, Lautrec, and it was all Theo's engineering. He had Uncle Cent's support, his father's brother, always generous with Theo, educating him in the art world, sponsoring him in his gallery, promoting his career with generosity. Uncle Cent had sponsored Vincent as a dealer years back, but Vincent couldn't—wouldn't—embrace the company's way of doing business. This was the first mortifying failure for Vincent, and it spread unease about his future. Now with the passing of Uncle Cent, and Mr. Goupil himself aging, the company was ready to sell. The books had to look good, it was not a great time for long-term investments.

Everything at Goupil was decorated with traditional elegance in mind. Paintings carefully hung in designed groupings—landscapes, still life, and portraiture, the naturalists, the Barbizon, the classics— all equal distances apart. Plush, traditional furniture was gathered in small conversational units. A highly polished French provincial desk, without even a scrap of paper, was centered against the back wall.

Convincing Mr. Goupil to expand into modern art was an ongoing negotiation. But Theo had found some success, and the popularity of Monet was a very important achievement.

It had been a battle for Theo selling the impressionists—the critics were only just coming around—and already painters had moved forward again. Dealers were also changing sales strategies. Durand-Ruel, Theo's biggest rival, invested heavily in impressionist art and was developing the business aggressively to exclude more modest competitors with fewer resources, like Theo. Durand-Ruel gave the artists money up front, paid for their groceries, rent, and medical bills, and demanded exclusivity in return. They hired the best writers to review the work, they set up viewing rooms in their own homes, providing easy access to all the art. They created a network of relationships across Europe and the United States to get the maximum exposure to wealthy clients. And, the biggest innovation, they created solo shows, each show featuring only one artist. All with backers financing the whole operation.

Theo watched all their business innovations carefully, adapted and innovated on their practices himself. Theo was younger. He knew which artists would serve as the symbols for their generation. But wealthy buyers of new art were rare. The risk of failure was high, and bankruptcy was always a looming fear. Collecting work, hording it, solo shows—all were expensive propositions.

Change is inevitable. This was his opportunity.

The upstairs gallery was loaded with paintings, in stark contrast to the pristine organization downstairs. Every inch of wall space here was covered, and paintings were stacked back-to-back, leaning against the walls—all new, all modern, some of the oil paint barely dry.

"My benefactor, Gustave Arosa, said you are the best person to represent me, to arrange sales," said Paul.

"Yes, Mr. Gauguin, Gustave is a great friend, a marvelous collector. He must see something special and unique in your work to sponsor you." Mr. Goupil shifted his weight and placed his hands in his pockets. Goupil would behave politely long enough to see the new paintings, if only to recount the tale of the difficult new painter, with all his eccentricities, at his next social gathering. It was Theo who would bring buyers for Paul's work.

"I do not follow the instincts of others," said Paul. "This does cause great suffering, but as we have learned, it is suffering which begets great art."

"Well, shall we get to it, Theo?" said Goupil.

Theo swung an arm out high, in the manner of a grand stage introduction of a beloved personality. He indicated an empty easel in front of one of the street-facing windows.

Paul accepted the invitation and, standing even taller, head so far back on his shoulders he might be staring at the ceiling, placed the painting he'd brought on the easel. He worked carefully, as if unwrapping a glass egg. Theo had high hopes for Paul's new work. Paul had spent years studying with the great impressionists and could ape each of his teachers' unique styles. He understood Cezanne's individualistic brush work, his colors, the same with Pissarro, with whom he had also studied. But he hadn't yet developed his own approach, one that would distinguish him as more than a talented painter—as an innovator, a modern master.

Theo held his breath, hoped for the best, but was prepared to make whatever happened a pleasant experience for Paul and Goupil.

Paul stepped back and admired his own work. He didn't bother to gauge Theo's or Goupil's reaction.

"The light is better downstairs," Paul stated. He started to remove the painting.

"No, Mr. Gauguin," Goupil said, "all the new work is kept here. The downstairs is for the Barbizon. You have a unique approach, Mr. Gauguin, another innovation in the impressionist movement."

Theo exhaled with excited relief and grasped Paul by the shoulder. It was a painting of two nude women together in the woods by a stream. Their backs were to the viewer, and one sat, one stood by an emerald pool. The large size of the vertical composition invited you to immerse yourself in the fantastic colors and spy on the women as they bathed. The sitting woman was holding her bright red hair in a ponytail exposing her cream-colored back, vibrating with shadows of yellow, orange, and green, creating her shape. The other girl stood slightly bent over, one hand on her knee, balancing herself on an orange rock, her entire backside exposed, but only a tantalizing curve of a hidden breast. Theo instantly saw the brilliance of the design. Their positions created a diagonal across the composition. A purple-shadowed tree with a deep green canopy sheltered the girls and separated them and cut a large vertical down the left side of the canvas. The women's bodies were painted with pastel colors and the woods around them in deeper tones, focusing all the light on the women. Some would find their bodies androgynous. Good. Controversy sold paintings to adventurous buyers.

You wanted to get closer, see their expressions, imagine what they were thinking. But you couldn't, and this created more suspense and longing. And the young girls didn't look at you, so it would be more comfortable for some to stare at the painting, another clever choice—erotic.

Yes, Theo thought, a masterpiece. Paul had evolved a new painting technique. He used a simplified line, bright and dark, pure colors, not grayed. The rendering of the skin was smooth, but not blended. Pure color brushed against pure color. A clever painting, a surprise—finally all his own. Should Goupil decline, he could buy this art himself, offer an exclusive agreement, or provide Paul cash up front in return for a guarantee of more paintings.

Gauguin was selling Mr. Goupil his artistic vision. He had moved beyond the impressionist obsession with nature and light, but he had kept the colors and developed a narrative approach. But Goupil wasn't listening. He shifted his hips—maybe the image was affecting him, Theo thought. Or maybe he was bored.

Paintings once told stories, everything was symbolic, a meaning in every gesture and object. This was new and old together. How to sell it?

"I am at the forefront of the new modern movement. I have invented 'symbolist,' and it is a narrative approach," Gauguin explained.

"Symbolist, I see. Very good," Mr. Goupil broke in. "Theo tells me you are a former accountant?"

"Stockbroker."

"Remarkable. Makes for a compelling story. Wouldn't you think so, Theo?"

"No," interrupted Paul, "it is a dreary story of corruption and commerce. There are more important concepts to present. I have royal Incan blood in my veins."

"Truly, but you are French?"

"I am from many places, have lived in many cultures. My wife is Danish. I spent many years in South America. My mother's family was politically active in the—"

But Goupil had heard enough. "Mr. Gauguin, this is really Theo's area. He handles our modern and impressionist work."

He held his hand out to Gauguin. "There is something new every day in avant-garde circles."

They had a brief, perfunctory good-bye shake.

"Wait," Paul said. Out of his pocket, he took a small, autographed photo of himself and handed it to Mr. Goupil.

Goupil took it with raised eyebrows and then made his exit.

"Let's continue," Theo suggested.

"Mr. Goupil exudes a noxious, ominous air. He doesn't care about new painting. He might be better at selling undergarments. He is a pimp." Paul looked down at Theo, eyes turning into black lines. "Who are you selling?" Paul asked.

Ah, always the constant challenge, Theo thought. He was glad he had been born with a calm disposition.

"Monet, Lautrec, Seurat are selling. I see possibilities for your new work. Have you brought other paintings to view?" Theo looked at the large, leather portfolio Gauguin brought, stuffed with unframed canvasses. *Let me see them all,* he thought. But he stayed patient and smiled, waiting.

Gauguin carefully repeated his unveiling of more paintings from Martinique—farmers, and landscapes. Now Theo saw and wanted everything.

"I think the work is impressive. I will confer with Mr. Goupil and make you an offer from the gallery."

"How much? I need money."

No surprise, he was desperate. Those were always the words Theo hated to hear. Selling quickly meant selling cheaply, especially for an artist who was still aspiring to establish a clientele.

"Should the gallery decline, I will represent you privately. It will be the standard pricing for new work, depending on size and subject."

"I require more, only because my family is joining me here. You will give me one hundred fifty francs for another, and I can deliver in a month."

"All in Paris together—wonderful."

Perfect, Theo thought. These new Gauguins would add to Theo's growing personal collection, and soon he could open his own gallery of modern art. He would be master of his own destiny, and Johanna would be his wife.

5

Vincent

My loved ones treat me like a disgraced prisoner. In jail there is no pretense, you are caged. Home, here, now the bars are their questions. My parents' stares betray fear, and worse, disappointment. What are you going to paint in the fields, Vincent? Who is your model, Vincent? The priest forbids girls to pose for you, Vincent! Where did you get the wine Vincent? I will explode, God help me. But I brush them aside and stay focused on my future, my dream.

I am one with nature here in the country. Beauty surrounds me in the fields. Staring across the horizon, I feel energy from the sun and sweet air. Inspiration overwhelms me, and I work like a madman until my cramped hand won't clasp my pencil. Then I sleep right there, under the stars, and breathe the night air. I feel a peace so great, the spirit I have been searching for overwhelms me and I surrender completely. I imagine what Millet saw, his delicate balance of color, his harmony of composition. I wonder if my best paintings will be here, in my mind, while I rest, smoking my pipe, staring at the stars.

I stand in the same spot where hundreds of painters have stood and bask in the glory of this perfect profession. Nature, perfectly rendered, the earth, and people, are one, and God on earth. Pure people, their simple tasks, are the truth.

Then I return home. Wait, no, here comes their attack. It is sure to begin because it is a new day. The light changes, and their ceaseless haranguing grows. Just months back with my beloved family, after they forced me to leave Clasina and the baby… this home is failure.

I sit at the table waiting and won't look at them. Father stares, appraising me in a tense silence he will soon brutally break. My poor sister Anna runs into the kitchen and runs out when she sees me. She fears she will be blown away in the coming screaming storm. She has struggles of her own—no man, no children, no job, a mouse running for crumbs to stay alive. "Ha! Good morning to you, too!" I shout at her back as she scurries away.

They all blame me for their turn with misfortune. Mother chews her food slowly, endlessly mouthing it due to her missing teeth. I pick up the bread from my plate, push back from the table.

"Vincent, what will you do today?" Father says every day, and it is the match to light the fire.

The provocation— "What will you do today?" Disguised as an innocent question.

"I have only one thing to do, and that is to steadily improve my drawing and painting, the same as every day. This is a beautiful day, so I will paint outside. I have a model coming." I leave and hear them calling after me, like I am a child. Their voices fade behind me as the door closes.

"I hope it's not a woman," Father is calling.

And Mother is huffing, "Why do we repeat this every day?"

"Vincent, we must have a serious conversation about your future."

There is a woman next door, Margot. She is the light in this dark turn.

We hide from our families, in the fields, in my studio. When she escapes to me, she will help me paint. I hope she finds a clever reason to leave the house and stay with me for the whole day.

Andries

The café was quiet due to the early hour. Andries knew it would not stay calm for long. Business was booming everywhere in Montmartre, the section on the edge of Paris that was rapidly converting from ancient to modern. The medieval city still existed here, there were a few gleaming boulevards, but mostly quiet, narrow streets and alleys, spreading out from the base of the hill. At the top of the hill, the Butte offered the greatest view of Paris. Surrounding the hilltop and scattered along the hillside were windmills and farms.

Diners would be nearly shouting when the restaurant filled, and what Andries had to say about Theo and Jo must be said quietly. Right now, the only interruption was an overly attentive waiter. Andries listened to Theo, waiting for his chance to discuss Johanna, but the business of art always opened and closed every conversation. Theo hadn't told him he was going to ask for Johanna's hand after only two meetings. It seemed an impetuous move for this man Andries knew to be calm, deliberate, and logical in all ways.

"You know Gauguin will be a very important painter," Theo said.

"Hmm, I know him as a pretentious failed stockbroker. He lost his sponsor. That's the gossip."

"Yes, and that makes him a great opportunity for us. Trust me, forget about past failures."

"How do you know?"

"Intuition. Do you like the painting?"

"I like the painting if you tell me to like the painting."

"I am going to buy them myself if the gallery doesn't. Have I earned a sale from you?"

Andries didn't want to talk about painting now. He looked down at the table, thinking of how to change the subject.

"Trust me," Theo said. "I would never do anything to jeopardize your investments." Theo leaned back in his seat, smiling. "There is virtually no risk."

"I've spent every penny I have on your selections. Obviously I trust you with art. I need to discuss a personal matter."

"Johanna?"

A stunning redhead approached the table. *Oh hell, Vivienne again*, Andries thought. *There goes my chance to ask about the sudden proposal.*

Vivienne was exactly the kind of woman who loitered about causing trouble, the kind of trouble Andries wanted to protect Johanna from. She smiled at the two of them. Slowly, Andries and Theo rose and nodded a very reserved greeting.

"Good evening, Vivienne. How are you this evening?" Theo's tone was blasé.

Why does she keep pursuing him?, Andries wondered. Theo ended their romance months ago.

Andries barely nodded to Vivienne, and she in return gave him the same wordless, hostile nothing. Her eyes, a brilliant green, quickly recaptured Theo's. She was proud, challenging, and gave Theo an unabashed, appraising look.

Again, this flirtation. The constant come-on, a temptation from hell. Andries rocked on his heels and stuffed his hands in his pockets. Theo stared back at Vivienne with a forced smile, Andries noticed with some relief.

Finally, she preened, "Theo, here in Paris you are supposed to say, 'Vivienne, you're looking so ravishing tonight. It's been too long. Please sit and have a drink with us.'"

"Vivienne, Andries and I are conducting business tonight. Another time?" Theo said, but it was not really a question and not Theo's usual magnetic voice. He had turned it off somehow. Vivienne made no effort to leave.

"Vivienne, I will find you another time," Theo tried again.

"Yes, Theo and I have business to discuss," Andries tried too.

The waiter with too few customers appeared quickly with a chair and placed it behind Vivienne, dramatically gesturing for her to sit. She did, gracefully, slowly, never breaking eye contact with Theo. The waiter snapped a napkin and placed it on her lap.

"Business—what else? Thank you. I will have an absinthe, please." The waiter bowed and left.

The table was silent.

"Buying more paintings, Theo?" Vivienne broke the chill. "Paul Gauguin, I heard, back from Martinique. News travels fast in our crowd. No more benefactor, many bills, many mouths to feed—now everything for Paul rests on Paris, maybe on you, Theo. What do you think of his new work?"

"He will sell to the thinkers with money. The critics will love his new work. He can't work the same way every day. Superstitious yet advanced in ideas."

"You have figured him out quickly. That's my Theo. And how are you, Andries? Still following Theo around with your wallet, financing your future with art?"

"Yes, *still* in the market." Andries half listened to Vivienne and Theo, wondering how quickly he could leave without seeming rude to Theo. Why Theo bothered with Vivienne, Andries had no idea.

After a few moments, Andries offered his excuses. He finished his wine in a hurried gulp, placed money next to his plate, and left the restaurant, but he didn't go far. He stood outside, smoking a cigar, staring into the restaurant, watching Theo and Vivienne. *When I'm not there, how does Theo handle her?*

He'd never liked Vivienne. Besides her beauty, she had nothing to offer.

He stood there among the couples ambling up and down the Boulevard de Clichy, a main thoroughfare, lined with the newest and most extraordinary entertainment Montmartre had to offer. Gas streetlamps cast a peaceful yellow glow on everything their light touched. The streets filled with carriages carrying tourists, Parisians in from the Champs-Elysees, and local artists mingling in the newest entertainment district of Paris. There was something for everyone here, haute and low alike, he thought.

Andries stayed in the shadows, in case that poisonous bird looked out the window. She was always spying for the next worm. His nerves were on edge, watching them sitting together. Women loved Theo. He was a sympathetic character, wearing his heart on his sleeve. They loved the way Theo listened, always leaning into them. Women also loved Andries—he knew it was his Dutch good looks.

Theo did nothing untoward, nothing animated or intimate with Vivienne. Then he reached up and out for the check.

Theo left the restaurant alone, and Andries fell in step with him. Theo, not surprised, thanked him for waiting. Now was the time to talk about Johanna, but Andries decided to wait until they got through the tourist crowd and onto their quiet residential street. Theo clapped a thankful hand on Andries's back, and together they barreled down the middle of the street at a brisk pace, artfully moving in and out of the oncoming traffic.

At the Moulin Rouge, a railway station–sized construction with a windmill on top, electric lights were blazing, and a larger-than-life statue of an elephant towered in the outdoor garden. The whole get-up was garish, Andries thought, but also amazingly good fun, especially the dancers. He watched Theo's face reflecting the changing colors radiating the scene: white, yellow, and red. They walked in silence, out of the range of the electric lights of the boisterous clubs and into the warmer yellow glow of gas lamps.

They slowed and walked around the base of the Butte, into the quiet winding narrow streets. Away from Haute Montmartre, the cafés and clubs emitted a darker glow. Prostitutes, pimps, men dressed like women, women dressed like men, and others in circus costumes wandered in and out of the gaslight, into clubs, around the back, and into the black gardens. Andries had to talk to Theo but stopping here would only invite more trouble.

When they reached Rue Lepic, almost home, Andries pulled Theo to a stop. They sat on a bench beside the vast construction of the funicular, a rail car that would travel up the side of the Butte to Sacré-Coeur.

"Theo." Andries wanted his voice to sound even, businesslike. He stuffed his hands in his pockets and tried to look casual.

"Don't think about Vivienne, she is just difficult," Theo said.

"I'm thinking about you and Jo. I refuse to see Johanna hurt."

"Don't you trust me?" Theo looked at him, waiting for an answer.

"I don't...not trust you. But why did you tell Vivienne you would find her another time?"

"I don't encourage her. I know you understand she is just ambitious," Theo said. He stretched out his long legs, rested his head on the back of the bench, and placed his hat on his lap. He closed his eyes.

"She was obviously looking for you."

"We'll figure out a way to get rid of her," Theo said softly, like he was falling asleep.

"Just say the word." Andries stood, trying to shake off the anger coming over him.

Theo was quickly up beside him.

"She thinks the avant-garde will be her way up. That is the sum total of Vivienne," said Theo with a wave of his hand.

Andries never wanted to argue with Theo, but he knew Vivienne was a dangerous woman who didn't care who or what stood in her way.

"Why didn't you tell me you were going to ask for Johanna's hand?" Andries had been alarmed when Jo told him of Theo's proposal.

"Ah." Theo took a deep breath, threw his head back, and stared at the sky. "Yes, I see, I should have. Forgive me, Andries. From the first moment I saw Johanna, I loved her. Her image swirls in my mind like a painting I will treasure forever. She is true, solid, smart, resourceful with work, beautiful. Johanna is the foundation for a new life. Tell her to trust me."

"Isn't that a bit too much? 'Swirls in my mind.' You barely know each other." Andries said with a chuckle.

"She will marry me. This will be a great time for us. We'll make our fortunes in Paris and go back to the north, rich and fat."

Andries felt this was a patronizing response he didn't deserve. And it was time to let Theo, his best friend and potential partner, know he didn't like it.

"Go back? Since when? You're good at changing the subject. Let's go." He stood impatiently and waited for Theo to get up.

"You are surprised I asked her to marry so quickly and now you are concerned?"

"You're a brother to me. And yes, I am concerned. Thanks for noticing. The lifestyle here is very cosmopolitan, not what Jo is used to. And Paris is not the place to raise a Dutch family. The expense alone, not to mention…well I don't think I have to mention the unique challenges here, do I? I am very surprised you didn't consult with me or even just talk to me like a brother would."

"Once again, please accept my apology. The proposal was impetuous in its speed, and you had already left for Paris. I knew more time might allow Jo to slip away from me if I am in Paris and she still in Amsterdam. I am not such a young man. I know now what I want when I see it." Theo rose from the bench and embraced Andries.

"Don't worry, you know women love Paris," Theo continued. "Help me make the match. I promise I will keep you close and Johanna safe."

"You think you know what Johanna wants? Tell me." Andries asked.

"Yes, I think I do," Theo said. "She wants the opportunity to do good work, live in a more sophisticated culture. She wants to help bring about the cultural change she dreams of and …who better than me to provide that for her?"

He was right on the surface. It all made sense to Andries as he listened to Theo and felt his sincerity. Yet it seemed naïve to him—a Parisian fairytale.

"Andries, do you know another man better for her?"

"No, at the moment, I guess I don't."

"Thank you, Andries. Help me make the match."

"God, you are too much." They continued down the darkened street, silently. Andries left Theo at Rue Lepic and walked to Rue Caulain Court, to his apartment building. He felt somewhat unburdened. He had been honest and said his piece, or had he? His mouth felt dry, and the cloying anxiousness still held him.

6

Johanna

The train trip from Amsterdam long. They would arrive just before dinner. She had a window seat with Fleur beside her. She feared that others, less fortunate, were forced to stand for the entire trip, some holding children. She didn't see them, but she worried they were there, in the back, their suffering hidden. Johanna rocked with the train's movement.

Nonetheless, the energy she felt for this change was unbroken. "I haven't been this excited or happy, ever," she said to Fleur. She leaned back from looking out the window and closed her eyes, blowing out a long breath.

"Same," Fleur said. "This begins our brilliant future!" She leaned into Jo and brushed back a stray hair. "You are tinged green. Why are you suffering? You need Fleur's original medicinal. Here, have a little, no one's the wiser." Fleur handed her a small flask from her purse. "I'm feeling queasy myself. Bound to happen, rocking with a train since the crack of dawn."

Johanna sipped Fleur's medicinal French brandy laced with spice-ginger and something else. *Mmm*—not easy with the relentless movement. Fleur took a taste. She looked forward to Paris and changing her life for a long time. The drug of independence she craved awaited her.

"Soon we'll see if you fell in love with a kiss or a man!" Fleur said.

"Did I say I was in love?" Jo knew she was close to falling, but two days and a few letters - she needed more. "I can't wait for you to meet him."

"Soon enough. No, I say you are in love. You've been a romantic since childhood…falling for every cause presenting itself, political and social and on and on. Well, while you are playing around with Romeo, I will be developing my baking career!"

"You will be a genius baker, Fleur. Allow me to translate your first cookbook."

"Naturally, or should I say, *naturellement*? Let's talk about shopping! What do we crave first?" They swapped French illustrations of the latest fashions for young women in Paris. Quite different from the Dutch.

"Fleur, we have to work on your French." Jo felt the brandy still burning the back of her throat. "I wish we were able to live together, then I could tutor you every night instead of watching Andries smoke his stinky cigars."

"And me, stuck with stuffy old Uncle. I bet he's a spy for my father." Fleur took another sip from her flask and raised a toast. "One day we will be independent. Until then! And now for the shopping plan."

"We need dresses, and walking suits in silk or fine linen." They were the rage. "Matching skirts with longer cut coats and shoes to match," Jo said, handing Fleur an illustration.

"Imagine lighter silk draping our legs instead of this!" Fleur said slapping her skirt.

Johanna and Fleur watched from the window as the train slowed and finally stopped. The air was thick with steam and smoke at the massive, soaring Gothic train station in Paris. They disembarked onto the wide platform, eager to stretch their legs and make the most of the rest of day. Even in the late afternoon sunlight, smoky soot filled the air with slowly swirling clouds of black and gray, instantly leaving a greasy grime on Johanna's skin. There were distant sounds of construction—hammers, saws, men's shouts—leaving her feeling like she was in a factory pounding out firing metals, not a train station in the capital of the world.

"Here we are." Jo felt loose and hot from the brandy and reached for her collar, wanting to tear it off. They stood together and interlocked arms, watching the commotion surround them. Men looked openly at Fleur, some speaking an informal French dialect Jo couldn't place. Fleur ignored them as usual. "I can't wait for you to see Theo," Jo said, scanning the crowd.

"The station seems smaller than I remember it," Fleur said. "But I was a child on holiday then, and everything seemed magnificent. Where is all that noise coming from? I smell filth. I'd forgotten the city air." She sniffed and mimed a small wretch.

Suddenly Jo saw Theo, and nudged Fleur. "That's him, with the bowler and shorter coat." He was a few cars down, looking into the line of disembarking passengers.

"He is good looking, Jo. Dutch but not too Dutch." Jo watched him, waiting until he saw her. She felt the familiar little pump in her chest when he finally saw her and beamed. He ran to meet her.

"Johanna! You're here!" He took off his bowler.

He looked pleased, with a big smile—happy and calm at the same time—so Theo, so sophisticated. He gave her a big kiss on the cheek and lifted her off her toes, hugging her very tightly.

"So wonderful to see you," he said, releasing her and kissing her hand.

"Let me introduce you to Miss Fleur Dutcher, my best friend."

"A pleasure, Miss Dutcher." Theo bowed to Fleur and shook her hand.

"So pleased to meet you, Mr. Van Gogh." Fleur gave him her splendid smile and while his head was still bowed, winked at Jo. Jo felt relieved at Fleur's instant approval.

"Oh, there is my uncle," Fleur said. "That was fast. Too bad. Well, tomorrow then."

Goodbyes were exchanged, and Johanna and Fleur hugged.

Theo offered her his arm and they walked through the station. "Let's collect your luggage."

"I sent it ahead."

Theo gently pulled her close. "Let me kiss you again. We can do that here in Paris, even in daylight."

Yes, kiss me again, in broad daylight for the world to see, Johanna thought.

He kissed her on the lips. They kept their eyes open, looking at each other. She blushed.

"Shall I escort you to Andries?"

"I would like to go the expo, have a look around." She wanted to see everything she could before being locked away under Andries's nose. It was still early enough, time for a little sightseeing, then dinner…then Andries.

"Smart, you want to see where you'll be working. When do you start?"

"The fair officially opens next week. We begin training tomorrow. Do you have time for a look at the fairgrounds and the Dutch Pavilion?"

Johanna and Theo rode the horse trolley from the train station through the city, following the Seine. Everything in Paris seemed to be under construction, in a rush to become Europe's first fully modern city. She could not move her head fast enough to keep track of all she was seeing. Everywhere she looked there seemed to be gaping holes in the streets, plumbing lines being laid down, the heavy pipes suspended from cranes. The boulevard next to the Seine was being doubled in width. New bridges could be seen half erected across the river. New trolley lines were being laid down. Almost every other structure she saw was either being torn down or built up, crawling with workers and the constant noise of machines and men. It wasn't glamorous, yet the energy floating off the construction was enveloping. She felt like an actress on a stage that glowed with energy.

They walked through the grand entrance to the Exposition Universelle, underneath the new attraction, La Tour Eiffel the gateway to the expo. She'd read there was supposed to be a restaurant and viewing platforms inside, but the structure was hollow—she could see the empty spaces between the gigantic steel beams. Photographs didn't capture the massive size and scale of the unique structure. In photographs it looked fragile, as if a strong wind could topple it. In reality it was overwhelming, powerful, modern.

A cowboy and cowgirl stood underneath the tower, posing for photographs. Johanna recognized Annie Oakley and Buffalo Bill, the famous American Western stars, here to perform at the expo. Bill began spinning a rope, jumping in and out of the whirling circle he created, while a swarm of fascinated children shrieked with pleasure.

Annie held a shotgun, its heel resting on the ground, and it stood almost as tall as she was. Her clothes were loose and easy. Her skirt was shorter, showing off heeled boots just like Bill's. Her calves were exposed. Her blouse didn't have a frill or touch of lace. It was a cotton fabric of bold red plaid, unbuttoned, exposing her neck. Her hair was long, loose—down past her shoulders. She didn't wear a hat. Now this was something—a woman with a gun, standing next to man, like an equal. She was a pioneer and made the world around her look silly, frilly, breakable. She radiated resilience and power. And she wasn't smiling. This was a woman making her own way, surely, standing her ground. Jo felt a thrill at Annie's wild, exotic boldness. Jo instantly knew she was in the right place. Paris, her new home, her new life. It was all up to her and whatever dreams she could make happen.

"The Dutch pavilion is this way." He pointed.

They walked past elaborate constructions of fairytale versions of each country's architecture, a trip around the world in a dozen spectacular blocks, all along the banks of the Seine. It was an amazing sight, glamorous and exciting. Johanna felt special standing in the center of it all.

The Dutch pavilion was a dark, oversized traditional house with an angled, pitched black roof. It was nestled between two opulently designed, bright, white sculpted-marble and concrete buildings. It looked like an ugly duckling sitting between two beauties.

"We look drab in comparison, don't you think?" Johanna asked. They sat down on the courtyard benches nestled against the river and stared at the pavilion.

"Yes, true." Theo held one arm around Jo and gestured a grand arc across the boulevard with the other. "This will make history!"

"Why did they have to stick it between these two palaces? That just makes it worse, doesn't it?"

"Forget it, now you are a Parisienne. Tell me, what will you do at the pavilion?"

"I'm lecturing on the history of Holland in Dutch, Italian, German, English, French, and Spanish. I conduct tours hourly from open to close, six days a week."

"Six languages, amazing. I hope you will spend all your free time with me."

"Yes, Theo." She felt herself turning pink again. "I need to speak with you, and I just want…" But she trailed off as she saw an Arab man with flowing white ornamental robes and head scarf, and a large shirtless African man with a monkey riding his back. They strolled by, their clothing elegantly swaying and the monkey chattering as they passed. A few children followed them, throwing crumbs at the monkey. It was a travel magazine photograph come to life.

"Yes, Johanna, I'm listening."

"I would like to have a…" She was about to say "proper court-ship" but caught herself. It sounded like something her father would say, a fate worse than death to her. "Let's get to know one another," she said, sounding boring, but not much sin in that.

They watched couples stroll the fairgrounds. Jo was drawn to the fine French fashion the women wore. Shimmering silk seemed to be the most popular, with matching-colored hats and handbags.

Suddenly Theo's attention was drawn to a nearby couple and two children. "That tall man in the unusual clothes is Paul Gauguin, one of my painters. That must be his family, I've never met them."

Jo noticed the man's black cape and beret that draped dramat-ically down the side of his face. Instead of boots he wore wooden clogs and seemed very bohemian. His wife by contrast wore more a silk suit more common to a middleclass Parisian woman.

"Hello, Theo. Yes this is my wife, Mette and my son Paul and daughter Aline."

"This is Miss Johanna Bonger."

Jo and Mette said hello and pleasantries were exchanged. Jo noticed the girl, Aline, and how tall she seemed, like her parents. She was perhaps ten or eleven and pretty with striking blue eyes. She was eating a sweet of some kind and leaning forward, staring into a refuse container, as if she had dropped something into it and was considering snatching it out. This was odd, Jo thought.

After a few more moments of small talk, they went on their way. "Shall we head to dinner?" Theo asked. "Get you a fine French meal?"

She thought about sitting in a fine restaurant in her drab clothes surrounded by a dozen women in silk.

"I should get to Andries. He must be wondering where I am," she said, but she didn't want to leave Theo.

"You told him I would meet you?"

"Yes."

"Then he won't worry. We're likely to run into him at dinner, in Montmartre."

"I think I should change into more formal clothes for dinner." She felt uncomfortable, embarrassed by her indestructible cotton and wools, created to last decades and so out of place and time. She caught him watching her again, smiling.

Theo's brow creased. "Trust me, you look very, very lovely. You're the most beautiful woman in Paris. Look around—your clothes are fine. Come, let's go."

She looked again at her clothes, not believing one word he said. "Where?"

"A special place for you Jo, trust me."

A horse-drawn trolley carried them down the wide Boulevard de Batignolles, into Montmartre, the Eighteenth Arrondissement, where Theo and Andries lived. Montmartre—so close to central Paris, yet completely different.

Jo held Theo's arm, and they walked around Haute Montmartre, passing the new galleries, restaurants, theaters, all the places that had suddenly become world famous, the new destination for tourists.

There was also low Montmartre—dilapidated buildings, sagging roofs, glassless windows, dusty parcels of land where buildings had been demolished, not yet rebuilt. The alleys were filled with cart merchants, circus tents, and young girls on blankets holding infants, selling heather.

On the hilltop the most famous of cathedrals was completing construction. The Sacré-Coeur, a magnificent design of white marble with five rounded spires, built by the Catholic church for the expiation of sins committed by slaughtering innocents during the Communard Uprising.

Theo took Jo to a Japanese specialty store. Art books, clothing, furniture, all from Japan, covered every inch of the tiny store. There was a general opulence—gorgeous colors on the fabrics. Theo held up a silk scarf printed with turquoise and yellow-gold flowers. He wrapped it around Johanna's plain, dark blue coat. The gold brightened her brown hair, the turquoise reflected green and gold in her eyes.

"You are beautiful," Theo said.

Johanna looked at herself in the mirror. The bright colors made her feel beautiful. Ostentation was not the Dutch way. But the women in Paris dressed very well. So should she.

"You would look ravishing in that kimono." A deep red kimono vibrated in the middle of the store window.

Johanna blushed. "Where would I wear something like that?"

The shopkeeper, without the slightest hint of impropriety, brought the kimono to her. With a flourish, he laid it across his arms inches from her face. It was a soft, luminous, shiny silk. Exotic geisha women wearing turquoise kimonos decorated the red silk. Small white flowers sprinkled in another pattern around the women. Gold vines twisted throughout. It was the most fantastic fabric Johanna had ever seen. Another photograph brought to life.

"Madame will wear the kimono at home in leisure, over delicate undergarments as a robe, or just by itself, the fabric is so splendid. It the most comfortable garment you will ever own. I can promise, you will come back for another. All my ladies do. Japanese design is the rage in Paris. I can't keep them in stock. You must have it today! It will not be here tomorrow. I can promise you that too."

He was so businesslike, so direct in discussing such an intimate garment. Johanna was flabbergasted. But she wanted it, and she let Theo buy it for her.

"Good evening, Mr. Van Gogh. Your usual table?" The maître d' wore a black tuxedo and carried himself with a formal elegance. The café was dark, candles glowing on all the tables. The floor-to-ceiling windows at the front of the building were open, letting the smoke out, the fresh air in. Not too busy, not too noisy. Theo had suggested a neighborhood place for a nice dinner. She was too tired tonight for one of the newer destinations filled with dancing girls, exotica, poets, and musicians that she had read about and were now the major tourist destinations.

"No, this evening just for two please," Theo said.

"But your companions are already here. They are waiting for you. Mr. Lautrec, Mr. Bernard, Mr. Seurat are at the usual table in the back."

"No, two tonight, please."

"Of course, this way." He led them to an intimate corner table.

Jo looked around. The ladies were drinking wine, and some were smoking. Several had bright red hair, highly rouged red lips and faces. The all wore lighter fabrics, brighter colors, many with thin stripes. She was instantly captivated. The tourist periodicals hadn't exaggerated the new freedoms for women in Paris. This was what she had hoped Parisian nightlife would be.

She was crazy for Theo—she felt it. Everything was new and exciting. She hadn't realized how dead she had felt before.

She took off her coat and left the silk scarf draped around her neck and shoulders. She held her precious kimono wrapped in tissue carefully on her lap. Theo was watching her again, always with his wonderful smile, and she wondered what he was thinking. He asked her if she might like to try absinthe. He really could read her mind.

Two men wandered over to their table, carrying chairs—and what an unusual sight. One was especially short, with broad shoulders but stunted legs that made him appear no taller than a child of eight or ten. He was very smartly dressed and youngish, in his early thirties or so. He wore a beard and large mustache and carried a tall hat in his normal-sized hand. Jo thought he must be very brave and proud, facing a judging world with a cheerful smile. The other man was younger, university age, sheepish looking, with long hair. He was also well-dressed but in a much more artistic manner. Standing together they looked a bit of an odd couple. The men crowded their chairs around the table and sat eagerly staring at her and Theo. They reminded her of children waiting for dessert.

"Why have you abandoned us, Theo?" It was a good-natured complaint from this small man.

"Good evening, Henri, Emile. You cannot sit here for long." Theo looked behind him to see if others were following. They weren't.

Henri Toulouse-Lautrec. Johanna recognized the name from her studies for this trip. She watched as he opened the top of his ornate cane and took a very long slug from it. It was hollowed out and inside was a flask.

"Why, who is this?" Henri challenged cheerfully.

"This is the woman I hope to marry: Miss Johanna Bonger," said Theo—with great enthusiasm, thought Johanna. He wore his heart on his sleeve with everyone, it appeared, not just her. How unusual for a man, Jo thought.

"Oh, Miss Bonger! A pleasure to meet you." Henri kissed her hand and examined her face in a friendly way. Theo introduced the other man, Emile Bernard. Jo didn't recognize his name. Emile didn't take her hand, but simply bowed, his long hair falling forward. He gave her a shy, childlike smile.

"Johanna is from Amsterdam," said Theo.

"Another from the north! Beautiful scarf, Miss Bonger. So, you have not yet agreed to marry our beloved Theo?"

"Behave yourself, or you will need a new art dealer," said Theo.

"Just asking! I see you have been holding out on us, Theo. I had no idea you were plotting a marriage."

Johanna listened to them all as she sipped her new, lovely licorice drink. Absinthe—green angel, she heard someone say. Theo had ordered it for her without her even noticing.

Henri was gracious. He seemed genuinely interested in everything everyone said, even the women who sauntered by for a few words. Emile was at least a decade younger than Theo and Henri.

He had a soft, round face and large, brown eyes, which held a permanent pleading kind of look. He was too sensitive for his own good,
she thought. He was hanging on every word Henri and Theo spoke.
She was torn between thinking these two new men were creative,
independent thinkers or just odd.

Johanna saw a woman with a parasol enter the restaurant alone,
scanning the crowd. Jo felt an odd jolt in her chest when the beautiful woman locked eyes with her and walked to their table.

The men stood up for her, laughing, happy to see her. Vivienne
was her name. Another chair was to be crowded around the table for
two. But outrageously, Vivienne sat down on Henri's lap. No one
seemed to think this was strange, not even Theo. Vivienne vibrated
in various shades of green, with blue and yellow trim, all setting
off her red hair and rouged cheeks. That shimmer could only come
from silk.

Emile inched his chair away from Vivienne. Jo could feel
Vivienne's continuous gaze. Jo gave her a friendly smile, but Vivienne
didn't smile back. She tilted her head, sizing Jo up, and ended with a
condescending smirk. She produced a cigarette and waited for Henri
to strike a match for her. Women didn't smoke in public in Holland,
because traditionalists considered it déclassé. Vivienne blew a large
grey billow across the table.

"Johanna, do you have the same Paris dream of fame and fortune as your brother?" she asked, so sweet, so musical.

Henri touched Vivienne's face, turning her chin toward him.
"Behave! Theo has already threatened us," he said in a teasing way.

She knows Andries?

"I am here for vacation and work," Johanna said.

"Vacation and work? Those are opposites. You must be a teacher,
having the summer off. Have you seen Theo's private collection yet?"
asked Vivienne.

"Yes, I was a teacher, also we have a family bus—"

"Yes, you Dutch are so resourceful. You are not married, so no children and…" Big smile and bigger pause. "You have followed Theo here for a courtship?"

Vivienne was quick, clever, and very rude, putting it all together so fast. She was instantly competitive, Jo thought. She could be in love with Theo and see me as a threat. Jo thought about challenging her back. With what? She didn't know Vivienne and considered herself above pettiness.

"I am considering a permanent move to Paris," Jo said and smiled into Vivienne's green glowing eyes. Jo thought the woman might be drugged.

"Wonderful, Johanna, I look forward to many dinners with you. Vivienne, you are hurting my feelings," Henri said. "Why don't you pay attention to me? You are sitting on *my* lap. *Not* our Theo's."

Theo put his arm around Johanna in a possessive way. "Vivienne's had too much." Henri laughed and Emile was giggling in a way that reminded Johanna of her troublesome teenagers at school.

She listened as the conversation turned to the newest scandals in Montmartre. An artist, jilted by his model and lover, had killed himself on the street in front of her as she left a café with her new painter-boyfriend. God-awful. Another, thankfully comical, was a row between students and a teacher over modern versus classical painting. In a fit of pique, the teacher, infuriated with his student's radical work and feeling it a personal insult, commenced a sword fight but using paintbrushes, ensuing in a brawl-riot that lasted hours. There was broken furniture and paint damage, and the land-lord demanded the school close, stranding the students. The school had refused to refund their money.

She had imagined the art world to be refined and intellectual, but here in Paris, the new world of modern art seemed like a free-for-all, with no rules, or perhaps the people who broke the rules won first prize. She felt relieved when Theo sent Vivienne, Emile, and Henri on their way, and they could finish their first dinner together alone.

After dinner, though it was quite late, they walked hand in hand to Theo's apartment in Montmartre. The glow of moonlight reflected across their dark path. The streets of Haute Montmartre were noisy with tourists and night revelers, and raucous music bleeding through the theater walls. The windmill atop the nightclub Moulin Rouge was brightly lit.

The absinthe made her head feel detached from her body, floating like a balloon. Her feet were tingling and numb. The absinthe also made the colors she saw blurry, swimming into each other. She held onto Theo's arm, and he guided her through the crowds. "Have you been seeing Vivienne?"

"No." Theo didn't seem interested in talking about Vivienne and shrugged an answer.

"She has eyes for you," Jo said.

"She wants Henri, he is the rage of Montmartre. Success is the best aphrodisiac."

She had seen a blankness in Theo's face when he looked at Vivienne, when he spoke to her. She couldn't really tell what he felt, but obviously he didn't love Vivienne now, if he ever had.

Theo's apartment building was newer than most, elegantly designed with a large entry foyer, a central staircase of carved wood, and very high ceilings.

They entered his apartment. "This is my parlor, where I show and sell privately." Theo, she was glad to see, left the door wide open out of a sense of propriety.

"Your private collection. Do you still work at Goupil?"

"Yes, I do, but I acquire pieces Goupil is not interested in. One day I will have my own gallery, so this is the beginning, and a little 'insurance,' so to speak. We all do it. A dealer must have inventory, especially in the beginning when he is trying to build a name for himself."

She walked around the room, looking at the art, listening to Theo explain the importance of each painting. There were three main rooms—the large entry parlor, a larger living room behind it, and a bedroom, which she couldn't see. The kitchen was to the right and spacious enough for a table in the center, with a new gas stove polished to a spotless, gleaming black. And the bathroom was large enough for the copper tub and sink with room to walk. Theo's interior design taste was just like him—elegant, not a lot of excess, few knickknacks, and many, many paintings everywhere.

There was a red velvet couch that would seat three or four, quite large enough to sleep on, in front of the fireplace. More velvet chairs were set to make a conversation circle. Oriental carpets of deep reds and blues covered the living room and parlor floors. The ceilings were high. She imagined the gas heaters were enough for the milder Paris winters.

She stopped in front of two pieces Theo hadn't discussed. One was a pen and ink intricate drawing of a farm. It was an unusually drawn piece—that much she knew instantly. Unique dots, dashes, simple forms filled the space. The artist's vision, simultaneously childlike and sophisticated, aroused her curiosity. The painting next to it, an oil—almost monochromatic—of a farmer struggling with a sack. The overall effect was sad and inspired deep sympathy for the farmer. She thought it must have been created by someone with both admiration and great empathy for the struggles of the poor, with no attempt to glamorize either. Someone who felt the same way she did about society's inequities. This artist had the power to change minds and open hearts to see the everyday differently. She leaned close to the painting, looking for a signature.

"The artist is my older brother, Vincent. You will love him." And he leaned in to kiss her.

She closed her eyes. She felt his warmth on her face. It was the beginning of a great kiss, until Andries announced himself in the doorway and ruined it.

"Well, hello there," Andries said loudly.

"Good to see you," said Theo, pulling away from Jo.

Andries threw his hat and coat on one of the chairs, in a familiar way. "I've been waiting at the apartment for hours, Johanna. I thought something had happened. I was about to cable home. Then I thought you might be here with Theo. Do you know it is after midnight?"

"I don't think we need to be so dramatic, do we?" Jo said quietly, wishing he didn't always interfere. She hadn't realized it was so late.

"Sorry, I was just about to bring Johanna to your place," said Theo.

Andries plopped himself down on the chair on top of his coat.

Theo put his hand on Andries's shoulder. "Where were you tonight? I thought we would run into you. Can I bring you a drink?"

"Where was I tonight? I was at home waiting for Johanna." He was almost shouting. "Johanna wanted to see your collection. A private showing?" Andries was sarcastic. Jo felt a flood of embarrassment and inwardly cringed. She walked around the apartment, gathering her scarf and bag. She stopped in front of Andries slouching in the chair.

"Ready?" She kept her voice calm.

"I am so sorry. I didn't realize how late it was." Theo was soft reassurance.

Jo didn't want Theo to see her and Andries squabble. She would leave and take this up with Andries privately.

"Thank you, Theo, for a wonderful day and evening. Andries will walk me. It's so late, and I have to begin work tomorrow." She took Andries's arm, still hiding her anger. She would go to sleep and dream about Theo's kiss.

7

Vincent

I am reveling in the deliverance of my dreams. I am an artist, my work improves daily. I can feel I have captured what is special in the peasants, work, and life. Brown and gray are beautiful tones, endless in their depth and usefulness. Warm gray and cool gray, one day I fall in love with warm, the way it melts away and quiets the storm in my brain, like Margot. Brown isn't as beautiful, but it is the color of the earth, and that is an inspiration. Brown and gray both work with my black. In my painting, the faces of the peasants are carved with black and brown. Shadows create the features and their poor feast—it is a dark harmony. I use the red, gold, gray, yellow, and a dark white to carry the light but not the energy of the scene. This morning, I will finish this painting. And then, I will find my new love.

I am reborn with Margot. She once was beautiful. She too has been beaten down and destroyed for years. Her family is horrible, four older sisters, bitter prunes who never married. They deny her the life they themselves can't have. We have a beautiful affair. This is our rebirth. When she looks at me, she stands tall, happiness in her eyes, an illusion of youth. She buys me expensive art books with her own money! She believes I will be an important painter. She wants me to hold her, kiss her, love her. She will marry me. No one approves, but this time no one needs to. I will never allow them power over me again.

"Vincent, they are coming," Margot shouted. "Look!"

"Hold on to me. They won't come out this far." Vincent hoped they had lost them in the fields behind the house. They were small but growing larger.

"This is always when it falls apart," Margot said. "Everything collapses around me when I start to feel happy." She never looked up, kept her weeping eyes downcast, like a prisoner of war forbidden to look at her guards. "I wish I could die right now. Before everything is ruined."

"Margot! Margot!" the voices screamed as if calling a runaway dog. Friendly, false, light on the surface, fury underneath. *I will protect her.*

She cowered and covered her ears.

"Oh, God help me, save me, spare me. I will never survive this torture, Vincent."

I didn't see her take the pills. I realized only after when she fell over, and her mouth—God, it was foaming white.

Johanna

"You wouldn't think playing a Little Dutch Girl would be so tiring," said Johanna to Fleur. The same lecture, the same questions over and over—it got tedious faster than she'd thought. But they were lucky to have these jobs, even luckier to have good apartments to come home to, which they could never afford here in Paris on the wages they were paid. Employment was scarce, and the wages for women were atrocious. The exploitation was criminal, Jo thought. The dance-hall girls, the waitresses, the artist's models—none of them earned enough. Prostitution was commonplace and, for licensed women, legal. It was a horrible side of Paris she and Fleur loathed.

They were changing out of their Little Dutch Girl costumes.

They laughed at them, traditional folk costumes no one wore any-more—ankle-length embroidered aprons, stiff wool, wooden shoes. But the worst were the white hats with flying buttresses, like the Notre-Dame, shooting out from their ears. The summer was hurtling by, and at the end of each day, they took out the false braids they wound into their hair and restyled it in the popular manner with curly bangs, upswept buns, and small, colorful hats. Outside of work, they lived in their new light, stylish, walking suits. They loved touring the elegant parts of Paris together and forgetting the poverty. They enjoyed the central city, which had the best shopping and easy transportation.

"Who is your date tonight?" Jo asked.

"Tonight, I'm seeing a pastry chef! I'm learning all his secrets. But after this, no more fun. Time to focus on a serious relationship. I can't be single with you married. Maybe Theo has a double date for me?"

"He has an older brother. And I haven't said yes yet, you know."

"But you will—he is everything you want—he is a man living in the future. An older brother—hmm, he could be something. What do you know about him?"

"Not much, his name is Vincent, and he is an artist. Should I ask?" Fleur was right. Theo was seeing a future she wanted.

"Do you think good kissing runs in the family?"

They walked together along the Seine toward the exit of the fair. It was dusky, hazy, hard to see, it might rain. The evening fair crowd was moving in. Buffalo Bill and Annie Oakley packed them in every night.

"Fleur, look. Over there, the children digging in the trash again." Children were allowed to run loose at the fair. It wasn't safe.

"Looking for sweets."

"You think that's all. They are very thin, don't you think?"

Several heads bent down and out of sight into the giant bin. Skirts were flying up, legs and rumps sticking out, as three girls rummaged through trash. One was familiar, her movements fast and purposeful. Something about her she recognized…

"Come on, let's get over there, this shouldn't happen," Jo said.

But long before they got close enough, the children had been shooed away by fair workers.

"Leave well enough alone, Jo, we've got dates, and we don't want to be moist."

Jo went on alone to meet Theo, and Fleur her pastry chef.

Theo and Johanna enjoyed a slow dance together at the Italian pavilion's outdoor café, but Theo kept breaking the step, bringing her to a stop, and pushing her to start again, with a quick glance to the heavens. Finally, he gently pushed her to follow, and said, "You like to lead?" with his usual way of speaking, making statements into questions.

"Oh, was I?" Johanna flushed hard.

"Just your instinct?"

"I don't know, I never realized. I'm sorry." She was blushing again.

"Don't apologize." He held her tight and whispered in her ear, "I like it, but not in public."

He was whispery, risqué, and proper at the same time, she thought. She loved being in his arms, his smell, his skin, his face. His touch was so light and firm at the same time. She dreamed about him. He listened to her. He looked at her when she talked, like she was a goddess. She felt natural with him. This was how she wanted life to be, in Theo's arms, listening to his voice humming in her ear.

Theo had a purpose, more than money. And he would allow her to develop her own passion, her own ideas, and create change. Change that would help people. It was indeed a mission in the new world of painting, and surely, Johanna thought, it was only a matter of time before Theo would make these young painters famous and his business future secure.

I am the stability. I will create a peaceful, organized home life. It was an impetuous decision, she knew. *When he asks me again, I will say 'yes'.*

His face so close to hers now—this was when she was happiest. So close, his breath on her face, warm and soft.

"The summer's almost over. How much longer will you stay in Paris?"

Put your face closer to mine, closer. Let me rest my cheek on your cheek forever, she thought.

"How about a kiss?"

"Yes."

They kissed and stopped dancing. No one noticed. Finally, she broke the kiss.

"Please stop. I might faint," she teased, waving her hand in front of her face.

"You love me. Are you ready to marry?"

"Yes."

Theo picked Johanna up and squeezed her tight. "Thank you," he whispered to the sky. "We'll get married right away."

"Shouldn't we return home and meet each other's families?" Theo still hadn't met her parents. Her father had been demanding a meeting for weeks. She only knew Theo's family by the photos in his apartment. Theo's father was a minister. He had a sister and his brother Vincent, the artist, with whom he carried on an extensive correspondence—thick letters, filled with fine sketches of farmers, weavers, neighbors, the people who inhabited the rural section outside of Amsterdam called Brabant, where they lived.

"We can leave our families out and just get married."

"Are you joking?"

"Yes, just avoiding all the question. 'Where will you two live?' You know how nosy parents are."

"Paris!" Where in Paris? Central Paris was out of the question—the expense, the distance from Theo's work in Montmartre. They should stay in Montmartre, but it was really two places. One was a unique blend of quarry workers, farmers, bohemians, painters, poets, sculptors, starving artists. Poorer families struggled, hungry children begged from tourists, and it wasn't very safe either. So different from life at home. It made her sad, angry, sometimes made her hate Paris. She looked at the slums and wondered how she could help. Especially the children, alone in the streets.

But in Haute Montmartre, life was enviable. And at night, a walk or trolley from central Paris, the large tourist section catered to big city appetites as lovely as a dream or grotesque as the worst nightmare. They would get a bigger apartment closer to the park, for their children, and farther away from the Butte.

A group of children lingered by the ornate concrete railing. Theo twirled her once as the song ended, and Johanna saw the restaurant, the dancers, the river. The children dug through the garbage.

One child grabbed something from the bin, immediately handed it to a smaller child beside her, and then dove down again. The smaller child quickly ate, scanning right and left, keeping a lookout.

Johanna stared at them. One of the children, with long legs and tall for a girl, was able to reach way down into the base of the bin. When a gendarmes appeared, she and her companions fled.

"Let's walk," Jo said, clasping Theo's hand. They made their way to the Seine and sat on a bench facing the river. Johanna nestled herself into Theo and leaned her head into his neck. The boats glided by casting shimmering beams on the water.

"What do you like about Paris?" Theo asked and wrapped both his arms around her.

This was what she liked most about Paris—being close to Theo, listening to his heart, and having his deep voice vibrate in her head. Sometimes she asked him nonsense just to hear his voice.

Theo kissed her then, in the dark on the bench, and her mind went blank, a happy swirling blank of nothingness and an anticipation of the thrills ahead.

A dark mass of children scrambled and squabbled around the bench, darting back and forth, squealing and giggling. It was the kissing, Johanna knew.

"Do you love the art?" asked Theo, his voice humming the question.

The art in Paris, vibrating colors and the stories behind them, every painting held a thousand thoughts. Paris was filled with the romance of the artist's struggle, she felt special to be a part of it.

One of the children was upon them, begging, a child's voice and somewhat familiar. Jo felt the recognition in her chest before her eyes could clearly focus in the dark. Theo let her go, he was digging in his pocket for coins.

"Thank you, sir. You, Madame, can you spare a franc?" In the uncertain light, Jo saw the long legs, the pleading eyes of the child. Was it Paul Gauguin's child?

"Miss Gauguin What are you doing?"

The child froze. A soft gasp came from her, then she broke and ran.

Johanna ran after her, but she wasn't fast enough. She looked for Mrs. Gauguin as she ran. She heard Theo calling to her. But she couldn't look back, or she would lose Aline.

"Johanna! Johanna!" Theo called and followed.

Theo caught up to her quickly and grabbed her arm. He was winded and wiped his brow with his sleeve.

"Johanna, God, you scared the hell out of me. What are you doing?"

"It's her, Gauguin's daughter. Don't you recognize her?. She's running around loose. I don't see her parents." Her throat burned gasping for breath.

"At the Expo, children run loose," Theo said and shrugged.

"But she was eating garbage. She was begging. You just gave her money!"

"All right," Theo said, nodding seriously. "Let's have a walk and see what we can see."

"Mrs. Gauguin must be here somewhere." Perhaps Aline was simply playing at begging with the other children. She couldn't imagine Mrs. Gauguin allowing her to—

"You've made a mistake. It's dark, everything blends in the dark."

"No, I'm sure. You must have his address. Something must be wrong. We need to help."

Vincent

I lay on the floor of the studio, knees up, using my legs as an easel, paper on my lap, drawing. I knew he would come to fight with me, all the while claiming he was trying to help me. He wants me to behave like he does, and he wants to destroy my plans.

Father enters and scans with squinted eyes. Looking at all my work, thinking this is a mess. "This doesn't look like my parlor, the way a room should." He sees only debris. He will try to hide his disgust, but only for a minute, then his bile and rage will fill the room with heat, and we will both choke with screaming.

"Oh, I didn't realize." Father looked for a place to sit, as if there wasn't any place to sit. He pushed my sketches away with his foot and said, "Wasn't there a chair in here?"

"I burned it." *I didn't look at him. I keep my mind and eyes on my drawing, as a distraction. I am already half destroyed. First my brother does their bidding and makes me leave my Clasina. I am to go home, to the bosom of my family, and recover myself, resume my training with less expense, less shame for them. Ha! Now Margot! I am supposed to abandon her too.*

"Why would you burn a chair?"

"For fuel. The cold." *So I could lay with Margot in my studio and not have her shiver in the cold. I draw. If I look at him again, he will make me burn with anger.*

"We can thank the Lord she did not eat enough poison," Father said.

"Yes, thank the Lord. Margot will live, and we will marry. I am going to Copenhagen to help her recovery." *I report with every ounce of emotion out of my voice. They only understand worship as an emotion. Anything else is an indulgence they loathe, but they can't deny me this time.*

"She is in a mental hospital. She will be there for a very long time. Her family forbids you to see her, ever."

They are nothing to me, they can't tell me what to do. I am not a dog to lock outside. I won't even answer this evil. I will leave and I will be with her.

"I understand this has been another terribly upsetting situation for you."

You understand nothing, nothing. Keep the conversation in your head, don't speak to him, draw. Wait…There is more loving evil coming.

"I wonder—no, I believe…I believe this from the bottom of my soul, what I am about to tell you. I feel so strongly, and God is guiding me in my thoughts. I have prayed on this, and now I know the answer for you, Vincent." *He moves his hand slowly, gesturing to his heart, to the heavens, and then back to his lap as he speaks. Finally, he points with emphasis to me. His finger feels like a knife waiting to plunge.*

"You must have help with your illness, a place where they understand how to help guide you to an ordinary path. In Gheel, there is a hospital where you can recover yourself. Learn how to be a productive—"

I jump to my feet in one quick move. "You want to lock me up! Your own son because I don't think like you. I am an artist! This is an artist's studio! It will never look like your parlor." *He holds up his hands, as if I was going to hit him! He is the one provoking me!*

Father gets off his knees and with one foot, hikes himself back up to standing, using his arms as leverage. It is hard for him, and I hold out my hand to him, but he brushes me aside.

"Yes, Vincent, are you even trying to control yourself? It looks to me as if you are making no attempt at all to carry on in a reasonable fashion. You need help."

"Help with what? You are my problem!"

"Vincent, look at this room. Does this look the way a room should? This is not the way a grown man behaves. The outbursts of screaming and anger. You *must* find an ordinary path. You must pray for a better life, and the Lord will help you."

"What is an ordinary path, Father? I despise ordinary. Don't you understand -- I am a man. I need a wife!"

Father puts his hands over his ears and bends over like he is the one in pain. "I can't hear you when you scream, Vincent."

"Then I will scream louder and longer until you can hear me!" Father left me in the studio. I followed him, watching. As he left, he limped slightly, one shoulder noticeably lower than the other. When he reached the house, he was red-faced, breathing heavily, saying, "I'm going for a walk," to Anna. She must have been spying on us, waiting at the door, listening to our shouts. He reached for his hat and cloak. They both saw me watching and ignored me.

"Wait, let me come with you." Anna clutched her shawl around her and hurried after him.

"I want to be alone," he said.

"I'll wire Theo to come tonight. He will help." Ah beloved Theo again to save the day.

Father didn't answer and walked away toward the fields behind the house. Fifty yards ahead, he staggered and then fell stiff like a tree, face first into the earth. Anna ran, her voice howling. "Father!" I ran faster and got to him first. When I turned him over and wiped the dirt off his face, his eyes were half open, and his mouth a circle without breath. Anna fell on him screaming for help.

Johanna

Death and destruction surrounded Jo the second she walked through the entrance of the Heaven and Hell nightclub, the newest cabaret in Montmartre. The doorway was a twelve-foot-round open mouth, garish, with oversized, protruding fangs, a bulbous nose, and high, arched eyebrows that met in the middle. Inside, the Cabaret du Néant—the "Cabaret of Nothingness"—was theatrically appointed as a dungeon. Waiters in flowing monk's robes, complete with rope belts and sandals, glided across the dimly lit restaurant.

Jo looked around. The space was shaped like an L, with one wall set aside for a stage. She walked through the L-shaped space but didn't see Theo or Andries. The staff spoke in contrived, morbid tones. More actors than waiters, Johanna thought. This wasn't going to be one of her favorites, and why Theo had chosen this place to announce their engagement to Andries was beyond her. Probably because it had just opened—be the first to go, enthusiastically on top of things, show them all a good time.

She sat alone at table, which she had never done in her life. And the table was a real closed coffin. All the tables were closed coffins. Her mind started to race on the good, the bad of women sitting alone, especially in such an ugly place, when a familiar voice caught her ear. The painters were here, Henri Toulouse Lautrec, Emile Bernard, and another she didn't know. And Vivienne too. The woman who patterned herself after the most cliché femme fatale. She was throwing her youth away, her nakedness, pandering to painters. Instead of developing skills to make a living.

"Madame, may I offer you a drink?" a waiter asked. "We have

kiss of the snake, spider bite, bloody dagger, bloodsucker, venom
bite—"

"Thank you," Johanna interrupted. "I'll try the bloodsucker."
That's what she felt like, knowing Aline was struggling somewhere
and she couldn't find her. She and Theo had gone to Gauguin's
studio, which turned out to be a space shared by many artists. He
wasn't there. No one knew where he lived. And Andries was back in
Amsterdam this past week, helping father, so she had the apartment
to herself. Fleur stayed with her those days, and they stayed up all
night reading silly French romances, playing with all the new cos-
metics. But still she ached to help this child.

"Yes, Madame, your wish is our command."

Johanna took in her surreal, grotesque surroundings and wondered why anyone would enjoy such evil. The walls were covered
with skulls, skeleton parts, gruesome battle pictures, and photographs of guillotines in action, rows of cannons and bodies from
the Communard Uprising of 1871. Many of the photos had been
taken not far from where she now sat. Montmartre, the mountain of
martyrs. Even the street where Theo lived, Rue Lepic, had been the
scene of barricades overrun, ambushes and assassinations.

Guests filed past her table to the open space in back of the dungeon to watch the stage show.

The monk put a large goblet down. "Here is your bloodsucker,
Madame. But beware, sip oh so gently. It is one of our most potent."

"What's in it?"

"Our recipes are very secret, but there is the green angel. This is
all I am allowed to share, otherwise, I shall be flogged to the bone."

Green angel—absinthe. She took a big gulp to calm the jitters
this evil place evoked. Suddenly she thought of Andries—he would
be happy about the marriage, wouldn't he? He loved Theo, he'd introduced them, they would be one happy group. And he would have
his apartment back to himself, not be responsible for her anymore.
And he was responsible, she realized after living with him. He was

often out late, maybe drank too much, but otherwise he was hard-working. He was up every morning, scouring all of Montmartre for art, and now Montparnasse, where artists were moving to get away from the tourists in Montmartre. He bought some work and started a minor branch of his father's business here, insuring galleries against theft and damage. And then regularly returning home to Amsterdam, he turned out contracts for his father. He was responsible and trustworthy.

Where was Theo? He was never late. Glancing around in the dimness, Johanna was drawn to watching the painters. Lautrec, Emile, Gauguin and Vivienne, sitting at another coffin ten feet away.

Something about all of them seemed perfect for this macabre, dimly lit setting, something in their expressions, dramatic, serious, brooding. They fit in this light.

She hated sitting there alone.

Suddenly Gauguin turned, eyes meeting hers, startling her. She quickly looked away. Alone, she didn't want to give him the wrong impression.

"What do you think of the names of the drinks? My favorite is Brain Rot. Shows some creativity," she heard Emile say. She watched them from behind her menu. Emile looked like he was trying to lighten their mood. There was a false lightness to him, he kept nervously throwing his head back and shaking his hair out of his eyes. She couldn't hear everything, the cement walls of the cell-like room played games with everyone's voices.

"Yes, let's work our way through the menu of cocktails," Henri suggested.

"I have an idea for you, Henri," Gauguin said, throwing his arm over the back of his chair. "Why don't you create a poster advertisement for this place?" He was testy, mean.

Emile and Vivienne looked down at the table, avoiding the fight. Henri tapped his cane at his side, and the glasses tinkled slightly as he said, "Paris is an empty desert for a poor man, isn't that right, Paul?"

"I imagine," said Paul, ignoring him, "that you would use many long strokes of bloody red, black, and purple, with Pepper's Ghost chrome yellow. But there are no women. What will you do with no women?"

"Excellent idea," Henri said breezily, "but my studio is full. How about if I put in a good word for you? You could use the work if you could find some free studio space. Are you still carrying around the photographs of yourself, handing them out for promotion? Sign one for me. I will offer the owners of this establishment your services."

"Life is easy when you have money for every little trinket your heart covets," Paul said, glaring down his nose.

"Oh, you are making a tiny joke? You are so clever. I don't think I've heard that one since primary school. Are you expecting me to pay your bill?" Henri aimed his cane at Paul and swished it quickly. "Get out of my sight."

Paul didn't leave, just swallowed his drink in one gulp as Johanna caught his eye again. She pretended to look at her menu.

"Have you examined all the photographs, Henri?" said Emile, gesturing toward the walls. "They are real images. Can you imagine living through such carnage?"

"I can imagine," said Vivienne.

"Why are you staring at Johanna Bonger?" Henri continued. "She is with Theo van Gogh. Good, Theo will be coming, brighten us up. She exudes a bit of intelligence, not your type, I think."

"Shut up, Henri," Paul said. "I believe I've met her."

"Johanna is Andries Bonger's sister. A possible customer. Why don't you go explore?" Egging him on.

Jo stiffened in her seat. Thankfully, Andries walked into the dungeon just then and joined her.

"Ah, Mr. Bonger and his fat wallet have entered the dungeon,"

Henri continued. "Two for one...But *restrain* yourself, Paul, give them at least a moment together. Show a little decorum."

Henri made eye contact with Johanna, offering up his glass, and motioned he would be over in a moment.

"Sorry I'm late," Andries said in Dutch. "You're all alone here, it looks terrible. Where's Theo?"

"I thought he was with you?" A small panic welled in her.

"He's not at the gallery. I swung by to pick him up. In public, Jo, smile."

She smiled for Andries. "Theo's never late." She tilted her chin. "Henri and some others are over there, fighting like children. *Vivienne* too, of course. What a parasite. No, she's like a hound from hell, a hellhound, or a hell bitch."

"Hell bitch? What are you drinking? Give it to me." Andries tested the drink. "Don't make eye contact, maybe we can be spared a moment of peace. The tall one is Paul Gauguin." He drank more of Jo's drink. "Absinthe and brandy—lethal. I am shocked you ordered it."

"Theo introduced me to Gauguin. I saw his daughter, Aline, at the World's Fair." Remembering the desperation in the girl's voice made Johanna flush with dread. "She was eating refuse from the bottom of a garbage can and begging."

"No, that's impossible—I heard from one of my gallery clients the family has returned to Copenhagen. Oh lovely, they are coming over. Just smile now. I refuse to pay the entire bill."

Jo's thoughts were still on Aline. How could she be here if the family had left? She wanted to speak to Mrs. Gauguin, find out what was going on—maybe this was an opportunity, if she could get a moment alone with the father.

Suddenly the artists were joining their table. Paul sat next to her, Vivienne on her other side, Henri and Emile beside Andries across the way. Andries made the introductions between Jo and Paul. They made small talk about Amsterdam for a few seconds before painting became the main topic. They talked about Gauguin's choice of colors—they were impressive, almost unique, a little of Cezanne's influence. The new landscapes, the images of the primitives were magnificent! Henri made it all sound friendly, and whatever fighting she'd overheard was over.

Something tickled in Jo's nose. What was the smell? It was a complicated and unpleasant. She pulled out her handkerchief and dotted her nose. Was it something sweet from Vivienne mixed with something rank from Gauguin? Vivienne's face—so much rouge again. Jo thought it was inappropriate, but in Montmartre at night brightly rouged faces were commonplace.

Henri tired of the banter first. "Where is Theo?" he asked.

Andries sipped his drink, squeezed Jo's hand now and then, and looked back and forth between the artists with a half-listening kind of smile. He never once looked at Vivienne, Jo noted.

"I don't know." Andries shrugged.

"Where have you hung my painting?" Paul asked Andries.

Andries didn't want him to know it was stuffed into storage at his family's office in Amsterdam.

"In the parlor," he lied and gently stepped on Johanna's boot under the table.

"What frame did you install?" Paul tilted his head far back on his neck, slowly drumming his long, thick fingers. Not a challenge, he wouldn't pester a buyer.

"Pepper's Ghost Show will begin in five minutes, take your seats please," said a monk, roaming among the tables to herd the guests into the back room, where the other waiters performed a disappearing act.

Andries smiled at Paul but broke the silence. "Anyone interested in the show?"

"Sit. The act is ridiculously bad," said Henri. "They throw a writhing, chained virgin into the fires of hell. Shall we see how revolting the food is? Pick something horrible sounding, and I will hail a monk."

"How is your family enjoying Paris?" Johanna asked Paul. Maybe she could establish a rapport with him, and then as they left this hellhole she could ask for a moment alone and talk about her concern for Aline. Another bloodsucker was put in front of her.

"My family has gone to Copenhagen to help a sick relative of my wife's," Paul said. The head went back, the chin out and the eyes two black slits.

"I saw Aline at the fair just yesterday," Jo countered without thinking.

"They have left Paris," he said loud and fast.

She felt pushed back, thought it better to say nothing, but she could feel the bile rising in her throat. Why would he lie?

Henri picked up the thread. "All urchins look alike in the dark," he said, and laughed.

Paul barked back quick as a shot, "My daughter is not an urchin!"

"Aline seems like a wonderful young woman." She felt even more concerned for the child.

"You were hallucinating, Miss Bonger," said Gauguin.

He was an absent father, maybe he really didn't know where his family was. Clearly, he a bully.

The bloodsucker was affecting her brain and she could be mistaken, Johanna thought. It was dark, children look alike. Like Fleur said, kids scavenging for sugar and just another girl begging.

"I was wondering where Theo is," she said, changing the subject.

"Children love the fair, don't they? What was Aline doing at the fair, at night, and alone?" Henri was using his sweet voice. He had put it together, Jo thought.

"I would know where my children are," snapped Paul. "My family is my business, not yours!" And then to Andries, "Tell Theo I must speak with him." He stood up, dramatically threw his napkin down on the table, and left.

"Ah, no good deed goes unpunished," Vivienne purred.

The group laughed loud and long, but Jo couldn't bring herself to join in. Nothing was funny about a child in distress.

"It's safe now, Jo, tell us what you saw. We are all friends, here to help one another," said Henri.

"I saw a child, eating out of the garbage and begging." She felt self-righteous and relieved. Maybe they would help Aline, bully Paul into…But Andries was reaching for his wallet, he was done.

"I thought this was going to be another dreary night," said Henri to the table, to another round of laughter.

"Paul is mad," said Emile, drunk and a little silly.

Andries stood up. "That's all for us tonight. We have early mornings." He threw some money on the table. "I'll go get Paul to calm down," Andries said.

"Sit down and let Gauguin enjoy his temper, it's good for his painting," Henri said. "Theo won't be concerned. Paul has nowhere else to go. You have bought one of his paintings, you might buy another. His temper is all for show."

Emile turned to Johanna. "He had a benefactor to support his painting, but that is over. Paul doesn't have enough money for family and paint."

"Mrs. Gauguin wants to leave, but Paul can't afford the train fare," Vivienne said. "We all know. It's so funny that you don't. I wonder why Theo doesn't tell you anything?"

Johanna felt herself flush red. What *hadn't* Theo told her?

Andries held out his hand for Jo and slid out from behind the coffin. She was leaving the table like a frightened little girl.

"Oh, you're leaving. I'm disappointed. I thought you knew you were picking a fight with a monster!" said Henri. "Brave girl. Let's change the subject. Andries, stay, tell us what is selling, and who is buying."

"I imagine Theo will be upset about Paul." Vivienne's green eyes held Johanna's. "Where is dear Theo?"

"Yes, why isn't he here?" said Henri. "It is late already, and I am ready for the crowd at Chat Noir."

"Vincent," said Vivienne, with dreadful, loud finality. "There's a new problem with the family and Vincent. I will put money on it." She rubbed her fingers together, looking at the table for a bet. "Theo has been called home again to fix Vincent. Ten francs he is en route to the north as I speak."

She and Andries hurried out the monstrous door. Vivienne, the monster, knew more about Theo and Vincent than she did. "I wonder why Theo doesn't tell you anything," rang in Jo's ears.

Theo

Theo had received the shocking telegram informing him of his father's untimely death while he was still at Goupil that afternoon. He caught the first train to Brabant, Holland, without enough time to send a message to Jo, to tell her he was leaving.

Life changes in a blink, Theo thought. His father, gone too soon, collapsed in the field only steps from home, his heart just stopped. Had he felt pain coming? Anna said only that she saw him walk from Vincent's studio after a terrible fight. His arm flew up, and he collapsed.

Later, after the funeral and with the guests all gone, Theo, Anna, and Mother sat in the kitchen. Anna stared out the tiny kitchen window at Vincent's cottage studio, as if by staring long enough some insight would reveal itself to her. Mother spoke desperate words in a fatalistic tone. What was to be done now? How would they live? They could rent out Vincent's studio, bring in some money. But what to do about Vincent?

"It has been terrible," Mother said. "Vincent won't do anything. He has failed at everything. Now with Father gone, we are impoverished."

"He's too special to work," Anna said, "and won't help around the house either."

Theo tried to break into the diatribe. "Vincent is studying to be a painter. That *is* a profession."

"He has made us pariahs in town. The shame is unbearable," said Mother.

"The service was very moving," Theo said, reaching for his mother's hand. "Every neighbor for miles has visited, brought you food, sat with you. Those are signs of respect."

Anna turned from the window, as if she had it all figured out. "Everything Vincent does causes enormous distress to us. I know he understands, but he just won't—"

Before she could get her entire sentence out, Mother broke in. "I can't speak to him. Everything is a fight. He refuses to do the normal, ordinary things. It is impossible to be in the same room with him. Now he lives in the studio, a filthy pigsty."

Vincent did reason, but emotion guided his logic—an unusual order for a man, emotion before reason, but not for an artist.

"He's your son, Mother. You know how to talk to him without provoking him."

"I don't think I can!"

"Don't you want to try?"

"I fear he doesn't care about anything…but himself." Despite her emotion she was monotone, fatalistic. "You know Father was going to have him committed to a mental institution at Gheel." Sadness and frustration further deepened her heavily creased face, drawing her eyes and mouth down.

Theo put his arm around his mother, he kissed her gently on the cheek. "Don't worry, Mother, we can sort through all this together." Putting Vincent in a mental institution would have been a fate worse than death. Hospitals were prisons, places poor people without families to care for them went to die. Mental hospitals were worse. Putting Vincent in one was an overreaction. His father loved Vincent. He just didn't understand his temperament.

"Vincent was born this way," Mother said. "One moment a loving child and the next, his heart exploding. I love Vincent, but I don't know what to do. Nothing I do eases his pain."

Theo vividly remembered his childhood and how he'd worshipped Vincent. Vincent was exciting, he saw the world around him differently from everyone else, always creating something fantastic from virtually nothing. An empty summer day would float before them, and when chores were done, Theo would follow Vincent in a fantastic world Theo didn't know existed. They created a fantastic menagerie of bugs together, they collected beetles, spiders, moths. Vincent meticulously arranged each dead insect in a small wooden box, positioning each looking at the other, giving meaning to things that couldn't possibly exist. Bugs didn't really talk to each other, love each other. But he made them look like they did. He collected small dead animals—birds, a squirrel—cleaned and kept their bones. He used wildflowers and made wonderful weavings of them, braiding their stems and branches together. He spent hours and hours on such things. He read aloud to Theo every night. Even then, Theo could see Vincent was unique, different from other boys in his thinking, his questioning, his designing of the world around him.

His parents were well meaning, very hardworking, but so essentially dull and relentlessly serious, without humor. His uncle Cent, his father's brother, was the excitement in that generation of the family. Uncle Cent lived a rich intellectual life as a very successful art dealer in London and Paris. He became the beacon for both Theo and Vincent. They wanted to follow in his footsteps, to get out of Brabant, to live in a modern city, a life centered upon creativity, accomplishments, and individuality.

Vincent had fallen on hard times now. He just needed the right environment to harness his strengths. Vincent would do something amazing in a creative environment with other artists to engage with.

He needed a clear path to take off, and with success he would be able to accept the daily frustrations of life. It was the failure that was destroying him. Wouldn't failure destroy anyone?

Theo and Anna stood outside Vincent's studio, just twenty steps from the main house. Theo had his hands in his pockets, staring at the ground, listening to Anna's whispers.

"We should think about what Mother wants, we could have him committed, if you sign, me, and Mother. We could get him to Gheel in a few days."

"No, she exaggerates. They love each other. He just needs to focus on his work. Paris is ideal for painters and easier for me than trying to sort through everything here. Some success will enable him to withstand the frustrations."

"Take me to Paris," Anna said quietly.

Theo shifted one foot out, looking up at Anna.

"Ahh," he said, looking to the heavens, "what to do about Anna?"

"I don't think you understand what this has been like. You haven't been here!"

"I think I'm getting the idea." He put his arm around her, pulled her close to him. She was so hard and stiff, every muscle tight, her thick blond hair pulled tight, her mouth a bitter line.

"The thought of Vincent loose in Paris—I think you're being very naïve. You do business there. And Mother is counting on you now."

"Don't worry." He looked at the cottage door. "Don't come in with me. Go, do something for Mother," he said. Seeing Anna's exasperated expression, he added, "Get her to take a glass of wine."

Theo rapped on the studio door, called to Vincent in a business-like way and without waiting for a response, entered. Theo took in the squalor of the studio. Vincent sat on the floor among open books and reams of drawings, his back against the wall, leafing through his sketchbook.

"Anna and Mother blame me for Father's death," Vincent stated, without looking up.

"His heart gave out. They can't really blame you."

"They think his heart gave out because I drove him mad with fury." He continued to study his drawing.

"It was his time, I suppose. His brother suffered the same fate just a year ago."

"Mother thinks I'm a filthy dog that can't be allowed in the parlor. Shaggy, disgusting, filthy with dirt. And Anna—God help that poor woman."

Theo walked around the small room, pausing to look at the drawings. He stopped in front of a painting Vincent named *The Potato Eaters* and studied it. He recognized the work from all the sketches and letters Vincent had sent. He had been working on it every day for months.

It was a large, dark canvas. A family of peasants sat around a table, eating potatoes. Their faces had some brownish, golden glows, but otherwise the painting was in dark earth tones. The family's faces—mother, father, children—all resembled one another and, even more, resembled the potatoes they farmed and ate. Vincent leaped to stand next to Theo and admire his work.

"Have I surprised you?" Vincent asked. "I'm almost done."

"Very good, Vincent. I think it's done."

"So, have I surprised you?"

"Yes. The people are the surprise?"

"I want to express the bond between nature and the peasants. They eat the food they grow with their own hands. They are connected in a spiritual way to the soil. The colors create the connection between the land, the food, the family. It is a spiritual bond—you see it?"

"Yes, I think you've captured it brilliantly."

"I speak for them. They are the reason I paint. Can you sell it?"

Theo smiled at Vincent and placed his arm on Vincent's shoulder.

"How long did you spend on this painting? Didn't I see sketches of this in your letters months ago?"

"Yes, this work has been my preoccupation. It's everything I know, everything I believe. Will you sell it?" Vincent took the painting off the wall to hand to Theo.

"It's wet, Vincent—my suit." He held his palms out and wouldn't take the painting. Vincent put it back on the wall.

"I walk through town, and they say, 'Your brother is an art dealer. Why doesn't he sell your paintings?' What do I answer? 'Your uncle was a famous art dealer. Why didn't he sell your paintings?' I must have ambition to succeed. One day I hope you can show my work without compromising yourself."

"Stop. You know it's not that simple. This is brilliant work—the theme, everything about it. But the subject won't appeal to Parisians. It's a touching scene, and you have unique qualities. But the colors are from the old Dutch school. The Parisian art scene…Well, we should talk about all this at the appropriate time." Theo let his voice trail off.

"You can't sell it. You won't sell it. What is the matter with it?"

Why can't I sell it? Theo thought. The scene was moving, a sad reflection on the hardship of peasant life…with Vincent's singular way of looking at simple things, imbuing them with his own stab-you-in-the-heart perspective.

He forced you to look at his images head on, and they got a hold on you, even if they weren't appealing. They stuck in your mind. You would worry for his family of potato eaters.

Theo turned away from the painting. He could never sell this work in Paris, not for serious money to a collector. The dour subject wouldn't appeal. The colors were old-school, painted with mud. He had tried to explain this to Vincent many times in letters. New color had to be seen. Even if he could find a buyer for this, what would it accomplish? No one knew Vincent, he didn't have a story to tell yet and a body of work to back it up. Selling one painting at a low price sets a precedent for future sales—a risk not worth taking to make Vincent momentarily happy.

"You know there are no shortcuts, you worked at a gallery yourself. You will sell when you have a new surprise with a modern approach. The impressionist and modern painters use a new palette, color, Vincent."

Vincent slumped against the wall again and sank to the floor.

"Vincent, trust me. Develop a modern palette. That is the future."

"I don't understand. Just because something's painted in a gaudier color, why is that better? I just don't imagine it."

"You can imagine color and light that you see every day in nature, exaggerated. Many different approaches, but the same ambition. We'll do it together. You will be my most important painter. Wouldn't you like to start over in Paris, instead of here at home?"

"Margot is in the hospital. I was planning to go there. Study, be with her."

"You need to come to Paris and see the new painting."

Theo sat in the squalor next to Vincent, collecting the discarded sketches from the floor and making a neat pile.

"Wouldn't you like to forget women for a while?" Theo again put his arm on Vincent's shoulder and pulled him in.

"Margot said she fell in love with me the first time she posed for me. Watching me work—that made her fall in love with *me*, Theo. Women flock to you." Vincent pushed back on Theo's shoulder, pushing him a bit into the wall, which was covered with charcoal sketches.

"Women are a challenge," Theo said, straightening himself up and checking his coat for charcoal smudges.

"All I wanted was a family, a purpose. I hate being alone."

"You have a purpose. You're a painter, and you will be with me.

Wait till I get a bigger apartment, it won't take long. I'll send for you. Mother needs to rent this space. Clean it out for her."

"I hate the city, the filthy air. I belong here with the peasants, in nature, telling their story."

"The Dutch school will not sell in Paris. Those paintings have been done, Vincent. You must reinvent. That is where the money will be."

"I'll have to see," he said stubbornly.

"Yes, Vincent, you must, together, like the old days, remember?" Theo put his arm around Vincent.

"The old days, Theo, I remember. We were happy together. You were happier then too, I think?"

"You did give me a very happy childhood. I believe in you, Vincent. We'll build a business together in Paris. You will be my greatest painter."

PART 2

8

Johanna

Jo had looked forward to this day. She was to meet Theo's older brother Vincent. Vincent was originally expected to arrive in a few weeks, after the sudden death of their father. But Vincent had surprised Theo by coming early. They would share an apartment while Vincent studied painting in Paris. Theo had hoped to get a bigger apartment first to give Vincent his own room, a studio in which to paint. Vincent sent a painting ahead of time, *The Potato Eaters.* When Jo first saw the painting, she was moved, and as she walked through Theo's apartment, she always stopped and starred at the painting, and the poverty of the family, the struggle of life purely captured in each face. It wasn't pretty and had nothing of the impressionist or modern colors Theo loved, yet the theme of poverty, of want, always avoided in society, this was destined to be her favorite painting. She knew a man like this would only respond to truth, would scorn the finer things.

Johanna and Theo strolled into the vast courtyard of the Louvre Museum holding hands. They were meeting Vincent there. Theo was more animated than usual. This was the first family member of Theo's she was meeting. And as he was the older brother, she wanted him to approve of their match. The Louvre was once the massive home to the French king and his art, in the heart of the city. After the revolution the palace became a museum, free to the public two days a week.

"He has reddish fair hair. A lot like me but shorter. And he will be wearing something appropriate for the country, not Paris—maybe a painting smock or a farmer's coat." He laughed. "He'll stand out, even among the tourists. There, he's here already." Theo pointed and ran to Vincent. "This is Miss Johanna Bonger, the woman I wrote you about. Both of my favorite people with me now—this will be a great time."

Johanna was surprised. What did she expect—someone tall, dark, and handsome like Theo? Vincent had red hair, stocky broad shoulders and chest, and was shorter than Theo. Their faces were similar but based on the portraits she'd seen in Theo's parlor, Vincent looked more like their mother, and Theo more like their father.

Theo and Vincent embraced. Johanna smiled and tried not to stare. Vincent indeed looked out of place, more country than city. She laughed to herself, remembering how she had bought everything new, to fit in.

His eyes were deep blue, and he stared at you and didn't appear to blink. He gave her a warm, bold smile, like Theo's with the lines in his face raising up to meet his prominent cheek bones. He was totally unselfconscious. Driven, happy. He was handsome but odd too. He looked like a boxer or a fighter, bouncing a bit when he walked, fueled by stored-up energy. She imagined him wearing boxer's trunks, laced tall leather shoes, and gloves, bouncing, jabbing, staring his blazing blue glare. His eyes shone so bright, with such intelligence and energy—this alone would unnerve anyone, she thought. Fix on the eyes, and you don't see the arm come up with the fist in your face.

Theo was talking softly, in a museum voice. He stood between them, took both of their arms, and led them farther into the museum. They strolled the lobby, deciding which direction to go, Theo and Vincent debating every option.

Walking into the first gallery, the two brothers strolled and lingered over every painting, talking rapidly to each other.

She listened. They debated a particular painting for a long time. It was an enormous Courbet. They analyzed every detail—the colors, the composition, the nature of the subject. They found meaning in every brushstroke, each stroke telling a small piece of an epic story.

It was fascinating to hear. She would never have put any of this together on her own. *"The beginnings of the modern movement, here with this painter."*

Johanna moved to a bench in the middle of the huge gallery, pretending to rest her feet for a moment. They didn't notice her stepping away.

She sat and watched them. None of the other patrons were interested in this painting, giving her an unobstructed view of the two brothers.

They spoke their own language, commanding each other's rapt attention. They laughed together one moment, then became intensely thoughtful the next. They had a strong bond. They were excited by one another, they held each other's looks, they jumped into each other's sentences, building new thoughts. Theo stood straight and still. Vincent bounced and danced. She felt their excitement rubbing off on her and drawing her into their unique private world. Their passion for painting was exhilarating. She carefully listened to their private language, thrilled to be a part of it all.

Theo leaned into Vincent, listening, enthralled. She loved this about him, his gentle manner, the way he spoke in polite questions, emotional in an acceptable way.

She resisted feeling like a third wheel. It was important for these two brothers to have their moment together. They continued the journey through the never-ending museum and the stream of talk about art and the future.

"This is our time, the dream is here, it is now for us, Theo!"

Vincent's excitement rung in her ears. Their happiness with each other was touching.

She walked around to another room. They wouldn't even know she was gone. She traveled to another gallery and found herself staring at the type of painting she hated most: medieval religious scenes. They were all repulsive physically. Men and women in elaborate robes, faces that didn't remotely resemble reality—beady eyes, pasty white skin, blobby, puffy fingers. The way painting used to be, reserved for churches and royalty.

She turned and bumped directly into Vincent. He had been standing behind her. She didn't see Theo.

Vincent read her mind. "He is on a personal mission. He will be back. What are you doing here?"

"The same as you, Vincent." She wanted to sound cheery.

"Why did you leave us?" He stared into her eyes, and it was unnerving, uncomfortable, too forward.

"I didn't leave," she said with finality. "I thought you two needed a moment." She looked back up at him, into the blue eyes.

He smiled. "Oh Miss Bonger, we will have many moments."

"Please call me Johanna, or Jo. Vincent? What will you paint?" Ask him about himself. Theo was always asking questions to get the artists engaged.

Vincent didn't answer, he only stared at her.

Johanna tried again.

"Will you study?"

"I have been studying."

"Teaching is so critical, don't you think?"

"No. I don't think teachers are *critical*, I believe teachers are *too* critical. At The Hague, the teachers dismissed the best work. They teach what was, thinking they know something. What I see is that the greatest and most dynamic minds of the century always work against the stream and don't listen to instruction."

Johanna instantly knew he was an independent thinker. Vincent and Theo were part of the revolution against the ancient ways, and now she would be too. Thank God I am alive now, she thought.

"My challenge is models. Will you pose for me?"

"…me? No, I couldn't."

"Why not? Don't you like art?"

"Yes, I love art. We studied music in my family. I play the piano. I'm learning so much from Theo. And the process, how you approach paintings."

"Art is life."

"Yes, his life, your life. This is why you're here in Paris, Vincent. Theo says Paris is the center of the art world."

"Yes, he wanted me here to meet other artists, to see the new directions he is dedicating himself to.

"Yes. You two are very close."

"Yes." Vincent looked at her, suddenly challenging. "We have been close since childhood, but apart for many years."

"How do you like Paris?" *Just make small talk*, she thought.

"I have lived here before. It's like all cities, they all become disillusioning in their own unique way after a while."

"I agree. Paris—so many poor people. Women and children especially. What don't you like about the city?" Johanna asked.

"Why are so you full of questions, Miss Bonger, am I in your classroom?" He laughed as if he had made a joke.

"No, I'm sorry."

"Let's forget the rest of the questions and find Theo." He offered his arm, in a rather dramatic way. She wondered if he had been a difficult student, alternating between needy and demanding, then sullen and walled off.

Johanna took Vincent's arm it but kept herself distant. He was just oddly frank and prickly, she thought.

After they found Theo, they returned to the museum entrance. Jo had to get to work. Theo discreetly kissed her good-bye. Vincent stared at them. Jo walked toward the trolley, wondering if she made a bad impression during their conversation. From his work, he seemed to be a man of great feeling and compassion for others. Yet to her, he was almost cold.

Theo

When Theo got to Cormon's Art School the next afternoon, Vincent had already set up to paint. He meant to meet Vincent there and help him to relax by making all the introductions, but business had kept him at the gallery. There was an enticing rumor that the Rand Durrell organization, the largest dealer, was struggling financially. Their biggest backer, Union Credit, was entering bankruptcy. Theo wondered who among Rand's artists he might tactfully approach for Goupil. He spotted Vincent in the front row.

Cormon's space was large, with great light and fresh air. Rows of students were neatly organized in a horseshoe pattern. Vincent had a good seat up front.

They all painted a statue of a torso, inclining at a challenging angle, difficult to capture the weight without arms or legs. Row after row of students in front of easels, equally spaced, each canvas reflecting the statue, with precise strokes, neutral darks for the shadows, warm medium tones for the masses, and bare white canvas for the lightest of lights—the same on every canvas, in every row. Perfectly arranged palettes were held in tense arms. Some beginnings were better than others, but mostly they were more alike than not.

And then he came to Vincent's station. Unlike some other artists, Vincent didn't start a work by sketching forms in varying shades of gray and umber. He leapt ahead, way ahead. Primary colors—red, yellow, and blue—covered Vincent's canvas. Emile Bernard and Paul Gauguin were at each side of him. Good, Theo thought. He had asked them to help get Vincent settled. He thought he could count on them and was relieved to see he was right.

Theo stood quietly just inside the entrance, no one had seen him yet. That was good, he didn't want to be a distraction. The instructor, Cormon, walked around the room, talking quietly, respectfully giving notes to individual painters. When he got to Vincent, he was silent. Theo held his breath. He hoped he would say Vincent's work showed potential. Cormon was very tolerant of differences and not overly concerned with academics, Vincent's Achilles' heel.

Cormon looked at Vincent's canvas, bold masses of paint filling the forms. "Who are you?" the instructor asked. He sounded kind but genuinely confused.

"I am a Dutchman, Vincent van Gogh."

"Oh yes, Vincent. Your brother, Theo, arranged the spot for you here. I should have guessed it was you. You have developed an unorthodox approach. Remind me where have you studied?"

"Amsterdam, The Hague. I have my portfolio." Vincent opened it, holding it for the instructor, who flipped slowly through pages of drawings.

"Your work is unconventional, I would even say unique. What do you want to accomplish here? We have many classes." He was done with the portfolio, he looked at Vincent.

Vincent searched for what to say, his brow creasing with thought. He remained silent for a moment too long, so Cormon continued. "Your family has a legacy selling art. We are happy to meet you, Vincent. Take your time, the answer will form. You are still hidden in the mist, but I see your potential."

"Thank you, Professor Cormon." Vincent smiled and nodded his head as if in thanks.

Theo breathed a sigh of satisfied relief. He left and went back to work.

When Theo caught up with Vincent at a café later, he was with

Gauguin and Bernard, and they were already halfway to drunk. The three of them were talking about art, and Theo knew it would be a different conversation than Vincent was used to. And this is what Vincent needed to learn. There would be several stresses for Vincent at once, Theo thought, joining them at the table. The judgment, evaluation of his work, and the new language of painting—this was what he needed to learn, and he was in the deep end already. They were looking at his portfolio. Gauguin would challenge him to articulate his intention and vision. The conversation wouldn't be about the same technical achievements the academic teachers obsessed over. What made him unique? Did he have an idea, and had he captured it in his work yet? Gauguin held the portfolio, silently turning the pages.

Paul and Vincent had a lot in common, Theo thought. They might be a good match, painting companions, maybe even friends. Both felt the intense need to paint and had come to painting later in life, after career setbacks, even outright failures. It could be good for Vincent to see someone else come to painting later and achieve success. All the younger men around the painting world could be intimidating to Vincent.

"A bottle of your best for my man here...um, for the table please," Emile said to the owner of the small, down-market café, who barely glanced at his patrons or wiped the wobbly wooden table. "And keep it coming, please." Emile handed him a large wad of francs and smiled at Vincent and Paul.

Paul was cool, handsome, almost regal in his purplish-blue double-breasted coat. He studied Vincent's portfolio, silently turning the pages without comment.

Theo caught Vincent's eye a few times, smiling, trying to keep him relaxed. Vincent was holding his breath watching Gauguin examine his work. Vincent drank his wine, shifting his eyes between Emile, the portfolio, and Gauguin.

Come on, Paul, Theo thought, say something and put Vincent out of his agony. Be kind if that is possible.

Emile kept asking Vincent questions, trying to engage him in conversation. But Vincent was having a hard time focusing, worried about Gauguin's opinion, Theo imagined.

Vincent stuck his unlit pipe between his teeth. Emile offered him a light.

He turned his empty pipe over. Emile raised his hand to request tobacco from the owner, but Paul offered his own pouch.

"Have mine, Vincent." Paul handed over his tobacco pouch, without looking up from Vincent's portfolio. Ah, this was a good sign, Theo thought. He will say something kind to Vincent, and we can all relax again.

"Why didn't you like studying at The Hague?" Emile asked. Emile was leaning in close to Vincent. Theo thought he was trying to get a closer look at the portfolio.

"They teach strict academics," Vincent said. "Everything from the past. The Dutch school needs reinventing. That's why I am here. How will we move forward if our classes stand still? I think artists are better teachers than the academics. If we all work together, help each other more, we would make faster progress."

"Paul and I have studied with Pissarro. Maybe he would take you on," Emile said.

"And then what?" interrupted Gauguin. "After you have learned what one painter knows, you know how to paint the way one painter paints." He tilted his head back and squinted down at Vincent. "The artist needs his own voice. Art is either plagiarism or revolution."

"What do you think of the impressionists?" Vincent asked.

"The impressionists lack form, substance," Paul said. "New painters are moving beyond. Impressionism lacks thought, their work won't last. Painting is more than a simple science experiment around color. Color—it is only a means to an end."

Theo was making good money selling impressionists, but he wasn't going to argue with Gauguin.

"You draw distinctively." Paul said. "The impressionists—most of them can barely draw, little chemists accumulating their little dots. To paint a story, you must draw."

Emile studied Vincent's portfolio. "I love your drawing, Vincent, it has emotion and power. I have never seen drawing so raw and true."

"Why do you paint? What will you paint?" Paul said again. "Your drawing is saying something already—your lines, circles, waves…expressive. But what is it beyond different? This is what you must explore. Anything worth doing is worth doing a couple hundred times," said Paul. "To succeed we must be willing to fail, over and over. Life is short, art is long. You know the saying."

"I find inspiration in nature," Vincent said.

"What about nature?" Paul asked.

"I am interested in nature, the relationship to man."

"No, nature is only a background for the story. It's not the story. What do you want to say, Vincent?"

Theo felt as much relief as Vincent after Paul's thoughtful and complimentary response. And they were off, talking about art for a long time, until they were all drunk, and Emile had spent all his money on wine, and everyone was hungry.

"Theo," Vincent said, "feed us."

Theo laughed at Vincent's changing moods. Earlier at Cormon's, he had been shy, quiet, intense. Then thoughtful, awkward while Paul looked at his portfolio. Now the wine lifted him high, dulling his fear.

"Paint outside with me, Vincent," Emile said. "I paint at the Seine. Others are there. It can be like your dream, everyone working together." Was Paul sneering at Emile, or was it just dark?

"Yes!" Vincent screamed. "Tomorrow! You too, Paul?"

Paul laughed and put an arm around Vincent.

"No, Vincent, I am busy in the studio. But yes for another time."

This is what Theo had hoped for. Vincent could join a community of artists and learn the new way to paint. He would reestablish his life here in Paris as a whole, healthy man.

Johanna

Johanna kept watch from the window of the apartment she shared with Andries. He was walking toward the building, not weaving thank God, but very loose. He was late again. She waited patiently at the door, her mind racing with a million questions she wanted to ask but knew better.

"What is all this?" Andries held a stack of letters as he entered the apartment. He flipped them around dramatically, checking the return addresses. "All for you, and from galleries and museums here in Paris," he said, snappish and challenging. He was a little sloppy—too much wine or absinthe at dinner with the artists again. She imagined Theo had been there.

"Never mind," Johanna said, quickly trying to take the letters.

But he held a few back, squinting at them with red, tired eyes. "Oh, have you written to the entire city? What is it?" His tone was hard to read. She heard curiosity laced with sarcasm.

"Give them to me." She wasn't ready to share her plans with Andries and hated talking to him in this condition.

He held them high, out of her reach, and swayed with them to the couch. Being slightly inebriated, he forgot once he sat, she could grab them all, and she did. His hands were moist and pasty, bloated.

"Andries, God, you reek!"

Jo walked to her room, quickly opening one letter from the Louvre. They requested an interview—she had passed the translation test! She opened another. An immediate offer to translate catalogs from a prestigious gallery!

My God, I am doing it, she thought. It's going to happen! Happy, she smiled and put the letters on her dresser. She almost wanted to celebrate herself. Her own business and a new sense of purpose.

And the last letter—another love letter from Theo. With his father's death, their wedding would be delayed an appropriate time for mourning. She saw him often here in Paris, though not as frequently now that he was dealing with Vincent. She didn't like it, but she knew it was necessary for Vincent to be settled in. She looked forward to Theo's love notes and dreamed of their beautiful future together. He was such a romantic and a beautiful writer. She couldn't wait to tell him her news. He would be happy for her.

She walked back to Andries. He was still awake—what a genuine surprise. Good, she was desperate to know what went on during these long evenings at the cafés. Maybe his drinking would loosen his tongue and she could find out about Vincent and Gauguin.

"How was tonight? You look worse for wear, per usual these days."

"Dinner and whatnot…" He lifted his foot, and she obligingly pulled off a shoe.

"Would that mean Vincent was there?"

"Yes. Please bring me water. I am completely dry and buzzing with that crap absinthe."

"Well, tell me. How is he getting along?"

Andries shrugged off the question. He held up his other foot.

"How about Gauguin? Have you found out anything about the family?" Aline plagued her. Jo wondered if Theo was angry about her confrontation with Gauguin that night, weeks ago. Her abysmal absinthe dinner, while she waited for Theo, who never came because his father had died. With the death overtaking events, maybe Theo didn't even know about the "fight" with Gauguin. Fleur said she was blowing everything out of proportion, that she had been right to confront Gauguin. But damn, there must be more she could do.

The image of Aline's face in the dark, begging, desperate, pleading left her feeling sick. Neither she nor Fleur had seen Aline loitering around the fair again. She prayed the child had gone to Copenhagen with her mother and her nightmare was over.

Andries flopped his foot down, and for a moment Jo thought he might be falling asleep, his eyes half closed. But no, he got his cigar lit. Johanna watched his hand carefully. One ash in the cushion, and they would burn in their sleep. He puffed on his cigar with his eyes shut, the blue smoke shrouding his red face, obscuring his expression. She opened the window, and across the pretty tree-lined boulevard was the Maquis, a shanty town of decrepitude. That was Montmartre, splendor and squalor together.

"Andries, what have you found out about the Gauguin family?" She went to the kitchen to get him a glass of water.

"*Stay out of it*," he said as Johanna handed him water. "Leave Gauguin alone. I don't need any more Jo messes to clean up. Why must you always pick a fight with the nearest bully? Can't you for once keep your head down, and just go along with… Oh wait, what are *your letters*? That smells like another pending Jo mess?"

'Jo messes' stung her. That's what her own brother thought of her for trying to do the right thing? She felt her back go up, her pride hurt.

"You're tired," she said. "We'll discuss it tomorrow." She didn't want to let on how much he stung her. "You were going to tell me about Vincent."

"No, I'm awake. Tell me, please, darling Johanna…about the letters." He almost batted his eyes at her.

"I have applied for translator positions here in Paris."

"Where?"

"Museums and galleries, catalogs mostly."

"Galleries?" he shot back. "I think both you and Fleur should go home. Stop gallivanting around." He paused, took a breath, and sank back in his chair in a defeated way. "Fleur…Do you know why she doesn't like me?" Andries stared at Johanna, suddenly wide awake and without his drunken snarl.

"I don't know what you mean." Jo was surprised, she and Fleur shared everything, always since childhood.

"Good, I begged her not to tell you. I felt a complete fool. Women usually say yes to me, you know. Is Fleur seeing someone?"

Paris men were very aggressive, not like at home. The workers on the street ogled and shouted at Fleur as she walked by. She thought they were disgusting. The wealthier men she resisted because she didn't like speaking French and she thought it gave them an advantage over her.

"Not…. seriously. Why, what happened?"

"She said I was handsome enough." Andries smiled with his eyes closed. "I was hoping I was handsome to her. It was remarkable to hear. She's so beautiful, the most beautiful woman in the world… Except for you, of course."

"Of course. So, did you try to kiss her?"

"Nooooo," he said slowly, shaking his head.

"Then what?"

"Fleur said I was a *sarcastic snob*, and *I* didn't have a sense of *humor*."

"Well, so you do know why she declined. Handsome can go a very long way. Your sarcasm is awful, and you are smart enough to develop a sense of humor." She wondered, could they be a match? She should have seen it.

Andries closed his eyes, took a deep breath.

"Humor. I thought I was humorous."

"You are so serious all the time. And why are you drinking so much?" This lit him up again and he began another sarcastic rant.

"Well, well, look who's talking! Miss Stony Face with 'I know what is right!' Miss 'Let's pick a fight with the artists!' And I am not drinking all the time, but it is hard to keep up with artists. They drink everyone under the table."

Then he got quietly morbid. "Am I disgusting?"

His condition was getting the best of him, unable to hold his thoughts together.

"You are not disgusting. But you need to stop drinking so much." She stood her ground.

He grabbed for the cigar again and puffed out two huge plumes of smoke.

"Gauguin's not the type to brag about an argument with a woman. It's possible everyone has forgotten, but in Paris gossip is the lifeblood of most conversations. You are now a lady with a reputation!" A lady with a reputation—she had to admit this sounded intriguing and it brought a brief smile to her face. Maybe it meant she stood out for saying the bold thing, the right thing. That was good in Paris, wasn't it? Which to ask about before he fell asleep—her reputation or information about Vincent?

"Tell me how Vincent is doing."

"You've met him. He's painting. What else is there to know?" Andries' threw her a sharp, knowing look like he'd said a mouthful. Then his head slumped back on the chair, his mouth hanging open. The snoring began.

Johanna took away the cigar, doused it with water, and put the whole thing in the sink. He would fall asleep in the middle of the conversation. She got little to no information. Nothing new about Gauguin, that just prolonged her agony over Aline. Nothing about Vincent, just that he was painting. What did she want to know anyway, what was scratching at her? Is he learning the new color theories...? She had visions of him painting the poor girls sitting beside the side of the street selling heather, coddling babies.

Fleur was right, Jo was too romantic and whatever Vincent was doing, it was none of her business.

9

Johanna

What could they all do together for fun in Paris? Everyone wanted something different. Theo acted the peacemaker, keeping the tension level low, the mood bright with the suggestions flowing, making the banter a friendly little squabble.

Vincent wanted to do something related to painting. Johanna wanted to tour the sights she hadn't seen or, as a woman, couldn't visit alone. Fleur wanted dancing and a really good meal.

Andries, unusually quiet, watched Vincent stare obsessively at Fleur. He wasn't doing well hiding his feelings, Jo thought. Fleur seemed puzzled by Vincent's attention. She was polite but clearly not interested in him.

No one said no to any suggestion, just a little silence and then another completely new idea would be thrown into the mix. How about Sacré-Coeur? Or how about the Musée du Trocadéro, or the Église Saint-Gervais Saint Protais? Or how about...

Finally, Theo decided for everyone. They would stay in Montmartre. For Vincent, a tour through the galleries. For Jo, the Basilica du Sacré-Cœur. And for Fleur, finally, food and dancing.

Vincent, Theo, Johanna, Andries, and Fleur ran and hopped on to the moving horse trolley at the base of the Butte in Montmartre. Vincent jumped on first and then pulled everyone on, easy and quick. The top of the Butte was a popular destination for Parisians and tourists alike reveling in the greatest view of Paris. The narrow horse path with switchbacks ran up along old heather farms, windmills, and abandoned quarries and vineyards. Both wood and stone apartments and houses stood just inches from the trolley path. If she tried, Jo could see the dwellers inside. Children and dogs darted out daringly, challenging the horses and driver, who paid no mind. The rickety wooden staircases between the buildings traversed the hillside, and children sat with their toys and pets.

Street vendors with large carts offered heather and vegetables from the meager hillside farms. There were painters too, crowded at the edges of the path, a few on the winding staircase. Theaters, poets, circus performers, singers, dancers. In the entertainment capital of Paris, everything was available, reasonable, and even the lowest of the low entertainment was respectable to attend.

At the top of the Butte, they disembarked in front of the construction site of the newest crowning glory, Sacré-Cœur cathedral, and from its grounds they had a view of Paris sparkling below. Fleur stopped at a vendor's cart loaded with fresh purple heather. She picked out two bunches, chatting with the child who manned the cart. Vincent raced to Fleur's side, digging through his pockets for money to pay for her heather. Some might think they were enjoying a moment together, but Fleur's gestures told Jo otherwise. Fleur, normally as flamboyant as an actress, stood straight as an arrow, looking at the ground, not at Vincent. Clearly, she sensed Vincent's interest in her and was gently trying to discourage him. Andries took a few steps to join them but was not in time and watched Vincent pay.

When they reassembled as a group, Jo was determined to get everyone moving together.

"The construction of Sacré-Coeur has taken decade, is that right?" she asked, trying to be like Theo, break the tension and keep a conversation going. Fleur nudged her in the side. She must sound silly, like a travel brochure—they all lived here, for goodness' sake.

They walked silently, she and Fleur, arm in arm. Theo and Vincent walked ahead. Andries strolled in the middle, moving back and forth between the groups. Every ten paces or so, Theo would turn and smile at Jo, and Vincent would turn and look at Fleur.

They rested on benches, and Jo thought she would try to engage them in a proper conversation.

"Vincent, I noticed all the painters on the Butte. Will you paint this for landscape studies?" She gestured toward the view, almost knocking her parasol into Fleur's head. "How do you see it, Vincent?" she asked, pointing at the glorious city of Paris stretched out below—the Eiffel Tower, the Seine, Notre-Dame Cathedral. Fleur nudged her again.

"We are standing on a graveyard," Vincent said. "Thousands killed here. The Communard Uprising, the second revolution. This is holy ground. Women, children lay down in front of the cannon, fighting for a belly full of food. This grand piece of white marble was built for the absolution of unforgiveable sins of assassination and murder, and it's now a tourist destination. You must know this from your tour studies?"

"Yes," Jo said. "Such great beauty out of such misery. The great painters of that era—they fled Paris to the countryside, to London, and returned at the end of the revolution and created Impressionism. Out of the horror, the great light."

Jo felt another nudge from Fleur and saw Theo whisper into Vincent's ear. She imagined Theo said, "*Is* there a problem, Vincent?" Andries stood off to the side, hands deep in his pockets, and smiled at her and Fleur, his eyes laughing, twinkling at them both. She felt warm, and she stood to catch a breeze. Fleur joined her, and they locked arms and walked away from the men.

"What did I tell you? Isn't Vincent... strange?" Jo said. They talked quietly but with big smiles in case the men were watching.

"He is very raw," said Fleur. "Theo is so polished. Vincent wants to see me. He didn't even make any small talk, just came right out with it." She laughed and looked out at the view below.

"A meeting with Vincent? When did he ask? You haven't even been alone with him."

"When he paid for my heather. I think they charged us double when they heard our accents. Anyway, he asked if I would pose for a painting."

"Will you?"

"No. I'm hungry, let's get going. And for God's sake, stop trying to talk to him, let Theo handle the conversation."

Theo and Johanna danced in the Moulin de la Gallette. Large opera chandeliers lit the vast room and were the major decorations. The dance hall had no windows, and an old miniature windmill stood off the center of the dance floor. It was a popular local place, with a diverse clientele—wealthy Parisians and local hillside inhabitants comingled in the old establishment.

Vincent and Fleur danced too, very strangely. Fleur looked miserable, with a pasted-on smile, her head as far back and turned away from Vincent as she could manage. Not a single flourish, no soft round movements—she was as stiff as wood.

Vincent knew all the steps, and he was an energetic, graceful dancer. Jo watched as Fleur feigned fatigue and left the dance floor. Andries watched them too from the table, sipping his wine. He had lost his winning smile, his lips in a firm line, folding in on themselves. He was less handsome when he sulked this way, Jo thought. She imagined he was annoyed that he was unable to get Fleur's attention with Vincent now in the picture. Jo excused herself to follow Fleur.

They loitered in the ladies' room. "I'm going home," Fleur said. "I can't dance with him anymore."

"Oh, no don't leave. What am I going to tell them?" Jo asked.

"Maybe I'm ill from too much sun. Think of something for me. I can't go back to the table. I'll just slip away." They exited the ladies' room.

"Wait. I'll get Andries to escort you. You can't travel the hillside alone." But Andries was now dancing with another young woman, having given up on Fleur.

"Oh, no, he's got someone dancing now. Jo, it's still daylight. I can hop the trolley myself. That is what I love about Paris, women unescorted, de rigueur! Oh, you know what I mean."

Fleur stopped short, pulling Jo to a stop with her.

"What is that?" Fleur asked. Vivienne was now sitting at their table, in between Vincent and Theo. Henri and Emile had arrived too, waiting for chairs to be added.

"That's Vivienne, the horror I've been telling you about."

"My heavens, Jo. She looks terrifying. What is she?"

"An actress and a model for Henri."

"A model? Of course! What else, with the rouge I can see from twenty feet away. I bet there is venom in those claws. Keep her away from Theo. I'll see you tomorrow."

Later, Andries was still enjoying himself, finding several young women who took turns dancing with him.

Johanna finally had Theo all to herself on the dance floor. Theo shouted in Johanna's ear.

"I was worried...what you would think of Vincent. But I knew you would love him because I love him!"

"I guess you have had your hands full, getting this all together for him."

"Yes, but we are all settled in now. Have I been neglecting you?" He cocked his head slightly and leaned into her. She loved having his face so close.

"Don't you like my letters?," he asked.

She did. They were a brief happiness at the end of the long days of hard work. "Does Vincent know we plan to marry?"

"Yes, Johanna, I told him and everyone—Henri, Emile, everyone! You are the love of my life."

Theo was saying all the right things, but Johanna still felt a nagging aversion around Vincent. She felt something had changed. The argument with Gauguin—Theo had never mentioned it. Theo was more distracted and preoccupied with Vincent. Even now, while she was dancing with him, he was looking over her shoulder at Vincent. He seemed to be concerned with Vincent's every move. Saving him from his chaotic side could take every thought, leaving no room for anything else.

The song ended, and they went back to the table. Vincent wasn't there. Maybe he had left, it was getting late. Henri, Vivienne, and Emile were sitting at the table, drunk. They looked like hysterical schoolchildren, convulsing with laughter, unable to talk, barely able to breathe. If this were anyplace else, Jo wouldn't want to sit down with them. But here in Montmartre, everyone was drinking too much, pushing to the edge and beyond of what was acceptable.

Theo looked around for Vincent.

For a horrible second, Johanna thought Vincent had followed Fleur home.

After dancing and the long day Jo felt sun-fatigued and thirsty. Henri's eyebrows raised in a questioning manner. Is he staring at me? she wondered. Did he just ask me a question?

"Better behave," Henri said.

The table bumped, the glasses shook, and Emile, Henri, and Vivienne made a quick grab to stabilize their drinks. Emile whispered, "Shhh," to his lap. Johanna felt a tug at her dress and cool air brush against her legs as her skirts were lifted under the table.

"Ah!" she screamed, shocking and mortifying herself at once. Her tablemates burst out laughing.

She stood, felt something crawling up her leg. She heard herself shrieking, out of control, "*Something* is grabbing...and..." She was toppled off balance and then was pulled back to her chair. Emile and Henri were shushing her.

"Johanna? What is the matter?" Theo asked.

She kicked, and her boot connected with something hard. She heard a guttural yell from under the table, and everyone around her went quiet. Her voice had developed a mind of its own, and she screamed even louder.

"There is an animal under the table—it attacked me!" She saw the large, bulky mound under the cloth. She thought of the dogs, scrounging for scraps.

Then an arm dangled out like a corpse from under the table-cloth. It was Vincent! She resisted the urge to scream again and recoiled, shooting upright, digging in her heels to push away from the table.

Theo lifted up the tablecloth, revealing a worse-for-wear Vincent, and bent down and whispered something short and terse to him. Jo couldn't hear. Vincent laughed and patted Theo on the cheek. He wasn't bleeding, but red-faced and slurring.

Andries poured a glass of water on Vincent's head. A crowd of waiters gathered. Henri held another glass of water for Andries to pour.

"Stop that, Andries!" Emile screamed and dabbed at the mess on Vincent's coat, holding his hand, trying to get him to sit up.

The maître d' had rushed over to Johanna. "Madame, are you hurt? Please!"

"No," was all she could squeak out. Half the restaurant was laughing at her. That wasn't an animal, Vincent was the wild dog under the table. She felt the flame in her cheeks and tried to recover her voice.

A group of waiters hoisted Vincent and carried him toward the exit like a bag of garbage. Emile followed, still holding Vincent's hand. "Gentle, gentle, be careful!" he demanded.

Andries and Theo helped Johanna up from the table.

"Alright now," Theo said reassuringly to her.

"Let's go home, Jo," Andries said, gently reaching for Jo, and Theo let her go.

At the curb, Vincent sat in the dirt and finally opened his eyes.

Theo knelt beside his brother just a foot away at the curb, trying to reason with him. He wasn't angry, he didn't even seem upset! Jo was mortified. Was she supposed to swallow this obscene behavior, because this was normal with the enlightened bohemian crowd of Paris?

"Theo, you need to put a leash on that," snapped Andries.

Vincent was completely out of control, Jo thought. How can Theo put up with this behavior? She felt a stab of pain for Theo. Vincent was obviously taking advantage of Theo's kindness. She must be an idiot, thinking she could talk to Vincent about painting, about the plight of poor girls sitting on the side of the road with heather to sell and babies in their laps.

Her new silk Japanese scarf was ruined with spilled wine. *I can't let myself hate this man.* She swallowed the thought.

Vincent

The impressionists don't use much brown or black paint. Instead, they use dark blue, dark green, and especially purple. There is no gray, instead I see rose, vermillion, a watery yellow, a middle green. I am working up to a yellow, one with gold.

"No, no, Vincent, don't blend the color. No, no, Vincent, don't blend the brush strokes. Place the paint and leave it." They love brush-strokes with texture, ridges, dots, dashes, lines, smears. "Vincent, make your statement with the stroke. Leave marks!" Knives leave ridges and the creation of texture will lift the color and catch light. I use my thumb to paint. The painters like the effect. Then I wipe my thumb off on my coat. They yell at me when I walk the street because my paint rubs off onto everyone who brushes past me.

They don't draw in Paris because the finest drawing has all been done. Lines are for holding the shapes filled with color. They don't want objects to turn in space. They don't care if there is dimension on the flat surface. The flat space is the best for the color and the texture. Color and texture are all we strive for, from morning to night. We make new colors and new patterns of colors and place them next to each other to make the composition vibrate.

I am floating in space here, traveling through all the studios and salons, my head expanding with colors I never saw, burning my eyes with color. The yellow bakes my brain and makes little explosions, firing, creating new ideas. My own ideas. I float above the streets stacked with people. I fly into one studio. I fly to the next. I don't know if I am speaking or listening. What I say to one is good. I say it again to the next, and he throws me out, cursing. But I am painting. I am always painting, even when I sleep. There is an invisible brush in my hand, and it is always painting. It wakes me up at night, and I paint.

Everything here opposes everything I have learned elsewhere, and now I need to forget. There is no authority, no academia, no individual to please. But a group as a whole, and each member of the group uniquely distinctive. Painters here live in opposition to the academics. It is a revolution and a race for the crown. Who wins will be the best. We are modern and close the door firmly on the past.

Here I am not ridiculed. I am welcomed and encouraged. Each man's uniqueness is his commodity. The women are not precious, they fight for their space, and they forcefully argue their points. Some painters are thick with talent and obsessed with art. Many have no talent except passion. You see the perfection and failure, and a clear path emerges for me. Because mistakes of others are easy to see, then your own work is better. The new path paints itself with enough seeing. New here is new unlike ever before. An exaggeration is the goal, and beauty is in the exaggeration. There is nothing in capturing reality.

There is always a drink on the table, it helps to paint better, free and loose. They use it here to help the table conversation, for painting, for sleep. It is food, it is our energy. And there is a new drink here, absinthe—it is another tool. You see the colors sharper, and you don't have to worry about the lines.

The light is brighter, and at night the electric lights buzz and burn a white, bright light on the streets. Every night is a party in Montmartre, and I am new and home.

Johanna

Jo and Fleur, shoulder to shoulder, eyebrows crinkled, watched Vincent and Emile paint at the Seine from inside the picture window at Dutch Pavilion. Vincent had chosen their positions for the best view of the river, which just happened to be directly in front of the Dutch pavilion, Jo noted. She and Fleur talked low to each other, sipping their tea, and avoided their fellow guides who were lounging through the lunch hour. The summer season gone, the fall season winding down, the fairgrounds had lost their spectacular vibrancy for Jo and Fleur. What had been special and then ordinary was now a place they were soon moving beyond—Jo to do translations, and in a few weeks, Fleur would join a bakery business back in Amsterdam.

Vincent and Emile were among other painters dotted up and down the boulevard. Some enjoyed talking to the tourists about their work. Vincent didn't. The crowds had thinned considerably, now the tourists were older. Couples calmly walked the expo, having the best places in the city to themselves.

"Vincent sent me an apology note. I should go and thank him for it, and you should come with me," Johanna said.

"I can't believe I left and missed the debacle! I can see it though, Vincent grabbing you under the table!"

"Theo said Vincent was too drunk to know what he was doing."

"Oh yes, we could all see Vincent was drunk."

"What I should say is, 'Vincent, you are intolerable. When are you going to learn to behave appropriately? Stop all your nonsense immediately!'"

"You sound like an old schoolteacher and that would be Theo's job." Fleur took off her flying-buttress hat and pulled the pins out of Jo's too. They worked on normalizing their hair.

It seemed impossible to have a reasonable conversation with Vincent. Theo put himself between her and Vincent, obviously trying to protect them both. Theo had begged her to forgive him. She felt for Theo, the chaos of living with Vincent was showing on his face.

In a way she was glad Vincent drank himself under the table. In her mind Vincent, talented, even brilliant, was still a bullying child on the playground, needing discipline. Now surely there was no denying how difficult he was. Crazy or undisciplined and inappropriate, it was a distinction without a difference. Didn't everyone see that? She'd felt like an idiot, screaming at full voice in public!

"He was looking up your skirt, Jo."

"He thought it was your skirt."

"I need to stay as far away from Vincent as possible. He is way beyond 'inappropriate behavior' in my opinion. I wonder if he can function without Theo. Say what you have to say and hurry so we can still make our little shopping expedition. I will wait around the corner." Fleur didn't like shopping alone. She thought all the shopkeepers were cheating her because she was Dutch and didn't speak French well. She would watch what other customers paid, and make sure she was getting the same price. She had an annoying reoccurring dream, that she was in the greatest shop ever, with fantastic clothes, everything she wanted, and not knowing what anything cost, she got one of everything, got home, and realized it had cost her everything she had.

"Vincent is a man obsessed. *You* are why he is painting here in front of the Dutch pavilion," Jo said.

"In a few days I'll be back at home, and he won't have to worry about pursuing me. I am afraid, dear friend, you have to do this yourself."

Something was getting to her. Fleur didn't have bad moods. But she didn't look happy, her brow constantly wrinkled. She was snappy, losing her patience with tourists, complaining about Paris. The expense, the smelly air, dirty streets, the men whistling at her. Johanna felt a little wave of Fleur's disquiet creeping over her, like the grimy air of the city.

"Come on, Jo, if you're coming with me." She cocked her head to the door and waved her arm. "We don't have much break time left." Her characteristic head gesture had changed, usually highly comical, head and shoulders both cocking to the door, as if she was about to bash it in. Now it was just a small tense nod.

"Yes, I'm…nervous."

"You have never ever been afraid of anybody, Jo, and especially not someone like Vincent. He's all bark and no bite. But I feel for him in a way. Theo has a big heart, too big for his chest."

"I don't think he likes me for Theo." She wanted Fleur to pat her on the head, reason her out of it with a joke and a smile.

"Well, Vincent has a big problem then, doesn't he? Just stand ten paces back and say what you have to say." Fleur grabbed Jo around the shoulders and gave her a pull.

Johanna adjusted her hat and dawdled a moment at the window again.

"Come on. You will both learn to get along. Rehearse the line and say it. Don't engage in any conversation or light his fuse." Fleur cocked her head again at the door.

Johanna framed her face in a smile she thought made her look optimistic, not the dour schoolteacher Vincent thought she was. Vincent and Emile looked like teacher and pupil, Johanna thought. Emile, ten years younger, hanging on Vincent's every word, watching every brushstroke as if it were the first time he had seen someone paint. He leaned in very close to Vincent, breathing in his pipe smoke, glowing with boyish admiration. Vincent benefitted from Emile's infatuation, Jo thought. He looked happy, confidently holding his brushes and palette, pipe crushed in his jaw, jutting straight out. He moved with big, graceful strokes, rarely pausing, one moment leading directly to another in a cascade of colors on the canvas, attracting attention from the tourists. But his emotions fluctuated wildly. One moment his heart was spilling out over everything, everyone, happy with the painting. Then he'd mutate into fury and anger at some tourists, shooing them away with swooping gestures, or fall into odd silences.

Which face would he show to her? Right now, he was looking pleasant, but a moment ago he'd yelled and waved off nosy tourists. Please, no humiliating public scenes today. Jo watched Vincent staring at Fleur as she exited the Dutch pavilion.

Jo approached them slowly, thinking it would give Vincent and Emile time to collect themselves and be pleasant. They were deep into a conversation, Emile nodding continually, pausing only to push his long hair back behind his ears and adjust his beret. She slowed down even more, hoping they would see her.

"Yes. Now, if Seurat is right, if we create upward tilting lines and use the chromes, it will make us happy. Let's try."

"Aren't you happy, Vincent?" Emile stared hard at Vincent.

Vincent put his paint-covered hand on Emile's shoulder and gave him a manly jostle. "I am happy we are painting together." Emile placed his hand on top of Vincent's and held it there and held Vincent's unblinking stare.

"Good day," Johanna said to Vincent and Emile. Fleur, true to her word, walked without getting close enough to necessitate a greeting.

Vincent stood to watch Fleur, forced a teeth-covering smile. Jo caught his heartbreak at watching Fleur slowly disappear down the wide boulevard.

"I wanted to thank you for the note. Your apology is accepted, and I completely understand how too much wine on an empty stomach can cloud one's ability to think and behave. Thank you again." Good, she'd got it all out, without a stumble, and she turned to leave and catch up with Fleur but heard Vincent call her.

Vincent looked at her with his piercing eyes, nodding. "Where is Fleur going?"

"She has an appointment. Good day." And she turned to leave again.

Vincent sat down and resumed painting.

"Would you tell me, where is she going, Johanna?" Vincent shouted.

Johanna stopped and struggled for an answer. His heartbreak was contagious. She felt immediately sorry for him, and she could barely stand him.

"To the market," Jo said simply. She had only the truth, they were going to buy rouge pots. The Paris colors were vastly better than in Holland. They bought them by the dozen.

He didn't look at her, but Emile did. His face reminded Johanna of a student after being scolded, sullen, eyes downcast, bottom lip pushing out. What an emotional young man. All emotions showed in his mouth, it had its own revealing way. Whatever ached in the brain confessed on the lips.

Tourists began to mill around Vincent and Emile again, asking questions, examining their paintings. Johanna moved out of the way.

"What are you painting?" they asked in Spanish.

Vincent and Emile didn't respond, so Johanna interjected, translating, "They are asking what you are painting, Vincent." She could be helpful, she thought, watching Vincent study the tourists, scanning their belongings. The ladies wore the Paris rage, brightly colored Japanese scarves, and all their parcels were covered with printed wrapping paper with Japanese motifs. She thought of her kimono and Theo.

"We are constantly interrupted out here," Vincent snapped through his pipe. "This is our work. We are not a tourist attraction."

Then maybe you shouldn't paint at the expo, Johanna thought but didn't dare say. The tourists continued firing questions at Vincent and Emile in Spanish. Johanna translated for them, but Vincent shot her a glare, warning her to shut up. He leaped up and screamed at the tourists to leave. Did he mean her too? Emile reached out to him to calm him down.

She stood there, the rudeness just intolerable. The tourists looked her up and down, recoiling like she was part of this unpleasant duo.

"Will Theo visit you here today?" Jo asked. She knew Theo wouldn't take the time away from work, but she thought asking about Theo would calm Vincent down.

"No, he's busy with Monet. You've heard of him?"

Before Johanna could say a word—of course she had heard of Monet—Emile jumped in.

"Monet is a painting machine. He paints five canvases at a time."

"Monet will be wrapping paper too." Vincent laughed. "Monet is the best artist at Goupil, otherwise, they would only sell tulips." He looked at Johanna just for a moment and then went back to painting.

She stood there for a lonely, long second. Why, Johanna thought, is he comparing art to the tulip craze, when everyone who invested in bulbs that went bust? She wanted to ask, but they wanted her to leave.

It was clear to her now. It was time to set a date and get married. They would finish the year of mourning, the custom required after the death of a parent, but there wasn't any reason not to set a date. Nine months left, so now was the time to sit with Theo and get down to making real plans. What Vincent thought or felt about her just didn't matter, but if the situation didn't improve and he wouldn't learn to behave himself, they would have to come to a better understanding. *I am the wife. I can lay down the law with relatives. Theo will stand beside me and see that this man is simply* out of control. She would run and catch up with Fleur, she was only a few minutes behind. Crazy or inappropriate—it was a distinction without a difference.

Theo

Theo struggled with his packages, climbing the stairs to the apartment. He paused at the door, balancing the bags of food. He took a deep breath and cocked his head, trying to listen through the door. He looked at the heavens and said a silent prayer before he stepped inside. *I am exhausted from a long day of work. I would love to lie down on my bed and rest my eyes. After I would like to see my beloved Johanna for a quiet dinner and listen to her plans for her business. My clever Jo, I miss her. But wait, Theo, calm yourself. When you open the door, who knows what will greet you? Happy working Vincent full of enthusiasm, new ideas, and brilliance, or the Vincent we dread, tiptoe around, and wonder why we can't help make whole?*

Theo's perfect parlor had been transformed into a sprawling studio for Vincent. Piles of garbage, food, papers, paint littered the floor. Theo surveyed the squalor and forced his face into an expressionless mask. "*But, Theo, everything is where I can find it easily, without wasting time opening drawers, searching through shelves!*" Theo didn't want to argue. Vincent's work was proceeding—that was more important.

"Thank God you're back," Vincent said. "I am out of everything." Vincent grabbed the packages and began rummaging through each one without first cleaning his paint-covered hands. "No paint! No canvas? No wine! Food, Theo! I don't need the food," he said, pushing the bag back.

"God, I just walked in the door."

"I need paint. Have you paid my color bill? I go out on the street and people say, 'Vincent, why doesn't Theo sell your paintings?' What am I to say? I can't go out!"

"I would like to have a showing here for you, but how can I bring anyone to this mess? I see you didn't clean, as I begged, *and* we agreed you would."

Vincent kicked the garbage out of the way and sat stubbornly in front of his half-painted canvas.

"I'm sorry, Vincent. What have you worked on today?" Theo said calmly, unpacking the bags.

"Why should I clean? Paris is disgusting with filth everywhere." He held up a freshly painted floral canvas.

Theo turned to see it and was at once transfixed. It was a still life of tall, red poppies, with blue, creamy-white, and ocher flowers exploding against a blue wall. A vase, multicolored in blue, steel gray, and white held the explosion on a gold-green ground, flecked with orange ocher. The spaces between the flowers were deep purple navy and forced the white buds into the front.

The painting was not big, but the subject was. The flowers filled the entire canvas, with petals spreading to the edges. Nothing else but flowers, vase, and tabletop made up the whole painting. It was a close-up view. This was also new—surprise, surprise—not a speck of brown, gray, or black on the canvas. Vincent had taken the color wheel and spun it into new heights of color harmonies and contrasts that made little explosions in your head. Red against blue, green to gold to yellow to orange. This approach would command attention!

"Another brilliant floral, Vincent. Congratulations!"

He would need more paintings, a dozen to start, Theo thought. Then a show here, in the apartment, could happen soon. Vincent could be on his way to a successful painting career. He understood the impressionist approach and was developing his own color palette, and modern composition style.

"You think I will be more successful than your Monet?"

"Yes, possibly, one day…"

"*One day, one day*, that is all I ever hear from you. Can you sell it? Can you even show it?" Vincent said. "Well, it doesn't matter. I'm going to organize my own show with Emile, Gauguin, and others. If we could all help each other instead of conspiring against each other, we could make some real progress. That's for you too, Theo. You should be on your own, your own business. Get out of the tulip trade at Goupil."

"Organizing your own show! Vincent, this is wonderful news!" He kept his voice upbeat, hoping Vincent would calm down. It was great news. He would get exposure and benefit from the association with up-and-coming painters. All on his own. *I don't have to worry about people saying I am a nepotistic shill, losing my integrity.*

He finished unpacking the groceries, noting Vincent had drunk an entire case of wine in less than three days. *Better not begin a conversation about his excessive alcohol consumption now when he's almost boiling.* Theo rolled up his sleeves and began to clean up the kitchen, working first on getting the oil paint off the counters and cabinets before it dried.

"'*Vincent this is wonderful news,*'" Vincent said, clearly mocking Theo.

Ah, so this is what it will be tonight, another endless series of provocations and maddening, irrational conversation about nothing. "A show with Gauguin and Bernard—you are in excellent company, Vincent."

"And you don't have to be associated with it and compromise your Goupil company!"

"One day I will have my own business. You will be my most successful painter. This work is excellent. Truly well done." That had been the plan, so easy to say, so much harder in reality without significant financial resources. With Vincent all was a double-edged sword, the good with the bad. Everything good had an opposing bad. Vincent was a talent, a workhorse, painting vivid compositions rapidly, a collection would grow quickly. And Vincent was helping

Theo grow closer to some new painters who were skeptical of the established dealers. They saw Vincent's new approach with paint and admired a true eccentric without artifice, a man whose heart was full and who would sacrifice himself for a friend.

And then there was the other side, painters who Vincent screamed at and battled with. As much as he had a trail of admirers, he had a long trail of those who thought he was intolerable to be around and loathed him. Everything was either black or white with Vincent, there was no middle ground. He couldn't see reality the way it was, only the way it felt to him in his hyper-sensitized mind. Compromise was evil and weak. Negotiating, arguing was useless and would only end in a volcanic eruption. This is what Theo had learned in the six months he'd lived with Vincent. It was a horrible, painful acknowledgment that all his family's complaints about Vincent were tragically true.

Theo cleaned the paint off the cabinet and counters and set the debris on the floor. Cleaning was a good distraction while talking to Vincent and helped keep his own temper from igniting. The worst nights caused him to collapse into a catatonic state, hiding under his covers, like a child from a monster.

"What do you like about it?"

"I'm sorry, Vincent. I thought I told you." This was one of the stranger new habits Vincent had developed. A conversation was never done. It always circled back, and every aspect of it was revisited, until you were mad with it. "I think you have the essence of the thing, and you've imbued it with your own unique personality. Very clever design and a modern palette. Do more. A still-life theme—it will make a good show. This will be impressive, but where—" Will the show be, he was going to ask.

Vincent jumped in, "You know, I was thinking, Theo. There are two ways of reasoning about painting—how to do it and how not to do it. How to do it with a great deal of drawing and not much color, how to do it with great amounts of color and not much drawing.

When will you settle my color bill? I need paint and tobacco and wine. Then I can continue."

"Vincent, you must eat. Enough of wine and pipe. Have you been out today? How about some fresh air? Women?" Theo hoped he could find a woman who could preoccupy him and get his mind off Fleur.

"Yes, out, I saw Johanna today."

"Really, where? I wish I had seen Johanna today—or any day. Where did you see her?"

"At the Seine, with Emile, we were painting."

"Did you speak to her?"

"She *recited* a precious little thank you for my note. Fleur was with her."

"That was generous of her, considering your behavior. Working, I guess?" She was on her last days at the pavilion, soon she would be a bona fide businesswoman.

"You didn't speak to her for me," Vincent said. "Will you talk to her for me?"

"What?"

"You said you would speak to Jo for me, about Fleur?"

"Fleur." Theo shook his head, looking patiently at Vincent. "Vincent, Fleur is a very popular young woman with many suitors."

"You are lying. I can always tell. Everything about me humiliates you, doesn't it?"

"No, Vincent, I love you. I promise I will speak with Jo about Fleur." It was going to be a night like so many nights with Vincent alternating between praising his thoughts, shouting his rebuttals, attacking his business, his health, his life, and his loyalty. The good with the bad, Theo reminded himself, but there must be an end to this chaos, with Vincent overtaking his life and future.

Johanna

"Are we prepared for the gauntlet?" Johanna asked her new

friends. Translating for the Louvre was an exciting and rewarding job. Her fellow translators she met through the Louvre and galleries were visitors in Paris like her. Most from northern European cities and a few Americans. Two of the women were American painters, who copied masters at the Louvre as part of their artistic studies and worked on translations to pay their expenses. They had all become fast friends, each day at lunch filled with laughter. Like Fleur, her new friends thought the shopping was a huge attraction, especially the new department store in central Paris, Bon Marche.

Most days, she worked from the moment she woke until bedtime and then dreamed about everything she needed to do the next day. When work allowed, she and Theo would spend their evenings together. She missed Theo. She hadn't seen him in days because of her schedule. Her lovely Theo still sent her letters, one every three days.

Some nights she would be free, but Theo would have an obligation, and she would spend the free evening with her new friends. They loved exploring Paris nightlife as a group. Montmartre was everyone's favorite. Tonight, they hired a horse-drawn trolley from the Louvre in central Paris to Montmartre. The local trolley slowed but didn't usually stop for passengers and running after a trolley and grabbing on wasn't what wealthier people were accustomed to.

The "Gauntlet" was a must-do for all who wanted to go to Le Ciel, a hugely popular nightclub in Montmartre. Tonight, they would dine at Le Ciel and enjoy the poets and singers. After dinner, they would stroll down to Moulin Rouge, the newest, most elaborate, and most popular of the nightclubs. There they would dance, drink, and watch the scandalous stage show.

Entering Le Ciel, 'The Sky,' meant surviving the Gauntlet. It consisted of a maître d' assaulting you with personal insults, which you must endure to reach your table. The maître d' was a very notorious and popular actor from the Montmartre theater. There he'd spent decades playing popular villains thrilling the crowds with his cartoonery. Now retired, he spent his night lobbing insults, again thrilling the dinner audience, who regularly stopped to listen and applaud his most successful efforts. The best dressed patrons and diners with signs of wealth were treated to the worst of the insults. However, once seated, you were treated well.

The waiters were all dressed like angels with diaphanous gowns, and the waitresses wore wings and spoke in heavenly soft tones. The room was bizarre. Large scandalous nude paintings and statues ornamented the space. The furniture was old French empire, ornate, overdone, and out of fashion, pre-revolution silly frilly. The center of the room was an elevated stage, and tables surrounded the stage, but there were smaller alcoves off to the sides, where larger parties were served. The nightly entertainment was completely bohemian—poets, singers, and dancers, usually with highly political performances.

"Yes," they shouted back to her. "We are ready for the Gauntlet."

She warned them, "Don't take offense. Best to laugh at everything thrown at you and hold your head high and wait for the signal to follow the maître d'. Don't try to push past him, and don't argue. And, ladies, expect to lift your skirt to show your ankles. They love howling at the blue-stocking ladies come to slum in bohemia!"

When Johanna first came to Le Ciel, she was with Andries, Fleur, and Theo, of course. Andries got the worst of it, being so handsome, Theo, less, and Fleur got nothing. Jo thought the maître d' was struck speechless by her friend's unsurpassable beauty. Johanna got an earful—she was asked to show her stocking, which she did, enjoying the sport.

Here we go, Jo thought, but she knew the intelligence and good humor of her group would successfully run the Gauntlet. And they did.

"Oh well, well!" the maître d' shouted when her group walked through. He started on the men first, their clothes and hats—fat penguins he called them, troll faces from Holland! He made fun of the Dutch and German accents, making clipped guttural singsong sounds. Birds from the north! But her friends smiled and tipped their hats to him. And the ladies—they did lift their skirts. None wore blue stockings, but they wore expensive silk, just bought here, and mostly he picked on their white faces—they didn't wear the popular rouges. Puffy white penguins! He ran to a table and pulled tulips out of a centerpiece and offered them to the ladies, harpooning the calamitous Dutch obsession with the flower. And he saved a good one for Jo—queen of the trolls! But Jo was happy, they were given a front table with a perfect view of the stage, and they were immediately waited on.

The first performer was a sad female poet, a Zola heroine, pleading in poetry for the plight of the average female in Paris. It was a heart-wrenching tale of the reality of the poor young women, doomed to poverty in the hell of the Maquis. Young women could not make enough money to survive. Their employers were evil with greed, and as Zola said, they had two choices—work for unfair pay and slowly starve to death or turn to prostitution. The poet was beautiful, plainspoken, drably dressed as a working girl but with a harlequin hat on her head. She received a raucous standing ovation. A group of men from the audience pulled apart their flower centerpiece and gently threw them all around her, as she bowed to her applause. Next was a sad ballad singer with a violin accompanist.

There was laughter, lots of it, coming from the front room.

A tuxedo-clad magician made an understated entrance onto the stage and commanded their attention. "Welcome, Ladies and Gentlemen, to my magic," he said in a soft, flat voice. Though it was a slow act, her group looked engaged enough.

Smoke filled the room, and the magician began. Jo slipped away. She had seen this act before.

The crowd was becoming obnoxiously loud throughout the dining area. Annoying, irritating—they didn't like the magic act, she supposed. When she returned to the table, she mentally reviewed the plans for their next stop, Moulin Rouge. She had the tickets. She checked the time to stay on schedule.

The booming laughter from around the corner of the dining room continued. The laughter felt rude, considering the surroundings. Rude and familiar. Despite reprimands from the angel-waiters, like a group of nasty kids, they wouldn't be controlled.

She recognized the loudest voice.

Damn, it was Vincent, his voice coming from deep within the alcove. He was shouting a long, rambling toast, buoyed on by shouts of laughter and encouragement from other familiar voices. Henri, she recognized—who else?

Then she heard him too, Theo—where else would he be? She could hear only bits and pieces, something like, "Vincent, we can all hear you, bring it down." Theo's resonating deep voice, usually elegant, now sounded smudgy, words blending into words, contaminating one another, unlike Theo. Now he was obsessed with taking care of Vincent, a grown man.

Johanna walked around into the front room and saw the large howling group, forming a long table. The painters were all there. Henri, Emile, Paul, Vivienne, Andries, Theo, and Vincent.

And there were more women—women Johanna didn't know—very flamboyantly dressed, like Vivienne, no hats, red rouge you could see in the dark from a distance, long, loose, gleaming hair like Vivienne's, their clothes, the makeup, so much red, red lips, red cheeks, clothes, nails, hair, even red drinks, bright in this dark café.

Vivienne sat between Vincent and Theo. Theo's head lay resting against the wall, staring at the ceiling, turning to face Vincent, listening, leaning in to listen to Vivienne, then back against the wall, eyes closed.

Vincent stood at the table to make a toast. "My main theory for much misery among artists lies in their discord, not cooperating. Not being good and honest. Being false to each other." He is proud, Johanna thought. His boxer's shoulders back, his arms outstretched to the table, welcoming, drink in one hand. He was drunk, loud, and inappropriate. And the others encouraged him.

Who were those women around the table? Models, sure, of course, but what else? "No, not models, Johanna," Fleur had said. *I am an idiot.*

Henri stood and made another toast. "A toast to our brothers from the north! Our futures are entwined. You are right, Vincent, we all need each other, and we can progress better together." Everyone was sloppy, screaming drunk. Gauguin was with one of the red women. She was leaning in, her hand moving on his chest, disappearing beneath the table.

Vincent's arm was around Vivienne now, but she was leaning toward Theo in an outrageously intimate way, her hands unseen, their heads back.

There was something truly awful about the three of them together sitting like that. It was so dark and hard to see, even harder to stay calm. Shadows played across everyone's faces. Her immediate instinct was to barge over to the table and get Vivienne away from Theo. Fleur's words echoed to her, "keep those claws away from Theo." But she didn't want to be seen with such a scandalous table.

Andries looked angry. He leaned over the table at Vincent and Theo, and something smashed loudly. She couldn't see, but she could hear Andries, snapping loud and vicious, a terrifying voice she had never heard. She wanted to get closer. She looked toward the room where the show was happening. The magic show was still going.

She looked back at the table with Theo and *that crowd*, and—smack—Vivienne's eyes locked onto hers, accompanied by a smile so vile it beamed through the dark and found home in Johanna's chest, slicing open the anxiety she had been pushing away.

Behind Johanna, she heard her friends call to her. Johanna snapped back around and joined them as the lime-green absinthe was warming on the table.

She sipped her absinthe and listened to them make fun of the magician, one of them imitating him a bit. They gobbled up the food and their drinks.

Johanna's mind was combusting. What was Vivienne doing between Theo and Vincent? Locking eyes with Vivienne—what was that look? Smug, patronizing, and worse, it had been friendly too, conspiratorial. She understood, didn't she?

Another crash. The angels took long strides, their robes billowing to the front room. Johanna gulped down her drink. The first two sips were bad, but the last gulp went down well.

More crashing noises echoed through the noise of the crowd. "Oh, someone is going to pay tonight!" one of her friends said. They laughed and passed around the last of the food.

Fury. She felt the prickle of it climbing, crawling around her head, felt her smile hard and frozen. The image of Vivienne between Vincent and Theo. She was sick with disgust. "I'm glad you enjoyed the absinthe," she said brightly to her friends. "You know there is a drink—half absinthe, half brandy—called the tornado. The painter Lautrec invented it."

A woman screamed. A large bang, another crash, another scream. The restaurant went completely silent, anticipating the next event. Which was immediate and appalling.

Andries burst backward from the alcove, dragging Vivienne, screaming, toward the exit. He had her by both arms. He was pulling her, she was resisting. They jerked back and forth, grappling in an odd-looking dance. Vivienne tried to kick him and missed, and he turned around, dragging her behind him.

Vivienne's light musical voice had transformed to furious and guttural. The other "models" got up and struggled to fend off Andries. They shouted at him, throwing silly punches. He roared back in their faces, and they jumped away. He had the stronger pull, and he would get her out the door.

The angels pounced, trying to alternately claw his arms off Vivienne and push the entire group of Andries, Vivienne, and the models through the exit. The maître d' came running, both arms out wide to keep everyone else at bay, like a referee, and allowing Andries to drag Vivienne away.

The absinthe was sabotaging her brain and she squinted, trying to focus. Was she hallucinating? Her group gawked open-faced at the spectacle, like children at the zoo watching the standing bears clash furiously.

Johanna had never seen Andries like this -- her brother in a fight with a woman, her fiancé in a scene of crashing tables and intoxicated artists. She had to get out of there.

"Drink up and let us depart The Cloud!" Johanna rose, but way too quickly, and became dizzy. She thought she was moving in slow motion. "Phew, this was a bit of a drink."

Yes, they all agreed and moved slowly too. The Dutch had good tolerance. "Yes, please, I'll have another" was the national anthem. But absinthe was something else entirely.

Out on the street, Johanna looked around, confused about which direction to go, though she had done this walk countless times. The cooler air didn't make her feel better. Andries was there, straightening his coat, arguing with the waiters. Vivienne was there too, still screaming and kicking her legs up at Andries, the waiters holding her back.

Andries saw her, they shared a thought, *Keep moving.*

Come on, brain, think. But no thoughts came. She scratched her head and said to the group, "Time for Moulin Rouge. Onward!" and raised her arm in a charge-like gesture. She turned one way and then another, trying to remember which way to go.

One of her group opened her purse and held up the guidebook. "We can look it up," she said.

But mostly they all stared at the pretty woman and handsome man, now fighting again at full throttle.

Vivienne shouted at Andries, "You don't tell me what to do!" And she attempted to reenter the restaurant. Andries barred the door with his arms.

She screamed, "How dare you!" She then shrieked at the top of her lungs, without any self-consciousness, "Gendarmes!"

The waiters seemed to be on Andries' side and prevented Vivienne from reentering the restaurant. Her gorgeous red French knot was lost to the fight. Loose curls flew around her face and atop her electrified-looking hair.

The maître d' stormed out of the restaurant. "Yes, the gendarmes! Get your friends out of here now!" he yelled at Andries. He handed him a bill. "Never come back!"

Andries snatched the check and squinted in the dark at the bill.

"Who are they?" her friend asked. "Is that one of the painters from Montmartre?"

Johanna was barely listening as she watched her brother pay up and storm off down the street, alone.

Angels held open the doors, and the entire chaotic party scene paraded proudly onto the street.

Gauguin was the first. He walked past Johanna without noticing her, his face slack with drink, and he dangled a redhead on his arm.

Next, Theo, in a controlled stagger, swaying smoothly, with his long stride, almost walked past her.

"Theo!" Johanna said, sounding a little more alarmed than she meant to. She reached for his arm and pulled him to a stop.

He stared at her, confused for a moment.

"Johanna, what are you doing here?" He was not slurring, thank God. "It is you, isn't it? I didn't think you were with us."

"Yes, it's me. What's going on here?"

"Here? Nothing. Some things got broken, it's all paid for."

Vincent followed next and, without a word to Johanna, grabbed Theo's arm and pulled him down the street.

"Theo, wait a moment," Johanna said. She compulsively took steps toward Theo. "Wait…" she said again, sounding desperate to herself.

"Shush, not here. You're with your friends from work? I will find you tomorrow. Or I will write you." Theo put his hand over his heart briefly and bowed in a sloppy, droopy way. Vincent dragged him away, laughing loudly and shouting at the group ahead.

Johanna watched Theo disappear down the dark street.

Theo—no greeting, no kiss, no hug, nothing. She was chasing after a drunk man. Her group was staring at her, some shocked with open mouths, others smirking. She felt like an idiot.

The young American painter from her group, Sarah, came up to her and took her hand.

"Let's go to Moulin Rouge," Sarah said, smiling, and they all walked as a group toward the glowing, electrified section of Montmartre.

Johanna felt a nauseating wave of anxiety and lost her breath. Walking was difficult, her body ridged yet fragile like glass about to shatter against the pavement. Act normal, act normal. Her throat was closing up and the absinthe kept climbing up the back of it. She developed hiccups that wouldn't stop and struggled to hide them.

Her friends were all talking, happy, cheerful, replaying the scene leaving Johanna's role out. "What a cast of characters" and so forth. For them nothing was wrong—only she knew everything was.

The red and yellow lights of the theaters, cafes, and noisy streets pressed in and buzzed around her head. Every other woman on the street had flaming red or maroon hair and lips. Men were holding hands, or was it women dressed like men holding hands?

It was hard to stay together, with all the stopping and gawking at elaborate displays outside the theaters. Johanna felt a tug on her arm, a push against her back, ordinary street bustle. Just outside the Moulin Rouge, they gathered in front of a huge double-sized elephant that towered in the garden, brilliantly illuminated by the new electric lights. The noise in the garden was equally electric, the outdoor stage filled with young ballet dancers skipping across the stage in white tutus, showing miles of arms and legs, petticoats covering their thighs just to the knee.

Atop the building the windmill was decorated with colored lights throwing red shadows across pedestrians and the street. In front, children begged and greeted the theatergoers with pleading eyes and appeals for help. Johanna stared, appalled at the begging children. Most of the women opened their purses. A tug on her sleeve interrupted her.

"Please, Madame, money for food?"

Johanna blinked twice and gasped loudly, causing her friends to look, and saw Aline's lovely face, now sunken with hunger.

Aline recognized her too late. She tried to run away, but Johanna was quicker and pulled her back.

"Aline, what are you doing?" Johanna tried for her stern school-teacher voice, hoping the firmness would hide her panic.

"Nothing." Aline stared at the ground.

"Where is your mother?"

"Home."

"Home where? Your father said you had gone to Copenhagen."

"You saw my father? Where is he?"

"He was just here. Why are you out alone at night?"

"Where?" Aline looked frantically, one direction and then another. But there was nothing to see except the hordes pushing to enter the theaters.

"Poor child, let me help you."

"I'm hungry," Aline cried.

Jo's friend Sarah bent over Aline. She handed the child money and whispered something in her ear. Aline hugged her and ran away.

"Johanna, the child is starving."

"Her father said they left—"

"He is obviously lying. The child needs help."

She felt a stabbing in her head and fought back the acid roaring up her throat. The world blurred and she might have fallen, but Sarah took her arm and moved her gently into the theater. Everything in life was suddenly spinning out of control. She sat in her seat and none of show registered. She saw Theo, Vincent, Vivienne, Andries, and tried to reason away what she had seen, and what others had seen her do.

Staying busy with routine tamped down her panic. But she was losing the battle, poison thoughts pushing her into a spiral of darkness. She wasn't sure if she'd slept the night before. Aline, Theo, Vivienne, and Vincent took turns haunting her. Johanna waited for Andries to get out of bed. It was Sunday lunchtime.

She placed croissant, fish, butter, cheese, and coffee on the table but couldn't sit. She moved quietly through the apartment, stopping to listen at Andries's door, wanting to knock but knowing she shouldn't. She paced around the apartment: kitchen, parlor, and bedroom. Finally, he strolled into the kitchen.

"What do you want, Jo?" He sounded tired and irritable, his face not looking handsome today.

"Who were those women last night?"

"Models."

"Why were they with you?"

"Theo and Vincent, entertaining painters, making connections, creating inventory, taking over Paris—you ought to know by now." He rattled it off with boredom.

The problem was, she didn't know. Theo told her nothing about Vincent and his plans—she was beginning to realize he never had. "Why models?"

"The painters bring them."

"Why were you quarreling with Vivienne?"

He lit a cigar and opened the window. "How was the show?"

"Fine. Tell me about last night, it was a terrible spectacle. Tell me please?" She was begging.

"Vivienne," he said her name with a disgustful, sarcastic sneer. "Is… a very difficult woman."

"Is she with Vincent now? Why were you fighting?"

"Me? No, I never fight."

"I know what I saw, Andries."

"No, you don't."

"Will you please tell me what happened?" She knew her voice betrayed the panic she felt.

"I don't like her. Actually, I don't like any of them today. We had an argument."

"What about?"

"She is destructive and manipulative. Let's see…She gets her way because she's beautiful. Everyone knows better, but everyone falls for it. I was protecting you."

"From Vivienne?" She looked at Andries staring into his coffee, puffing on his cigar. He wouldn't meet her eyes. "Please tell me not Theo." She couldn't be wrong about Theo. She was building a new life with him.

"Theo doesn't love her," Johanna said flatly.

"No, he loves you." He picked up her hand, held it for a moment. "But I wonder if he is the best thing for you. Sometimes I think we should just leave."

She snatched her hand back. "Well, this is out of the blue! Of course, Theo and I are going to marry! Vincent is a terrible influence on Theo." She hadn't expected such a shocking statement from Andries, and it chilled her.

"Theo sees it differently."

"How does Theo see it?"

"He loves his brother, and he's trying to help him. And Vincent is helping Theo—he says so at least—with new painters."

"Why doesn't Theo promote Vincent's work, sell some of it?"

"I imagine he thinks Vincent's work isn't ready. I haven't even seen much of it. And…It might compromise him professionally."

"It's only about time and money, isn't it? He'll be successful, live independently. You should buy a painting from Vincent."

"Buying one painting won't make any difference for Vincent's prospects, short term, long term, or otherwise. Vincent is…" Andries held his tongue and changed tactics. "I guess we are going to have to trust Theo on this. We should stay out, we're the outsiders."

"He's going to marry me. A husband's first responsibility is to his wife."

"Vincent does exactly what he wants, without regard to anything or anyone else. That's how it is. Theo is completely loyal to him, and Vincent cannot survive without Theo."

"That's ridiculous. Vincent is a grown man. He just chooses to be difficult."

"That's what you think? This behavior is an intellectual choice on his part? The drinking, the constant quarreling, the slovenly dress, the fanatical moods, hysterical—"

"Yes, I do. He's a grown man. He will have to change. Has anyone ever tried to reason him through? Set limits?"

"Jo…Keep out of it. Trust Theo on this."

She handed him his eggs and toast. She didn't answer back. She was right about Vincent. Set limits, reason, do the right thing—all this is necessary. She does it, doesn't everyone?

"Jo, did you hear me? *Just go along and let Theo handle Vincent.*"

10

Johanna

Spring rain had made the streets of Paris shiny and slippery. Johanna walked with Sarah around the remains of the fair. They walked slowly through an on-and-off gray haze, with an occasional streak of yellow sun to warm them and brighten the day. The fair reminded her of Fleur and how terribly she missed her. Fleur had only been gone a few weeks, but time had slowed. She had an irritating feeling she was missing something. She would not let her life spin uncontrollably this way. She hadn't seen Theo since the incident with Vivienne, but he'd sent another letter as if nothing had happened.

They walked up the promenade, Sarah talking to all the artists about their work. Vincent was there too, at the Seine in a new spot not far from the Dutch pavilion. Just seeing him her tension rise. What had she seen with him and Theo and the witch Vivienne? It haunted her and made her question her instincts and Theo's intentions.

She had resisted the urge to run. Run where? Back to London? She had lived there for a short while, doing translations for the British museum. At the beginning it was wonderful, but it got tiresome. It was the most segregated, classist society and terrible in its treatment of the poor. Then she and Fleur set their sights on Paris.

And now here she was. She was not frozen in place, and she would not run. She would plan, think, set it all right. Restore.

In the week since the horrible night when she saw Aline and Vincent and Theo, she had made her plan. She would get to the bottom of the chaos with Vincent and Theo, help him set limits, and plot a new course of action for Vincent. And Andries assured her the purchases he made with Gauguin would help provide for his daughter.

Today, there were two painting stations. Emile's was momentarily vacant, so Vincent was alone. He stooped over his palette, squeezing out enormous gobs of paint.

Johanna and Sarah approached him. If Vincent could see she could be a help to him, maybe they could start over.

"Vincent van Gogh is another very promising new painter. He is just recently studying, like Gauguin." Jo said.

"I know the van Gogh name, Sarah said. "You are a family of art dealers. It's in your blood. What are you painting there? Is that the Seine?"

Vincent stopped painting and looked her over. He smiled. He nodded. He held his pipe clenched between his teeth and puffed slowly. Then without removing the pipe or putting down the brush he said, "I am painting the Seine. Obviously."

"Yes, you are painting quite quickly," Sarah stated.

"Maybe you are looking at it too quickly," Vincent snapped.

"Imagine, think of buying one of these paintings today, like a Monet, growing in value," Johanna said, trying to smooth over his edginess.

Sarah moved away, bored because the painter would not talk. But other tourists moved in toward Vincent.

Johanna leaned down and whispered in Vincent's ear. "I'm only trying to help you. Tourists are interested in art and enjoy talking to painters."

She straightened. "Vincent," Jo said, projecting her voice so the others could hear, "you said you wanted to reinvent the Dutch school. How will you do that? What is your approach?"

Vincent was silent, he stopped painting. He looked up at the tourists as if he might say something. He raised his hand with his brush. But no words came.

"You aim to start with the primary colors? Explain your vision to us, Vincent, everyone is interested." All the other painters relished the attention from the public.

He looked at her, staring, unblinking. "Miss Bonger, I would like to continue without interruptions," said Vincent quite stiffly but reasonably.

"Everyone is waiting to hear from you. Maybe you will sell something." Jo said cheerfully.

"You're ruining my concentration. I don't have time to chitchat with tourists. There is only so much daylight."

The group got the message and moved back and out of the way. Vincent smiled at their retreat. He returned to painting, puffing his pipe.

She felt her old schoolteacher voice screaming to the front of her brain. "You can't talk to people like that," she whispered to him. Don't you want people to be interested in your work? You know better, you are not a child." She was done tiptoeing around Vincent. Why should he be allowed all this ridiculous self-indulgent behavior?

He ignored her.

"This is the perfect place to attract attention. All the painters present their ideas here." This was good for their business, some even sold paintings right off the street.

Vincent looked back at Johanna dumbfounded and waved dismissing her. She felt her face turning red. His rudeness was inexcusable. He took out a flask and drank.

"Look Vincent, I am just trying to help you. Practice a speech about your vision, what you aim to do. Create a few phrases. I could rehearse with you."

Vincent jumped up from his stool. Frustration and anger gushed out, his face beet red. Johanna stepped back. She saw Emile running toward them.

"What did you say to me?" he screamed, lunging toward her.

Johanna jumped back but not fast enough.

"This is my art, my business and Theo's business. You are nothing. And this will never, ever be your business—not ever!" Vincent exploded, inches from her face. His breath blew hot and putrid, his teeth exposed as he narrowed his lips in fury. He smelled an unbreathable mixture of paint, solvents, pipe, alcohol, and sweat. Flecks of his spittle burned on her face.

Johanna calmly moved back a few paces. Vincent followed her move backward with one large aggressive stride, his face lit with fury.

She felt the stares of everyone. Time felt like it was standing still.

"Theo is my brother! It is our business. You should never talk to me again—ever! Get away from me. You are all wrong for Theo! I won't allow it. Father is gone, I am the eldest. He won't marry you without my permission!" He started to walk away.

Johanna impulsively grabbed Vincent's arm and pulled him to a stop, like she had a thousand times with a difficult child. Vincent shook her off.

She tried to spit out a few words, but her mouth had gone dry. She was trying hard to stay calm but could feel her knees buckling and tears on her cheeks. Then her brain kicked in and reverted to its old basic skills. She spoke in her sternest schoolteacher command.

"Vincent, turn around. Look at me." But he didn't. She walked toward him and stood her ground, just inches from him. "I love your brother. He loves me. I'm just trying to help. You're a grown man. You may not speak to me in this way." She reverted to Dutch so only Vincent could understand.

"You know nothing about life…about suffering. You are a bourgeois…a schoolmarm!" He screamed so loud the entire block could hear him.

"Vincent!" Emile shouted, trying to drag him back from Johanna. But as he did, Vincent lost his balance and rocked back, his free arm smashing up through Johanna's jaw, knocking her to the ground.

She lay there a moment, not moving, the wind gone from her lungs. Sarah ran to her and dropped to her knees to help.

"Johanna, are you hurt?"

"Run for the gendarmes," someone shouted. Then another voice.

"Oh my God, are you hurt?"

"Can you get up? Let me help you up."

"Vincent, we have to get out of here now." Emile struggled to lead Vincent away. He glared down at her.

"She fell." Vincent turned and shouted back at her. "Are you hurt? I'm sorry ---You shouldn't talk to me that way. Just don't speak to me again."

"Get out of here! You're a madman," said someone in the crowd.

Johanna lay on the ground. She put her hand over her mouth and tried to breathe deeply in and out.

Breath and sobs came together, and she fought humiliating tears. She allowed a pair of hands to pull her up. Sarah dusted her off, smoothing her hair, consoling her. Vincent and Emile packed up and fled.

"My umbrella—bring it to me, please. I must have dropped it." Jo said.

"That man is crazy, unbelievable, carrying on that way," Sarah said.

She got up stiffly and put on her professional, 'nothing bothers me' face. "Well, that's enough of that. Time to go."

And without looking back, Johanna moved down along the Seine and didn't talk to any more painters.

He was filthy, drunk, quarrelsome, unreasonable beyond the measure of any man she knew. What Fleur and Andries said was true. He is allowed to be a brat yes, but he is also a lunatic, and he hates me, and he will hate me forever and never allow me to marry Theo. And there it is, she thought, I've misjudged everything. Theo doesn't understand Vincent is beyond reason.

Andries

Andries stared down at two letters on the kitchen table, one addressed to him, the other simply to "Theo." Next to the letters was a plate of food, covered with an upside-down bowl.

He didn't pick up the letter. He knew. Still, to be sure, he walked into the silent living room, scanning for any sign of Jo.

None.

He lit a cigar without opening the window and sat on the couch, staring at the empty desk. After a few deep pulls on his cigar, Andries checked Johanna's bedroom. The room was cleaned out, her clothes and books gone, the dresser empty. On top of the dresser, another note, this one just said:

Please give this letter to Theo. You will see him before I do. I just can't. I am sorry. Love, Johanna.

What had possibly happened to provoke this dramatic action? It had to be Vincent, but when would Jo have seen him, and even be alone with him?

I don't want to be in the middle of this, he thought. Andries smoked his cigar and walked toward his mission with dread. *But I am and have been since the beginning. This is a bitter end. She deserves better. Johanna doesn't have the thick skin and killer instinct needed to survive the snake-pit world of modern art.*

His heart was filled with agony for her and anger at Theo. This was exactly what he had feared. She would be heartbroken. He must get back to Amsterdam, see how she was. But he had to get this done first. Endings are such misery.

On the grand boulevard in Montmartre, Andries checked all

the cafés, bars, and restaurants, but Theo wasn't in any of the usual places. He hated to try Theo's apartment, afraid he might find Vincent instead, and he was already in a bad mood.

When he arrived at Theo's apartment, there was a bouquet of flowers sitting outside the door in a bucket of water. He knocked and waited what felt too long a time. But he could hear movement behind the door. Damn. He knocked louder. Vincent opened the door.

"Good evening, Vincent," he said, upbeat and as friendly as he could pretend. "Can I bring these in for you?" He indicated the flowers.

Vincent peered around the door and looked at the flowers.

"No, leave them," he said with a self-satisfied smile.

Vincent stepped back, opening the door. He made a half gesture with his hand for Andries to enter. "Theo isn't here."

"Do you know where he is?"

Vincent walked back to his canvas and sat at the easel. A still life of a brown vase with a large bunch of yellow flowers chaotically leaning in every direction was arranged on the table, with gaslights throwing patterns against the wallpaper.

Andries followed, carefully picking his way through the staggering amount of debris and paint-covered garbage everywhere. He trod carefully, protecting his clothes, his shoes, and everything else. He wanted to lift up his trouser legs, so no paint accidentally brushed the fine wool.

"It's very good, Vincent," Andries said, and he meant it.

"Really, you like it?"

"Yes, I think you're on to something new and different."

"Sometimes I think I am. Truly new and truly different."

"Poetic." Andries took a step closer to look at Vincent's painting. There were others, lined up against the wall behind him, several hanging on the wall. They were still life's, in something of the classic composition—bowl, fruit, tabletop or vase with flowers. The painting on the easel was hypnotic. A thousand pulses of yellow, gold, bronze, orange, and every hue in between, ten thousand more—cobalt blue, turquoise, green—sharply contrasted, causing the whole painting to hum and vibrate almost as if the flowers were moving.

On the wall, tall red peonies swayed in warm tones. Contrasting colors and close-ups were the hallmarks of all the canvases. Vincent had learned the new visual style of the impressionists, vibrant colors and flamboyant brush strokes. Maybe he had done them one better.

The subjects, the flowers, the fruit in close-up view, so close, clever—no wonder the other artists put up with him. He was on to something, the colors more vibrant, with even sharper contrasts. So fast, Andries thought. Part of the new world of painting, in his own way.

Perhaps he should buy? He turned away from the array of paintings and looked at Vincent, in front of his easel.

"Brilliant, Vincent."

"Thank you. What do you like specifically?"

"The viewpoint, close-up—this is new? The colors are exceptional, yours alone."

"Thank you. I can't think of a time when I have done better work."

"Yes, congratulations, all of this is truly brilliant." He seemed calm, pleased with himself Andries thought. Then suddenly Vincent got loud.

"Why are you here? Are you trying to reason with me?" Vincent stood up, putting his hands on his hips. "It wasn't a fight. Is that what she told you?" Vincent stared at Andries, eyes unblinking, challenging.

Ah ha, yes, that's it. She had a run in with Vincent. She never could tolerate being bullied.

"She hasn't told me anything. She thinks you don't like her. So where is Theo?" He kept his voice matter of fact.

"Selling tulips someplace. Turning Monet into wallpaper."

Vincent lit his pipe, drank his wine, and resumed painting. He ignored Andries.

"I have checked the usual places. Do you have any idea where he might be?"

"No. Why? Do you need Theo tonight?" He turned and stared with his endless hard stare, more a glare now.

"I don't need him. I just haven't seen him."

"You are lying." Vincent laughed. He returned to his painting again.

Andries wanted to leave, but he put a smile on his face that said, everything is normal here, we're just having a regular conversation, hoping not to provoke him.

"You are duplicitous like everyone else in Paris. I wonder if Theo knows how evil you are." Vincent spat out this outrageous betrayal.

Andries hated emotional outbursts.

"Why would I lie to you, Vincent?" He tried to hide his annoyance and now growing anger.

"You would lie to me. I know you lie to Theo. Because you want everything to work out. You want everyone to be happy, to get along. Happiness is not important. Theo is all the family I have, and art is my only purpose. Those two things…I will fight to the death for both of them."

Andries smiled again at Vincent but felt ridiculous. Vincent was agitated, his anger no longer a nagging nuisance but a bundle of horror about to explode. Andries, acquiesced, his hands up and out, imploring for calm. He only hoped to leave as quickly as he could.

Vincent turned his back on Andries and continued painting.

Andries kicked the garbage out of the way, sending some of it flying back up at him, and dodging his own blowback headed to the door.

In the hallway, feeling exceedingly mean spirited, he stole the bucket of flowers meant for Vincent to paint, carried them down to the street, and dumped them in the gutter, throwing the bucket, watching it clatter down the alley. But he felt no satisfaction from such a petty action and hoped no one had witnessed his outburst. *I must find Theo.*

Andries walked off his nagging anger searching for Theo. He found him finally, alone in the darkest corner of an obscure neighborhood café, on the outskirts of Montmartre. Here, he was guaranteed not to run into any acquaintances. Theo looked exhausted, staring down at the table. Andries put his hand on Theo's shoulder.

Theo looked startled to see him and then happy to see a friend. Andries had seen Theo become a different man over the months, worry lines had appeared and gotten deeper.

But this was his sister's life. Jo had to come first. Perhaps Theo might think it was for the best. Not having Johanna in Paris would be one less worry for Theo. He could focus on his business, the artists, gallery owners, and his brother.

Andries reached into his pocket and pulled out the letter from Johanna and leaned it against Theo's wine glass.

Theo's face said it all. "Aren't you at least going to sit down," he said with uncharacteristic bitterness.

"I'm sorry, Theo." Andries sat and waved to the waiter.

Theo didn't pick up the letter. He coughed a loud, racking, congested cough in a napkin and choked. Andries reached across and rested his hand on his shoulder.

It was a small, dingy bar. The waiter was watching, and he was giving them a moment.

When Theo was able to speak, he said, "A public place for a painful, private matter. You want the conversation kept to a minimum. Jo wants no conversation at all. Without warning, you hit me from behind."

"I haven't done anything," Andries sounded defensive and

immediately regretted it. He rubbed his forehead with his hand. The waiter delivered another bottle and a glass. Andries filled both glasses. "I'm sorry, Theo. I wish…I wish I could wave a magic wand and make everything work out for all of us."

"I love you, Andries, and I love your sister. It's been so hard with Vincent, his crazy behavior. And Goupil selling to Brossard. They want their investments paid out quickly. Selling quickly means selling cheaply, never a good idea."

"I love you, I love my sister more, and so what, we all love each other! But we have a bad situation. I can't help but think this could all have been avoided."

"Why so harsh? Has she left Paris?"

"Yes." He hadn't meant to sound harsh.

"Why?"

"Read. I don't know."

"I don't believe you." Theo stared at him hard, looking like Vincent. It was unnerving.

"I came home, she was gone. Maybe she's taking another job translating…London…America. Why learn five languages if you don't travel?" He knew he sounded ridiculous.

"You do know."

Andries remained silent.

"You have been against this match since the beginning."

He sounded just like Vincent for a second, Andries thought, the recriminating tone wasn't like Theo.

"No, I agreed, remember."

"I'll do anything for her," Theo said, looking up at the café ceiling.

"Yes, so you say." Andries surprised even himself with this bit of sarcasm.

"I must have Johanna. She is my future. I promise you this will all work out."

"Jo left because she didn't like what she was seeing. She has to think about her own future. This is a simple ending—that's all."

"This is a crisis!"

"This is my sister. I must protect her."

"From me? The future is all I think about. You don't know the future. I do! That's why you do what I tell you to do! Someday you will have a fortune in art, worthy of any museum in Europe. I will be the preeminent dealer. Change is the certainty. Emotions are contagious, color will win out. We will have money enough for one hundred families."

"Enough diatribes on modern art! Which family, Theo? The one you want or the one you have?" He snapped.

"What do you mean? You mean I have to choose between my brother and my love?"

"God, you are blind, my dear friend. Have you even talked to Vincent?"

"I can't bear to be around him anymore. I go home late when I know he has drunk himself into a stupor. He's slovenly and quarrelsome with everyone, especially me. And do you know what the worst part is? He's almost happy. He has gone over well here in Paris. His work is unique, brilliant. His friends see the achievement, the artists he admires respect his work. He has helped me with a few new artists. They trust me, think I am authentic, not just a tulip trader. Andries, help me."

"Read your letter."

"Tell me where she is."

"Read."

Andries took a deep breath and watched Theo open the letter. He read it and dropped it on the table for Andries to read. He looked to the heavens and mouthed something Andries couldn't make out.

Dearest Theo, I am sorry, but I have to leave Paris. Circumstances have changed, and I find I am no longer certain Paris is where I belong. I am very unhappy here and have been for some time. Endings are very hard, and the less said now, the better. I must start again and focus on building my business. All my love, Johanna.

"I'm devastated. This will do me in." Theo said hopelessly, and carefully folded the letter, placed in back in its envelope, and placed it next to his heart inside his jacket.

Johanna

Emotion is power, the personal is universal in the modern world of painting. Theo taught her that. That is why she had loved the new painting. Freedom, emotion—they were a powerful drug in the new world. Emotions didn't need to be hidden away, they were glamorized, celebrated. But not here in Amsterdam. Her father was watching her, out of the corner of his eye, as he sorted mail. They were all watching her, the staff, from their desks. She stood quietly behind the counter, staring down at contracts to be filed.

She looked the same and was functioning. The slaughter inside her was not visible, she thought. She had failed to create an independent life for herself, full of purpose.

She felt in a sickening flash how all the recent drama had changed her for the worse. Her life had been stolen out from under her. She had lost. She hadn't done anything wrong, yet she was being punished. She was back home, trying to put one foot in front of the other, work, recover. Thank God for Fleur. Jo spent every minute she could in the back of Fleur's new bakery, talking out the pain.

At night, the lonely black hole pressed on her when she tried to sleep and dream of the future. No marriage, no Paris, no career, no purpose. She needed to start again, again.

She acted happy to be home. Pretending was exhausting. Everyone knew she had failed, and this was a walking death. She forced herself to smile. She rolled up her sleeve and discreetly drew a long winding *S* on the inside of her wrist and then pulled her cuff over it. The S shape, the movement was supposed to be a desirable design in paintings, a wide horizontal S movement or long, deep vertical S, of color and light across the canvas, dragging the eye through the composition.

What could she have done differently? The endless spiral of thinking what was done and would never be undone, and how terrible she felt and whatever could she do to feel better? She had asked her brother to give Theo the letter—she was a coward on top of everything else. She didn't think, she just ran. What would Theo think of her argument with Vincent? She couldn't bear to lose his respect. Better for her to break it off than for him to reject her. Vincent told her to leave, and she knew he would make things worse for her. She didn't see a choice, and she had lost herself.

Her father called to her to go to the back room, the contract storage room, to bring him a file. She hated that room. More new paintings were there, the paintings Andries had invested in. The paintings were a bloodsucking animal, just having them around drained her. She stood in front of the stack of carefully covered paintings. She had a letter opener in her hand, sharp and long. She wondered how easily the canvas would slice.

She took the cover off the first painting. It was a Lautrec, a nude, likely of a prostitute. It was rich with deep colors, contoured with sleek modern lines—a quintessential modern painting. "Modern"— she used to love the word. It was an important word, it was the critical notion of the times, and she loved it when Fleur would joke with her, "Jo, you are so modern." Modern was the way forward, the leaving of all the past, easy comforts, and once you stepped into the modern world, there was no going back. You either embraced the new things or you didn't. Either you were the enlightened one, the risk taker, or you weren't, and you were a lesser person. Modern, it was the place where all the self-proclaimed smartest, most talented men resided. Women elbowed in too, thick-skinned and determined.

What does it mean to be modern? To turn a blind eye to others' indiscretions? To allow oneself to get carried away in displays of vulgarity? To let your children beg while you buy tubes of paint?

She was once almost one of them.

She imagined her letter opener was a knife and put the tip to the drawing of the woman's head. She wanted to slash it to bits. Would she have to sweat and saw, or would it cut cleanly? She imagined slashing all of them, one at time.

They are not better than me, she thought. Everyone will have their turn in the end, that is the nature of things. This suffering will make me wiser. When I recover, I will be better than ever and will have moved forward. Then I will get my choices back and stand my ground. I should move all these paintings of chaos and color out of sight to the basement with the others, not here, reminding me of everything I have lost.

She heard the door quietly open and close behind her, and her father cleared his throat. She had forgotten about his contracts.

"What are you doing?" Her father stood at the door and whispered to her. His alarm bled through his whisper. He never tolerated displays of emotion, a woman with a knife would get his blood pumping.

She couldn't bear to turn around and meet his eye, she thought her misery would betray her, and she would break in front of him.

"Johanna, Mr. Van Gogh was just here. I didn't think you were expecting him. I told him you weren't in, to come back in an hour," her father said softly, surprising her.

Theo was here, he had come. Her heart started pounding. *Be strong, Johanna, be proud, you didn't do anything wrong.*

"I hope I did the right thing. What do you want me to tell him if he comes back?"

Her father sounded so comforting, and that almost made her crack. Theo had followed her. If she had the scene with him, the one she had run away from, this would bring about the final unhappy ending she dreaded. She would sink into the black abyss. Would there ever be a way to recover, to be happy again? She had seen her happiness as this perfect thing. Why wouldn't everyone be happy for her too? Why did her happiness have to bleed like an acid and ignite another's pain?

Theo

Theo stood on a drizzly, gray street corner in Amsterdam that was the home of Bonger Insurance. She was there, Theo thought, and she's hiding from me. It was too soon to panic and fear the worst. Let's see what has happened and what can be done or undone. The letter had said nothing, but he felt destroyed. She had to be there, where else would she go? He took off his hat, shook the droplets off, and smoothed his hair. He took out a handkerchief and wiped his face and hands. Last, he arranged his coat, making sure everything was in the proper place. Bonger had said she wasn't there, but his body betrayed him—he looked around nervously. She was there, in the back.

He looked down the alley and saw the partial silhouette of a woman. Jo was there and avoiding him. He walked slowly, trying to be quiet. He came to the turn where the alley opened up into a little courtyard. He saw Johanna standing there, head tilted back, staring up at the gray overcast sky. She looked so sad.

"Johanna," Theo said quietly.

She jumped. "Oh God, Theo, you're here. You scared me!."

"What's going on? How could you leave me like that?"

"I thought a letter would be more manageable. I didn't leave you. I just needed to leave."

Theo stepped carefully to Johanna. "I've been frantic. Let's get out of this alley. Let me hear what is happening." Theo offered her his arm. "Shall we? Anything you need from inside?"

But Johanna didn't move, and her face betrayed her. She looked to the ground, turned her back to him, and put her hand over her mouth, covering half her face. She was trying not to cry. "No scenes. Let's stay here," she said.

He walked around her, took her shoulders and then, lifting her face to his, said, "No scenes, what does that mean? Johanna, you're going to marry me." He failed to hold on to his usual calm and his voice broke on "marry me." He sounded like a child to his own ears.

She was silent and pulled away from him.

"You want to marry me." He held his breath.

"I…won't marry you. I'm sorry." She wouldn't look at him.

"Why not?" He said it too quickly and again his voice broke in an odd childlike way. He was losing his grip.

"When I agreed to marry you, circumstances were different. I can't build a future with you the way things are."

"The way things are. What is different now? Tell me. You love me still?"

"Yes. But I must have a calm, respectable household. I'm only prepared to handle certain things."

She didn't sound like Jo.

"Jo, what do you mean 'calm household?' Why aren't you being honest with me?"

Johanna didn't say anything.

"All right, what things can't you handle? Come back with me."

Jo stayed silent, face frozen, staring at the ground.

"You want me to move my business here? Sell art in Amsterdam? Why don't you tell me what's going on?"

"This is hard for me, Theo."

"Can't we please get out of this alley? Isn't there a private space inside, an interior office or something?" If he could sit with her, hold her, and speak quietly, he could discover why she had fled and how to turn her around.

"No, there are employees inside. We won't be alone. The walls are thin."

"Alright, I'm listening." He put his hat on the chair.

"It's your brother. He hates me."

Theo traded places with his hat and collapsed in relief on the chair. He laughed breathily for a moment, a smile spreading across his face.

"He doesn't hate you. His heart is too big. He loves you. He loves you because I love you. He gets overwhelmed, confused…" He waved his hand in the air and looked at Jo. He smiled at her, relieved he could turn this around.

"No, he despises me."

"That's impossible."

"He hates me. He told me so."

"When was this?" His relief vanished in a heartbeat and Theo felt another flash of wretchedness and wiped a bead of sweat off his top lip with his already rain-soaked handkerchief.

"It's such a mess with him," Jo said. "Everything is out of control, all the time. I feel like I'm walking on eggshells when I'm around him."

"When were you alone with him? Was he drunk? He'd had too much to drink, no food probably." Oh no, another "misunderstanding" with Vincent, and he was angry at having to clean up another Vincent debacle.

"He's always drunk, Theo! And filthy. Surely you've noticed," Jo snapped.

Theo felt stricken by this angry tone he had never heard from Jo.

"When were you alone with him?"

"I wasn't alone… with him. I was with a colleague at the Seine. Vincent was there in his usual painting spot." She paused, exhaled deeply, and slowly began again. "We were talking to the artists. I tried to talk about his painting. He screamed at me. Maybe I said a wrong thing or two, but I didn't deserve to be humiliated! He said I was a woman who didn't know anything about art or life or suffering. I was wrong for you, and I could never give you what you needed. He called me a bourgeois schoolmarm. He said he would never approve of our marriage, and you would never marry me without his approval."

Theo looked to the heavens. Despite the dramatic words, her delivery was reasoned, unemotional, to the point.

"I'm sorry Vincent said those things. This is a misunderstanding. I will clear this up immediately. Vincent didn't mean any of that and none of it true. He was distracted from his painting and got agitated. I would have to kill him if he said anything like that." He chuckled, but Jo didn't crack a smile.

"That is exactly what he said, Theo. You are always with him. We almost never see each other."

"I need to stay close to the artists and be part of the circle. There are other dealers now who are interested, and the artists are fickle. I need to manage Vincent better, I understand that."

"This is why I left, partially...."

"But you will come back. Partially.... What else?"

"There is an American company needing..."

"America, no, you can't go there, no one ever comes back from America. Please, Johanna, come back to Paris with me."

"This is so sad, Theo. He's completely dependent on you. Does he even try to stand on his own? Or even get along with anyone? How can we have a marriage with him sniping at me?"

"Please, Johanna, trust me, I'll handle Vincent." *How am I going to handle Vincent?* This was spinning beyond his control. In the back of his mind, he felt the onslaught of depression and failure.

"He's a terrible influence on you, you must see that at least."

"Yes, maybe I do. But I also see brilliance. I thought you loved his painting. I thought you might learn to love him. I know he is—"

Johanna walked to the door. "There is something else too," Johanna said.

Theo stiffened, took a breath, and waited for the blow. He opened his arms to her, begging. "What?"

"I saw you with *her*," Johanna said.

"You saw me with whom?" Theo asked.

"You never ended it with Vivienne."

"Vivienne, for God's sake, Johanna, she is the devil on the earth! It was over. I never, ever loved her." Theo clasped his hands together.

"Le Ciel, with Vincent, the three of you together, in public. Disgusting."

"No, that didn't happen. I wouldn't let that happen."

"Theo! Andries dragged her out to the street. You wouldn't even talk to me!"

"The absinthe...whatever you saw...I don't remember, and it meant nothing."

"You are always with them, and it did happen."

This had been his life for so long, the endless party he didn't even like.

Johanna yanked the door open. Her face held an expression he had never seen. Love and horribly, disappointment. Lines drawing down her trembling mouth, her eyes teary. Yet she held her chin up and head tall, defiant. She was going to leave him, and he couldn't stop her. She would close the door and she wouldn't look back.

"Johanna, forgive me." He begged.

"I feared you were too good to be true."

"Don't leave me. Please, Jo."

He cried as she closed the door behind her without looking back.

"Where have you been, Theo!" shouted Vincent, without looking up from his easel.

Theo didn't answer but gagged on the smell in the apartment. On his way to the window for some fresh air, he saw a rustling under the debris and froze, his eyes glued to the spot. He stamped his foot, and a rat ran past him, squeezed through the door and out of the apartment.

What a wonderful welcome back to Paris and this handsome apartment, Theo thought. Vincent left his easel and stood in the middle of the squalor.

Theo looked around—and saw utter squalor, covering every inch of the floor, ruining every piece of furniture. The walls told the tale of hard work, brilliant creativity, and enduring beauty.

"God Almighty, this was a nice apartment," Theo said.

"We waited for you at the café for two nights, Theo." Vincent ignored the mess and embraced Theo.

"Who paid the café bill?"

"Henri paid. Where were you?"

"I traveled to Amsterdam to see Johanna."

"Oh, Johanna." He sighed.

"Yes, Johanna. You understand I love her, don't you?"

"You don't. She is a mistress of duty. No passion, no fire."

"I love her, Vincent. Why would you be awful to someone I love?" If he talked gently, suppressing the anger he felt, maybe he could make Vincent understand.

"She was awful to me. I was showing her the truth."

"I just told you the truth." He caught the edge in his voice and forced a thin smile.

"You will never marry her. She is too precious for you. I'm just trying to help you, little brother. You are better off with someone like Vivienne, someone who understands art, is engaged in life."

"Vivienne is a whore. That you would even compare Johanna to Vivienne is inconceivable. Johanna is the love of my life." Keep it all reasonable and get Vincent to understand. There was too much love between them, wasn't there?

"She doesn't understand art."

"Johanna is my future, which makes her your future. And if you ever say another unkind thing to her again—"

"What? Are you threatening me? There is nothing you can do to hurt me! You made me give up my family, you won't do the same for me?"

"You fool, that was long ago, and you don't see the difference?"

"Yes, yes, I see the difference. I lost the child too! That is the difference!"

"So go back to her then and figure out your life. Possibly you two will still recognize one another!"

"What about our dream, our business together! We only need each other. Don't you see that?"

"No, we both need more."

"Johanna left you, didn't she?"

"She'll return." *I will get her back. I will figure out what to do with you, find money to set you on your own, and get Jo to marry me. I have let this all go on too long, and now my life has spun out of control.*

"You are better off without her."

"Stop, Vincent, you're depressing me!" Theo went to his bedroom and took off his shoes and overcoat and lay on the bed with his suit on, the back of his hand covering his eyes.

Vincent followed him and stood over the bed.

"I am talking to you." He nudged him a little. "You are depressed because you do not control your own destiny. You are a handmaiden to others. Sell my work, and I'll go south and start my painting cooperative."

Stay calm, Theo, calm down. You will get her back. Time is the only enemy. A plan will emerge. The painting cooperative in the south—always with Vincent, a good idea, get him out of Paris, out of my daily life. How am I going to pay for it? I could cash in the inheritance from Uncle Cent. I could sell some of my private collection. I could leave this apartment, find a cheaper one. I could break into my savings...

"But that would compromise you, wouldn't it? You have become a bourgeois art dealer, selling tulips. That is what Johanna has done to you! That's why you're depressed. If you were serious about our business together, if you lifted one finger to help me, our business would grow."

"What would we sell the paintings for, Vincent?" He sat up on the bed. He patted the side of the bed for Vincent to join him. *Calm, slow down, stay calm. Let him do the screaming for both of us.*

"We sell the paintings when they are worth selling," Theo said. "When you have positive notices from the right critics, when collectors of note become convinced you will be an important painter, when every painter in Paris knows your name, when any gallery would be proud to have your show, when you can speak about your work with conviction. That is when we sell the paintings! You above all should know this, understand, and work to make any of this happen! We are not going to give them away for the sake of a sale. Is that what you want, just to say you sold a painting? Now, leave me, Vincent. I'm not feeling well. It has been an exhausting, depressing time. I must be an objective arbiter, otherwise my clients won't trust me. I'm not here to push your work." He pulled a cover over himself, still fully clothed.

"Did you say, 'push my work?' I knew it. You don't like my work!" Vincent shouted and jumped off the bed.

A neighbor pounded on the walls. *Boom, boom, boom.*

Vincent screamed in the air, "Boom, boom yourself!" and stomped his feet across the floor to the wall, and pounded loud and hard, three times.

"I love your work. Do more—the more, the better. Get out of the apartment. Enough still life—go for landscapes. Stop that pounding, or the gendarmes will come again, and we will both spend the night talking our way out of jail. Do you want that?" Theo put a pillow over his head, hoping to muffle Vincent's uncontrollable rant. God help him this could go on until daybreak. Theo felt for a moment he might lose his mind and then all would be lost. He had to keep a grip, get Vincent to quiet down, give him some peace.

"You need to renew yourself in art, Theo. It is the only way."

"I know Vincent, that is what I am working to achieve. Please, leave me alone, you are harming me, don't you see!" Say it calm, let the words speak. If you yell, this is the match that will erupt the volcano, and the screaming and circular argument won't end until dawn. "Vincent, brother, I love you, but you will kill me with this madness. Let me sleep. I need to rest and think. I need to renew myself in money, that's what I need—more money."

PART 3

1888

11

Johanna

Johanna worked hard to keep up the meaningless, endless small talk with her customer as she stood behind the high wood counter at Bonger Insurance. Chatter never used to bother her. Now it was enormously tedious, and smiling was almost painful. She often redrew the *S* on the inside of her wrist, trying different sizes—a long, winding one, a fat zigzag, a swirl. Sometimes a painting would flash in her head, a Vincent floral mostly. The bold colors and chaotic swirls transported her momentarily, a feeling of energy returning to her step. And then despair overcame her. Maybe it was better to live in ordinary dullness than to live a fantastic life and lose it.

The chitchat in Amsterdam was excruciatingly dull. The same conversation, the weather, the boring local events, the gossip that disguised itself as news because the people were too hardworking to spend valuable time on inconsequential gossip. But this was home.

Then a little lift. The postman was approaching. He was wet, the rain was back again.

She rifled through and saw the letter from Theo, which put a cautious, anxious energy in her step. He wrote to her, he never stopped. He hadn't let go. He reasoned, he pleaded, and often recounted his days and plans, hopes for the future. Hope for what? She couldn't live that life, around a man who despised her.

She started the kettle on top of the potbelly stove and looked through Theo's letter, waiting for the kettle to come to a boil. It was many pages long and contained a flyer advertisement for a show called Le Petit Boulevard. *Meet the artists — Vincent van Gogh, Paul Gauguin, Emile Bernard.*

Johanna dropped the ad on the counter and returned to the letter. The first line was *Johanna, I beg you to return to me.*

The door chime rang out.

"What a nasty mess out there!" Mr. Bonger quickly entered and shook the rain off his coat.

"Let me bring you a cup of tea." Johanna stood.

"Thank you." He saw the flyer sitting on the table. He picked it up and looked it over. "From Theo? Looks like progress, thank God," he whispered sweetly to Jo. "Painters of Le Petit Boulevard—what do you think that means?" he asked.

"It means they are not the Painters of the Grand Boulevard. They are the new ones, aspiring to be grand."

"Aspiring to be grand. Hmmph. Will you go?"

"I don't know."."

"I hope you don't" he said and turned away stiffly, moving into the office and saying hello to the employees.

She looked at the flyer as if it contained clues to something special that more looking would reveal. Maybe it was a compulsion, and seeing the names conjured a storm in her brain. It was a messy brochure- blotches of color stretched across the pages. Not well produced she thought, but the chaos spilled energy off the page.

She stood leaning behind the massive counter and began to read Theo's letter.

Dear, darling Johanna,

Once more I beg you to return to me. Arrangements are underway for Vincent's move to the South of France.

The room darkened with the increasing storm. The storefront bay window was transformed into a warm, gray cloud of rain and thick mist, a noisy, careening pattern of torrents of water. The rain was mesmerizing in a deadening way, mimicking her feelings.

Then a color flashed by the window—someone running to escape the downpour. The bright color popped in her eye, and she chased it out of view, hoping for another.

"Color has an energy and urgency all its own." Someone had said that to her, one of the artists. She didn't remember who, it was all an old blur she only remembered now when she lay down to sleep, like colorful pages from a children's book.

She missed Theo. Her chest ached, and she felt dead all over. Vincent was leaving for the South of France. *The brighter sunlight is ideal for landscape painting. I will be alone again,* Theo had written.

Jo watched as indistinguishable masses of gray moved past the window.

The bell on the door rang again, the happy little noise bringing Johanna back to life. Fleur paused in the entrance, radiant and wet in her vibrant red wool coat, with her yellow-and-blue umbrella.

She stared at Jo and cocked her head back at the door, a gesture that said, "Time for lunch, let's go."

Yes, Johanna thought, let's go.

"You need to go back to Paris and see for yourself," Fleur said, sipping tea and nibbling on a small sandwich. As soon as Jo told Fleur that Theo had arranged for Vincent to live independently, Fleur blurted it out. Johanna listened to Fleur as she picked at the flavorless lunch in front of her. Did she have the stomach to try again? Uproot again to Paris?

Fleur read her mind. "You don't have to stay. You don't have to talk to anyone. Go to Paris, that's what my Jo would do. 'Go' is the only decision necessary. What do you have to lose?" Fleur kept talking before Jo could wrap her thoughts around the question. "You know Jo, I've learned a lot from baking. When we first arrived in Paris, I had a brioche, and I thought it the most delicious thing I ever tasted. I wanted to bake one myself. It took me dozens of tries. All I needed was the chance to do it again, but differently. And eventually, *et voilà*! Perfection."

"Jo, are you listening to me?" Jo was listening, thinking about Paris. She only needed to go and see. Fleur was right, one step at a time, one decision would lead to another. Vincent and Theo seemed ready to make changes. With Vincent away she wouldn't have to worry about fighting with him again.

Theo

Theo was laying out rolled-up canvases upstairs at the galleries, once Goupil, now Brossard. He coughed wetly into a cloth hand-kerchief. He resisted the urge to check for blood and tossed it to the garbage. He mopped his wet brow and took a lozenge. Soon it would be spring, and the warmer weather would clear up this infection.

More rest, less wine, better food. He was making slow progress, the fever had stopped, soon he would completely recover. And he hoped he'd recover his mood, which needed improvement. Vincent kept him on edge. Something had happened to him in Paris, some-thing wonderful and awful. His painting was beyond Theo's highest hopes and dreams. He was tireless, worked constantly, and had achieved a massive leap forward in painting. But he was impossible to live with. Vincent having everything he wanted made him even more unlivable. Here he had friends who shared his excitement, women who liked him, enough paint, canvas, food, drink—way too much drink—and there was no way to deny him anything. He compared himself to everyone around him. He was never satisfied. And he craved light. The winter in Paris was gloomy, gray. He craved sun, talked about sun all day, all night.

Theo needed Johanna, to start his own family that he could love and make happy. He carefully unrolled a canvas and put an L-shaped frame sample on the corner.

A young staffer quietly appeared at the top of the step. "Mr. Van Gogh? Mr. Brossard would like to see you."

Theo straightened himself up, checking his attire. This was unexpected, and likely not going to go well.

Theo sat at a French-provincial walnut desk. Mr. Brossard had a furrowed brow and superior countenance, waving his hand when he wanted Theo to speak. He wasn't going to waste any time with small talk.

"Theo, you need to make your case for further investment in the impressionists and especially in the moderns." He waved his hand for Theo to come forward.

"We have the opportunity to become the preeminent dealer of modern art," Theo said. "Sales have been steady. There is remarkable new talent arriving every day and we have an edge in their representation. We are one of the few representing with these new artists. Our reputation and longevity in handling the realists and Barbizon school made us known to painters. Our success with Monet—"

"I hear many of them like Vincent. They admire his determination, dedication. They like to carouse with him. None of my business, not my expense." He stopped for dramatic emphasis.

"Yes, he has developed many friends in the painting community," Theo said.

"I don't see enough return. And I hear you are collecting on your own, on the side."

"Yes. Only painters the gallery has looked at and declined. Many of these artists need money up front. That is not our—your—policy." *This is standard, all the dealers do it. If he objects to this, I have a larger problem than I thought.*

"My policy choice is your opportunity?"

"If you want to put it that way."

"Where are your loyalties, Theo? Are you committed to this business?"

"I believe in modern art. I think that benefits this organization."

"*Believe* is an interesting choice of word. Modern art is a risk. We need popular, established work to sell. This organization is not seeing the return, you know the benefit is minimal, at best. We need you to make the realists, the Barbizon school, your first priority. You know this is what pays the bills, your salary."

"Impressionists will eclipse Barbizon. They have created a revolution in painting. If we invested a fraction more, you would have—"

"Revolution?"

"Yes. Each artist has a unique—"

"Then what would happen to the classic collections we have? It is in our best interest to keep those prices high. Don't you see?"

"Art reflects society's changing tastes. We can take the lead. Modern works create value overall for the company and ultimately the greatest return." *This man will never see it unless I bring in a fortune fast.*

"The greatest return, really? Theo, have you seen the latest *Paris Art Review*?" He threw the paper to Theo. "They call this work anarchy, with social implications leading the culture into decadence. That is the overwhelming conclusion from the collective art establishment. Why would someone endure that in their home? Individuals with money want real art, not speculation. How will you compel critics to write positive reviews? Where is your plan?"

"Mr. Brossard, modern art is gaining traction, there are many new collectors throughout Europe—"

Brossard held up his hand for Theo to stop. "Where Theo? England? They don't want it. You need a plan, otherwise we will load a steamer and send it all to the nouveau-riche Americans and be done with the lot." Theo thought to reply how well the Americans paid and that this might be an excellent opportunity, but Brossard waved his hand up and down, back and forth, for Theo to go away. That was it, he was on borrowed time.

He slowly climbed the stairs, trying to keep his breath, up to the gallery piled high with modern art. He was selling but not fast enough. The company wanted double the sales monthly. The end was coming with Brossard, and he needed to prepare. He was committed to modern art. Not only because of his personal inclinations, but it was also the only way to break through in the closed business of art dealing in Paris. He needed to take a new path. Could he buy back all this inventory? So many personal and professional challenges, all intertwined in an unhappy chaos, all to be solved, one by one.

Think and do the math later. He must get ready. He had an appointment with Gauguin.

Paul Gauguin burst into the Brossard gallery, sniffing the air. The receptionist took his coat and led him upstairs, where Theo was waiting.

"I need money. You can't set another low price."

Does he think I like selling at undesirable prices? He needed money, selling low was the only option he had.

"It is best to wait and ignore low offers, but as I am trying to accommodate your needs, we set the price accordingly."

"Who is that downstairs?"

"That is one of the new owners, Brossard. Goupil has retired."

"I think Brossard exudes an ominous, noxious air."

Theo smiled and repeated, "Ominous and noxious, hmm. I think you said those exact words about Goupil."

"Women's undergarments are more interesting to him. Merchants and pimps."

"We are the preeminent dealers in the world's capital for art." He offered Gauguin a glass of wine.

"I know cold-hearted bean counters when I see them. Vincent told me you are storing some of his work here. Show me." He drained the glass in one gulp.

Theo uncovered one of Vincent's best vibrantly painted florals. It was not part of the Brossard inventory. Vincent had painted over two hundred canvases in Paris, and storage was a challenge. He preferred not to show it in this haphazard manner, spoiling the surprise, but Vincent wanted Gauguin to see.

"I am impressed." Paul nodded enthusiastically. "I had a feeling about Vincent. This is better than the Monet of the same subject. Will this show at Le Petit Boulevard? Idiotic name, don't you think?" He held out his empty glass for a refill.

Theo knew it was good work. Was Paul jealous? He gave him a refill.

"Le Petit is fine for an intimate café show."

"'Intimate,' huh. Well put. Will Vincent trade?"

"I can arrange a trade, but not for this. We'll see." He is jealous, a trade is high praise.

"Good, now to my business. I need financing for my next trip—Martinique."

"Martinique. A long trip. Expensive," Theo said.

"Pristine, unspoiled. Very inexpensive."

"Once you get there."

Paul looked at Theo with his characteristic gesture, head back, chin jutting forward, sneering at everything in the world. "I belong in the tropics. You must front me money, three hundred francs a month, for a guarantee of one painting a month."

"That's a fortune. I can't recoup the expenses from the prices you are getting now. I can get you out of Paris, possibly, but I must have a say in where you go and with whom."

"Tonight, over dinner, Theo, just the two of us."

12

Theo

"Vincent, why are you dressed like that?" He is a filthy mess, Theo thought, but pointless trying to convince him. Just live with it, Theo, only a few more days. Tonight, the café show, and a few days after that, Vincent will be on a train to the South of France, just in time for spring.

He watched Vincent look himself over, smile, and pose in the mirror. "Try a clean coat? Where is the blue one?" Theo scanned the messy room, looking for the coat, and checked the closet—no coat.

"The coat has gone missing," Vincent said.

"Try one of mine." Theo kept looking, under the bed, through the crumpled, filthy sheets.

"What do you care what I look like? No one cares, and anyone who does care I wouldn't want to stand with. I look like a painter."

"You look slovenly. This is an opening. Critics have been invited. Please try."

Theo went to the kitchen, washed his hands, and saw the coat under a pile of food debris on the floor. He picked it up—it was destroyed with paint and filth. He slammed it into the garbage and had to wash his hands again.

"You think everyone cares about appearances, but I don't," Vincent said.

"Try this one." Theo took off his own coat and offered it. Vincent took it and then dropped it to his foot like a ball and kicked it back up at him.

"Let's go. I think I will sell tonight!" said Vincent.

"I hope you do. Have you prepared your statement?" Theo shook the coat and put it on, looking at himself in the glass.

"Yes, you would *hope* I do!"

"Behave, Vincent. And if you do get an offer, don't take it, unless it is rich, otherwise, you will never get over the low start. Better find me first and tell me."

"I need some Dutch courage." Vincent went to the kitchen and slugged back some wine. "We need more wine."

"And stay sober, Vincent. No one likes a sloppy, slovenly, quarrelsome painter."

"I am always sober. Give me a hug. My nerves."

They embraced.

"The work is strong, brilliant, unexpected—many surprises on every canvas. Everyone will say so. I'm very proud of you."

"Thank you. I am proud of you too. It is because of you. You sent me to Cormon. He said then, 'The sun is beginning to shine on you, but you are still hidden in the mist.' No more! We have done something special, and soon the world will know."

"Vincent, this is a small café show, a good first step, but the world will take longer."

Theo stood among the artists, scanning the room, sipping wine, evaluating the crowd. Café Cliché was a good choice, an avant-garde part of town, good street traffic, with wealthy tourists. He prayed Johanna would show up. And more importantly, leave with him.

He had a plan for them to be together. He had written her, she hadn't responded in time, but Andries said she would be there. Jo was the most important piece in neutralizing the chaos that had overtaken his life. He could win her back tonight. She would see Vincent's brilliant work and know he is talented, with a future, he would not be an endless burden. And best of all, she would hear him announce his painting cooperative in the South of France. It was an expensive proposition but worth every franc for Theo to get his life back with Johanna. He had cashed in his inheritance, the bonds his uncle Cent had left him, to finance Vincent's trip south and to set up his house.

It was a cast of characters, the unusual mixed in with the wealthy and more traditionally dressed. Pink and red rouged women were smoking and drinking as they pleased. The crowd was growing, it was getting harder to see the front door and street windows. A large, eclectic crowd would favorably impact the critics, if any showed.

Paintings were hanging in the café hall. Easels had been placed in the center of the room with tables pushed to the sides.

"Henri, you'll recognize them. Tell me when you see one," Emile Bernard said, referring to writers and critics. He was nervously patting his long hair behind his ears and then shaking it loose, adjusting his billowy clothes, struggling to be still.

"This is a small café show. I doubt many critics will show up. Please spare us the heart on your sleeve" Henri put his hand on Emile's shoulder. "Just imagine we are playing chess—strategy and action, move by move. Keep your emotion out of it. Once they know you care what they think, you are finished. They will lose all respect for you, on the spot." He poked his cane in the air for emphasis.

"You need to tell these people what to think," Gauguin said. "And if they don't like it, why would you even care?" He threw his head back, staring down at Emile.

"Because I want to sell, and we're all subject to their opinions, no matter what you say."

"We have set a new course, broken with the past. Critics write for

each other and only praise what has already been praised. Critics…"
Vincent said and gestured rudely.

"Critical success makes my job easier," Theo said. "Some will
show."

Then he saw her, standing outside, her back to the window,
looking up and down the street. She was beautiful, even not smiling.
He had held his crackling nerves down, but now seeing her, he felt
warmth surging through his body. She had come, he could convince
her to marry him now. It had been a long year without her. He wrote
to her nearly every day, and she wrote back, less often. There was a
brief happiness just reading her letters.

Theo left them whining about the critics and prepared himself
in the men's room. She was waiting outside for Andries, she wouldn't
come in alone. She must be nervous. He thought that a good sign.
He closed his eyes and said his silent prayer.

Johanna

One decision at a time. She was back in Paris. She stood outside
the gallery, the opening of the Painters of the Petite Blvd. She waited
for Andries. Theo had written that Vincent was leaving, they could
be together. "Come see the paintings. Come see me. Be with me,
forever, here in Paris." She did want Theo, but not the madness of
Vincent. And Paris, the good, and the bad. She'd arrived earlier in
the day and dropped off a small overnight bag at Andries's apartment. He wasn't there. She spent the rest of the afternoon restock-
ing the rouge pots she and Fleur liked and hunting down the most
fantastic readymade eyelash paint. It had a small wand that sat in a
little screw top bottle. Shopping always calmed her nerves.

"Hello, Jo!" Andries kissed Johanna's cheeks. "Why are you
outside standing alone? It doesn't look right."

"I was waiting for you."

"I'll protect you. Who are you dreading the most?" Andries offered his arm.

"Ha."

They walked in together, but Johanna pulled Andries to a stop before they got too far.

"Are we going in or not?" Andries asked.

"I was hoping to see Theo first. Then look at the paintings. I need to hear Theo say Vincent is leaving Paris."

"He's here and has been completely miserable without you. And I told you, Vincent is leaving Paris. Come on."

The minute she entered she felt a charge of glorious energy. They joined the line of patrons walking slowly through the exhibit. She alternated looking at the unusual work and watching for Theo.

Some artists stood in front of their work, talking with customers, describing their paintings, their intentions, accepting drinks. Some stood off to the side in quiet conversation. Each painter was dressed distinctively, like an actor playing a part. Some made it work well, confident and charismatic. The outward appearance of the artist had become important currency in the Paris art scene.

Well, she laughed to herself, now they know what it is like to be a woman.

Henri wore his usual fancy three-piece woolen suit, elegant top hat, and carried his carved cane—the gentleman painter. Emile's long hair, beret, billowy shirt under a fancy navy silk jacket, and traditional wool trousers radiated some confusion. Was he a dandy or a gentleman, an artist or perpetual student?

And Paul Gauguin, in the same flamboyant ensemble he must live in. Long flowing cape, clogs, beret, embroidered jacket. She watched him dramatically swing his cape over a chair. His head tilted as far back as his spine would allow.

For a moment Johanna felt for them, standing in front of their work. Their hearts and minds were melded on canvas, screaming, "Look at me! It is good, I am great!" Their potential patrons were not a captive theater audience. Artists must earn a long pause in front of their paintings. How depressing when no one stops to see.

They passed Vivienne, posing in front of a Lautrec nude. She was the model. They nodded polite greetings and didn't stop to speak. Vivienne beamed. Jo thought light might be emanating from beneath her skin.

They came to a stop in front of Vincent's work. Vincent had five times as many paintings on the wall as any other artist. But he wasn't there.

Jo's first impression was of massive blocks of contrasting colors -- still life, fruits, flowers, and Paris landscapes of Montmartre and the Seine. They were extraordinary. The colors were lavish and took you over, so many color vibrations, overwhelming your eyes. It was very surprising, she thought, and energizing. The paintings accomplished what he'd said he wanted -- to reinvent the Dutch still life. But unlike the polished, refined Dutch work, these paintings had a frenetic, racing quality which captivated her. It was as if every day Vincent woke up dreaming of nature, spun the color wheel, pulled out his paints to play, and created fireworks, frozen on a canvas.

Johanna listened as others crowded around laughing, drinking, oohing and aahing. Some spoke in intellectual language. *Classic composition, neoimpressionist color and brushstroke.* Others' reactions were more basic—*I love the colors. I want that color for my next dress.* Looking at the work she wanted to pick up handfuls of colors and play, as free as a child. She surrendered to the outrageous people and color. Color everywhere.

"I'm amazed," she said, again scanning for Theo. Something special has happened here—something good, very good. Vincent has real talent...and has worked very hard to develop it. "Will you buy Vincent's work…. which one?"

"Yes, absolutely. But Theo wants to wait for higher prices," Andries said.

They moved toward the next mini exhibit area, Gauguin's, but he was not standing in front, playing the barker.

The colors were flat, deep, and contrasting, and fantastically rich. There was a compelling self-portrait, Paul's broad features, handsomely defined with pastel for highlights and deeper primary colors in the shadows of his nose, under his eyes, the contours of his cheeks, soft edges, careful strokes highlighting his face, fewer dark lines traveling through the edges, with mashed, flat color. She squinted trying to see more in the dim light. He pulled her in. There were some odd figures, posed in symbolic scenes from religious art she didn't understand. And a magnificent nude of a "primitive," scandalous and spectacular.

"What do you think these are about?" she asked Andries, indicating the religious-themed work.

"Only Gauguin knows. Let's not loiter, he'll come over. I can't bear another speech about the 'primitive,' and I already own enough Gauguin." Andries glanced around. "Look at them all, preening like peacocks. They carry on as if they don't care what anybody thinks or says, but opinion is what they prize most."

Johanna carefully scanned the crowd, smiling, unafraid to catch anyone's eye. She still didn't see Theo. She scanned the room again and again. She was looking forward to seeing him more than anything she could remember. The feeling was frightening, like she might do something she wouldn't be able to stop.

She saw Vincent then, standing by his paintings, Emile at this side. If someone could look manic and frozen at the same time, Vincent did. He spoke quickly, with broad gestures, pipe in hand, referencing his approach with an unselfconscious smile. He stood tall in front of his work, seemed to blend into his wall of painting. His broad shoulders, square and back, his flame-red hair glowing against all his blue backgrounds. Emile fed him glass after glass to keep him loose.

Then she saw Theo join Vincent.

She would wait for him to approach her. She listened to Andries droning on.

"They all crave power, prestige, even though they pretend to hate it. They brag their appearances don't matter, but you know, I think that is all they care about. They all have these carefully calibrated personas, like a caricature, a competition to see who can be the most unique."

"Some are sincere," Jo said. "This is all finally getting old to you. You should marry, before you lose your looks. A wife will improve your mood."

"Possibly." Andries smiled. "I want to marry a Dutch woman." They exchanged a glance. Fleur still, Jo thought. His face was vulnerable, maybe for the first time in his life.

She studied Theo while he stood with Vincent in front of his paintings. It had been months since she had seen him, and she felt instant concern for him. Even from across the room, he looked thinner and gaunt in the face. Andries took her arm.

"Ready for a pleasant chat with the riffraff? Gauguin's seen us and he's coming over." Andries smiled.

"Hello, Andries, Miss Bonger," Gauguin said. "Buying tonight?"

"You don't waste any time," Andries said.

"I don't have any to waste."

"Mr. Gauguin," Johanna nodded back. But she was watching Theo. He was getting lost in the crowd.

There was an awkward silence.

"What do you think?" asked Gauguin stepping back appraising the room.

"A wonderful show, many interesting new paintings. Johanna is here from Amsterdam to attend." Andries rocked on his heels a bit.

"Amsterdam. You wanted to see the paintings?"

"Yes and attend to some business. I think the show is spectacular—especially Vincent's work…and I admire your self-portrait."

Johanna said. Paul raised his glass to her and looked behind her to see who else was in the room.

"I have other business here in Paris," Jo said. "There is a new machine, the typewriter. I am investigating for our insurance business."

At the word *insurance*, Gauguin's eyes seemed to glaze over. He walked off, just as she spotted Theo across the room gliding to her, but he was pulled to a stop by Vincent. They were getting ready to make remarks. She and Andries moved deeper into the room and took good positions to better hear the speech over the noisy café. They stood next to Emile and Henri and had a quick little reunion.

Gauguin joined the group at the center of the room and said, "Vincent should begin, his work is the best." He shouted to the crowd.

She could tell Vincent was struck by this praise from his idol. Theo patted Vincent on the back. And then Theo saw her. He placed his hand over his heart and from across the room, he bowed to her. Jo smiled back, and she knew returning was a good decision. She watched Theo work his way across the room toward her and halfheartedly listened to the conversation around her.

"You think he means that…Vincent's work is the best?" asked Emile. "Or is he just sucking up to Theo?"

"He might mean it this minute. He's right. Vincent's work is the best," Henri said. "He wants the trip south, all expenses paid, but can you imagine living with Vincent?"

"Yes, I can," Emile said.

Henri smiled at Emile, put his arm on his shoulder. "Let me get you a drink, Emile. I will bring you something special."

Vincent stood in the center of the room and lifted his glass. "I believe artists should be cooperative, work in a collaborative painting arrangement. Imagine how much progress painters can make if we work together and do not compete. This is the new approach of the painters of Le Petit Boulevard. My dream, our dream, is to have our own studio where we can all collaborate, working together and sharing expenses, a studio in the sun, in the light. We will create the new painting for the new century to come."

While Vincent continued his toast, Gauguin made his way back to Emile. They stood together. Andries and Jo stood to the side, quietly listening.

"Will you go with him?" Gauguin asked.

"Will you?" countered Emile, asking Paul.

"It is a financial question for me," Paul said. "You want to go, don't you?" he asked Emile, dry as a bone.

"I might, but I don't know if I will be invited."

"Why?"

"Because he admires you."

Vincent and Paul living together. Didn't seem like a good idea, they didn't treasure the same things, only age and painting in common.

Theo found her while Vincent was still talking, surprising her.

"May I kiss you, Johanna?" And then not waiting for an answer he kissed her, not his extra special kiss but a wonderful kiss in public, and she let him. He hugged her. And in one kiss the warmth of Theo came flooding back.

"Thank you for coming." He smiled wide, his eyes glued on her. They held hands.

She had missed him. It was like she just woke up after a nightmare.

Vincent continued his speech. "We are done here in Paris. The new art will be made in the country, in the true light, with true people who live off the land, away from the tulip traders, the scoundrels who manipulate and steal."

A coughing fit broke up Vincent's speech. Henri joined him in the center of the room.

"Thank you, Vincent, well done. A toast please! To the painters of Le Petit Boulevard! And our dearest friend, Theo van Gogh."

Good applause. A round of toasts. More artists and more

speeches. Each complemented the other with rounds of applause leading to calls for more toasts.

Jo thought Theo received all the attention gracefully but carefully steered it all back to Vincent. She listened, quietly sipping her wine. Vincent was a success. All these talented, remarkable painters were singing his praises. Henri, Gauguin, Bernard, the others—they all sold, so that meant Vincent would sell too. He would lead an independent life financially, and he would be hundreds of miles away in the South. Maybe she had just met Vincent in a low point in his life, recovering from sad love affairs, his father's death, false starts in his career. She had compassion for him, so painfully shy yet speaking in a strong voice, about his unique plan of a painting cooperative.

She was happy back at Theo's side, watching his face in shadow and light, his deep voice humming in her ear, casting its spell on her.

Finally, Johanna and Theo were alone at a tiny table. "Congratulations, Theo. Vincent could never have done this without you. Painters of Le Petit Boulevard will make news."

"Yes," Theo said. "Small news—this is barely an exhibit. Do you like his work?"

"Yes, I love Vincent's paintings."

"Thank you, Jo. He's worked very hard."

"Didn't he say he would begin with the primary colors?"

Theo didn't answer, but he took her hand and pulled off her glove. He kissed her hand and placed it for a moment on his cheek and took a deep breath. "I'm so happy you're here. For the first time in my life, I have felt lost. I fall asleep and dream something terrible is on me. I know you are my salvation. The depression is terrible."

"Vincent's moods are contagious—that's all. When is he leaving?" Up close, Theo looked worn out, like a flu or exhaustion had got hold of him. His pallor was gray, his eyes bloodshot as if he hadn't slept. Vincent had run him ragged. He needed her.

"Soon."

"Best for him to stand on his own, plan his own life."

"Yes, he will be on his own. We can be together, believe me. He has done well here, but it's time to change, or he won't progress. He'll travel through the South of France, paint landscapes, settle down someplace there."

"Painting is his life."

"Yes."

"Your life too, Theo." Johanna said.

"Art is my profession. You will be my life, Jo."

She wanted to reach over and kiss him. Daring, a woman initiating a kiss in a crowd. She did, in the middle of a crowd. Her second decision, and it was another good one.

"Johanna, thank you for the kiss. Shall we go? Can I escort you home? Or a late dinner?"

"Yes, dinner and a walk home."

"How long will you stay in Paris?"

"Forever, I hope."

Theo's face registered instant relief and happiness, and he kissed Johanna again. He rested his forehead against hers, so close, and said, "Together forever, Johanna."

Andries and Vincent approached the table and paused to watch this intimate moment. Before Vincent could offer a polite hello, Theo cut them both off.

"I would like to have a private dinner with Jo. I'll see you both tomorrow at lunch."

Johanna nodded a smile to Vincent. She placed her hand on her heart and said, "Brilliant work, Vincent. I'm so proud of you."

Theo held Jo's hand, and they left the cafe. Jo turned back for one last look. There was Vincent, watching her and Theo walking away. She couldn't see his expression but saw Andries clap him on the back and lead him back into his show.

Theo

"Only a fool wouldn't see how deeply you love her," Vincent

said to Theo. It was a slushy, gray winter day. Steam from the trains circled around the tracks and the platforms.

"You have no idea, Vincent, how happy I am to hear you say that. Johanna is my destiny."

"Then she is my destiny too." They hugged.

Theo clapped Vincent on the back. "Write me every detail and send every sketch and painting. I will build your persona from here."

"I'll make you proud, Theo. Come with me, just until I get the house together?"

"I can't, Vincent." Vincent had been begging him for days to come with him. He was nervous, Theo knew, but he also knew Vincent must do this on his own. "I remember it was you who said to me, 'What is a life without courage?'"

Vincent laughed and said, "I think it was 'it takes courage to get anything great accomplished.'"

The conductor walked the platform, calling, "All aboard!"

But still Vincent seemed frozen in place, surrounded by his easel, suitcase, and paint box.

"Go on, Vincent. What you have done will always remain well done. I'll dream of you creating the modern landscape of the South. Remember you are my secret weapon. Ah, but not so secret anymore!"

"We did it together, Theo. I see you in every canvas. Thank you, brother."

"I love you, Vincent."

"I wonder who will be happier, you kowtowing for every franc in Paris? Or me, free from the duplicity of ambition."

"I pray it will be you. I have put a lot of money into this venture."

"Don't forget me."

"Never." Theo smiled and hugged him once again, and gently pushed Vincent toward the train door.

13

Vincent

I found a yellow. It was mine. I dreamed about this yellow for months. I won't give it up. I have caught fire with my yellow. I am the painter of sunflowers. Paul wanted red. Red, red, red, red. Red. Red. Red.

    There were the mistrals, the winds from across the sea. And rain. And painting outside is impossible for Paul. I can do it, but he can't. He doesn't care about nature. He only sees what is in his own head. And it's always with red.

    I put the sunflowers exactly the way they should be, and I move in close. And I paint as fast as I can move. I use my yellow. He stands over me at his easel, mocking me, painting the flowers. Because he hates me. I think if you like the painting, you should like the man. He says he loves my sunflowers. More than Monet's sunflowers. Then why does he challenge my brush?

    I work hard against his red glare. I can feel him out of the black corner of my eye, the bars growing and blurring into my yellow. If I press into the yellow, the gold, so close, I can deny his face glare glowing in the black. I need another drink.

"What are you doing there, your nose in the canvas, Vincent? Do you hear me? Why are you messing around with all that paint?" *Paul says things like that to me all day long, all night long. I hear him in my sleep. And I drink myself into a stupor to blur his face and deafen his voice.*

"This is how I paint. I choose a color, and then I experiment with the values—"

"Experiment, no! Vincent, have intention! What is your intention there? You must paint from memory, Vincent. Art is abstraction. Don't just brood over nature. See it and then reimagine it—it's the only way to create like our divine master."

And he keeps on and on and on and on until I break what I am doing and answer him.

"I need to paint what I see in the flower. What it makes me feel." *I take deep breaths to stay quiet and calm and lean farther into the flower.* "I want to capture this." *I point to my sunflower.* "I know I must wrestle with nature, there is nothing else, and we are all powerless before nature. You start with a blade of grass…to learn about man. You see?"

"You are a slave to nature. Paint the flower from your memory. Slowly, Vincent, think…Using all that paint, so quickly, you will get distracted by your own ostentation."

Ostentation. "I work these flowers in one sitting, before they wilt. I prefer to wrestle with nature rather than reason. My intuition mixes with the essence of the flower."

"If you do it the same way every time, you get the same result. How will you grow? Why am I here, Vincent? To teach you! Listen to me, Vincent."

"Nature is the only truth. It never deceives you. Emotion, truth, nature—this is what guides me and pushes me so strong that each touch of paint leads to the next. Sometimes it isn't like this, a difficult day, without inspiration. That is the day to try something new." *I sound reasonable, and I am not yelling. He is the difficult one.*

"Try one from memory. Then you will learn to see."

I ignore him, pushing into the yellow. Why does he always challenge me? He said he liked the sunflowers. Then why doesn't he like me?

"Try it my way."

"Later…outside, when the rain stops."

The rain stops. I walk through the little town to the post office. I get your letter. I know your marriage news. You should have told me in person. I won't go, you don't want me to go, or you would have told me sooner. Fine, I will stay away. I need to make progress faster.

How does Paul know you are going to be married? He is blurring in front of me.

"I am not upset." *I scream at him over and over.*

"Johanna Bonger—he will marry her. Put it out of your mind. We need to get back to work. Is there any money with the letter? Look, Vincent, we need a drink or two. Let's go. We can talk this through at the café." *He thinks he is helping me.* "I understand what you fear. Wives are expensive. Then the children are more expense, and the women are warriors for them."

"Why are you lecturing me?"

"Listen to me. Create your story."

"I am not a story."

"Vincent, they have the money, the connections, and you have the talent. They are nothing without us. We will convince Theo to show your work. We can look at painting differently, use the resources more reasonably."

"I don't paint with reason."

"I am going to the café. I won't sit in this house and disintegrate with you. Theo will always be there for you." *He says he needs to leave. I think he's leaving.*

I use the knife to get the red, to make him happy. See—I am trying his red, and I am using memory. Red, Red, Red. Everywhere. See Red, deep red. See my red now! It is everywhere. But I don't know where he is, he is gone. In the café. I lie in the red, swim in the red, and know red represents the vile passions of men. All the beauty is in nature, and it is yellow and blue and green…

1889

Johanna

The carriage was loaded. In three days, Johanna would be Mrs. Van Gogh and enjoying a honeymoon retreat on a beautiful lake in Holland. Theo, Andries, and she were on their way to the train station, splurging on a private carriage, a treat from her brother. By the end of the day, she would be with her family and Fleur, the new baker in Amsterdam and caterer of her wedding luncheon. She had planned everything, nothing could go wrong, and then she saw a messenger hand Theo a telegram.

Oh no.

Theo's telegrams were almost always bad news from Vincent. The little annoyances of Vincent were part of what she had signed up for, but they were coming with alarming frequency. Was he kicked out of another café? Had he fought with another traveler? He was with Gauguin, and despite her initial concern she heard they worked well together. Theo said Vincent admired Gauguin She watched Theo reading the telegram, looking for a hint. Something he wasn't expecting. Yes, his look to the heavens said it all.

She shot a side glance at Andries. Maybe he knew something? Theo jumped into the carriage and closed the door abruptly, leaving Johanna and Andries outside.

He reread the telegram sitting in the near privacy of the carriage. Johanna saw him drop the telegram to his knee and turn to stare out the opposite window.

"A well-wisher for the wedding?" she said to Theo in Dutch, knowing it was not. She said it only for the benefit of the driver, who was watching impatiently.

"Goddamn it," Theo said from the carriage. Andries reached through the carriage window, grabbed the telegram, and read it.

Quick to anger, quicker to hide it, he folded up the telegram and jammed it into his pocket.

"All right, all set then—let's go," Andries said, as if nothing had happened.

But it was obvious to Johanna something very bad had happened.

"What's the matter? Did they burn the house down? Cheat a prostitute or something?" She knew she sounded flip, but she was eager to get to the train. She looked first at Theo and then at Andries. No, not a minor annoyance, it was something much, much bigger, she thought with horror.

"Christ," Andries whispered.

The telegram messenger was still standing there waiting with his hand out. Johanna gave him a coin and he ran off.

Theo was staring down at his lap, trying to slow his breathing. Clearly his mind was racing.

Johanna whispered to Andries, "He isn't dead, is he?" *Oh my God, please don't let him be dead.*

"No," Andries said as he copied Theo's gesture of looking to the heavens as if saying a prayer. Johanna took the telegram from his pocket and read it. Then she climbed into the carriage and covered Theo's drumming hand with her own.

"Vincent will be all right," she said. "They'll help him at the hospital." She felt relief. He was at a hospital, not dead, thank God. What had happened? The telegram didn't say more.

"I'll meet you in Amsterdam in two days." Theo sounded anxious and weary at the same time, now tapping his heel and rubbing his forehead.

"Theo, Andries and I should go with you. You shouldn't be alone."

"Go ahead, Jo. I'll go with Theo," Andries said.

"No, you go with Johanna."

"What are you going to do?"

"Help him. No one in the family needs to know anything."

Theo

> *I am to be in two places at the same time,* Theo thought, *my wedding and pulling my brother from a shattering crisis. I carry two opposing feelings in my brain at the same time. I love him and I am drowning in his darkness. The mystery of his unhappiness and his pain only increase. I thought his pain was loneliness, but loneliness is just the beginning of a deep well of blackness. He was lucky he didn't bleed to death.*
>
> *He is a broken-hearted man who will never heal. And he leaves a wake of chaos in his path. Now, with Vincent, I know good will be followed by even worse, in an endless chain of misery.*
>
> *His pain will never end, and his painting is better than great. I won't stop loving him.*

Theo watched as Vincent sat in front of a work in progress, a self-portrait, complete with the white cloth bandage encircling his entire head. He munched on his pipe, alternately sucking and biting it, moving it from side to side, though it held no tobacco.

He played with his paints, mashing oil into them to refresh them and keep them from drying out. "We loved the peasants and worked like them, painting from dawn till night," he said to Theo.

Theo didn't respond, just walked around the rooms of the Yellow House, looking carefully with his appraising eye at the paintings on the walls.

Vincent tried again. "Fortunately for me, I can promise you my paintings will get better because that is all I have left. I'll make progress, faster now."

Theo knew Vincent was trying to guess his mood.

Outside noises created a low rumble in the house. There were knocks on the door, voices calling, more knocks and loud voices from the street. Again, another knock.

Theo looked out the window, saw the lone gendarme engaged

with some passersby. He was directing people on the street to move along. Theo couldn't hear what they were saying, but it appeared Vincent was the talk of this small town.

"Leave it and they will go," Vincent said. "They are nosy, disgusting people." But the knocking persisted.

Finally, Theo gave up and answered the door, putting on his professional manner. The conversation was brief and disturbing. Theo did his best to listen and placate.

"The peasants are restless, concerned about your condition. I assured them you are recovering and won't cause any more trouble," he said, returning to Vincent.

"They don't bother to hide their monstrous curiosity. I've lost my privacy," Vincent snapped.

"They will calm down. Avoid them. So…What happened to your ear?"

"I think I would feel depressed if I did not fool myself about absolutely everything."

"You look depressed, you're not fooling me. Are you going to tell me what happened?"

"I am well, and I'm painting. That is critical for us, that I keep painting."

"Why did you fight with Paul?"

"His name is a knife in my chest."

"He said you pulled a knife on him. You could have bled to death. Thank God for that woman. Why did you give her your ear? Who is she?"

"She is a woman I saw a few times. I don't know why. I didn't think we were fighting. I don't remember. And I still have my ear, Theo!"

"Why don't you remember? Were you drinking?"

"I don't want to talk about it. I'm painting. That's all that matters, isn't it? We tried it with Paul, and it didn't work. Maybe somebody else. You should have…"

Theo could tell Vincent was putting on his brave face and trying to keep his temper in check. Theo finally sat down, a few feet away from Vincent. "I should have what?"

Vincent remained silent and continued to paint, slowly alternating staring at himself in the mirror, then at the canvas, and then back at Theo for reassurance. He was moving in an uncharacteristically slow way. His shoulders drooped, hands loose and leaden.

"Here we are again, Vincent," Theo said.

"What do you mean 'here we are again?' I don't think you've ever been here. You've been in Paris."

They stared at one another. Who was madder, Theo wondered?

Theo slapped his hands on his thighs, stood up, breathing in deeply. *I don't have much time here*, he thought. *Finish the matters at hand, and salvage what I can.*

"Vincent, did Paul leave any work?"

Theo began his search around the rooms of the house. He walked into the bedrooms and kitchen.

"You can sell his but not mine? Don't you want to see my work?" Vincent shouted after him.

"Show me. I'm looking for the work," Theo called back.

He looked around Vincent's bedroom. Blood was everywhere, the floor, the bed—everything covered in blood. Footstep patterns on the floor had dried with crusty, caked-brown blood. It looked like a murder scene, preserved for a gendarme's inspection.

Vincent slowly followed him, hanging back, still nursing his head like he was balancing a box of eggs on it. He gently leaned on the furniture and the walls as he moved for support.

Theo brushed and scraped his foot over the dried blood. "We need to clean this up. The landlord is coming back."

"Will you give Paul money to go to Brittany?" Vincent asked.

"No, I don't know where he is. He promised me paintings. If there's a canvas, finished or not, I would like to salvage something. This Yellow House—it's been very, very expensive."

Theo found a portrait by Paul of Vincent painting a sunflower. "Is this it?"

"Yes," Vincent said and sat on his blood-stained bed. After a moment he slowly lay back against the wall.

"There must be others. Do you have anything to say about this debacle?"

"It's your debacle. I thought we could collaborate. I tried a few canvases his way, but he didn't want to look at nature. He is only interested in memories. I thought because he loved the sunflowers, we could help each other."

"Very disappointing for you. Maybe it couldn't be helped. He has a bad temper, an egotist. Henri says he's a monster." Theo walked over to Vincent and leaned over the bed, putting his hand on Vincent's shoulder.

Vincent put his hand atop Theo's. "He wanted a trade for the sunflowers. I put sunflowers in every room."

"Yes, brilliant work, Vincent. Sit back and rest. You've lost a lot of blood." He patted Vincent again, got up, and moved around the room, calculating the mess and what had to be done.

"I only have until the morning. I need to clean this out, prove to the landlord you are fit to stay here until the lease is done. Then think of what is next. We have creditors and they must be paid. Money is tight. Where are your cleaning supplies? Can you think of someone who might come in to clean?"

Vincent shook his head.

"You aren't in any condition to help. I'll do what I can, but I must go in the morning." He took off his suit coat, picked a painter's smock off a heap on the chair, shook it in the air several times, and covered himself. He looked at Vincent. "What is it?"

"Why are you leaving first thing?" Vincent sounded like a scared child, begging a parent to stay.

"To attend my wedding," he said, smiling.

Vincent threw his paintbrush at Theo but missed. "That's where the money is going—to her! Creditors...Who is more important? The creditors or me?"

"You are, but they must be paid. Money is *the* issue most days. That's my world."

"Let's see what kind of humanity you have."

"That's how you repay me, questioning my humanity?"

"Who is more important? You cannot deny me. We had a deal."

"We had a deal, and we *have* a deal. But you must find a way to get along without all this trouble." Theo waved his arms around. "Do you have any idea what this investment meant to me? To my future? Do you even care about me? All you ever say to me is 'Theo, you are a tulip trader. You need a better woman!' You treat me like the garbage strewn all over this house. I will not be trod over anymore!"

"If you would only listen to me...Renew yourself in art."

"Shut up, Vincent." Theo got on his knees and began scraping and scrubbing the blood stains off the floor.

The arguing went on and on. Theo cleaned, and Vincent railed from where he lay in bed. And it went like this for a long time, until the floor was clean enough.

When the earliest morning light hit the window, Theo awoke from a wooden chair. He decided not to wake Vincent, and instead left a note with all the money he could spare.

14

Andries

"For a moment there," Fleur said to Andries, "I thought we might have a wedding without a groom!"

Andries laughed and flashed Fleur what he hoped was his most appealing smile. Fleur was right, Theo had just gotten back from visiting Vincent that morning. Andries concentrated on giving Fleur a lovely dance, keeping a polite distance, and not sweating or breathing on her. She looked so bright framed by the arboretum-filtered sunlight, surrounded by abundant flowers and every shade of green.

They danced together, faces flushed red, eyes smiling and glassy. He resisted leaning in before leading her into a turn, using just his hand for pressure, and wished he could pull her closer.

Fleur smiled. "You're quiet today, Andries. This is a wedding party, isn't it?"

Andries lost his usual confidence but finally, after clearing his throat, said, "I'm trying to think of something funny to say."

"Why funny?"

"Because you said…oh never mind. You're looking well. I hope you don't mind me saying so. How is your baking business?"

"It has been an enormous success. I'm invincible! The Dutch love French sweets."

"Congratulations, I am not surprised, you have great talent."

"Thank you, you are sweet to say. How is Paris working out for you?"

"Paris has been a wonderful place to visit. I'm applying to study the law. I will be the oldest student by ten years!" Being a lawyer had been in the back of his mind for so long. Now was the time. He had a nice collection of art. He'd sold a few pieces and could finance law school.

"A lawyer— I can see it, yes."

The blue eyes stared into his, and it was hypnotic. He felt himself fall into a trance controlled by her eyes.

"I noticed a new gallery in town—modern work, isn't it?" he asked.

"Yes, Dries, new work, with the modern light and colors you like. The owners studied in Paris and are now back here. I think you and Theo are right, all the new approaches could be catching fire."

Ah, she called me Dries, my informal name, and so intimate. "Would you like to go with me? I can take you to lunch afterward if you have time."

"Yes, I will make time for you. When do you think?"

"Tomorrow we'll go."

She said yes! This is a fine day. What is she saying? Yes, she is saying something…

"Have you heard me? After this dance, you should dance with Anna."

"Anna? Why?" *I don't want to dance with Anna. Did she just brush her cheek against mine?*

"She's the sister of the groom. Someone needs to dance with her, and you are the best man," Fleur reasoned.

"I don't want to give her the wrong impression."

"Well, you can work that out, can't you? Smart man like yourself?"

"If you want me too." Anna was sitting with Mrs. Van Gogh, Theo and Vincent's mother.

"Two dances, then you'll come back and dance with me." Even with her light voice, it was a command, and he felt it in a wonderful place.

"I will." He breathed deeply, smiled, and felt himself falling into Fleur's blue eyes. Light explosions were erupting in his head. He felt weightless, everything and everyone looked bright and lovely. What was this feeling? Not wine, he'd only had one mouthful. Then he remembered…happiness.

"Yes, good."

"Yes, very good," he blubbered out.

"Did he really cut off his ear?"

"No one is supposed to know. He just sliced part of it."

"Why?"

"Because he's mad."

"Awful! Poor thing. And imagine Theo, just before his wedding."

Andries approached Anna and Mrs. Van Gogh, who sat quietly together at one of the small tables surrounding the dance floor. Anna tapped her foot to the music. Mrs. Van Gogh held herself stiff and sad, her mouth dragged down. She wore black to the wedding, still in mourning.

Andries thought he would chat with them both for a moment, compliment the lovely wedding, the beautiful couple, and then ask Anna for a dance. But Mrs. Van Gogh had another topic to discuss.

"Why doesn't someone tell me where Vincent is, Andries? Don't I have a right to know? I hate to think of him all alone out there. Theo promised me he would protect him. What's happened to him?"

"He's traveling the South of France, painting—that's all I know, Mrs. Van Gogh." He hated to lie.

"It has been so long since I've seen Vincent. My heart will break if anything has happened."

"He's all grown up, Mother, he can stand on his own," Anna said. "He doesn't need protection and Theo buying him out of every little scrape. It just prolongs his difficulties really."

"He needs protection from himself," said Mrs. Van Gogh.

True, Andries thought, waiting for them to finish.

"It's Theo's wedding day, so for once let's not argue about Vincent," Anna said and looked away from her mother to Andries.

"Anna, may I have a dance with the sister of the groom? I'm the best man, it's only appropriate. Please join me."

She looked so pleased. He felt the pain of her loneliness as he led her to the dance floor.

Anna was a lovely dancer. He hoped to keep the conversation off Vincent, for once.

"Do you know where Vincent is? Theo is lying to me and Mother, obviously."

"Creating masterpieces in the glorious sun of the South of France!" And recovering from blood loss and God knows what else. Another terrible ordeal, and it could be another step closer to the catastrophic ending Andries feared.

15

Vincent

Dear Theo,

His red has overtaken me. My yellow is hiding. All I have is the painful feeling of collapse instead of progress. And always, it arrives, duplicity. There is a general evil under the stronger sun here in these towns in the country. And the southern mistrals make the villagers mad. I am at the mercy of evil peasants who have locked me out of my own home.

It is my duty to resist it. Everyone here scares me now, and I shouldn't be around them. This blasted artistic life is shattering. There is no cure but work. But only in that it helps me get the day done, I have no ambition anymore, I know I won't ever do anything important. I would rather have a downright illness like this than the way I was in Paris, while this attack was brewing. Life passes and time does not return. Opportunities for work do not return.

I am starting to believe there is such a thing as too much. Wanting is better than having. There is no reward for hard work, pain, and enduring your humiliations alone. Cruel, when you get what you want but the mistral returns, in fuller voice, and all the dreams wrapped in color are carried away.

I know now I must delude and fool myself about everything and everyone. Success, whatever I thought it would be or would mean, is never final. My plan now is to be alone, as much as I can bear it. Alone, I won't have these problems. I am defeated, my mind shattered completely.

If I am not mistaken, your letter seems late to me.

Yours, and best to my sister Jo

Vincent

Theo hates doctors and hospitals. That is why he won't visit me in this asylum. It is not so bad here. I can leave and paint if I want. They feed me and help me. My body is getting better, my strength returning and my desire to paint and draw, is a compulsion, and the drug which heals me. I am painting religious art. Then a brilliant stroke from the universe when I dreamed I painted a new painting of a star-filled sky.

I saw the painting out of the corner of my eye. The colors were always with me keeping me company and calling my name. In bed at night with my pipe, it stared back at me and became my obsession. It was the starry night sky, the stars, the moon, the town comforted and consoled, enveloped in their brilliance. The night sky has more colors than the day. Dark hues of blue and purple. I painted outside at night. This is better for me because the fields are unbearably lonely. Some people watch me, thankfully they are quiet. Some see I need wine and buy me a glass and I can keep painting. Drinking isn't allowed in here. I am taking note of when to expect another attack. It is my new clock. My change and the changing seasons. I need to conserve my energy for the night. For the dark, and my yellow. Swirls of eternal stars light up my night, peaceful eternal golden stars, the velvet of the night sky. The moon's fat smile gifting us the light in the night.

When I woke up, the nuns were calling us to breakfast, and my new painting glowed on me from my easel. I felt such joy and my old energy returning, another glimpse from the corner of my eye of something new to look forward to. I can't wait for the dying daylight to finish my Starry Night. I need to eat as much as possible, drink lots of water, and conserve my energy. This is everything I am, my anguish, my rapture. The day is fleeting, my night is eternal. I pray I die tonight.

"Cries and screams are contagious," Vincent said to Emile, who had come to visit him. "One of the inmates broke into my dream and others jumped to his rescue because it took a long time for the nuns to come. If the screaming doesn't stop, we all scream, like screeching monkeys, imprisoned in the zoo. We go to the screaming one, hold him, talk to him, and we take turns sleeping next to him until a nun comes.

"This light is strong from the south and lights the room all day, so I can work all day. But look at them, Emile. They sit all day on benches and stare into space, no work in their hands or cards, checkers, no pencils, papers, nothing. Some walk in circles, like the lions pacing in the zoo. Why don't they do something? You are not cattle, do you hear me? You're not cattle! I shout this out the window every hour, but…"

Emile tries to get me to sit down next to him and open his presents.

The linseed oil sparkles amber against the bottle, creating the illusion of an inviting glass of wine. I squeeze paint into my mouth and sip the linseed that looks like wine.

"Vincent, don't! Spit it out, Vincent, my God!"

The paint stuck together like a glob and wouldn't break down enough to swallow. Finally, I could spit it out the window.

"Look at what you're doing. Put the water here and the oil there. Please be careful, Vincent."

Emile rubs my neck and shoulders. We sit on the bed in silence.

"We need you back at work. I know a place for you that's closer to Paris. Everyone can visit you."

"After the Yellow House, one of them called me a communard… That color made me mad! They put me here. I guess I belong here for now."

"You look well, you have recovered. I miss you. I want you closer to Paris, all right?"

His long hair falls forward as he hugs me tight.

"I work, all day every day, Emile. From morning till night, like a peasant. I can't leave."

"Vincent, let's make plans together. You once said, 'I do not know the future, eternal law says everything changes. One thing does remain, and one does not easily regret having done a thing, and I would rather have a failure than sit and do nothing.' Remember, Vincent?"

"Theo hasn't visited me. I haven't seen my brother in a year."

"He writes and he sends money. He's gotten your paintings into many shows and is having some success."

"I know, he writes. Johanna is pregnant."

"Theo is frantic with work and sick, always fighting something off. Look—I bear many gifts from your friends."

Emile puts the packages on my lap and calls them an early Christmas. I let the packages sit.

"I want you closer to Paris. Theo will visit."

He opens the packages for me.

"Look—from Henri."

He tears off the brown paper.

"Ah wonderful, Japanese! Your favorite. New prints, the latest journals. The new book by Zola. More images for your walls. Why do you have religious cards up there?"

Emile doesn't like my postcards. I don't know what to say, sometimes it is easier to copy than think about something new. The nuns like the cards, they let me paint them, and I think it helps them be nice to me.

"New paints, pencils, a new sketch book, Vincent."

"I can't make plans for anything. I am better now, but hope, the desire to succeed, is gone. I work because I must, so as not to suffer too much mentally, so as to distract my mind."

"Why, Vincent? Don't you want to leave?"

"No, I can't. They scream all night here. One night I awoke in the black and heard the screaming, and everyone was on me. I didn't recognize the sound of my own voice. Where can I go? Who would live with me like that?"

If I were to dwell on all the disastrous possibilities, I would paralyze myself. Across the distance and as time goes by, all my good memories have a kind of heartbreak in them

1890-91

Johanna

Jo felt the happy pregnancy weight of the baby digging into her back. It wouldn't be long before they were three. In the parlor of the apartment, Theo and Emile carefully rolled out Vincent's canvases on a large table in the middle of the room.

She listened to Theo and Emile conversing softly in their language of art, awestruck by the new paintings. She was glad Emile was there, helping Theo with Vincent. Vincent was in and out of institutions. Jo could only imagine how horrible it was for him. Theo never went to visit.

No one seemed to understand what had happened to Vincent, why he had collapsed. It all weighed on Theo, and money was again becoming an issue.

Vincent sent letters daily. Before Theo opened them, he always said a silent prayer, calling on God to help Vincent.

"Vincent said the red and green express the terrible passions of humanity," Emile said.

"I see. Not a new thought. But he has done something new with it." Theo held a painting up for them all to see.

"This is Vincent's best. *The Starry Night* is… The painting is brilliant, beyond all else. He has reached a new level, his alone." Jo noticed a slight tremor in Theo's hand while he held the painting. It was unlike any she had ever seen. The night sky was a mass of swirling blue with bright stars of yellow—a fantastical scene, and she wanted to lie under that image and feel the beauty of the night. It was his best, she thought, and it made her happy to know that despite his problems he was creating magnificent work. The work entranced her. It struck a deep chord she could almost hear…and she thought he must be feeling better.

"He is inconsolable. Can't you visit him, Theo? You haven't seen him since before the wedding." Emile stole a glance at Johanna.

"I can't bear those godforsaken hospitals, everyone rotting. I'd rather be dead" Theo said oddly, almost snarling. Jo put her arm around his waist, and he kissed her forehead. Only she knew the agony that Vincent had caused Theo. The guilt of knowing he couldn't help a person he loved. Vincent didn't realize he was drowning them both, but Jo did.

"I can't leave Johanna with child." He coughed, his hand shaking as he rolled out another canvas. "I correspond with him weekly, send him every tube of paint, book, brush, palette knife. I take in all the work and pay all the bills. I have gotten his best works in two exhibits, with good notices. Vincent needs to come to terms with Vincent, himself."

Jo thought he sounded guilty, like he was defending himself against something.

"But he *misses you*, Theo." Emile avoided looking at Johanna. "Please?" he whispered.

"Is he still slovenly and quarrelsome with everyone?"

"He only cares what you think," Emile said. "There is a doctor just outside of Paris, close to us. He works with artists, and he specializes in brain disorders. He is willing to take Vincent. Pissarro vouches for him."

Jo felt Theo's forehead with the back of her hand. Every winter he got a cold, he said, and it wouldn't go away until spring. This cold hung on, taking some of his energy, and Jo wondered if it was affecting his compassion. It had been a long break from Vincent, his guilt was clear to see. *We should both go visit*, she thought.

"It sounds ideal, doesn't it, Theo? Let's visit and cheer him up," Jo said.

"You? Go out at the end of your confinement?"

"Why not? More and more I see women who are expecting out on the street. And in the suburbs, I am sure it is a common sight. We should go Theo…it's time."

"Yes, cheer him up," Emile said. "Give him courage."

"Thank you, Emile. I'll get it arranged." He sounded hopeless, Jo thought. And why would he still be running a fever?

16

Johanna

Theo stood and beamed proudly, reading aloud from an article about Vincent by a prominent critic.

"'Vincent van Gogh is a worthy descendent of the Dutch masters and the most innovative artist of his time'—this from Albert Aurier! Ladies and gentlemen, we will be rich!" At the breakfast table Johanna, Andries, and Theo's sister Anna exploded in applause. The baby jumped in Jo's arms at the sudden noise. Theo had gotten Vincent the first important piece of acclaim they all knew he deserved. He had done it!

Rich! What would they do with more money? Jo had never thought about becoming rich. Money was tight, but she always had what she needed. A bigger apartment would be nice. Willem could have his own room, and maybe even a room for visitors like Anna, helping with the baby. More room—that's what she would like, and a vacation in the country during the brutally hot Paris summers.

Vincent had recovered after a few peaceful months with Dr. Gachet and was traveling back to Paris to see his family meet his new nephew. It would be a fresh start and a reunion. Vincent had begun his correspondence with friends again and was serious about working and getting paid. His friends had helped him get three portrait commissions. It was a new beginning.

A month's visit—it would be crowded, but it was a chance to begin again with Vincent.

Andries checked his watch. "Soon, Theo," he said.

Theo mopped his brow. "Yes, I know. While we are all together here, I want you to promise me something. We are a family, we love each other. Vincent needs us. We love him, and we must work very hard to understand and accept the ordeal he has been through. Everything is turning around for Vincent now. This wonderful review, three portrait commissions…and greatest of all he is feeling better."

"You mean we should not pick a fight with him?" Anna asked.

"God, Anna, let's keep everyone calm, try to have a simple reunion. Can you promise me that?"

"Of course, Theo. I'm a guest here too."

"I think it would be best if I pick him up at the train and bring him here. Johanna, if you and Anna could visit the park, let me get him settled?"

"Yes," Johanna said and patted Theo's hand.

Theo kissed Jo's hand, stood, and looked at Anna. He pulled his jacket off the back of the chair. He looked at Anna again, waiting.

"I promise I won't do anything to set him off," Anna said. "But that doesn't mean he won't explode. He only cares what you think." Anna's voice had a colorful trill to it. Johanna had noticed it when Anna moved here to Paris, to help Jo with her confinement. At home, Anna's voice had always seemed flat, like her mother's.

"He'll be here for weeks. He needs you to be on his side."

"I'm just saying, you never know what's going to set him off."

"Don't ask him about his health, his treatment, Gachet, his painting. Don't say anything critical about his appearance or anything critical period. And don't bring up my business plans. Just think before you speak, count to ten, do whatever you have to do to make this a happy visit. He has earned it."

"What's left to talk about then?" joked Anna.

"Talk about Willem. He's very excited to see his nephew. Agreed?"

Johanna and Anna spent the morning meandering through the park with Willem while Theo got Vincent acclimated back into Paris and their apartment. Johanna prayed Vincent's recovery was true and he would achieve the success he was entitled to. And let everyone live in peace and prosperity.

"When was the last time you saw Vincent?" Anna asked.

"At Gachet's. He was… gentle."

"I saw Vincent in hospital. An awful place. If you weren't sick to begin with, just being around the insanity would do you in."

They walked through the park together, the baby in his pram Children, mothers, and nannies congregated around the swings and benches. Jo recognized a few mothers, her "playground friends" she called them. She missed Fleur and her home. Paris was more fun with a friend and money in your pocket. But she didn't wallow in any of that. Willem was a dream baby, and he made her very happy. It was a warm, sunny spring day. Children stripped off their jackets. Piles of them lay strewn about the playground.

Johanna and Anna sat side by side on a bench and watched the children run and play. Anna chatted absentmindedly about Theo and Vincent, when they were little boys playing together, how close they were. Johanna sat listening to Anna about those years, little Theo and Vincent, setting up a menagerie of bugs and animal bones.

Anna's voice sang up and down. "They were always close. They saw things the same way. Theo always chased after Vincent, doing everything Vincent did, a little mime. Theo was always overly attached, I say."

Her up-and-down rhythm was relaxing, easy to listen to, and didn't require the usual counterpoint of "oh…yes…ah-ha" and so forth. Talking with Anna or listening to Anna talk was peaceful. She had become a good friend.

"Thank you for coming, Anna." Anna had been seeing a man back home in Holland, they planned to marry the next year, when he was done at the university.

Theo was leaving Brossard, negotiating his exit and which of the inventory he would buy. They just couldn't see eye to eye. Brossard was pushing him back toward the old school, forcing him to take a chance on his own. The modern art world was growing in value, but slowly in Europe, faster with the Americans, who seemed to have an interest in impressionism.

Who was collecting, who was selling, which paintings to sell, which to hold, how to be competitive without an established gallery behind him. And Vincent, always a worry. So many expensive setbacks. But if Theo was right, Vincent's art would sell, and that would lift the biggest burden.

She prayed Vincent would work hard on his commissions and earn his way. Work gave you purpose, organized your thoughts, out of your own monotonous thinking into another world of people and problems to solve.

Johanna thought of work and how she missed it, and surprisingly, she felt the little knife in her chest, and she lost her breath. From out of the blue, without any warning, and the anxiety of loss. But she had a new purpose now, her husband and her son.

She felt the sun flushing her face red. She closed her eyes and hoped for colors to brighten her mood.

"Ouch, Willem, little prince, let go," Anna sang, arching her head away from his tight fist. Willem held fast onto Anna's thick, bright-blond hair.

"He likes your hair color." Johanna untangled his tiny fingers from Anna's hair, but he protested.

"Maybe he will marry a blonde!"

"Time to go. Let's pray for a happy conversation with our brother," said Johanna, standing to leave.

Vincent's paintings covered every inch of the walls, from floor to ceiling. Emile teetered on a ladder, hanging more. Henri was there too. Thankfully, no Vivienne, thought Johanna. Vincent's paintings also lay carefully draped over every piece of furniture, tabletop, bed and floor. The furniture was covered like decoupage, pins holding the canvas carefully secured to the upholstery.

What was going on here? When Theo said he wanted to get Vincent settled, she had no idea "settled" would leave her home transformed into a tornado of color. All the paintings stowed under the bed, the couch, every cabinet, hundreds of them packed away, were now out on display. Her home was transformed into Vincent's painted world.

Patterns bounced and danced from every corner. Small paths were choreographed in a specific pattern around the hundreds of paintings throughout all the rooms of the apartment.

Theo kissed Johanna hello, took Willem and carefully walked down the tiny path to Vincent. "Vincent, your nephew greets you!" Theo sounded happy.

Vincent looked well, healthier and stronger than Theo. Theo had recently developed a little stoop in his shoulders. It was all the worry he carried, she thought, all the changes ahead were weighing on his mind.

Henri was comparing the transformed apartment to Paris's most magnificent stained-glass church, Sainte Chapel. "Better," he said, "this is our modern church of color."

Johanna listened, trying to understand. "They sing this way, the yellow scale next to the blues, the green scale next to the reds," she heard Vincent say.

The paintings were arranged according to color scheme. Johanna walked the tiny path through the kaleidoscope of color. So many, so rich, all, the colors blending, bleeding into the next color.

She stopped in front of a golden green-blue painting she hadn't seen before. It was a poignant scene—a small child working to take her first steps to her father, a farmer who had dropped his hoe, down on one knee, arms outstretched to catch his daughter. Something about this one focused her attention. She didn't move from her spot, transfixed.

Theo called to her, "That one is a copy of a Millet, but Vincent's will be more famous. Come this way."

She listened to all the artists. Their voices pitched in high, clean energy, talking fast, talking over one another, giddy and fantastical, praising Vincent. She didn't realize until now, seeing them all together again, how she had missed them. These days she stayed home, cozy with the baby in the evenings. Theo still went out, but less often. Everything was more serious now. Theo was watching expenses, saving up for his own gallery.

More paintings came out from under the bed, from the top of the standing closet. Emile carefully unrolled each one. Vincent pointed to where it should go. Emile gingerly walked the small path and carefully placed the painting in the exact spot.

"Vincent," Emile repeated, over and over, with such passion and love, staring at the paintings. His joy transformed him from a worried, soulful young man, with his petulant edge, to a joyous, love-struck child with glistening eyes, a lumpy throat, and giddy voice.

"God, this is remarkable," Henri cried. "Vincent, in my entire life I will never see a body of work like this, ever! Smile, man, you have done it! We need drinks. Where is Andries?"

Johanna stared at the spectacular sight, tiptoeing carefully through the vibrating colors, bright, brighter, brightest, glittering paint everywhere.

"I'm going blind with color," Anna sang up high, the bright colors reflecting on her brown wool dress.

Suddenly the energetic chatter died down. Johanna saw a new face in the crowded apartment: a critic.

The art critic, Albert Aurier, walked with Vincent though his rooms of color, his notepad hanging at his side, listening to Vincent talk about each painting. Emile followed behind Vincent and hung close to his every step, trying to touch him whenever he could, whenever there was a logical reason to. "Careful, Vincent," Emile said, grabbing his arm, so he wouldn't step on one of his paintings. "Watch behind you," he said as he gently steered Vincent away from an obstacle. Emile moved like he was attached to Vincent with strings.

"We will have the greatest modern show Paris has ever seen. I will design the poster, introducing *Vincent van Gogh*!" Henri raised a glass.

Willem began to fuss in Jo's arms, rooting for her breast. Where to find some privacy?

Johanna walked carefully past Vincent and saw in his face not joy, not the excitement and wonder everyone else wore. He looked nervous, eyes darting, not smiling. He was overwhelmed, like one of her students before a presentation. They'd all worked hard to make him happy, yet with all this attention he seemed as manic as ever.

"Do you think we can ask Monet to have a look, maybe give us a quote?" Emile asked. "What do you think, Theo?"

Johanna sat in the kitchen nursing Willem, listening to the conversation. They were using the word *modern* over and over, and it was resonating in her head: *modern*, modern composition, modern color, modern Vincent. The infectious mood overtook her, and she felt euphoric. Emotion took hold of her, tears welled up in her eyes as she looked at her baby. Anna sang behind her as she put together cheese and biscuits to pass around.

Vincent and Theo edged their way into the kitchen with the critic. She wiped her tears and laughed, covering up. Vincent handed Johanna a package wrapped in plain paper. He bowed a little.

"It is for Willem. A birth gift I painted for him. I hope you like it."

Johanna let more tears spill, handed Willem to Theo, and opened the large painting. It was a simple composition, branches of an almond tree in blossom, covered with pink bundles of flowers against a cloudless turquoise sky.

"It's magnificent!" Johanna said. "The colors are so...so...As usual, my words fail me. It's wonderful, Vincent!"

She felt awkward. She didn't know how to describe the work in artful terms, she could only come up with the most basic statement. "Now this my favorite color." She thought they might laugh at her.

"Yes, a turquoise sky. I wanted it for Willem, so he could see what the country is like. Every morning, first thing when he wakes up, he will see the beautiful sky."

The blue was gorgeous and irresistible, it made her feel excited and calm at the same time. It was like the real sky, but better, the way you wish the sky was. She was lost in it, and in that moment, she felt finally like she belonged, just a little, in Vincent's colorful world.

"Color expresses something all by itself, doesn't it?" Vincent waved his hand over the painting. "If one intensifies *all* the colors everything comes to a point of harmony and calm."

"I feel happy just looking at it. This is the most special gift, Vincent. Thank you. We will cherish it always," Johanna said.

"I wanted to express with painting something soothing and consoling, like nature, but more exultant...what music does for the soul. That is what I am aiming for, that feeling, through color."

"That is the perfect emotional statement, so expressive of you. I feel it so completely." She held out her arms for permission to hug him.

He looked relieved, his piercing blue eyes held hers, not in a challenge but soft. He held his arms out to her, and they slowly came together and held a true embrace.

A truce and now peace, all forgiven and forgotten—it was a great beginning for Vincent, for the family. The critic's pad stayed up as he wrote. The critic copied every word Vincent said. Theo and Emile discreetly watched over his shoulder.

"Vincent, what will you do today?" Anna asked. "Oh no, I didn't mean to ask that. I mean, Johanna, what are we doing today? Shall we go to the park again?" Vincent, Theo, Johanna, and Anna crowded around the breakfast table. Andries stood at the tiny counter, sipping a coffee.

"I am going to visit some clients," Vincent answered and stared at Anna directly, sucking on his lit pipe.

"How wonderful you have clients! What are you going to paint?" Anna asked, trying to sound light in her singsong voice.

"Portraits. I have commissions. Andries, for one." Vincent looked to Andries, who struck a pose with his coffee cup.

"What do you think, Vincent? Does this capture the real me?" He slapped Vincent and Theo on the back. "I'm off, meeting one of my gallery clients. See you later." Andries left, and after a quiet moment, Vincent broke the silence.

"I think…." Vincent began, speaking slowly, methodically, as if giving an instruction, emphasizing every word. "I'd like to paint men and women, capturing their unique eternal quality, symbolized in the past with a halo. But now, in a new style of portraiture, I want to convey radiance through the vibration of our coloring."

Jo listened carefully, remembered all the medieval portraits she loathed: white, fleshy people, all awful.

"Oh really, wonderful. Commissions…means they pay you, better than a swap?" Anna said.

Vincent twitched at Anna's questions. Johanna knew artist's swaps were high compliments, sought after, and in some ways better than an exchange of money. She wondered why Theo didn't jump in to explain.

"The artist exchange is the highest compliment one artist can pay to another," Johanna said. "Vincent, can I get you breakfast?"

"Thank you, I'm not hungry."

"What an amazing evening, all those paintings, all the applause from your friends. You must be thrilled," said Johanna, trying to change the subject.

"Eat something, keep your strength going for the long day," Theo said. "Jo makes excellent eggs."

"All right, an egg, thank you."

"Some toast? Are you thrilled, Vincent?" Johanna asked again.

"It is hard for me to believe. I can't accept it."

"Why can't you accept this good news? What did that critic say?" Anna asked.

There was silence from Vincent, he just looked at Theo.

"He was *very impressed* with Vincent, the quality of each painting, the overall quantity of the work, the ideas, the technique. We have validation. Vincent will submit to shows across Europe. And we start looking for important collectors."

Vincent looked empty, depleted. Johanna put a plate of food in front of him. "There, eat. You need your energy."

"You should have waited before inviting him in. I need another year to develop stronger drawing, better composition."

The edge in Vincent's voice brought out in the open the unease that had been simmering. Almost happy last night and now this morning, he seemed morose. Johanna ignored Vincent's warning tone and jumped in to change the subject. Was this a sign of another of Vincent's attacks?

"Theo, what can I get you?" Johanna asked.

Theo didn't answer Vincent's statement or Jo's question. But both his hands came off the table, and he threw an arm over the back of his chair, staring at Vincent.

Willem fussed, coughed, suddenly red-faced, choking, crying. Johanna picked him up, pushing back alarm, wiped his nose, and touched his skin. "Feverish, I think," she said, and walked him over to Theo.

Theo placed his hand on the baby's head. "Maybe a little, don't worry, he's fine, just a cold."

Johanna put her hand on Theo's head. "I think you have one too. Both of my boys with fever. I don't like it."

"I hope we don't all get it," said Anna.

"You do look terrible, Theo," Vincent said. "I was shocked when I saw you. The country air is better for the body. Paris is filthy, I had forgotten how dirty. It is no wonder you are both sick. A move to the country would do everyone good. If you don't have your health, you have nothing."

No one said anything to that.

In the kitchen, Anna said, "I will make you something, Theo. What would you like?" She got up and busied herself fixing food.

"Why don't you believe in yourself?" Theo finally responded to Vincent.

"It feels far away from me. I am not ready to embrace it."

"You have done important work." Theo sounded like he might be pleading.

"Wait till Mother hears!" Anna trilled.

Both Theo and Vincent glanced at Anna, sharing a conspiratorial look. "Has Mother ever been excited about painting, or anything?" Theo said. Vincent laughed. Anna cracked a smile too.

"I feel a disgrace and a failure. Theo, I need to talk to you about the future."

"What you have done will always remain well done. You have risen above. You are the envy of a thousand painters."

"The success you want for me is the worst thing that can happen for a painter."

Willem suddenly coughed up vomit all over Johanna and the kitchen table.

"Theo, we must get him to the doctor." She jumped up, frightened.

"Can't Anna go with her?" asked Vincent. "I need to speak with you, Theo."

"Later."

"When?"

"This afternoon or this evening. I also need to secure studio space for you, for the portraits."

"It is critical. I must speak with you now, alone." Vincent was demanding.

"I understand. We have a full day. I have a gallery to arrange. First the baby. We will talk alone, I promise."

"I'm here, Vincent, if you want to talk," Anna said. She put her hand on his hand, and they sat together in a peaceful moment.

Jo and Theo exchanged cautious glances. Was it safe to leave? They had no choice. The baby was sick.

Theo

Theo and Vincent sat close together in front of the fireplace. It was late, and they were the only ones left awake. Theo rested his head back on the settee and closed his eyes. He'd had good progress today. The baby's fever was gone, and he had found a shared studio space for Vincent. His own business was progressing. He would strike a good bargain for the modern inventory from Brossard, and best of all, his clients would stick with him. Financially it would still be tight, but with Vincent doing better, Theo and his young family would progress on every level.

"I'm sorry. It's been chaos. Where to begin?" Theo said.

"I miss you, Theo."

"I miss you too." His tone was low and sad, not encouraging. "What is it, Vincent? Aren't you happy here with us? I have found you studio space, for the portraits. We can see it together, tomorrow."

"I want to go home, back to The Netherlands…I want to travel and paint my way home."

Theo opened his eyes and rolled his head to look at Vincent. "What about your commissions, Vincent? These are serious offers, a profitable opportunity."

"I can't. I need to get out of Paris as quickly as possible. I have another plan. I will paint my way home in a way I never could before. I want to paint the colors of the north, of home, in our new, modern way."

"The new gets old quickly. Is that it, Vincent?"

"One songbird doesn't make a summer, and a new idea does not destroy finished work."

"So?" Theo took his jacket off, smoothed his hair, and rested his head on the settee and closed his eyes again. This whole idea was impossible. How to begin explaining this to Vincent? How to avoid a volcanic explosion, especially now with a small child, his sister, and Jo all crammed together?

"I could be the first to paint the northern lights."

"It's a good idea. One day we can put a trip like that together. Right now, none of that is possible," he said, resting again, his eyes closed.

"Why not?"

"What about your treatment? On your own, traveling through the countryside, who would be there to help you? I have a family to support, a new business to finance. Dr. Gachet is close to Paris. We can visit as often as we want."

"What if you moved to the countryside? We could be closer, and it's cheaper…and better for everyone's health. We'll be together."

"I can't sell art from the countryside. We are ready now. We'll exhibit during the fall season and then, the grand opening of the Van Gogh Gallery, with the premiere of the newest, greatest modern painter, Vincent van Gogh. Hang on now, the worst is over."

"I need you. This attack doesn't feel over. I can't go back to

Gachet. It is the blind leading the blind with him. A rather queer result of this terrible illness is I have no hope left in my mind, no desire, and I wonder if this is how it feels when passions lessen, and you descend the hill instead of climbing it."

"You have come further than most, don't you see? Don't you believe your friends?"

Vincent paused and took a deep breath. "You must listen to me. You will have to make a catastrophic choice."

"I hope nothing so dramatic lies in my future. This is not a choice. We all need money."

"I can't paint myself whole. Questions, questions, and more questions about painting. Isn't seeing enough? Why will words make the work meaningful? What carefully thought-out words would you have said?"

"I was there, Vincent. I heard. Aurier believes in you, everyone believes in you. He is a critic, and he admires your work. He thinks he has discovered you. You gave him something to write about, to make himself unique."

I want to wait another year for the exhibit, until I have another year of work, when I have more characteristic things with decisive drawings. There isn't anything worth mentioning now. It is absolutely certain that I shall never do important things."

"You are important, and a success. You're just nervous and doubting yourself."

Vincent stood and headed for the door. "Don't you see, success is the worst thing for me now? Success is the enemy of art." He headed for the door.

"Where are you going?"

"I need a walk. I'm exhausted."

"It's past midnight."

But Vincent left anyway.

17

Vincent

I can't think about the past without drowning in a sad longing. I am underwater, looking through the green to blue-white clouds. I reach for the cloud to pull myself out. I see my hand above the water, glistening with green, reaching. I sink deeper, forgetting how to swim. My world is darker and turning black. I am dreaming, I think. I wake up, drenched in an oil slick of sweat, my heart painful in my chest. I am afraid of more nightmares and won't let myself sleep.

Theo thinks my heart was born broken. I have a sensitive nature. I must follow the emotions swelling my head. I tried to make that work for me, for others, for painting. Theo thinks I have won the argument, that what I have done will always remain well done. But I know success is never final. We are flimsy, and all of this is just a storm in a teacup.

Perhaps it is from the sick we learn how to live. I see hope in the end, and you will be happy with me again.

See, I am grateful. I will have the stamina to bring an end to my chaos, no longer be a coward before pain. I remember the expenses that will never ever be recovered, so much wasted I can't bear to tally the total. There is not another future for me. I have no skills, except chasing swirls of color.

I have always felt I am a traveler, and I am certain of life beyond the grave. Every artist holds a torch, a light into the future. I have faith another will see mine and carry it further. My brother, we were one, he was mine. My brother, come to kill me, come to save me, come to hate me, to be ashamed of me. He is shackled to me, and I don't know how to live without him.

Theo

Theo lay across the couch, his foot nudging the cradle where the baby snoozed.

Johanna was cooking in the kitchen, dropping chunks of biscuit dough into simmering stew. This was the new routine on Sundays. Andries and Theo were planning their gallery. Jettisoning the weight of managing a doomed relationship with his employer had improved Theo's mood. Vincent seemed to be doing well with Dr. Gachet, and paintings and letters still arrived daily.

Andries talked to Theo about a gallery space he had seen in Montmartre.

"It has southern light in the front. The back gets northern light, but another building is blocking some of the windows. And the upstairs has large living quarters. You can live above, work below, it's very practical. There are even rooms in the basement and attic to rent out for more income."

"Practical," was all Theo said listlessly, and this got Jo's attention.

Johanna brought Theo tea. She checked Theo's head for fever. He always seemed to be hot to her touch.

Andries picked up Willem, held him high in the air. "My, my, my little nephew, aren't you looking fat and handsome! Who do you look like today? Every day you change. Today, you look like Vincent. Maybe tomorrow you will look like me?"

There was a knock on the door. They froze and looked at each other thinking…Oh no, now what?

"Oh God, it's Vincent again, I know it." Theo looked up to the heavens and mouthed a silent prayer. It was another telegram, and even before it was opened, adrenaline flooded through them all.

Within minutes Theo was gone, running for the train to Dr. Gachet, to save Vincent again.

He doesn't look so bad, Theo thought with relief when he saw Vincent. Vincent could be saved. He was in time.

Gachet sat in a corner, sketching Vincent lying in the bed.

Vincent lay smiling in his bed, pipe in his mouth, bandages brown and red with blood wrapped around his abdomen, his chest exposed. His eyes sparkled when he saw Theo, and his smile grew. Vincent reached out for Theo. *He is smiling. Good, he will recover.*

Theo climbed into bed next to Vincent, just like when they were children.

"Light my pipe, Theo." The bleeding had slowed to a trickle, the bullet still inside. The damage didn't look fatal, Theo thought.

"What happened, Vincent?" Theo lit his pipe, and the smoke wafted in Theo's face, prompting a slow, continual cough. He spit into his handkerchief.

Vincent half waved his pipe smoke away. "Theo, you ought to get that cough looked at! You look sick."

"How is the pain?"

"No pain," Vincent said and closed his eyes and kept his smile.

"What happened?" Theo asked again.

"He's had medication, he shouldn't have pain," said Gachet.

"Theo, listen to me. This new business, remember, the sun may set on you, but renew yourself in the core of our profession, of painting and dealing, and have your own business."

"Awfully organized words for a wounded man. I'm glad you approve of the plan. When is the surgeon coming, Dr. Gachet?"

"I have been thinking about it. I am so happy now," Vincent said and opened his eyes.

"Why are you happy now?"

"Because I am dying."

"You're not dying. Where is the surgeon?" Theo asked more urgently.

"No surgeon. My sadness is over," Vincent said. He tried to take a sip from the cup Theo held for him. Vincent coughed. Theo could see the liquid would not descend his throat and instead gushed back out of his mouth, followed by a small drop of blood trickling down his chin. Theo wiped it away.

Vincent reached for Theo's hand. "This sadness will last forever." Vincent closed his eyes, and his pipe dropped to the bed. His mouth went slack.

"Yes, rest, I'll stay right here," Theo said, taking Vincent's pipe from the sheets. Vincent's words—'this sadness will last forever'— echoed in his mind.

"No, Vincent, there will be no sadness. Stop this right now!" Then he stood and barked at Dr. Gachet. "When is the surgeon coming?"

"Vincent declined the surgeon. I begged him!" He put down his sketch of Vincent.

"No, you fool!" Theo shouted and grabbed Vincent's head as it slumped down onto his chest. He lifted Vincent's head back upright. He pressed his ear to Vincent's chest, praying to hear a heartbeat.

Nothing. He pressed in harder.

He hugged Vincent tightly and felt his own body shudder and convulse with uncontrollable sorrow and rage. It came so suddenly. He couldn't breathe. He climbed back into bed and hugged Vincent closer and closer to him. He had failed him, his voice shrieked in his head. His body convulsed against Vincent's warmth and stillness.

He had failed him. He had failed, he had failed, he had failed.

Johanna

Theo, Johanna, and Dr. Gachet cleaned out the rented room above the café near Dr. Gachet's house where Vincent had been living. There were letters, papers, prints, and Vincent's belongings, including unsent letters to Theo. Theo was not discerning between junk and things of value, packing everything. His hands were shaking noticeably, arousing concern from both Jo and Gachet.

"Let me do that, Theo, you are stiff from holding vigil," Gachet said. "May I have a look at you in my office? I can help with the cough, your tremor."

Jo had worried about his cough, his fever, now his tremor. He had a lingering winter cold, he said.

"I am a magnet for every sniffle." Theo's voice had lost its magnetic quality. The deep harmonies were just flat, with a tinge of something sharp, impatience maybe, Johanna feared.

"Vincent was concerned for your health. He asked me many questions about various—"

Theo suddenly snapped. "Vincent said his therapy with you was 'the blind leading the blind.' Those were his exact words, Doctor. Why didn't you save him?" He sounded rude, and aggressive, Johanna walked to Theo's side and put a hand on his arm to calm him.

"I tried," Gachet said. "He didn't want help in the end, you saw for yourself."

"Didn't want help, really?" Theo brushed Jo's hand away and got to his feet and stood directly in front of Gachet, who took a step backward and bumped into the wall of the tiny attic room.

"I am truly sorry, Mr. Van Gogh."

"Theo." Johanna walked to his side, trying to soothe him, "Theo..."

"Why was he here in this hovel of a room above a tavern and not at your home? How was that helping him, *Doctor*?" He screamed, full of bitterness.

"Theo…" Johanna said again. She had never seen him utter a loud word. The harshness in his voice frightened her.

"*What, Johanna, what?*" He turned to her, his face leaning into her, his eyes black.

She felt a thousand stabs at Theo's mocking scream. He had never screamed at her, never even raised his voice.

"Yes, Mr. Van Gogh, I failed him."

Theo turned back to Gachet. "And you sat sketching him on his deathbed! Where is the drawing? I demand it, now!"

"Yes, I'll give it to you. I am so profoundly sorry, believe me. Success is never guaranteed with these psychological matters. But we tried." Gachet handed the drawing to Theo.

"Get out. I don't want you," Theo said. Johanna felt her knees buckle. She followed Gachet out of the room, thinking to say something to blunt Theo's horrible, uncharacteristic behavior. But her mouth had dried out and she feared shouting down the staircase. Gachet stopped and turned to look at her. Their eyes locked. He said nothing but gave her a compassionate smile and nodded his head to her. Was he asking her to come with him? Did he want to talk to her? She turned to look back at Theo. She could leave him for a moment. But he was staring at her, waiting impatiently. He waved her back in the room and handed her drawings.

She had never seen Theo behave this way. He was always in control, getting his way without screaming and never lashing out. He was upset, losing perspective in this tragedy…understandable, she thought. She needed to get him back to the comforts of Paris. But another dismal day lay ahead. Tomorrow they would travel home, to clean out Vincent's old studio at his mother's.

18

Johanna

"What are you crying for?" Mother van Gogh stood in the tiny kitchen of the van Gogh home in Brabant, holding baby Willem, his hands flailing in the air, his voice piercing and shrill as if a thousand needles were stabbing him. She spoke into his face, loud and monotone, and then put him on top of the kitchen table, flat on his back, while he shrieked. She sat down herself.

Anna reached out to console Willem. "Shush, don't cry, baby."

"Leave him be. It is better if he works it out on his own. He must have the illness."

"He's only a baby, Mother." Anna reached for the child.

"I told you to leave him *be*," Mother snapped, her voice rising. Anna dropped her arms back to her sides but sang an old nursery rhyme to Willem.

Johanna sat in the small parlor off the kitchen, sorting through the boxes of Vincent's letters and documents. Vincent's painting of purple irises glowed from the wall. He had sent this and several others to his mother. He had painted it in the asylum, and it was one of his greatest. The colors, the composition, the simplicity, the brushstrokes. She tallied all the innovations. If only we could all be so glorious in our pain. Willem cried from the kitchen. *Why do they*

235

let the baby cry? she thought angrily. She dropped the heap of dirty, dusty letters and went to the kitchen.

Willem still lay on the kitchen table, crying and red-faced. Johanna sang and cooed, letting him know she was on her way. She washed her hands and picked him up, fast and gentle, over her shoulder, soothing. Her face rubbed his cheek, her hand gently patted his back.

He stilled instantly, and Johanna took a deep, calming breath. Vincent's painting, the copy of his beloved Millet, flashed in her mind. *First Steps*, he called it, the farmer, arms outstretched to his darling daughter as she toddled toward him. The farmer's arms out so far, down on one knee, and even with the face obscured by a hat, the joy and excitement flowed through his pose as he anticipated his baby in his arms. The baby's arms reaching out across the gold and green ground. The mother, behind, gentle, helping keep her upright as she takes her first steps to her father—so much feeling right there in just the arms. How had Vincent done that?

It flashed in her mind, all the colors and emotion. The sweetness of the reaching arms made her pause, bittersweet. Poor Vincent. She wondered how fast she could get out of here, back to Paris.

"Why do you let the baby cry, Mother?" Johanna asked, working extra hard to sound pleasant, a tight smile covering her annoyance.

"He's sick and you'll catch his illness. If he's just fussy, then let him cry it out. Everyone knows handling babies spreads germs, that is why our Theo can't lose his cough. I am surprised you don't know."

Nonsense, Johanna thought. So cruel, these old notions about handling babies, spreading illness, more quack medicine. A baby, sick or not, can't reason its way through pain.

"Mother, I need to pack up Vincent's work now. Can I have the key to the studio?" Good, hold your temper, don't bother arguing with her. Collect and preserve. That's what Theo wants, that's why we're here. The faster I move, the closer to home I will be.

"I'll take him." Anna stood next to Johanna, her arms open

for the baby. "I won't let him cry. I promise." Anna's face was soft with concern, but she lost her entrancing singsong voice around her mother. "The packing will go faster that way. The studio is too filthy for the baby."

Anna took the baby from Johanna, cooing to him and giving him a gentle bounce. Willem gave her a half smile and grabbed a fistful of her yellow hair.

"I'm coming, wait." Theo, up from his rest, entered the kitchen. His hair was uncharacteristically unkempt. His face was bloated, eyes swollen, as if he had cried a million tears for Vincent.

"This should be interesting, all Vincent's old drawings." His voice was returning but still hoarse and weak sounding.

"Let me do it with Johanna," said Mother, blocking the door. "Nothing but dirt in there and you'll ruin your suit."

"You know we won't be staying long, Mother," Theo said, pulling out a kitchen chair and having a seat, as if he'd forgotten what he was going to do. "Later, after the holidays, we'll set up in New York City, and we'll send for you then."

What was that? There was a pause, a long silence. Johanna looked at Theo, but he remained silent. Anna and Mother exchanged confused glances. Jo froze, confused, and a little slice of panic hit her. When had Theo decided they were moving to America?

"You're moving to New York?" Anna was the first to ask what everyone was thinking.

"I thought maybe London," Johanna calmly responded. "This is the first I'm hearing of America." Theo wasn't making any sense. He once said they should consider moving to London if the market for modern art improved.

"Not London, they had their opportunity, and they lost the chance. America is the future for modern art. They love Monet. Nouveau-riche collectors are excellent prospects."

"This is a bit out of the blue, isn't it, Theo?" Johanna gently touched Theo's head.

"Like I said, many wealthy industrialists!" He shook off her hand. Jo felt her panic growing. He still looked terrible. He hadn't bounced back from the funeral. And they still needed to clean out the studio, pack and ship the rest of Vincent's work. Maybe Theo was dreaming about America.

"Theo, lie down. I'll handle the studio. Maybe Mother can make you some tea. I know what to do, and I won't throw anything out."

Mother jumped in. "Theo, I'll show Johanna. Anna, you make the tea."

Johanna sat on the only piece of furniture in the studio, a painter's three-legged stool, wearing workman's gloves and a smock covering her dress. She combed through piles of old drawings and Japanese prints, packing everything into shipping boxes. The papers were dirty, disorganized. Was this work Vincent had cared about?

Theo wanted to move to America? The best place for modern art and Jo felt she was the last to know! Did Andries know? Of course, it must be New York, it was the only civilized city there. Because of the Dutch.

Johanna had always hated housework, cleaning, washing. Nothing about it occupied her mind. Mrs. Van Gogh walked nervously around, handing over more debris for Johanna to sort through and pack away.

It might be easier and faster if Mrs. Van Gogh wasn't there and if Jo didn't have to keep up a conversation

"This is what is left. He never sold anything you know." Mother rambled on and on, driving Johanna mad. "It has no value. All the oil paints—they are expensive, aren't they? All Theo's money and now nothing. Why bother with this? I worried Vincent would impoverish the family. He didn't know what would sell, and he sold nothing. I knew he was too troubled, I always told Father he was.

He broke my heart. I loved him, I tried everything. He only listened to Theo."

"Theo said at the funeral that the painters think Vincent was brilliant, a genius," Johanna said. "That's what they all said. Everything must be treasured, it's all part of a master's work. Didn't you paint yourself?"

"No," Mother said in a dismal voice. "Not like Vincent. I couldn't see the world and paint the way he did. I love my Irises, you can't take them, but the rest here…you can take it."

Johanna was shocked. It seemed as if nothing had been cleaned out in decades. All Vincent's debris was strewn across the room.

"I needed to rent the room. I begged him to clean it out. I needed the money. He wouldn't lift a finger. Oh, my poor Vincent."

Johanna stared at an old drawing of a nude woman, *Sorrow*. She thought it might be important.

"There is more out back. Come on."

They stood in front two large garbage pails filled with debris. Johanna's eyes widened, and she gasped.

"You can see, nothing worth keeping," Mother said.

Johanna found sketches, prints, and what might be rolled-up canvases covered in burlap. She was overwhelmed.

"Garbage, all old garbage, from his room. Childhood things, schoolwork, other things, shipped here from God knows when and where. He traveled, sent everything back here."

I need to purchase more shipping boxes, Jo thought. "Don't worry, I'll take care of everything."

Finally, all the packing done and on the way home to Paris, Johanna cuddled next to Theo on the train. Every muscle ached from the cleaning and gathering of all Vincent's work. Theo held Willem on his chest. She relished this moment of quiet and closeness.

Theo talked on about Vincent and the great solo show of his work he would create. This would be their priority. Then they would open a new gallery, with a permanent installation of Vincent's greatest works. Some paintings they would sell, some they would hold, and some works they would save for museums.

She loved to hear him strategize and share his thoughts. It gave her a sense of purpose. She didn't care where they lived. His voice vibrated in her ear as she rested her cheek on his shoulder. This is the peace, the love, the life she had wanted, always. They had come through a terrible ordeal and were now going home.

The baby bounced in front of her on Theo's lap. Willem seemed thrilled to be in his father's arms, always trying to reach his face. Theo's color was ruddier. He seemed thoughtful, more like himself. He was recovering.

Her body moved with the gentle rhythm of his breathing. Does this look inappropriate, she wondered, in public, sitting so close?

"He was happy dying, I told you. We can begin again. Did I tell you his last words? Oh, I'm sorry, are you really sleeping?"

The peace was broken. Johanna had heard these words many times. Vincent's last words, "The sadness will last forever." For a moment she imagined Theo at Vincent's bedside, Vincent saying those words. "The sadness will last forever." To his brother, the person who loved him the most, who sacrificed the most, believed in him the most. Sadness and forever—two words that should never be spoken together.

Theo fixated on Vincent's last words. He repeated this dreadful phase relentlessly, never able to understand the intention. Johanna would talk about it to the end if only it would give Theo peace.

But it didn't, and he began it all again. How could Vincent do this? Didn't he know or care how deeply this would affect Theo?

"He said, 'The sadness will last forever.'"

"I know. Terrible words." She opened her eyes and lifted her head. She touched his head. He was a little sweaty, but the train car was warm.

"But he wasn't *happy* in his sadness," Theo said. "Whose sadness was he talking about? His or mine? Can you take him? Want to go back to Mommy? Yes, Mommy, here you go."

Theo handed the baby to Johanna. "What do you think, Jo?" Theo's hands shook without the weight of the baby. He rested his head back on the seat and turned toward her, waiting for her response.

"Vincent shot himself in the diaphragm, not the head," Jo said. "He walked home. He wouldn't let the doctor treat him. Why do you think he did that?"

"Why don't you tell me what you really think?" Theo said.

"I think…" Johanna looked at Theo closely. Should she say exactly what she thought? Vincent could have killed himself instantly, with a bullet to his brain. She thought Vincent wanted the deathbed scene with his brother. It made her angry because it hurt Theo, he was guilt ridden beyond any measure of reason. Then she had to remind herself, Vincent never saw the world the way everyone else did. This was what had made him so special and so difficult. Theo knew this better than anyone.

"I think Vincent wanted to say good-bye to you. He loved you more than—"

"You think he wanted me to feel bad?"

"No. He was a lonely, sad man. That's why he killed himself, to end his own suffering. Everyone knows you're not at fault. You did everything, but you couldn't cure him. He didn't know what he was saying. He was in agony, and he had to make it stop."

"But do you think he wanted me to feel guilty?"

"No. You loved each other, and he wanted to say good-bye. Nothing makes sense when you're sick. We were all working together to make Vincent happy."

"No, I didn't do I everything I could," Theo said. "I couldn't let *you* go." His voice was suddenly ragged, sarcastic, a tone she had never heard from him.

"He didn't want you to let me go. He called me 'sister' and hugged me. He loved the baby."

"He wanted a family. Once he had a family. God, I am exhausted by this. I don't deserve you."

"What family?"

"I don't know. I need to get this out of my head. I just wanted everyone…" Theo began to weep, in public, on the train. Johanna sat up and tried to block his body, so no one could see. She was startled. What in the world was happening, crying here, now, in public?

"Theo, shush. Please. It's all over."

"I don't know why I can't stop. I feel like I'm fading, dying. I see what's coming, and I can't stop it. It's so painful. I'm…overwhelmed, with a weight on me so heavy, I can't hold upright."

"Here, take the window seat, switch seats with me." They exchanged seats, and Theo turned toward the window and rested his head on the glass.

"Close your eyes, get some rest. You'll feel better. This is over now, we're moving on. Can't you feel it?"

"No. Promise me, Jo."

"Of course, Theo, I promise you will feel better." She touched his brow. It was warm.

"No, not me." He waved her hand away. "Promise me you'll help me with Vincent."

"Of course, Theo. I promise. As long as it takes. Whatever you need me to do."

He leaned in close and whispered to her, "'We fix what is broken, restore what is lost, we save the day…'" Repeating Jo's words about the insurance business from long ago, the day they met. Why would he be remembering this now?

"Thank God, Johanna. Thank God for you. Marrying you was

the best thing I ever did. Johanna Bonger, Bonger Insurance. You're my insurance." Feverish thinking.

His pain was growing, and they kept having this same conversation over and over, the horrible repetition of the agony and never an end or closure to it. It was just like Vincent, the endless circle of—*oh my God, I need to get him to a doctor. Andries will help me.*

"No, promise me you will take care of Vincent. Get him treated the way he deserves."

"I will." She petted his head the way he liked. He seemed to calm down and stopped speaking. His eyes closed but tears still came.

Get him to a doctor. She felt a queasy fear. Whatever was wrong, she prayed it wouldn't be what had happened with Vincent.

Theo refused to see a doctor until he finished setting up the retrospective of Vincent's work. They worked day and night organizing the exhibit, and Theo grew worse, weak with a constant fever. The memorial exhibit of Vincent's work would be in the parlor of their apartment. There was a large table in the middle of the room where Vincent's unframed canvasses and drawings lay stacked in separate piles.

"Theo, who is this?" Johanna asked. The ugly drawing of a pregnant woman in an undignified pose had bothered her since the first moment she saw it in Vincent's old studio. It had clean lines, she supposed, but ultimately was a depressing portrait. Theo walked over and had a look at the drawing.

He looked at it a long time, as though it was hard to see.

"*Sorrow,*" he said. "Where was this?" He dropped it down on the table.

"At Vincent's old studio at your mother's."

Theo worked his way toward the red settee in the living area behind the parlor.

"Are you limping?" She followed him, studying his gait. He was dragging his foot, slanted sideways.

"I'm not. Just too much sitting and lying down. Not enough progress. We have to move faster, Jo."

Theo sat down and quickly fell asleep, his head drooping. Johanna covered him up with a blanket, feeling his head. He was sweaty. She wiped his forehead with a cloth.

She looked at Willem, sleeping in his cradle by the fireplace. Theo mumbled something incomprehensible. She watched him talk in his sleep, unable to understand his words.

She continued cleaning and organizing while the two of them slept. She laid out each piece on the table, carefully dusting each painted canvas with a fine brush and then cleaning off any grime with a solution Theo had given her. With the drawings, she only dusted and placed thin tracing paper between each one.

Theo came up from behind and startled her.

"Oh! Feeling better?" Theo was looking at the drawing of the woman again. "Who is it? Do you know her?" Johanna asked.

"Don't bother with that one. I don't want to show it."

"Did you know her?" She went into the kitchen and began preparing lunch. Theo talked to her from the table.

"Her name was Clasina. She was a faded prostitute Vincent thought he loved. She was pregnant. It might have been Vincent's baby," he said.

"Why did he leave her? What happened?" Johanna came back to Theo and stared at the drawing.

"She was wrecked, wretched, ruined from the start. Very sad, I guess they all died. But if she didn't, I'll be a perfect gentleman when she shows up. She will ask for more money. We don't have any to give. We have to tighten our belts. Everything is for the new gallery. Put that one with the letters."

"What do you mean when she shows up? Did you say she was dead? I'm confused."

"Her name is, or was, Clasina Hoornick. I remember—how about that! When she comes we'll ask her what happened to her babies."

Theo went to the bedroom, but he stopped first to touch Willem, sleeping in the cradle. Theo lay down on the bed slowly, like a very old man whose bones ached. Nothing Theo had said made any sense, and worse he sounded cavalier and mean.

He is ill with fever. Andries will have to force him to go to the doctor with me.

"All right, rest, we'll talk later. Can I bring you lunch in bed? You must see the doctor." Johanna bent over the bed and stroked Theo on the head the way he liked, up and down, then side to side. Theo snatched her hand and held it very hard. "Ouch," Johanna said and tried to pull her hand back.

But Theo held on to her hand and continued to squeeze it painfully. He looked her directly in the eye and snarled like an animal.

"What are you doing? Stop!" she said, trying to pull back.

He finally let her hand go and Johanna burst into tears. "Oh my God, what is the matter with you?"

Theo held the back of his hand over his eyes. "He left them for the painting. Get out, leave me alone."

Theo grew worse, yelling at her and Andries and talking about things that didn't exist. Finally, she convinced him to go the doctor. Jo and Andries sat in silence on either side of Theo, waiting for their turn with the doctor. When she could think clearly about it, she knew he was very ill. He never got back to normal. His voice had changed—his deep baritone had become a lighter version of itself, with a little rattle, a watery sound in there behind his words, causing a haunting echo. The extent of the change was upsetting. The understanding, the caring quality, the empathic tones that swirled in Johanna's head—these were all gone.

They all stared into space, waiting. Johanna rested her hand on Theo's thigh. He let her. Sometimes he patted her hand and gave it a squeeze. And sometimes, now and again, he sharply pushed her away.

After a time, the doctor saw them.

"Why are we here?" Theo sounded annoyed, the monster creeping back in.

"He has been fighting fever for months," Andries explained to the doctor. "He's dejected over the death of his brother. A tragedy for the family, of course. No other illness in the family, except his son had a cold this winter."

"Yes, I understand. But there may be something more. We need a full physical examination to see what can be seen."

"What about the tremors? The other day he could barely walk," Johanna said.

The doctor turned from Theo, who sat sullenly staring into space.

"Let's have you and the baby examined," said the doctor as he continued to evaluate Theo.

"Yes, you both should be looked at," Andries agreed. He whispered to Johanna, "I will pay."

"How will that help Theo?" Johanna walked over to Theo and moved the overgrown hair out of his eyes. Theo swatted her hand away. Johanna jumped back. Startled, she looked at Andries and the doctor—didn't they see? She didn't have tears this time, just an ongoing, overwhelming dread.

"I wouldn't rule out melancholia certainly after a tragedy. Your husband is acting in a way that is not typical for him?"

Andries and Johanna nodded. Theo stared sadly back at them both and huffed.

"Mr. Van Gogh, you are not feeling yourself? Would you describe how you feel?"

"I feel like I see where I want to go, but I can't get there."

"What about walking, Mr. Van Gogh? You have difficulty walking? I see you are running a fever."

Theo didn't respond.

The doctor continued. "Let's begin with a full physical and possible observation in the hospital. Is that agreeable with you, Mr. Van Gogh?"

"I agree, Doctor. I think we should leave him here under your care." Andries looked to Johanna for confirmation.

Theo exploded. "Will you all stop talking about me like I'm not here? Do I have a say in my own life anymore? Are you running everything?"

"No," Johanna jumped in. "Maybe we misspoke."

"Maybe we misspoke." He mocked her, sounding just like Vincent. Maybe he had the same thing as Vincent. *Oh God.*

"I think I have work to do, work you all need me to do, so you can all do what you want to do! And I don't have money to waste on more hospitals, *Doctor*!" He got up to leave the office.

"Theo, wait." Andries tried to take him by the shoulders. Theo violently shrugged him off. "Please, you're ill. You're right, you've been working too hard. Think...a place where you can get some rest, no baby crying..."

Theo screamed at the top of his lungs, "An asylum You won't commit me! There is no way in hell I will ever go to an asylum do you hear me?" He looked around the room, struggling to catch his breath. "Where is my hat?" He saw Johanna holding it and grabbed it from her.

"Theo, wait, please, the examination. Where are you going?"

Theo half staggered, half stormed out the office, the entire left side of his body lilting downward as his left leg dragged behind, his foot slanted to the side.

"Andries, go after him!" Johanna demanded, and Andries followed in Theo's path.

"Mrs. Van Gogh, this isn't typical behavior for your husband?" asked the doctor.

"No, for God's sake."

The doctor came over to her, looked in her face, and held up a tongue depressor. "Mrs. Van Gogh, do you have any blisters or rashes?"

"No. Not now, please." Johanna waved him off. "Just give me some medicine for him, please."

"You must get him back here immediately. Have you noticed any blisters or rashes on your husband?"

"No, I haven't."

"We should examine you and your son as soon as possible. In the meantime…" He handed Johanna a package of medicine. "A sedative will help him get some rest and lessen his agitation." Johanna took the bag.

"Mrs. Van Gogh?"

"Yes, I have to go, please hurry." Johanna moved toward the door. But the doctor gently blocked her path.

"Mrs. Van Gogh, please wait a moment."

"What is it? I have to catch up."

"You must not have relations with your husband until we know more."

"What did you say?"

"Mrs. Van Gogh, your husband is obviously ill. As a precaution, until we know more, please do not have marital relations with your husband."

No relations with my husband. No relations with my husband. It repeated in her brain as she stared at the doctor, trying to read his inscrutable face.

He said it calmly enough, matter-of-factly, she thought. The room was suddenly whiter, her head lighter.

"Yes, Doctor, thank you."

She raced the halls of the hospital looking for Theo and Andries. The slicing feeling in her chest pierced through to her spine. Sweat poured down her face into her eyes and onto her high woolen neckline, and the hallways of the hospital were an ugly blur of faces.

Johanna sat at the kitchen table feeding Willem. Focusing on his perfect face made her feel better. She was exhausted but smiled at her baby as he played with his food. He took the spoon as it neared his face and placed it in his mouth by himself. He drooled half the food down his chin. Johanna wiped it off. They started again.

The parlor and living areas were decorated with Vincent's work. All the furniture was stuffed into the bedroom, piled one piece on top of another. They had worked day and night, placing the paintings the way Theo wanted. She had been a complete partner to Theo, attaining his trust, and respect for her judgement. Nonetheless Theo was miserable with everyone, and she fought to hold her own mood.

Andries stood in the parlor, now transformed into a gallery for the grand showing of the selected paintings of Vincent van Gogh. He walked to the bedroom and poured a drink for Theo. He pulled a chair from the pile and sat next to Theo.

Theo lay in bed, fully clothed, staring blindly at the ceiling.

"Maybe I'll get the apartment back to a livable condition," Andries said.

"Do whatever you want," Theo barked.

"Stop sulking, Theo. It won't help anything, you know," Johanna whispered to herself. She smiled at the baby. What in the world was wrong with Theo? It was a bad, bad time, and no light at the end of this black tunnel. Thank the Lord, she and Willem hadn't caught the cold or influenza or whatever it was.

Theo was angry, mad over one thing or another. Or on a good

day, just sullen belligerence over God knows what. Nothing made him happy, or even consoled him. Everything right was wrong, everything wrong was normal. Always planning the exhibit, the new gallery, the move.

My world is collapsing, and everything is upside down. Why can't we go back to the way it was? What is Andries pleading with him about now?

"It's a good show, no matter what you think. It was well received," Andries said.

"No one came."

"Yes, they came."

"The right people didn't come."

"The writers were here," Andries said. "It will get written up."

"You fool, we won't get the right notices!"

"Theo, will you please stop attacking everyone!" Johanna said from the kitchen. "We're all on the same side here!" She was going to crack.

"I spent a fortune on frames alone. Oh, and thankfully I ran out of money before we could spend it on advertisements!" Theo shouted back.

"You did a good job. You know better than anyone how challenging the market is. There are a thousand painters vying for the attention of—" Andries was cut off by Theo's sudden screaming.

"This was…No, wait, this is…*This will forever be a total failure! I can't change it, so it will always remain a total failure!*" He screamed so loud he raised himself up, his voice howling with fury. "*That's how it will get written up, if it gets written up at all. You two promised you would help me. And if you don't stop lecturing me on how I should feel, I'm going to jump out the window!*"

When he was finished yelling, he slowly lowered himself back down.

Johanna put her hands over her ears, and Willem's eyes widened. He began a fearful cry and held his arms up and out to Johanna.

Johanna picked him up and bounced him around. She tried to hold back tears, but they flowed silently as she smiled at the baby.

Someone pounded on the floor or wall.

"Theo, for God's sake, you are exaggerating. I am trying. Jo is too. We are both trying to help." Andries sat on the bed next to Theo. They stared at each other for a long tense moment.

Andries rested his hand on Theo's shoulder. He stayed close all the time now, always reaching out to help Theo, even with small things like right now, rearranging the furniture in the living room back to its proper positions after the "failed showing" of Vincent's work. He led Theo around, holding his arm, never leaving his side, as if he were a cripple about to fall. The horror of watching Theo disintegrate into such profound unhappiness was unbearable. He wouldn't return to the doctor. He barely went out at all.

"If you need advertisements, I can pay. I have had offers for the Lautrec nude." Andries spoke softly.

"I know you mean well. I have to think about what to do next." Theo's voice had a fatalistic tone.

Johanna came in holding the baby and stood next to the bed. She reached for Theo. The four of them clustered together, everyone holding and touching someone. Deep frowns of concern creased all three faces. Only the baby was calm and serene.

Theo covered his face with his arm. He reached for Willem's head and cupped his hand around his skull.

"I think I'll take Willem out for a while," Johanna said. "Are you feeling better?" She held up her hand to feel his forehead but waited for his welcome, which didn't come.

"My fever is my best friend. It's how I know I'm alive."

"It's after dark, Jo," Andries said, pulling her to a stop. "Where are you going to go with a child at this hour?"

"Oh, I didn't realize."

"Would you two mind closing the door?" Theo snapped from the bed, meaning he wanted them to leave.

Johanna and Andries left the bedroom. They picked up one of the couches and began replacing the furniture around the main living room and the parlor.

"Just leave it! I'll do it tomorrow," Theo demanded from the bedroom.

"Yes, Theo, just a few pieces," Johanna said. "I need someplace to sit beside the kitchen."

They got a few pieces of furniture arranged.

Johanna and Andries sat in front of the fire, staring at each other. In that silent moment in front of the fire, she looked to her brother. Was it as bad as she felt?

Andries signaled his departure, buttoned his coat, patted his pockets, but didn't take his eyes off Jo. He seemed to be hesitating. Then they heard Theo. He was moaning loudly, then shouting in a voice that wasn't his own. Andries hesitated at the door, as if to go in to help settle Theo down, but instead placed a chair under the doorknob, so Theo wouldn't be able to leave the room without making noise.

Jo finally cracked. The panic she had been containing watching her beloved Theo transform into a bitter, mean-spirited man was too much to bear.

"Please, Andries, don't leave me alone with him."

Johanna woke from a deep sleep—what was that noise? She rose from the settee, her makeshift bed, and checked on the baby in his cradle near the fire. She heard Theo talking angrily in his sleep. She removed the chair blocking the entrance to their bedroom. Andries had told her to replace the chair after he went in to sleep next to Theo.

She touched Theo's head, checking for fever. His pillow was soaked, so she carefully put a towel under his head, trying to lift it without waking him. Her hands were wet with his sweat, so she left the door open and cleaned her hands in the kitchen. She checked on the baby again, still fast asleep. Checked the fire—still going strong.

She went out to the parlor, looking through all the work. She pulled her silk Japanese kimono tighter around her and looked at the piles of letters from Vincent and put them in a trunk. She looked at the drawing of Clasina again. If he loved her, why would he make her ugly?

She stared at the picture, wondering about the woman. She was ruined to start with, Theo had said. Why would he be so cavalier? How could Vincent have left her? Theo had said "babies." Was it in the letters? Poor Clasina. Looking at the drawing of her had become a compulsion.

Suddenly a dark shadow crossed over the drawing. She looked up just as Theo crashed his fist down on her face, screaming at her.

"*I told you not to come! You are not welcome here! Ever!*" Theo cried down at her, his face a horror of menace. She was staring at the ceiling. *Bang*, the floor was against her face, the fire inches away. She was on the floor…What was happening?

She put her hand up, but the breath was knocked out of her. Theo was hovering over her. He kicked her in the ribs. He kicked again. She heard herself screaming.

"Theo, stop, wake up!" she wailed up at him from the floor. Willem was shrieking, and like a magnet Theo turned toward the baby.

"*I told you to get out!*" Theo screamed.

"Wake up!" she shrieked again, but when he reached the cradle he kicked it over, and Willem tumbled out and across the floor, inches from the fire.

Silence. Time stood still. In the darkness she could see her son, motionless.

The fireplace poker was in her hand, and on her knees, she crawled and swung it at Theo, aiming for anything to connect to get him down and stop his madness. She cried out for Andries as Theo fell to the floor.

She crawled to Willem and clutched him and got to her feet. Theo was breathing, his eyes half open, making a horrible gurgling noise. He raised his hand like he was reaching for something or pleading for her.

She dropped the poker. And he moved in a flash and grabbed it and hit her from the floor.

She saw his face. In his eyes there was nothing she recognized as Theo.

He was pulling her down. He had caught her kimono. In seconds she would be on the ground with the baby, and he would kill them with the poker.

She kicked him square in the face. She screamed and kicked him over and over. The blows didn't matter. Theo got to his feet and grabbed her with one hand, the poker in the other.

He will kill us now, Johanna thought, and raised her free arm to block the blow, screaming.

"Theo! Theo, wake up!"

A shadow jumped on Theo, and both crashed to the ground in a thud and the sound of air rushing out of lungs. They struggled inches from the fire for the poker.

Andries got his knees on Theo's chest and the poker across Theo's throat and choked him unconsciousness—or to death—Jo didn't know which.

Andries

The police station was half-filled with a sad collection of unfortunate Parisians down on their luck. Johanna sat on the long wooden bench, her back against the wall, the baby sleeping at her breast, her vacant eyes staring into space. She was the obvious victim, perpetrator.

Everyone here was suffering from misfortune of some kind. Johanna stood out. Everyone noticed her, but she saw nothing, she was in shock. She didn't remember Theo's delusional attack on her and the baby, just hours ago. Her amnesia was a blessing. The room was dim due to the late hour, with pooling gaslight. Johanna's face showed growing bruises. Her left eye was beginning to swell shut. Her mouth had blood, dried and fresh, dripping down her chin, staining her coat and silk scarf. Bruises on her cheeks were beginning to bloom and swell.

"I understand, but we will not be pursuing this matter. Mr. Van Gogh is seriously ill, requiring hospitalization. I will arrange his transfer in the morning." Andries tried to sound professional, matter-of-fact, in charge. As if it were normal that a man would violently attack his wife and infant child.

"Yes, I'm working as fast as I can," said the gendarme, filling out paperwork.

Andries saw a dozen ladies, prostitutes, lined up across the station, waiting. Some had power, confidence, engaging with the officers, carefully edging for a favor. And some were broken, acquiescent. Finally, the officer handed Andries the papers they needed to leave.

Andries reached for Johanna on the bench.

"We're done here." He wrapped his scarf around her face, trying to obscure her wounds from the staring undesirables milling about the station.

"Come, you need a doctor."

She sat still, eyes closed, unresponsive. Andries leaned over to her and whispered in her ear, taking her arm. "Johanna, can you hear me? Open your eyes."

She said nothing. He tried to gently lift her, and she shrieked a loud, long, singing moan, growing in intensity. Something else was wrong with her that Andries couldn't see. He thought she might have a concussion but also something internal, cracked ribs? He released her.

She opened her eyes and sighed heavily. "Oh my God, what are you doing to me?"

"Johanna, you're in shock and I must get you to a doctor." He felt the stares from the line of ladies glaring at him, assuming he was the one responsible for her wounds.

A reporter entered the room and mingled with the ladies, jangling coins in his pocket and handing out cigarettes. One cocked her head toward Johanna and Andries. The reporter scanned the large room and quickly locked eyes on them. He gave a sniffing look in their direction.

"Let me lie down," Johanna said.

The reporter was looking at them without any hesitation or courtesy. Andries stared back, trying to intimidate him, but that only increased the reporter's curiosity. He buttoned Jo's coat and encouraged her to stand. The gendarme came over and looked at her closely.

"She needs to be looked at. I'll get help."

"I have a carriage waiting downstairs to take us to the doctor. Thank you. She's in shock. Please keep the reporter away." Andries cocked his head toward the man.

He stopped speaking in French and addressed Johanna in Dutch. "Open your eyes and get up slowly."

"I can't, it's too bright. Andries, please."

"Come, it's time for Willem's cold medicine, we can't miss an administration."

"Oh, yes." She squinted her eyes open and, with Andries's help, got up.

"Where is Theo? We can't leave him."

The cages for the prisoners were in the basement, out of sight.

"Theo is home. That's it, slowly. Quietly, don't wake Willem."

Johanna grimaced and moved like an old woman whose every step was agony. With one arm, Andries held Willem, and with the other, Johanna. Step by step, carefully they inched toward the door.

As they reached the door, Andries worried how he would get the door open without letting go of Jo and the baby.

"Good evening, sir. May I?" The reporter politely opened the door.

"Thank you." Andries spoke as if nothing at all was out of the ordinary.

"Excuse me, sir, what happened here tonight? You look like you need help. Oh, watch those steps…Here let me." The reporter took Johanna's other arm and helped her down the stairs.

"And what is your name, lovely lady?"

"My name is…my name is…Fleur."

"How lovely, Fleur. I see quite a bit of bruising there, don't I? Is this your husband, Fleur? Has he been drinking tonight?"

"For God's sake, you bloodsucker."

"What is your last name, Fleur? Who hit you?"

"Don't answer." Andries lifted Johanna into the carriage and placed the baby with her. He took cash out his pocket and smashed it at the reporter.

Andries held Johanna and Willem cuddled together, rocking with the swaying cab as they traveled the deserted cobblestone streets. Still the middle of the night, he thought. Only two hours spent at the station. Now, the doctor. Then back to her apartment. How to avoid the questions? Neighbors may still be up, gossiping about what just happened. Too many nosy neighbors, too many questions.

His thoughts flowed nonstop. We should go to my apartment. Stay away from Jo and Theo's for a few days, buy new things for

Willem. Go back when no one will be around. I need a story, something that will answer the screaming. Who was screaming exactly? What would be a good explanation? Theo was delirious with fever, still sick with grief over his brother's death.

And now what will happen to Theo? What a bitter reward from the universe.

Yes, keep it depression and illness. The tragic suicide of his beloved brother, causing depression, igniting an illness, causing delirium.

Andries heard the knock and got up to answer. He held Willem in one arm and opened his apartment door with the other. His hair was unkempt, he hadn't shaved.

Anna rushed in from the hallway with uncharacteristic quick movements and energy. She carried two heavy suitcases and a face stiff with fear. They didn't exchange greetings, just short bursts of questions for immediately needed information.

Anna began a scan around Andries apartment, where nothing had ever been out of place. Everything was now chaotic. She grabbed for Willem, relieving Andries. She held him and unbuttoned her coat simultaneously.

Andries helped her take it off. "Thank you for coming. I'm sorry I couldn't meet you at the train."

"I can manage myself," Anna said. "Where is Theo? Tell me everything." She held Willem out and turned him in the air, inspecting him. The baby grabbed a hunk of her yellow hair. Even though she dodged his grabbing fingers, he was faster.

She walked to the bedroom and found Johanna sleeping.

"Oh my God, what happened to her?" Johanna's face was swollen with purple bruises. One eye bulging, her mouth engorged, and cheeks swollen, she was almost beyond recognition. Andries stood behind, trying unsuccessfully to unhinge the fingers from Anna's hair.

"The doctor thought she might have a bruised rib, and shock, maybe, concussion and amnesia. She isn't making sense." Johanna rolled over and looked at them. Her hands automatically went to her ribs. Then she reached to Anna and for the baby. Anna carefully placed him on the bed next to her.

"Anna. Where is Theo?" Johanna asked.

"He's in the hospital," said Andries.

"Is he worse?"

"He's doing better. I'm going there now. Don't worry, everything's fine."

"Are you going to pick up the test results? The cough turned to a fever and…now he's…ahhh…" Johanna tried to get up, but the pain pulled her back down.

Andries sat in the chair next to the bed. He poured some syrup into a spoon and got Jo to take it. She closed her eyes. He gave Willem back to Anna.

"Was Theo attacked too?" Anna asked.

There was a knock on the door. Andries glanced back at the door and then to Anna.

"We won't answer that. Shush, don't make any noise," he whispered and held his finger up to his lips. Anna rocked Willem slowly, and he stayed quiet.

Moments passed in silence. Anna looked around. The small alcove kitchen was full of dirty dishes. Towels lay on the floor, leftover food on the table, half cups of tea, glasses of water, wine were on every surface. Piles of soiled baby clothes overflowed a hamper under an open window.

More rapping on the door. Anna could hear a muffled voice outside but couldn't make out who it was. Andries again put his finger to his lips.

"Are we not answering any knocks or just not this one?" she whispered when the knocking ended and footsteps receded.

"Don't answer the door, no matter who it is." He put on his coat and hat, ready to leave. At the window he looked down to the street.

"I have to make arrangements. Keep her quiet and in bed." He pointed to the liquid he'd just given her. "Give her more of this when she wakes up again. It's from the doctor, to help her rest. Her rib will heal only with rest."

"What is it?"

"A sedative."

"Oh, how much should I give her?" Anna said, looking at the bottle. "Where is Theo? Why does Johanna look like that?"

"You see why I need you, she can't be left alone, and I'm going to help Theo now. Just keep her quiet."

Anna sat down next to Johanna and felt her head. Jo smiled back at her.

"What happened, Johanna?" She looked closely at Johanna's face. Andries jumped next to Anna.

"No, please. Don't ask her that! She doesn't remember what happened. She's in shock. Wait to talk to her until I get back. And I'm sorry, thank you again."

"You're not telling me what's going on here, Andries."

"Please. I'm counting on you. We need someone we can trust."

"Why does she have amnesia? There really isn't any such thing, is there?"

"Yes, there is." Andries looked at the mess. "I hate to ask, but I'm desperate. Could you organize things here a little, but quietly?"

"Of course. You can count on me."

Andries left, to organize all that had to be done to protect his family. At the bank, while signing his name to cash withdrawals and close-of-account forms, he noticed he had filth under his nails. He realized he hadn't bathed, shaved, or changed his clothes since… before Theo went mad and attacked Jo, two days ago. He scanned himself, looking for something else wrong, blood, torn shirt. He noticed teeth marks on his hand, where Theo had bitten him. Theo's eyes had glowed red with the reflected fire, as he turned into a devil—Theo without reason, no longer Theo, now a monster.

Forty-eight hours later, Andries' panic still drove him through the arrangements. And the constant refrain in his head—Thank God I was there, thank God…to save her and the baby. He ticked off the next item—hire a private carriage, collect the monster.

Johanna

Jo woke up to screaming, and it was a moment before she realized it was her own voice. She tried to sit up, but pain burned in her ribs.

She saw Anna stir from sleeping on the sofa, and Andries woke in the chair. Willem fussed and cried. Johanna tried again to sit up but screamed again, pain doubling her over.

Andries and Anna ran in to the room. Johanna struggled out of bed with the lamp.

"What are you doing? Please lie back in bed." But Johanna pulled herself up and limped out of bed. Andries and Anna grabbed her on each side.

"Johanna, do you need the pot? Let me help you…Johanna?"

"Get me to the mirror," she said.

They helped Jo to the mirror and held up the lamp to her face. One eye was black and blue, swollen shut. Her lips were misshapen, swollen red. The rest of her face had more bruising on her head and cheeks.

She remembered more.

"Come back to bed…Johanna," they were saying over and over, but she couldn't move.

Finally, she found the courage to speak. She looked at Andries and couldn't recognize the expression on his face. He was crying.

"Did you kill him? Did you?" she shrieked again.

"No, he's in hospital."

"Oh my God...you...saw...This is true...He did attack us?

"Come back. Lie down. The baby needs you."

"Why would he do that?"

"I don't know."

Oh my God, he's gone mad like Vincent, she thought and burst into tears. They led her back to bed and placed the baby beside her. She stopped crying when she saw him, examining every inch of him, he wasn't bruised. Then they made her take medicine, and she lay back on the bed and sobbed.

19

Johanna

"I think I should tell him I forgive him. Families forgive, people who love each other forgive," Jo said to Andries.

Johanna's face was better, still blue and yellow, but face paint and rouge pots made her decent. Her rib was still sore.

"Yes, we all need forgiveness," Andries stated with extra compassion, a tone Johanna rarely heard from him. She knew he was hiding things from her.

"What's wrong with him?"

Andries was silent.

"Why did you bring him back to Holland? We are hundreds of miles from Paris. How are we going to care for Theo here?"

Andries remained silent.

They walked together up the endless steps into the Utrecht hospital. Her ribs throbbed. Andries held her arm, allowing her to set the pace.

Why would a hospital require sick people to climb stairs? She remembered to take shallow breaths, move slowly, and keep calm. Crying was as painful as laughing. The medication Andries gave her made her feel removed from herself. She was in someone else's nightmare, none of this was really happening. There would be an explanation, and she would fill in the puzzle pieces. All the bad things had happened, now good must follow.

"Whenever you don't respond to a question, I know the answer is going to be terrible."

Andries held the heavy hospital door open for her. "Utrecht is easier for his mother to visit, near home," said Andries. "It's affordable, we can't keep him at home in this condition. I'm sorry, Jo, the doctor is expecting us."

"Why would he attack us?"

No answer.

They entered the building together, hand in hand. The world inside dissolved into black-and-white, ugly, with rays of pale sunlight bleeding through small windows, creating hopeful patterns on the floor. Everything looked clean enough, yet the smell of ammonia was overpowering, unrelenting. They were given the number of Theo's bed.

As they walked deeper into the hospital, the shadows on the floor grew longer, reminding her of prison bars. They needed kerchiefs to block the increasingly foul smell. Andries *knew* the way. Johanna's mind went blank.

They found the bed number, she stared, what she was looking at? This couldn't be Theo, he seemed too small and frail. She looked around to ask for help, but there was no one except Mrs. Van Gogh. Theo's mother sat silently by the hospital bed. Andries kissed Mrs. Van Gogh gently on the cheek, and left, he said, to find the doctor.

Mother van Gogh was silently praying, her lips moving without sound. Then Mrs. Van Gogh nodded a silent greeting. Johanna moved closer to the bed. Theo looked at her, his face sunken, deformed with slack, sagging skin, bloodshot half-open eyes, squinting. Theo, devoured by disease.

He lifted his hand to her. She knew the hand, the long slender fingers reaching out to her. But she was frozen.

"Johanna." Weak, breathless, only an echo of the deep, vibrating voice of Theo, his hand held there in the air, wavering, waiting for her to hold. Mrs. Van Gogh clutched Theo's hand.

How could this happen so fast? We packed, traveled here. How long had he been alone like this? Why haven't they helped him? He is worse.

Mrs. Van Gogh said "Finally you are here. How is Anna? Little Willem?" She spoke in her monotone voice, but quieter. "I wonder if he knows me today." She placed Theo's hand gently back on his sheeted body. She dug into her bag and handed Johanna a small cloth holding a lock of Theo's hair. "For you," Mrs. Van Gogh said to Johanna.

Jo took in a deep breath to calm herself and instantly gagged on the smell. Andries returned with the doctor.

"Mrs. Van Gogh, I am sorry I wasn't able to meet you earlier," the doctor said. "But now you see how he is. We are doing the best we can for him." He began looking Theo over, then he turned to Johanna. She fought back panic. "How are you feeling, Mrs. Van Gogh? There are symptoms you must be watchful for, both you and the child. We will pray you haven't contracted the disease. We must remain hopeful."

Theo mumbled from the bed. The doctor wrote in a chart.

"He is suffering, you have to help him," Johanna choked out.

"We try to ameliorate the pain. He doesn't really know what is happening to him. That is why he attacked you. This has gone to his brain, causing the dementia, hallucinations."

"What has gone to his brain?" Johanna asked. She felt light-headed and like she might faint, and then a surge of prickly adrenaline. "What has gone to his brain?" she choked out again, feeling her throat close.

"I thought you understood. I am so sorry."

Andries jumped in. "Doctor, is there anything you can do for my sister? She's been confused for days…"

"Likely the result of the concussion."

"He attacked me. He attacked me and his son. Why did he?"

"Hallucinations. He didn't know what he was doing."

"Why hallucinations?"

"Theo has advanced syphilis," the doctor said. "I'm afraid he has had it for quite some time—years. And now the disease has traveled to his brain, causing the delusions and violent behavior, and now paralysis. It is the final stages. I'm afraid he will pass soon. There is nothing we can do but try to keep him comfortable. We will move him to the syphilis ward. He will be cared for."

"*No*, he does not have syphilis. He has a mental condition like his brother."

"This has progressed, as you can see. You might be a carrier. You are at risk and must be very cautious. The disease can be dormant for many years. Late-stage syphilis is not necessarily contagious, so we can still be optimistic. Offspring too can carry. You must be careful with your health—diet, fresh air, out of the city would be ideal. Blisters or rashes must be evaluated immediately. We have no cure yet but are working on one. Mercury treatments showed some promise. This has been an epidemic in Paris, many families affected, tragically. Mrs. Van Gogh, many do just fine. We don't know why. Hopefully you will be an old woman before this might cause you any issues. By then, there will be a cure."

"You said many do fine. He can get better?"

"No, ma'am. I'm sorry."

The baby, my baby, our baby. Syphilis. Syphilis, a death sentence. Johanna felt sweat pouring down her face, washing away the face paint. She was going to be sick.

They were talking, Andries and the doctor, but her head buzzed and she couldn't follow. She watched Theo, his head moving back and forth slowly on the pillow toward the direction of the voices.

The doctor was talking to her, blotting her head. He put something under her nose. "When did he get syphilis?" Jo asked, trying to sound businesslike but her voice cracked.

"Many years ago, Mrs. Van Gogh. The disease can last for many…"

She had stopped listening. Get out of here, get me out of here. Theo never wanted the hospital, didn't visit Vincent in the hospital, would rather be dead than get treatment in the hospital. Now dying in this hell. She snapped her head to the sound of Theo moaning. He was speaking gibberish. His mother held his hand and stroked his head. Jo swallowed her horror and picked up his other hand. "Theo…" she whispered close to his ear. His hand felt so familiar, but no comfort, cold and weak. Then she felt him squeeze her hand. God, was he still in there? Could he hear? Did he understand what was happening to him, what had happened?

"Does he understand he is…ill?"

"He understands he's very sick and he recognizes his mother and you, clearly. I believe he can still hear, and he can speak with difficulty. If you want to say something to him, you should."

She felt him squeeze her hand again. He knows I am here. I must tell him I forgive him.

"Theo…" She couldn't breathe. She tried again, squeezing his hand, and he squeezed back again. "I am sorry, Theo, you'll get better. Don't worry, we are here. The baby is well. I love you." That was all she could get out. His hand went limp in hers and let her go. She wanted to stay but couldn't wait to leave. When he appeared to be sleeping and stopped reacting to their voices, she nodded to Andries it was time to go.

Johanna and Andries left the building, walking slowly down the long entrance steps. She held her face down. She couldn't speak and walked leaning on Andries, with her limbs trembling. The thought gripped her, Theo was dying, and his death would be a blessing for him and agony for her. She fought back sobs with choking coughs as she tried to remain composed.

"Keep moving. Let's get home, Jo, don't stop. Let's go Jo," he was saying over and over.

She stared at her feet descending the steps. She breathed carefully to help forestall the surging emotion she couldn't control. At the bottom of the horrible steps, she dared look up. And she saw Fleur—an image so surprising and perfect. Her face coursed with a rush of warmth, and she began to sob uncontrollably.

Fleur ran toward them. She hugged Johanna gently. Andries had told her about the rib.

"I came as soon as I got the cable! My dear, dear friend, let me help you. Tell me what to do."

Andries looked at Fleur, said nothing, shook his head, and stared at the ground with tears in his eyes.

Syphilis. Her breath was gone, no air in, no air out for a harsh moment. And then it came back in loud, bellowing, keening sobs.

"Oh my God! Ah, what could be worse than this!" Johanna cried. Fleur cried too.

"I am so sorry," Andries said. "I'm sorry Theo is here. I just didn't think we could care for him at home. Johanna, I promise you I will take care of everything. I won't let this happen to you. I won't."

"What are you saying?" Fleur asked.

Andries was pleading. "Let's get home, please keep moving."

She would watch her beloved husband die here. Then she would die here…her precious son…die here. Her knees collapsed, and she dropped like a stone caught between Andries and Fleur. They held her arms and elbows, her rib burned like fire.

They struggled to hold her up, but she dragged Andries and Fleur down with her. Andries gave up last, placing Johanna on the pavement and kneeling beside her.

No more pleading to walk and get home. Still, together on the ground, weeping. Johanna felt like she was floating. The world tilted around her, everyone moving at odd angles.

She saw black shadows everywhere. She could see through the darkness that strangers were towering around them, but she could only hear a growing squeal, the noise growing louder and louder until it seemed like a freight train boomed in her brain.

Fleur cocked her head at the onlookers and scolded them to move on, her arms flying at them, angrily shooing them away.

A carriage appeared, the smell overpowering, large wheels and horse legs filled Johanna's dark vision.

Andries and Fleur lifted her. She felt nothing as she heard, "Utrecht Inn, please."

Agony organized her every day, watching her beloved Theo disappear inside the hell hospital. What had he ever done to deserve this horrible death?

His cold, limp hand—it was the only part of him she could recognize. Johanna wore gloves and was covered in a white sheet for protection. She knew the sheet was pointless. But there were often horrible messes around Theo.

Theo breathed, slowly, one breath clearly perceptible from the next. Inhale, pause, exhale, pause. His chest was a hollow cavity, his eyes were half open. He didn't appear to look at anything. Fleur pulled back the curtain that created the hospital room where Theo lay dying.

Jo closed her eyes. Fleur was here, it was safe to sleep a moment. Johanna dozed in the chair, head nodding, chin down to her chest.

The room is dark with only firelight. They sit in the parlor, kissing. Theo, a silhouette, his arm wrapped around her waist, stands up, offers his hand, and she takes it. They stand together in front of the warm fire, faces so close, so tempting for another kiss.

But it's time to go. Where, she doesn't know. "It is time to go," he says, stroking her face, down to her neck, and her body hums peacefully with pleasure. "One more minute by the fire."

He turns her face to the light of the fire. "Johanna, isn't it so beautiful, all the colors." But she wants to look at his face, not the fire-light, so handsome, his cheekbones high, and his eyes serene.

Then his hand circles her neck, and with all his strength he strangles her, lifting her off the ground, his face so close.

She woke with a startled breath. The same dream again, over and over. When would that dream ever end? That wasn't even what had happened. This sadness would never end.

Had Theo known this wretched death in a stinking hospital was coming? No, he would have thrown himself in the canal.

She remembered the strange things Theo had said and done after Vincent died and he began his own decent. The snarling monster he slowly became, and her ignorance beat her like his fists—she couldn't get the horrid visions to stop repeating over and over. She never dreamt Theo had syphilis—and the horror she felt thinking of when and how he had contracted such a vile disease. She realized, painfully, this explained everything about Theo's final days. The wearing down of his body, the declining mental and emotional health, and finally delusions. Had she been such a fool not to see? Or too much in love to really look? It was all so fast—and so shockingly awful, she wanted to hide.

When Theo was quiet, she would sit motionless trying to forgive herself her failure and confusion. Her thoughts drifted to the future without him, and the feeling of disloyalty and guilt swept over her. She forced her mind to empty and stare at the pitiful sight of Theo living in the hell of this betrayed body. *What am I going to do? How will I pay the bills? Where can we live?* She had found her true self in Paris, an exciting place full of change and art. Her life with Theo was centered on his love of art, which she came to share. She imagined her love of art a lifelong dedication, as her love for Theo. But Paris was expensive. She couldn't go back to her parents' house. Her independence was paramount. Could she do what other widows did? Open an inn or boarding home? What about all the paintings, Willem's legacy, all that was left of Vincent and soon all that would be left of Theo? Paris was indeed expensive, but it was also the home of modern art.

She heard the whispers of her parents—for Andries to dispose of the paintings. She was unable to sleep, alternating nightmares of Theo's sunken, tortured face calling for her, and her father throwing Vincent's paintings on a bonfire. She would wake up nauseous, sweaty. Andries wouldn't let them destroy the paintings, would he? Would he even consider such a disloyal travesty? The paintings lived in her heart and must be saved at all costs.

PART 4

Holland, 1891

20

Jo sat quietly in the bedroom in the Utrecht Inn which she and Fleur had been sharing during Theo's final days at the hospital syphilis ward. The air was stale in their room, as if the worn-out innkeeper never opened a window or beat the rug. An innkeeper—was this in her future too, one of the ways widows made ends meet? She took the brandy Fleur offered, relishing the dulling of her mind. Sleeping Willem lay on the tightly made bed. Making room for her, Fleur put Willem in the cradle.

"You lie down yourself. Let's have nap before the trip back to Amsterdam for Theo's memorial." She covered Willem with the crocheted blanket Theo's mother had given as a birth gift.

Jo lay back and stared at the ceiling, sleepless. Her thoughts were a jumble of past and future, shrouded with black. Fleur extinguished the lights and lay down next to her. "Jo, do you want to stay with me in Amsterdam?"

"Thank you, Fleur, a night or two, but then I am going back to our apartment in Paris." There was much to do to put her life back in order and move the pieces into place. She would take up where Theo left off.

Fleur sat up on the bed. Even in the dim light, Jo could see Fleur, always beautiful, looked a woman who had walked a hundred miles. Her upswept blonde hair was matted flat, her eyes, cheeks, lips usually beautifully lightened with her expert hand, were pale with tiny lines.

"Paris…alone?" She sounded alarmed but recovered and put her arm around Jo.

"I have Willem. Andries will be nearby most of the time." She took a deep breath waiting for Fleur to cut right to the core of her Paris plan. She didn't want to debate her decision. Fleur didn't know the art world like she did.

"Theo didn't sell any of Vincent's paintings," Fleur said, kindly. "It just was the timing. But what has changed? You will be alone."

"I won't starve, Fleur. Just because you didn't like Paris. Vincent found himself there. The art world is there. I need to be there."

"I did like Paris—I discovered a lot about myself there too. I brought what I liked about Paris back with me. I understand your impulse to pick up all the pieces and move forward…but Jo…"

"Don't argue with me," Johanna snapped, and Willem stirred in his cradle.

"I am not arguing with you. I just have some questions. You will need help…."

"Yes, you are arguing with me, and I don't need help. What happened to, 'no one is better than us?'" Johanna turned her back to Fleur and stared into the darkness. "I'm sorry. Everything has been so horrible."

The memorial reception was mostly family with a few of Theo's old friends from Paris. Henri, Emile, a handful of others. She felt unbearable pain. She moved in slow-motion and mostly let Andries, Fleur, and Anna do what needed to be done.

She hadn't seen Paris in months since taking Theo to Utrecht.

Vivienne held Henri's shoulder. He leaned on his cane, now

more than just a prop, sadness on his face and sagging shoulders. The changes to the Paris crowd had not been kind, Johanna thought.

Emile stood apart, alone, and stayed that way, always at the edge of the group.

They gathered at the Bonger Insurance Agency. She had the main office cleared, everything stuffed into the back rooms. It wasn't unheard of, a reception at an office. Unusual perhaps. Her father stood stiffly, but polite, bruised by the bullying of his wife and children.

They all stood holding glasses of tea and talking softly to one another. A small buffet sat on the large, ornate reception desk. Fleur baked some of her famous Paris pastries, all of which were devoured first. The space was bright with sunshine spilling through the large room.

Fleur sat between Mother van Gogh and Mrs. Bonger, holding Willem. "Mrs. Van Gogh, are you hungry?"

"Why are we here? This is an office, isn't it, the Bonger family business? It's the money, I guess."

"I made the cakes myself. Let me bring you something?" Fleur offered.

"We offered the house," said Johanna's mother. "But Johanna thought this was so much closer to the train, for the people from Paris, the artists. I know it is strange, in a way."

"This is my third loss in…how many years? My husband first, then two of my sons in six months."

"I am so sorry, this must be unbearable for you," said Johanna's mother.

"Theo held us together. It is a blessing Father went first. We shouldn't bury our children. I live under a dark cloud. It follows me everywhere." Jo let Fleur respond to all the statements and questions.

Jo wandered the reception accepting condolences. Thank God everyone had the good taste not to bring up the tragic illness at his end, she thought.

Henri approached Johanna with Vivienne at his side, Emile behind. Jo had always liked Henri the most. *I'm glad he came*, she thought. He seemed sympathetic, sincere, and she had missed seeing everyone these past months.

Vivienne and Henri both looked worse for wear. Vivienne's red hair showed brown roots. Her ivory complexion was tinged yellow around the eyes, and reddish-brown blemishes bled through the white powder on her face. Her round eyes had fallen, with the upper lids dragging down. Wrinkle lines bled into her mouth. Crimson lip paint caked into them. The decline was quick, Johanna thought.

From a distance, Henri looked dashing in his odd way. But up close, even his beard couldn't hide his face, bloated with alcohol. She imagined his hands would be moist and puffy, but he wore light woolen gloves.

Emile was handsome as ever, but he had lost his youthful energy. Why? She knew Emile and Theo were not especially close. Maybe it was something else. Maybe he wasn't selling. Still, it was good for him to be there.

Gauguin wasn't there. *Why should he live, and Theo be dead* she thought, fighting anger.

"How are you, Johanna?" Henri said in French. "A terrible, terrible loss. I am destroyed by this."

Here in Holland, she hadn't spoken French in many months. She felt hopeful for a moment. Maybe it was the French, it reminded her of Theo and Paris. Henri stared at her deeply, with true empathy. His face evoked so many beautiful, happy memories of evenings in Paris. Looking back, it was a perfect life—but now it was all dead, all the good things, gone forever. *The sadness will last forever*, Vincent had said on his deathbed.

"Yes, terrible," Jo said. "He's at peace now." Andries came over and shook Henri's hand, barely nodding to Vivienne.

"I know you did the best you could for him," Henri said.

"I hope so. Thank you for coming. I know Theo would be pleased to have you here. Your friendship meant so much to him."

"Theo was honest, a good soul. I admired him. A tragedy, and so fast, after Vincent. Theo touched so many lives—a pioneer in modern art. There is no one to replace him."

"There are so many dealers," said Johanna. But Henri was right, none like Theo.

"You have all the paintings, Johanna?

"Yes, in Paris."

"Thank God. I wondered. Andries told us neither your family nor the van Goghs wanted them." He was right, the families were not interested in preserving the paintings. "What will you do now?"

"I will go back to Paris and pick up where Theo left off with Vincent."

"You plan to sell Vincent's work?" Vivienne asked, amazed.

Henri ignored Vivienne and kissed Johanna on both cheeks, hugging her tenderly. "I am at your service, for anything. I am sorry. You are determined—you are thinking big, revolutionary, I dare say. I like that." He worked his way over to Mrs. Van Gogh but turned back twice to look at Jo.

Emile walked closer to Johanna. He was weeping.

Andries put his arm around Emile. "Emile."

He is crying, this is too much. Johanna was fighting for control herself.

Emile held out his hand for Johanna to take. She did, and he fell into her arms and embraced her in an overwhelming hug.

"I am trying to recover, but I can't." He sobbed into her shoulder.

Johanna let him for a moment and then gently pushed him back. "Time, Emile, you need more time." She patted his back.

"I can't paint anymore. I miss him so much."

Of course, he means Vincent, she thought. He's talking about Vincent. Vincent again, still dead. Vincent and *Emile,* she had forgotten. So far away now—Emile's unrequited love for Vincent.

"How will we ever recover from this endless disaster?" Emile said. "This epidemic…it is…evil. I'm heartbroken," Emile said. "I loved them. I knew their genius." He was breaking down.

He tried to collect himself. "I want to prepare a show of Vincent's work, in Paris. I need help with money to rent a good space." It was rude to bring up business at a time like this. But because of his deep love and conviction, it felt appropriate. Her funds were limited, but a show in Paris would be worth the money. She could invite all the dealers who were displaying more modern work. One of them would be interested, she knew it. Vincent would have a gallery space in Paris, and she could sell paintings. And she would not starve. A plan was coming into focus. She had to succeed for her son and to make the van Gogh brothers live again.

21

1892 Paris

This was the meeting Jo had been nervously waiting for. The most important, successful art dealer in Paris, Durand-Ruel was the dealer who could make a career. Underwriting, world sales, beautiful exhibition space. Theo had corresponded with the owner, Paul Durand-Ruel before his illness. This was who she was going to meet now, to light a fire in the city of lights for Vincent.

Waiting in the windowless reception room of Durand-Ruel, she recognized many of the paintings on the walls: Monet, Seurat, even a Gauguin. All painters Theo used to handle. The familiarity of it all, the paintings, the gallery, put her at ease. Vincent belonged here, she could see it, she could feel it. This would be a great new beginning for the van Gogh brothers' legacy. A young man came out to bring her into the interior of the amazing gallery.

"Ah, Mrs. Van Gogh," the assistant said, while leading her out of the reception toward Durand-Ruel's office. "First, Madame, let me say, please accept our condolences." He half-bowed.

Mr. Durand-Ruel's office was opulent and housed many antiques and more paintings. He seemed a kindly older gentleman with crinkles at his eyes, a sincere smile and very warm hand. He offered her a seat not in front of his desk, but on the settee, then sat next to her under a magnificent seascape she thought was a Boudin.

"How is it, Mrs. Van Gogh, that we have never met? This seems impossible to me."

He was charming, and she felt an equal. "My son, Willem, keeps me very busy. And Theo's work with Vincent."

"Yes, Theo was incredibly special. Completely dedicated…I always admired him, and you know…he gave me quite a run for my money!" He gave a good-natured laugh. "I am deeply saddened by all this tragedy. Life, ah…you must be so grateful to have your son… and Vincent's namesake, wonderful."

"Yes, he is a gift. You have a magnificent gallery, Mr. Durand-Ruel."

"Thank you, Mrs. Van Gogh, it has been my life's work."

"Thank you for seeing me. I found correspondence between my husband and yourself regarding a possible exhibition of Vincent's work. I was hoping to continue this discussion with you." Was she moving on to business too quickly? Should she let him take the lead?

"Yes, we did have discussions some time ago. I only know a few of Vincent's paintings. Camille Pissarro, our client, was very fond of Vincent personally and an admirer of his work. He also spoke with me about Vincent—did you know?" He didn't wait for Jo to answer. "I am not able to create this exhibit for you now, Mrs. Van Gogh. I wouldn't rule it out in the future. My gallery is full, and a long schedule before me."

This was not what she had expected. In one minute, a total change had come over the meeting. At first so personal and warm, now suddenly all business, hard, sharp, direct. She felt her shoulders slumping with disappointment, but quickly straightened up.

"I don't understand. Vincent is so special, his work so unique. I know a gallery like this is busy, but you won't rule out a show in the future. How far in the future, do you think?" She tried to keep the conversation alive to change his mind, or at least get more information.

He nodded, as though he had expected her to protest, and he understood.

"I don't know what the future holds. But I have advice, if I may."

"Please," Jo responded. She worked hard not to sound deflated

"I would like to help. You control the collection, and sadly there will be no more van Goghs. Most established galleries, should they represent your collection, will require an exclusive arrangement with you. You control all the paintings, so they will not benefit with only a few. You understand they will want all the paintings and to establish all the prices, the pattern of showing and selling. Are you prepared to grant control over the entire collection?" He paused and she met his eye.

"No. Control of Vincent's work must stay with the family."

"I understand how personal this is for you. Art is a reflection of the artist, the deeply personal view. Vincent's art is so new. No longer art painted as 'descriptive,' he is expressive."

"Yes, I agree completely. This is why I love Vincent's work, and the world will love it too."

"The world may take a lifetime. I must tell you, and I tell you this to help. I am on your side in this. I always side with artists. This is painful to say, but you should be aware many here in Paris," he paused again, "feel Vincent's work is very specific to his health difficulties."

She knew the rumors about Vincent and his "difficulties." But she didn't think this was cause for him to be dismissed outright.

Jo replied, "He has reinvented the Dutch school. These who complain about his temperament do so only to diminish his work. I cannot allow less talented, less productive artists besmirch Vincent's achievements. You must acknowledge his achievements are monumental." She must sound shrill and defensive.

He held up his hand and smiled, shaking his head.

"I apologize," Jo said. "I'm sorry, thank you for your honesty."

"True or not, you will need to address and change the perception.

I will, if you like, hang a few van Goghs here. Not to sell, but to showcase and help build Vincent's name. Pissarro says I must see the landscapes from the South of France."

"Thank you, you are kind. I would appreciate any effort on your part. Theo's and Vincent's friends will stage a show soon. Henri Toulouse-Lautrec and Emile Bernard. Please come."

"I will visit. It is a pleasure to meet you. And if I can be of any further help, please don't hesitate." He bowed to her.

"Thank you again for your time, and your honesty."

She walked home, worrying. She needed more money. Theo's beautiful apartment was expensive. Paul Durand-Ruel—why had she been so optimistic? He knew everything she was going to say before she even sat down. She still had another opportunity. She would invite all the dealers to Emile's show. Not all of them would see Vincent's difficulties, but some of them would recognize his greatness. If she could sell some paintings, she would get more time in Paris to light Vincent's star.

The street to Pere Tanguy's shop was crowded and filthy. Men loitered about smoking and yelling at one another. She dodged her way down the street and felt greasy grime grow on her face.

Although she had never met him, Tanguy and Vincent had been close friends. He sat outside the door in Montmartre in a small chair, his shop of paintings, art supplies, books, and prints all flowing outside his store, occupying the dirty sidewalk.

"I heard you were back, I am sorry for your loss, Madame van Gogh. Terrible. I pray you got my letters. I am too ill to travel these days."

His voice was very guttural and baritone despite his small stature. Grizzled with a deeply lined face, he looked old, but not frail. He was a local hero in Montmartre. He had been part of the communard revolution and somehow, he survived the battles and prison. Now he was a paint supplier and a minor art dealer. He'd also been Vincent's dear friend. He rose quickly from his chair, and they entered the store.

"What can I help you with, Madame van Gogh?" His voice boomed in the old musty shop.

"Please, call me Johanna."

He offered her a seat. There was barely a spot to walk, much less sit down. She hated to brush the seat before she sat, and didn't, focused instead on the Cezannes, Japanese prints, and paintings she did not recognize which hung sparkling color from floor to ceiling, others leaned against walls. He displayed several van Goghs, which she imagined Vincent had gifted him. One was new to her, a portrait of Pere in this shop, prominently displayed. It perfectly captured the individuality of the man. Another was a floral, possibly painted in Theo's apartment. The surprise of seeing them enveloped her.

"I need advice," Jo said. "I have been to see Mr. Paul Durand-Ruel." And many other dealers in Paris, but she didn't bother to mention.

"Ah," Pere interrupted, "He won't give Vincent an exhibition? I suppose no one else will either."

"You are very direct."

"Did he give you a reason?"

"He has many committed shows and several of his other painters are concerned that Vincent's state of mind at the time…" She faltered for the words, but Pere waved her off.

"He was being honest with you. Many painters here think Vincent was a colorist. But a madman for color. And his work a product of that insanity—here in Paris that is."

"But some admire him. You for instance, you loved Vincent's work. Lautrec called him a genius! Why does Paris reject Vincent's work?"

"The art world is filled with many bourgeoise who despise

audacity," he said. "They are sheep in their hearts. Vincent was my
comrade. And his story, his heart and mind. They are afraid of this
mad painter." He lit an already half-smoked cigarette, making the air
in the cluttered shop thicker. He blew out a hypnotic shade of blue-
grey smoke and dust particles swam and swirled through the cloud.

"Why do you want to promote Vincent?"

She didn't expect a challenge from him. "I am the executor of
Theo's estate. All the paintings belong to our son, Willem."

"You don't answer my question, Johanna. I was an admirer of
your husband's work too. Why do you love Vincent's art yourself?"

"I just look and love, it's instantaneous. It keeps me close to
Theo. It's my purpose. I must get Vincent and Theo the legacy they
deserve, for their sakes and for my son. If I fail, Vincent will wallow
in an abyss and my son's mother is…I am…nothing.

"You are never nothing. In my life I have seen the boldest ideas
born not of thought but of feeling and intuition. What else do you
admire in Vincent's work?"

"Simple lines, color, expression of feeling. I look at his work
and I feel sadness, sometimes exhilaration. It is real, real people. I
feel when one has seen a van Gogh one cannot look at painting the
same way again. He reinvented the language of art. Vincent was the
beginning of a new movement."

"The movement—it's the future. I will tell you this, Johanna.
Have you heard of the American painter, Mary Cassatt?"

"I know her work a little." She had just seen a few at Durand-
Ruel's gallery.

"Mr. Durand-Ruel is a good man, very dedicated to art—and
he doesn't wish anyone ill, except us old communards. It took him
decades to build the Barbizon school and now it is taking him a
long time to build the impressionists and modernists. So much, too
much is based on impressions, personalities, image. This is France
after all. You know, despite his lovely home and galleries he was almost bankrupt. Because he gives money to all his painters –Monet,

Renoir, Pissarro, even Degas—otherwise they would starve. All his investment, poof! This must all sound familiar to you, Johanna. Without sales, Durand-Ruel was on the precipice of bankruptcy and no hope in sight to make money. For the artists, some might starve. Others of course come from wealthy families."

Johanna struggled to understand the relevance of this.

"But enter the American, Mary Cassatt. She has rich friends in America, and she is arranging sales for the artists in that country. The Americans, they don't insult the work, they buy and pay well. And they buy on Miss Cassatt's word."

"You think I should go to America?" She wasn't grasping the point of his story. What did he mean?

"No, I have confused you. What will you do, Johanna?"

"Emile has arranged a show for Vincent. I am hopeful he will sell. I have invited all the dealers in Paris. You should have received an invitation."

"If you don't sell, what then?"

"If I can't sell Vincent's paintings here, I image I will return to Holland, maybe open an inn." She felt blasphemous saying such a thing. Vincent had said going home meant failure. She felt the same way.

"Yes, exactly. You must realize failure surrounds us, and once the stink of it is on us it can last for a long time, until it doesn't. It may take years or decades to succeed. There is a world outside of Paris. That is my point. I always say, never underestimate a woman. You will find a way to make Vincent's star rise with the Dutch and then you can return to Paris if you want."

A lifetime, did she have that much time to give?

This was her last chance to stay in Paris. She trusted Emile but didn't know what to expect. He had chosen Le Barc de Bouterville to present Vincent's work, because the gallery was dedicated to post-impressionist paintings. Sixteen of Vincent's paintings were hung.

Jo recognized the painter Edgar Degas immediately. He was not a bohemian. He dressed like a distinguished gentleman. He was accompanied by Mary Cassatt, the American painter Pere Tanguy had talked about. She was most elegantly dressed in Paris silk with a velvet hat, matching bag and gloves. She and Degas strolled slowly around the room, leaning close to the paintings and talking quietly together. Jo was hoping to introduce herself. She looked for Emile to bring her over. Then Degas bought a van Gogh, a floral still life—right off the wall! Edgar Degas, the most prominent modern French painter! Johanna smiled to herself. She was elated and walked over and introduced herself.

They were pleasant, and when they left she chatted endlessly with whomever was around her. Henri was there with Vivienne in tow, visibly sick, pasty, with a relentless wet cough.

As the day wore on fewer people entered the gallery, not good for an opening. Independent gallery owners tried to engage her. They wanted money up front to stage a show for Vincent. She didn't have the money to spare, and they would not negotiate against future sales. She watched the street. Often passersby looked in but didn't enter.

After a few hours of lengthy and eventually forced conversation with Emile, she walked outside to get some air. A fashionable couple stopped for a moment and looked in the window of the gallery. She smiled at them, hoping to meet their eye and invite them in.

"Shall we?" said the man. The woman peered in and shrugged.

"It's empty." She squinted and looked longer at the painting of the peasant family sitting around a table, *The Potato Eaters*.

"It looks very grim," she said.

"He was mad, you know." The man answered. "That is why you feel sad looking at them." The woman laughed, and they walked away.

A wave of loathing crashed over Johanna, so overwhelming she had to restrain herself from running screaming after the couple. Like a dam breaking, pain came flooding back to her. Anger lit her energy. She walked back into the gallery, accepting for the first time what everyone else knew.

"Emile," she said without thinking, "I hate that they laugh at Vincent's work."

Emile stood tall and strong.

"Vincent needed a champion in life, and he needs one in death as well," he said. She saw his face soften, waiting for this to sink in.

Soon Fleur and Andries entered the gallery. Fleur had come for the opening of the show to support Jo. She had a quizzical expression on her face as she looked around the lightly attended space. She saw Johanna and walked over. They kissed silently.

"You will find another way," Fleur said casually. That was Fleur, always to the point, always right. "I will help you. We will do this together."

Andries shook hands with Emile, kissed Johanna and whispered he had a buyer for her apartment. Which meant she would have cash to buy a home for herself and Willem. Not enough for Paris, but enough and more for Holland.

She would find another way, like Fleur said. She would take a part of Paris back with her. She pushed it all into the back of her mind and said a prayer that a plan would come.

At the end of the day, she told Emile and Henri her new plan.

"I plan to buy a home, a boardinghouse in Bussum. Everything will travel with me. Then I will pick up where Theo left off. I will hang Vincent's star. Selected paintings will hang at the inn, until I can arrange proper showings in galleries. Then the creation of a museum in Amsterdam," Johanna continued.

"The work belongs in Paris. I just need money for more gallery shows—you know Paris," Emile said. "Vincent is getting some attention from critics, and he continues to attract the avant-garde group. Hiding the work in Holland is not an answer," he said, shaking back his long hair.

"Perhaps they want to see him just to copy him," Jo snapped. This was the worst nightmare of all. Not that his legacy would be ignored, but that it might be stolen.

"Hiding the work in Holland is not good for the cause," he said. "Vincent is not an attraction for bourgeois country bumpkins who don't know art."

"An Amsterdam museum. A good ending," Henri said and erupted in a wet cough, grabbing his silk handkerchief.

Vivienne had been listening in. "A Vincent van Gogh inn? Ha, you are joking," she sniped.

"The air in here...so much dust." Henri waved his hand and leaned back against an empty wall.

"Careful, Henri." Andries offered his arm. "Hold on." Henri wiped his face, opened his hollowed-out cane, and drank deeply from the flask inside.

Jo thought the boarding house was a good plan. First and foremost, she had her son's health and her own to protect. Clean country air, away from this filthy city where an influenza epidemic might break out. The second was money. She would need an income. She couldn't leave her son alone, so she needed to make money at home. She could do translations, but that would not pay enough. Taking in boarders was a very common way for widowed women to support themselves. But her inn wouldn't be just any inn, it would showcase the van Gogh work and cater to art lovers, with lecturers, salons, and the fabulous work of Vincent van Gogh.

"Dealers open their homes to show their collections. This isn't so novel an idea," Jo said.

"I agree. But why not keep looking for a dealer here in Paris?" Henri asked gently. He seemed unconvinced.

"Paris—with whom? Look around, Henri, we are the only ones here. Do you know a trustworthy dealer who wants nearly eight hundred of Vincent's pieces? I can't lose control of the legacy."

"Leave the work to professionals, Johanna." He was sounding reasonable still. "Paris controls the art markets, the journals, the galleries, the critics. Paris is where legend is made," said Henri.

"I understand, but this is a new day, a new circumstance."

"I am surprised at you, Andries, allowing this travesty of guess-work," Vivienne said.

"I don't care what you think, Vivienne," Andries responded, quick and sharp.

"Stop it, both of you!" Henri slowly got to his feet. "We must all jump in, do our part. I can talk to other dealers."

"Talk to dealers if you like but I will hold the art." Johanna said.

The group was quiet for a moment. Until Vivienne broke the heavy silence.

"Johanna, you should listen to Henri. He knows what to do," Vivienne said.

Jo had let so much pass with Vivienne, always turning the other cheek on her petty, harmless barbs, keeping the peace among friends. Vivienne had wanted Theo, too. Now with Theo gone the rivalry should be as well. "I know this is not how things are done," Jo said. "But I feel that I have a plan. I think the Dutch will be more open to Vincent's work."

Vivienne smiled and said "Well maybe you do have a new idea. I'd like to see a woman take on the man's world. Perhaps you will succeed after all."

"You can't stop me." Jo said. Her mother, holding Willem on her lap, was quiet in the corner.

"No, Johanna, I can't. I can reason with you." Father used his soothing voice. "We only want to help with this ordeal. You were a gifted student, pursued what you wanted, and we allowed that. You never were interested in what was expected, in what we wanted. You reached beyond what is normal for a young woman. But we must keep your reputation, your future intact. Let's look objectively at your circumstances."

"I don't need to review my circumstances. I need help. I need the Bonger Building basement to store my husband's and Vincent's collections. That doesn't seem too much of a sacrifice."

"Yes, and then what?"

"I will develop relationships with modern galleries here in the north and send Vincent's paintings to all the shows. With the sale of the Paris apartment, I will buy a home. Everything will come with me. The inn will showcase Vincent and will be a dramatic standing retrospective."

"We expect you to move home with us."

It felt like the same old fight she had endured with them for years. She folded her hands on her lap. Her father waited for her to fight back and when she didn't, he turned to Andries. "Is there any chance for a sale of the collection?"

"I don't think a sale is in the cards just now," Andries said, his voice a monotone.

"What about another dealer taking the collection? Andries, you know the community."

"We have hundreds of paintings. One would need to begin on a smaller scale. There is dealer, Ambroise Vollard, he might try his hand at a few."

"What is the point of selling a few?" their father asked.

"If those sell, he will want the entire collection. It is an endeavor requiring—" But Father cut him off.

"The idea is to dispose of the collection. Why is Vincent's work not popular? I trust you can be objective."

"I am in the good company of those who always admired—no, revered—Vincent's work."

"You both hold a romantic bohemian ideal. Is it your opinion Johanna should burden her life memorializing a failed lunatic painter?"

"Johanna is the executor of the estate, mother of the heir. She must decide what to do with Vincent's work. I have releases from the van Gogh family giving Johanna all the works."

"I would throw all the paintings away," Father said. "This is a burden no one should bear. In time a respectable man could be in her future."

"No!" Jo said. "I am the one who decides what do with the estate. This is a man's life's work! And my husband's as well. Their purpose, their meaning is now mine." She looked at her mother who stayed quiet, never saying what she thought.

"But Johanna, this is not a coherent plan for your life and son. You understand it will be hard to turn back from this decision." He thought he had summed it up well and folded his arms across his chest.

Andries, unusually quiet, stared out the tiny window. Her father was annoyed, angry, domineering. She had seen it all before and didn't care.

"Allow me use of the basement temporarily. If you do not, I will make other plans, incurring additional expense."

Her mother jumped in before another word could be said. "Why not allow Johanna to use the basement, dear?"

Her father went silent and left and left the room.

22

Theo's death left an empty space in Johanna's heart. His mission to make Vincent famous became her own. It drove her. His demand out of the blue... *'Promise me.'* Planning Vincent's future became a guard against the darkness breaths away.

She had the paintings, which consoled her. They were a part of her, filling the vast nothingness of a lost woman. She would not let disappointment turn to bitterness and overtake her. She had learned from the Paris failure. She picked up where Theo left off by establishing relationships with modern galleries across the north of Europe and sent paintings to group art shows and exhibitions. But sales were modest, prices low.

The housework required for running her inn was her existence. Her life had collapsed into a daily routine of chores, drearier than any housewife's, and she was chained to everything she despised. But her mind was occupied with Vincent and art. This was all a means to glorious end, she had no doubt. Her only doubt was in her ability to find a way to ensure Vincent's legacy. If she didn't, the tragedy of their deaths would remain forever.

There must be more she could do for Vincent's memory. But what? The question settled in the back of her mind as she went about her daily tasks.

Emile had said Vincent needed a champion in death. She knew whatever was to be done, she was the only one to do it. Why should other artists with less talent occupy museum walls? Redemption became her obsession. She wouldn't stop until every major museum in Europe hung a van Gogh.

How much time was left before the dreaded disease struck her down? Had Theo infected her? There was no definitive answer. Syphilis was raging in Paris and doctors had many theories. Only time would tell for sure.

Fleur was always there, helping her put her future together, piece by piece. Finally, as the months ticked by, life settled down and Johanna felt her future emerging from the blackness of terror. Her son wasn't sick, and she wasn't either. They might be spared.

Outside of Amsterdam, few had heard about the final horrors of the van Gogh brothers. She hid the truth about Theo's disease and death. She lied about Vincent's madness, too. He was an epileptic, she told people who asked. The asylum doctor had said so. She thought this was more acceptable than the continual charge of lunacy. She needed to protect Vincent's image and the paintings.

New painters stepped into the spotlight all the time, even here in the Netherlands. There was only so much time to create the first impression. If this was squandered in haste or poorly thought out, long years of failure could await until another opening in time.

She found joy in watching Willem change as he grew. He had lanky, long, lean bones like Theo, not Vincent's stocky boxer's build. He did have Vincent's green eyes and beautiful red-blond hair. Willem was a graceful boy who walked well, talked well, ran fast, and held his head high and straight. There were no coughs, no fevers, and especially no rashes or blisters. Three years in the clean country air was helping the whole family. His face was smooth and creamy. He was perfect. She doted on his every wish.

She dreaded to think what he would hear about his father's humiliating death and his uncle's tragic suicide, when he was older.

The inn did moderately well. The guests were not bourgeois bumpkins, as Emile had predicted. They were from all walks of life, attracted by fresh air, Fleur had come to live with them and brought her fantastic baking and the art of Holland's first modern painter. If they laughed at her, they had the courtesy to do it elsewhere.

One day when she was busy cleaning, a knock came on the front door. She wasn't expecting any guests. She opened the door to a young man in his late teens. He was wearing clothes uncommon in Holland, but universal among artists: a paint-covered worker's coat, the pockets loaded with pads, charcoal, and pencils, always necessary when the muse struck.

"Madame Van Gogh," he said, as he bowed. "I have a letter from Emile Bernard, to make my introduction. I am here to see the paintings of Vincent van Gogh, if you please."

She was struck speechless.

He continued, "May I also say hello to your young man." He gave Willem a smile and small piece of candy.

"If there is a better time, I can wait. I have walked from Amsterdam."

Just like Vincent, was her first thought, walking great distances without provisions, sleeping in the fields, and throwing themselves on the mercy of mother nature.

He followed her into the living room. *The Potato Eaters* hung above the fireplace, but she knew that like everyone else it was the colors he wanted to see. She took him to the wall in the living room, where she had placed *Sunflowers* and *The Night Café*, among others. The exquisite colors and compositions were like jewels in the otherwise plain, unremarkable room.

He stared for a long time. She thought about starting a conversation but decided silence was best. Finally, she left him there and got him a glass of water.

"Thank you. I am deeply moved. Is there more to see, please?" She showed him landscapes in the study and dining room. He sketched quick pencil copies. Willem watched in fascination as the painter drew miniature versions of the paintings. For a moment this worried her. But Emile wouldn't send her a forger.

He straightened and asked her sincerely, "May I return, madam?"

"Yes, of course."

"There are many painters, friends who want to see the work also. Mr. Bernard speaks all the time of Vincent's genius." His eyes settled again on *Sunflowers*. "I can see it. The suffering—so awful for him. So much power in his paintings. You knew him well?"

"Well enough to know painting was his life. And he hoped more than anything that his work would bring happiness and peace to others. Everyone is welcome to visit."

This was the beginning of an understanding, of possibilities. Of hope.

Soon more came. Some alone, some in groups. Painters, writers, students—they came from Amsterdam and Paris, walking, begging rides, or on bicycles, all to see the genius of Vincent. They wrote, and they spread the word. It was a light that fed on itself and grew all on its own.

Many painters throughout Holland, Germany and Norway traveled to view Vincent's work. They stared at Vincent's paintings, politely begging to see more, and they loved him. They sat for hours sketching his drawings, copying his swirling strokes. They were too poor to buy anything and so sweet, asking endless questions about Vincent's art, but never about his madness. They were his pilgrims. Vincent had always said art isn't for elites, art is for the people.

The train station at Bussum became her second home. Shipping paintings to exhibits was a difficult job. She contacted a network of galleries throughout Europe to display and sell Vincent's work. No exclusivity, no commitments, but a community of gallery owners interested in new art. The happy bonus was that Willem's favorite place in Bussum was the train station. The engineer and conductor became his best friends, taking him by the hand through the train, and best of all, letting him sit at the head of the train playing engineer. While she supervised the loading and unloading of the paintings, Willem wore a smile so big it lit Jo's heart.

She was constantly watchful over her own and Willem's health. A little sneeze, a cough. Could this be it? The onset of a new flu? Or more of the disease ravaging Paris, the ugliest of deaths?

Her mind wandered to the farmers Vincent had worshipped. Their pain, which he had memorialized. The family praying over their few potatoes at the dinner table. The peasant resting on a haystack. The farmers plowing the fields. The glory of the penniless peasants and Vincent's obsession with unfortunates.

23

After a time, Andries took over the Bonger family business and completed law school. He liked law and was very good at negotiation. He'd learned a lot from Theo. He traveled the French countryside buying back Vincent's stranded paintings.

She organized a retrospective of the work to reach the bigger cites of Holland. She cobbled together money and hired a professional art curator.

Richard-Roland Holst put together the small touring show of Vincent's sketches and paintings. She hoped the Dutch would embrace one of their own. The show was receiving some positive notices but no sales. She hadn't been to the show and felt guilty about not going. She couldn't leave Willem, she felt. Or was it really that she was afraid the Dutch would be laughing at the lunatic painter?

The large rug from the inn's sitting room hung outside on the clothesline. Johanna beat it clean with a wire rug beater. With every vigorous swing, she grunted. She felt grim, tired, and dirty. Willem beat the rug too with a stick.

With each stroke, Willem stepped into the cloud of dust from the beaten rug and watched the particles of dust settle on him. When he coughed and gagged, Jo felt icy needles on the back on her neck.

She dropped the rug beater. "Willem!" She gently picked him up, trying not to sound too alarmed. She carried him around to the front of the house. He didn't feel warm, no fever, but the cough didn't let up and his nose was running. Was he choking?

"Mama, stop bouncing me…. put me down," Willem said through her frenzied steps. Relieved, she put him down. She had to stop this constant panic over every little sniffle. She carried him to the kitchen in the back of house to clean him at the sink.

Fleur kneaded dough on the large worktable in the middle of the kitchen.

"What is the matter with our little man?"

"He was suddenly sick, choking!" She might be losing her mind.

"Really!" Fleur dropped her dough and began to examine Willem. Within seconds she stepped away, "No, you are just filthy from playing with that dusty rug, aren't you!" She mopped Willem's face and clothes with a wet towel and threw Jo a smile.

"I know, I just thought he might be choking," Jo said.

"Forget that old rug and take a rest." Fleur carefully placed a clean cloth over her dough to help it warm and rise. "I'll make you a cup. When is Handsomer-Than-Ever coming?" Fleur asked offhandedly, cleaning her hands, and taking off her apron.

Jo shrugged and grunted.

Johanna and Willem climbed up the back staircase, off the kitchen. At the landing were more paintings and furniture from Jo and Theo's apartment: the chair, the coffee table, the red settee nestled in a seating area off the staircase. Bedrooms were in the front, the side, and back of the house. The front staircase had a grandly carved dark banister. There was a smaller back staircase to the upper floors, with another landing where Jo kept her office.

She quickly changed the boy's dusty clothes and headed back down the staircase to the kitchen. She heard Andries's familiar step in the entryway and his call up the stairs.

"Hello! Where are you ladies?" he shouted. "I have returned, please hail the conquering hero!" He dropped his suitcase and opened his arms wide. "Jo? Fleur?"

"Oh, you are back," Jo shouted as she brushed by Fleur, who was freshening her face, checking her reflection in a gleaming pot.

"Uncle Dries!" Willem shouted and ran to him, and Andries swung him high, kissing him.

"Nice to see you too, Jo!" He gave her a warm kiss over the clinging Willem. Andries made his way toward the kitchen with Willem standing on his feet.

"Fleur?" Johanna shouted. "Fleur!" she shouted even louder.

"Really, Jo, I am sure she can hear you. How are you? You look tired."

Fleur came to the edge of the kitchen and shouted loud enough to be heard across the rooms to the entry hall. "I can't come in, I'm head to toe in flour! Jo needs more rest. She's up all night translating letters, working all day, exhausting herself per usual."

He followed Fleur's voice into the kitchen, wearing his best smile for her. Willem scrambled after him, and Jo followed them. "No, I'm fine." Jo said.

"Andries! Great, you are here! I'm in the middle of the bed, but I'll get you a room ready as soon as the sheet is on the rise." Fleur said, making no sense.

Andries raised his eyebrows and gave Fleur a happy wink. Johanna looked at Fleur with utter incomprehension.

"What's the matter?" Fleur asked.

"Nothing," Andries said, with total feigned innocence.

Recently Fleur's clever way with language disappeared when she was around Andries. "Never mind that," Jo said.

"I've brought a book I thought you might like. But I see you are covered in flour, so I will give it to you when you're ready," he said, eyes flitting up and down.

"Thank you." Fleur almost batted her eyes back at him.

Andries was a good ambassador. Over the past few months, he helped attract visitors to the inn, art dealers, critics, teachers from the university. Everyone loved Fleur's baking. Jo kept a lively conversation going, but she had managed to sell only a few paintings, and too cheaply—that was a problem.

"Any word from the northern tour?" Andries, preoccupied with the vision of Fleur, didn't answer. "Any news?" Johanna asked again.

Watching them, she felt a stabbing pain in her chest. What are they waiting for?

She left them that way and went upstairs to the third-floor attic to get back to work.

Nights in Bussum were dark and quieter than the brilliantly lit nights in Paris. It was hard to get used to at first. Now the soothing quiet and black outside helped her think of what she needed to do. Most nights she spent upstairs, working in her third-floor attic office while Willem slept. Here she kept Vincent's letters to Theo, along with some paintings and sketches she felt particularly attached to. Everything was artfully arranged on shelves and tables. Each table had a large card with a date, 1888 on one, another 1889. Vincent's letters were stacked across a long table. Theo had kept every letter from Vincent, he had wanted to create a book of them. Drawings were pinned on the walls, and a few canvases were rolled and placed neatly on shelves. The rest of Vincent's effects and work were still stored safely in the old Bonger offices.

Johanna sat at her desk and reviewed her letters to museum directors and exhibitors asking for space, for a solo viewing or inclusion in an upcoming show. And letters especially to writers and critics inviting them to see Vincent's work.

She was hopeful this new tour of Vincent's work would attract attention, but she had a sinking feeling the show was slipping through Holland too silently, attracting little notice. Richard-Roland Holst, an expert trained in Paris, had made most of the decisions. Now the show was almost done, and they were going to lose money on the venture.

Vincent's letters to Theo, all undated, comprised her nightly reading. His letters, like a diary, described what he was painting, reading, where he was living, what he was learning, eating, every detail about his singular life. His list of supplies, paints, canvas and his pleas for money.

And his insights, poetic and painful. To paint you have to see, to write you have to feel. Gifted Vincent could do both. If he'd had less talent, would he have had more common sense?

What was the difference? It wouldn't bring Theo back. Reading the letters, Vincent's voice gave relief to her own pain. She must go on, make something good happen from all this misery. If she failed, Vincent and Theo would fail, forever forgotten.

Anna was preparing her own article about Vincent and Theo's childhood, long before Johanna knew them. Anna now had faith that one day they would be world famous, and she would be ready.

Emile was publishing some of Vincent's letters in the better art journals. She didn't like him publishing now. Wait, she had told him, until his artwork was more famous. Vincent's work suffered under his biography, everyone knew this. She thought his work wouldn't be taken as seriously because of the horrors he'd endured.

Jo had tacked cards to the wall, each describing a necessary component of being a successful art dealer. Most of it she remembered from Theo. Exclusivity—the dealer should retain an exclusive relationship with the artist and in return pay expenses and salary so that the artist may paint. Hoard and carefully store the work, selling when the time is right. Hire writers to create articles about the artist's work and his importance. Solo exhibits—a whole show dedicated to one artist. Use a network of international galleries for maximum exposure. Find a large financial backer to underwrite the entire operation, a marriage of art and finance.

She read each of Vincent's undated letters to Theo, guessing at the year it had been written based on his travels and what Theo had told her. She stacked each in a separate pile for the year, and from there was guessing about months, based on the paintings referenced—indoors, outdoors, landscapes, blooming trees, the mistral winds. It was a puzzle, and it occupied her mind, hundreds of hours, night after night of the letters.

Above her desk she hung Vincent's painting of a skull smoking a cigarette, laughing. It was a dark painting, from before Theo introduced him to light, before Vincent became *Vincent*. Black background, browns, golds, a little red, warm tones, and a small light bouncing off the bones—it was one of her favorites. And Clasina was hanging on the wall too. Sad, ruined Clasina, her head in her hands, destroyed.

It had grown late. Jo took some of Vincent's letters and returned to bed. In her mind she saw Theo reading the letters, sitting on the settee, his foot slowly rocking Willem in his cradle, and it made her heart crack open.

> *I have always thought my life was a journey. I sought, searched for answers, but I never discovered anything. I study like the man at university, try to understand what shuts me up and what sets me free. Horribly they are both the same. A kind generous word, a nasty comment -- does it matter from whom? I study every detail of every exchange until I can't bear it anymore, and I put down the dark glass I see through, and I drink myself into oblivion. It lessens the pain, and there is freedom in the horrible bottle I am chained to.*
>
> *I need more light, I need less people, I can't listen anymore to these painters. My brother, come to kill*

*me, come to save me. I fear I am drowning you in
my darkness. You see now we are the same, chained
together as one.*

*We should be together, Theo, with Jo, Willem, you,
and me. I can see you suffering as much as me, more. I
hear your lungs failing. You must move to the country,
live in the clean air, away from the expense of Paris.
You will only recover here. Come with me before it is
too late for all of us, Theo.*

"Momma?" Willem stood in her doorway, sobbing quietly.

"Why are you awake? Come here, let me feel your head." Johanna tossed the letters aside. He held up his arms, and she picked him up and put him next to her.

"What's the matter, Willem? Why are you crying?"

"I don't know." He shrugged. "Why are *you* crying?"

Johanna was stunned. "I'm not crying. See, I'm smiling at you. Better?"

"Yes." He breathed a deep sigh the way children do.

"How about you, Momma? Are you better?"

"Yes, I am better."

"Are we sad?"

"No, we are not sad. Let's go back to sleep and have only sweet dreams." She hugged him close.

"All right, Momma." He climbed out of bed.

"You can sleep here if you want."

"No, I'm going to my own bed. Please don't cry anymore. I don't like it."

That took the breath right out of her. She stopped crying. She lay there listening to the creaking of his small steps, then quiet as he stepped on the carpet and into his bedroom.

There was more noise cracking on the stair but wide long silences in between. Dries—he was sneaking into Fleur's room again.

Was she letting everyone down? Was everyone waiting for her to live again? Vincent and Theo are waiting for me. I brought you home, but I haven't saved you.

24

The next morning, Jo entered the kitchen, with her small overnight bag. She tugged at her traveling suit then straightened when she saw Andries and Fleur at the breakfast table whispering quietly to each other. Willem was with them too.

"Andries, what is the word from the tour? What have you heard from Holst about the shows?" Jo didn't sit down with them and gave Willem a kiss on the head. No answer meant no news, which meant no sales. He shrugged, and she knew he had heard nothing. *Let it go, just find out for yourself, Jo.*

"Fleur, would you take Willem today? I am going to The Hague, to speak with Richard-Roland Holst."

"Excellent idea, you go," Fleur said. "I am in charge, little man, so mind me!"

"If you make me cake," Willem said.

"Are you sure you are up to the trip?" Andries asked. "I should go with you."

"No, I can do it myself."

She stood between them at the table, very close. They both looked up at her quizzically. She picked up Andries' hand and Fleur's hand and placed them together. She grasped her hands around both of theirs, holding them together. They looked surprised, waiting for her to say something. If she spoke, she would crack, and she couldn't in front of Willem.

She met Andries's eyes and smiled and cocked her head toward Fleur, trying to imitate Fleur's gesture. She felt Andries press harder on Fleur's hand and pull it toward his chest. She thought she might have heard Fleur breathe in a giggle, and her eyes were welling up. Willem sat oblivious, eating his porridge. But then he stuck one hand in the mix.

"Me too," he said.

"Thank you," Jo said, her calm returning. "I couldn't have survived." They were silent, shocked, she imagined. She kissed them all goodbye. And she walked out of the kitchen and into the hall to leave.

When she opened the door, she saw them outside on her lawn, more pilgrims, the artists who worshipped Vincent. One was lying on the grass, sleeping on his side, his hands cradled under his head, his knees pulled into his belly. Trying to keep warm overnight. The other was up, and already at work, sketch pad open, sitting cross-legged on the path, waiting for her door to open. When the artist saw her, he scrambled and nudged his sleeping friend.

"Mrs. Van Gogh," he bowed to her. "We've come to see the paintings." They likely didn't have a coin on them, Jo thought. They probably hadn't eaten either. Like Vincent, their clothes were utilitarian, and stained with paint.

"Please, Mrs. Van Gogh, we've come a long way." She imagined they had, with the Spanish accent.

"Yes, we're just open. Go in, there should be coffee." Fleur would give them something, and Andries would keep them company.

She left them and ran for the train.

The train ride was the first time she could remember when her hands were empty: no cleaning, no Willem, no letters. The Dutch countryside rolled along, green and sparsely populated, then houses darting up more frequently at the outskirts of The Hague. What could she accomplish at this late stage of the exhibit?

Looking out the train window, she remembered when Emile had visited her at the inn. He had traveled to the see the show when it opened in Copenhagen. He had come to the inn to express his unhappiness, saying it didn't capture Vincent's greatness.

He walked through the inn, staring at all the paintings as if he hadn't seen them before, lingering over each one. Johanna discreetly followed, watching him. He had changed for the worse, she thought. His youthful charm, long hair, and eccentric clothes had once given him an appealing quality. All of that was gone, and what was left was a still-young man with no youthful energy. Sadness dragged his eyes and mouth into a frown, and there was nothing decorative in his clothes, just plain wools any professor would wear. What had happened to him?

"I wouldn't have shown *The Potato Eaters*. It wasn't what made Vincent unique. He thought it was ugly, too sentimental. And the drawings—not yet. Show them to the students for now. Just use the space for the color, and for God's sake get them to hang properly."

The criticism stung, igniting guilt. She hadn't seen the show in person, she had turned everything over to Richard-Roland Holst, someone she didn't know well but who had been recommended, by whom she couldn't remember. To her every suggestion, he always had the same response, "Allow me, Mrs. Van Gogh, this is my business." He wore her down soon enough, and she went along with it all.

Willem sat on the carpet in the middle of the room, building another imaginary castle with blocks, tiny logs, and miniature men. It was a quiet day. Fleur baked in the kitchen, the house smelling deliciously sweet.

"Vincent said *The Potato Eaters* expressed his love for peasants," Jo said. "His desire to immortalize their lives, and he painted it here in Holland. That was my intention."

Emile sat down next to Johanna and paused a long while. She

thought he might be composing a thought, as he struggled to speak and then stopped and caught his breath. He slowly blew out some air, forcing a smile for her.

"What is it, Emile?" She touched his hand, like a mother nudging a son.

Emile burst into tears, shaking and sobbing.

A grown man crying in front of a woman and a child—unheard of. The clattering of pots and pans in the kitchen stopped. Fleur was listening.

Willem dropped his toys and jumped to his feet. He strode over to the man and grabbed his shoulders, shaking him gently. "Don't cry. Don't cry. You must stop." Emile took the shaking, didn't push the child away or stop crying. Jo reached for Willem to leave Emile.

"Willem, come for your chocolate!" Fleur called from the kitchen. Willem backed up two paces, looked at Jo, and after she nodded to him, flew out of the room.

"They were grown men," Jo said. "They made their own choices." His crying was unnerving. Theo had cried on the train in public, heralding the terrible spiral into hell she never saw coming.

"He was mine," Emile said.

"I remember," Jo said. She thought to put her hand on his shoulder, the way Theo would.

"I need to tell you about Henri." He continued to weep.

"I know, he's dead. Very sad. Pneumonia?"

"Yes, pneumonia and syphilis. It was fast."

"I'm sorry, I know you were close."

"We were true friends, so rare." Emile handed her the wrapped package he'd brought with him. "This is for you. A gift from Henri's mother. She asked me to bring it."

Johanna opened the package.

It was a simple portrait of Vincent in a café. Henri had captured all of Vincent's intelligence and magnetic quality and some of the unique oddities that gave him his own special charm. His staring, in profile, his leaning in, the shoulders of a fighter. And he made him romantic, dreamy. Vincent, surrounded by the color he lived in, warm and cool together in spectacular harmony, a glorious moment frozen in time, the essence of Vincent. Memories flooded over her, the feeling of the time, the place, of Paris, of love.

"How amazing," she said with admiration. "I am deeply touched."

"It is a remarkable likeness. It kills me to give it to you."

"You could have kept it. I wouldn't have known. You were always a good friend to the van Goghs, Emile. This is how we should remember him, Vincent at his best. Would you like to keep it?"

"No, it belongs with the collection. You must keep the portrait out of the light. If you hang it, use a dark room, out of the sun." Emile took a deep breath. "Is there more to see?"

Jo showed Emile her collection up in the third-floor office—the smoking skull staring out at them, next to the drawing of Clasina, *Sorrow*, and a self-portrait by Paul Gauguin.

Emile looked through all the drawings and letters neatly arranged on large tables throughout the attic. "Mrs. Lautrec is collecting all Henri's work. She is opening a museum completely dedicated to Henri, in their hometown, Toulouse."

"Those are all of Vincent's letters to Theo, years of them," Jo said, "at least two volumes' worth."

"In his hand and not dated. Hundreds of them." Emile looked carefully "You should publish immediately. I remember Theo wanted to publish the letters."

"I'm finding a method to the chaos and have organized them by year, then by month, and then by week. I think I should wait until his paintings are more famous. I don't want him known just as a mad painter."

Emile shook his head. "His own words show he was never mad." Talking about Vincent, Emile seemed to recover himself. "Vincent did have a theory, unlike what Gauguin tells everyone. He was pure emotion, the perfect embodiment of the personal. The essence of him, his painting, his philosophy, more real than intellectual."

"Vincent didn't save Theo's letters," she said. "Don't you think that's strange? Theo treasured everything from Vincent."

"He carried Theo in his heart always."

Emile slumped in the chair at the desk. He dropped his head back, staring at the paintings. "I'm happy you're doing well."

"I keep well for my son."

"Vincent knew all the falseness between men. If he had loved me, I could have saved him. Vincent used to say, 'if you love the painting you have to love the man.'"

"You tried to save him, we all did."

"Why not me? Why him?" He was looking at the self-portrait of Paul Gauguin. Vincent, Emile and Paul had all exchanged self-portraits, a sign of deep friendship and shared vision for new art.

"I think he admired Paul's painting."

"He worshipped Paul, how he manipulated ideas about painting in a way Vincent never could. Paul was jealous, and still Vincent worshipped him. Paul is a danger. The writers listen to him, even if all the artists call him 'the monster.' He is using his influence to damage Vincent's memory."

"Paul can't hurt Vincent anymore."

"Gauguin is favored by the critics, the writers. They are fascinated with his primitive persona. His star has risen. The man owes his very existence to Theo. What you are trying to do is impossible. Building a star, away from the Paris elites—truly it has never ever been done. I admire your gumption."

A compliment from Emile, she would treasure. "Thank you for telling the world the truth about Vincent. But I will get Vincent the recognition he deserves. What are you painting now?"

"I'm a student of Titian now. Back to the classics. And Jo, for many reasons, I am leaving France. I'm going to Africa. Algeria first, looking for the change of light. I fear conscription. I couldn't stand it if they took me for the army. There is liberation away from the main conversation. And there is another reason. My sister Madeline is in Algeria, and she is in trouble."

"Oh, I am sorry to hear this, Emile. But Titian? The classics? You are a pioneer in modern art."

"Once I was."

Now with Emile leaving, Henri dead, she there was no one left in Paris committed to Vincent.

Her heart sank as she approached the large picture window of the Gallery De Hague, Modern. She had envisioned this show would be like the galleries in Paris, rooms filled with color, magical. But this was entirely different. The prominent back wall, most visible from the street, showcased what looked like a black-and-white jumble of pen-and-ink drawings of landscapes of Holland. Roland had suggested a focus on landscapes people of the north would recognize. But now she could see it had been a mistake.

The side walls were poorly lit, hiding the dazzling Vincent color. Roland wanted to highlight the tamer work, the "more *rational*" work he called it, to avoid all the talk of his outrageous color, the symbol of his madness. The paintings on the side walls hung haphazardly by color, blue landscapes all stacked together and at odd heights. It was hard to focus. Some hung inches from the ceiling and others grazed the floor. The flowers were on the adjacent wall, and this was decent, she breathed a small sigh of relief. It was too late to change anything. Roland would argue with her, "…allow me, Mrs. Van Gogh…" Emile's exhibit in Paris had better cohesion, the way he grouped the colors, like a color wheel, moving across the spectrum. This show looked small and inconsequential. Already she knew it was another heartbreaking failure. She feared people laughing at Vincent and worried she might lose control and scream. Well, the hell with it, Vincent screamed and maybe she should too.

A young man with a pad and pencil caught her eye. He smiled and bowed to her. He reminded her of the student painters but with more money, better dressed and groomed. Back home, all the young painters in town knew her, they all bowed to her because they loved Vincent. They were a spark in her heart.

Roland the curator made a beeline towards the young man. Ah, he is a reporter, the young man with the pad and pencil. She had been warned by Roland to avoid the press. One false word and they can destroy anyone's reputation without mercy. She tried to keep all the horror of Theo's and Vincent's tragedies out of the press. But she needed to understand what was happening or, more to the point, what wasn't happening. She decided to go introduce herself before she could change her mind.

"What a pleasure to meet you, Mrs. Van Gogh. I am Johan Cohen. I'm writing a review of the exhibit. May I ask you a few questions?" Johan looked at Roland, his eyebrows up in a questioning manner, his pencil pointing at Roland, and said, "Could you offer us a few chairs? I wouldn't want to keep Madame van Gogh standing." Roland left abruptly, returning with chairs and a teeth-baring smile.

This was the end of the reporter's pleasantries. He began to hurl questions at her.

"How many paintings are there? When were they primarily done? How well did you know Vincent? Did you ever watch him paint?"

She wasn't prepared, she didn't answer strategically, the way Theo always had. Most of the questions required simple answers, so it didn't matter. She must make a note to think ahead, have these answers ready, and not fumble around.

"In Paris they say Gauguin is writing an article about Vincent and the incident with the ear?"

The ear. Paul Gauguin, trying to sabotage Vincent, just like

Emile had warned. Paint him mad and no one will ever take his art seriously. Two-faced monster.

"He would write about the most inconsequential part of Vincent. His left ear."

Roland gasped a little. The reporter broke out laughing.

"Yes, I completely agree with you, Mrs. Van Gogh. I look around and absorb all this magnificent work and feel so crass to ask again. What can you tell me about the ear incident?" His eyebrows shot up again, his manner calm.

"Nothing." She smiled. "I can't imagine this will be of much interest to your esteemed and educated readers." Intelligent men looking at a revolutionary in art and all they can think about is a detached ear!

"There is a rumor that he painted a self-portrait after the incident with his ear?"

"Yes, two in fact," Jo said. Roland's eyes bulged and he dropped his head as if he had been struck.

Johan wrote down every word, his pad resting gently on his crossed knee, but he never broke eye contact. He had learned to write without looking. What a good trick, Johanna thought.

"You knew him during this incident?"

"Yes." It was rude to ask again.

"Why do you think he cut off his ear?"

"Mr. Cohen, Vincent did not intend to cut off his ear, there was an accident. There is so much more to Vincent than this overblown drama."

"Did you think Vincent was mad, Mrs. Van Gogh?"

All of Vincent's words swirled through her head. She hoped some would come down and land in a sentence. Instead, she found her own.

"No, he wasn't mad. I think his pain was clear, absolute, and he couldn't ever turn a blind eye to the suffering of others. He saw the world through his sensitive lens, and I think this overwhelmed him.

And it gave rise to this great world of color around us now. Painting was his consolation."

Roland was staring down at his shoes. *He is embarrassed for me.* Johan wrote continually and watched her speak. Maybe she should leave now, with dignity. She stood, and Johan reached gently to her elbow.

"'A consolation,' very well put, Mrs. Van Gogh. Please, just a few more questions. Are the self-portraits with the bandage at your inn?"

"Mr. Cohen, you are welcome at the inn. But those portraits are not displayed."

"Has Mr. Gauguin attended any of the exhibits of Vincent's retrospective?" He looked to Roland for the answer. Roland shrugged gracefully. "Do you know Paul Gauguin, Mrs. Van Gogh? Theo represented him?"

"Yes, for years. I hope he'll visit. Vincent was an enormous influence on his work," Johanna said, as a matter of indisputable fact.

"Or was Gauguin an influence on Vincent?"

"Vincent is the creator of a new modern movement. He created hundreds of paintings using his own unique, revolutionary approach. This will all become clear in time."

"Ah, really, Vincent completed hundreds of paintings, you could fill an entire museum. Mrs. Van Gogh, how do you define expressionism?"

"Mr. Cohen," Roland interrupted. "Mrs. Van Gogh is not formally educated in art. That is why I am here, helping the van Gogh family."

Expressionism, Jo thought. The latest 'ism' invented by a Paris art critic. Did Roland think she didn't understand that? She'd hired him, he should be more respectful.

"Yes, but first I would like to hear more from Mrs. Van Gogh." Johan said quietly and waited.

"Vincent would say, art expresses the spiritual," Jo said. "He would say color itself is an emotion. And for Vincent, art would help sooth a troubled soul, like music. Vincent believed the vision of the painter captured his emotional state, coloring the subject he focused upon, not just the reality we all see." She waved her arm toward the wall of Vincent's extravagant flowers.

Johan was writing quickly and watching her, smiling. "The way we would like the world to be," Johan said. "Yes, wouldn't it be magnificent to live surrounded by Vincent's flowers."

"You must visit our inn, in Bussum. I will show you Vincent's entire collection of paintings, drawings, writings, everything. What you see here is a small sample of his work."

"Thank you. When shall I visit?"

Johanna left the gallery with sweat running down her back, her face red and damp. But she didn't care. She walked fast, her heart racing. She tried to rest on the train, but her thoughts kept her awake.

Then a realization hit her. She'd been fighting against the wrong thing. Protecting the wrong things, hiding, because she was afraid. There wasn't going to be a way to sanitize Vincent's madness. The more she hid the truth, the more she took away his power. Everyone understands pain and suffering. Most families have a vulnerable child.

There was no hiding from Vincent's madness, making up aliments, and swallowing shame, the most destructive of all emotions. No living in fear of the truth.

The truth was that Vincent's tortured insanity was what made his art glorious. His truth, his love, his pain was what he captured for the world to fall in love with.

I must stop dreaming about 'when,' Jo thought. When will Vincent have enough notoriety for a big museum show? When will he be famous for his work and not his madness? When will I sell to museums and collectors for decent prices? When will I recover and lose the desperate gloom that dominates my life?

I will plan a new exhibit, with bigger, better ideas, something as big and bold as Vincent. I won't hide his colors or his madness. Everyone thinks I can't do this. But I can. What is more modern than a woman without a husband, making her own way in the world, with purpose and power beyond filling a soup bowl?

This small, poorly executed traveling retrospective wouldn't do. A grand exhibit in Paris was impossible. But she had Amsterdam, and the Dutch were great art lovers. The new Stedelijk Museum, this is where Vincent belonged, a large prestigious museum in Amsterdam with an interest in modern art. They had said no before, but now she was not going to accept no. She needed the prestige of a big museum show. She was done with the smaller galleries with limited clientele. The northern tour had exhausted all those possibilities, and she had little to show critically and had lost money financing the traveling show, paying for advertisements in a dozen towns.

Jo made a list of his best paintings: *Starry Night, The Sunflowers, Night Café*, so many landscapes. She thought of the list of the things Theo said were needed to make an artist a great success. She had exclusivity, no one could ever take the paintings away. She provided easy access to Vincent's work, although only if you were willing to travel to Holland.

Theo said you need good notices from writers and critics. The critic Albert Aurier, who once proclaimed Vincent a modern master, had died. She would need to take a big chance.

What if she used Vincent's own words? Emile had said to publish the letters. Emotion is power, the essential brushstroke of a modern painter. Who needs the intellectual hyperbole of an elitist critic to describe the artist's vision? Real people don't read that rubbish.

Vincent will speak for Vincent. The letters will be his art review, his own personal art journal. The artist's vision is the emotional state of the painter, madness and all. The personal is universal in the modern world.

It's here in the letters. I will give it to the world with the paintings.

That's the plan. There will be a legacy, a redemption for them all. Vincent's story—the words that will enhance the mystery on the canvas, the artist's vision.

25

"Johanna," Fleur said, "I knew you would find a better way." They stood outside the Steldjik museum, the perfect venue for a Vincent van Gogh show. Mr. Jansen, the Steldjik's director, had once said "his museum" would not exhibit Vincent's work. But the young artists and students in Amsterdam were talking about Vincent and the works they'd seen at the inn, creating new interest. Jo finally cajoled Jansen into a meeting to learn about Vincent.

"Wear him down with charm, Jo. Just remember, when he bullies you, don't get angry." Fleur gave her a kiss on the cheek and pushed her into the building.

Jo wouldn't let herself be baited, but she always resented anyone with power over her.

Mr. Jansen's office was over-decorated with ostentatious clutter and not enough light, with a layer of dust covering the tall windows, odd for a new 'modern' museum.

"First, let me say, Mrs. Van Gogh, we are delighted to meet you finally." He crossed legs and brushed off the fabric of his pants and did not look up. "I do apologize for taking so long! At any rate, you are here now, and I am all ears." He finally met her eyes. "Your family legacy is so rich in art. Can we offer you some tea?"

"Thank you." She smiled ignoring his condescension and hid her flinch at his mention of ears. "No tea. thank you."

"I read your letter. Your concept is rather ambitious."

"In Paris, they know Vincent is an important painter. Did you read the article from Aubert Aurier?"

"Yes, some time ago. We are intrigued to view the work. You never know, there may be an opportunity to include Vincent in a future exhibition of local painters." He waved his hand dismissively. "Right now, there is little interest here in Vincent. We are looking at more prominent artists."

He is cutting right to his point, Jo thought. No, no and no. He feels he was bullied into this meeting.

"I plan a solo exhibition. Only Vincent van Gogh."

"Well, ambitious! Admirable. But as I have said, we don't see the opportunity for an exhibit. Possibly in the future when van Gogh has—"

"Vincent's significant paintings hang at the Van Gogh Inn. I have had many visitors, he is gaining in popularity, I'm sure you are aware. But my space is small. Vincent's work demands a grand space."

"The Van Gogh Inn, your own permanent installation—a novel idea, yes, excellent. I guess you know well the controversy surrounding modern art and the lives of some of the more flamboyant painters, ghastly deaths. Great interest, but many impressionist and modern exhibits across Europe are not well attended. And often receive critical reviews. Museum boards don't like bad reviews, ours included. The patrons are sensitive to word of mouth. An embarrassment is hard to live down. Why risk failure now before Vincent van Gogh's achievements are understood, and his reputation is secure? You understand the importance of first impressions."

She had heard it all before. He had probably rehearsed. Who cared what he thought of the "flamboyant painters," their "ghastly deaths?" She nodded and smiled showing appreciation at the unctuous diatribe. Johanna looked around at the dismal decor and decided now was the time.

"Yes, you are correct, there are many risks." She raised her eyebrows and nodded. "I have a suggestion, Mr. Jansen."

"Yes?"

"My proposal is to underwrite the cost of the show completely and rent out one of your magnificent rooms. No risk for you or the trustees either."

He smiled, surprised, and fiddled with the dusty knickknack miniatures of classic statues on his desk.

He thinks I am desperate for an exhibit. He doesn't know what is special about Vincent and he is nervous about his madness.

"I believe the Dutch, with our rich history in art, will appreciate seeing one of our own who mastered the new ideas of color and light. You will have a large, curious, appreciative audience. Vincent will bring a crowd. I guarantee it. I can hardly keep up with my bookings, you see. And Vincent's Northern Tour has been an enormous success." She lied, but well enough.

"Guarantee?" He nodded unconvinced and choked back a snort, then clearing his throat he went on. "I am happy to hear of this success for you, Mrs. Van Gogh." He is in a hurry to end this conversation, Johanna thought.

"Perhaps you need time to think it over," Johanna said. "Talk with your board. I have other calls to make with this novel idea."

"Really? Other calls? The Rijksmuseum would never consider such a 'novel' idea as you describe."

"All museums are looking for wealthy benefactors. And museums are not the only institutions with spaces large enough to showcase Vincent's work."

"None with our reputation."

"Yes, that is why I came to your museum first. With your reputation of embracing modern art, presenting the first exhibition of Vincent van Gogh, our very own modern master, is a perfect fit. But another organization might see this opportunity also. The north will be the first to embrace him. The only question is where the exhibition will be."

Jansen's smile was thin.

"To that end, I understand all your concerns," Jo said. "Empty rooms, poor reviews. None of that will happen." She waved her hand in the air dismissing them all and smiled. *Only risk for me, my family, my son's legacy.* "If you could clear your calendar for an afternoon, I would love to have a luncheon, in your honor, and show you the paintings at my inn. I have an excellent chef and acquaintances, art patrons, you would enjoy meeting."

Jo decided now was the time to mention the wealthy couple who had visited the inn, lured by the talk they had heard from the young artists.

"The Schmidt's, patrons of yours, have purchased two van Goghs. They are planning to come for luncheon soon. Maybe with you at the same time?" She smiled sweetly at him and picked up a tiny replica of Rodin's *The Kiss*. "What do you think?"

The mention of the Schmidt's grabbed his attention. "Yes, sounds excellent. I would be pleased to visit and view the collection."

"Please tell me about all the wonderful objects I see in your office, a little museum within the museum?" *Yes, hold my arm, walk me around this dustbin, and bore me silly with endless descriptions of ancient useless "excellent reproductions."*

It was a big, bold idea. How many tickets could be sold in a day? What should she offer for a room? She would make it work, she had to come up with the money. She could mortgage the inn. She would harness the controversy—the drama surrounding Vincent—and make it work for her. She must no longer run away from the madness. It was time to embrace what is true for everyone—*suffering.*

She would speak from her heart about Vincent, his love of painting and his desire that painting be for the people.

Next, the crowning glory, she would announce the publication of Vincent's letters at the grand opening of the Vincent van Gogh Exhibit at the Stedelijk Museum. First she needed to convince Jansen.

Her mind raced with the possibilities. But she kept calm and quietly descended the steps of the museum, looking for Fleur. What would Theo think? Déclassé, desperate paying for rooms, or clever? Would he approve of exposing Vincent's reputation to the taunts of madness? She took a deep breath and blinked, letting herself relax, and there he was, in her mind, Theo's face close to hers, his breath on her skin and his deep baritone soothing her. Her heart was full with Theo. She wanted to be alone, sit and remember every moment with him.

She found Fleur.

"Your face says it all, Jo. You will make this happen!" Fleur laughed. "Ready for something delicious? I'm starved." She took her arm. "Let's go, and you'll tell me everything!"

26

Johanna saw Paul Gauguin out the window and blew out a loud "ah-hha' putting her hands on her hips. Today was her special luncheon for the museum director, Mr. Jansen. She was introducing him to Vincent's work. They were close to agreeing on a reasonable price, she hoped to successfully continue their negotiation.

Gauguin paused to look at Willem playing beside the lawn. He had built an ingenious fort out of twigs, small blocks, stones, and mud. Little toy men lay in a pile. Willem picked them up carefully, one at a time, and placed them down, thinking before lifting each figure, holding it up and appraising the scene, placing, holding, and placing, then a final decision and placement. He didn't bother much with the very tall man walking up the path, who now stood in front of him.

Paul looked down at him.

"Hello. What is your name, son?"

"I am Willem."

"Stand up for me?" Paul bent down and reached out his hand.

Willem stood up quickly without Paul's hand. Paul appraised him closely, with a reassuring smile. He put his hand softly on Willem's shoulder.

"What are you making there? I am impressed, you are very accomplished."

"My fort—it's not done. I have more plans."

"I think it *is* done."

"*No*, I am going to dig a moat."

"A moat? Why?"

"To keep things out! For protection against invasion."

Gaugin hadn't gone to any of the gallery exhibits Vincent was included in or the northern gallery tour. Emile said he was disparaging Vincent in Paris. Paris was one thing, but now he was here.

She had even gotten the Schmidt's, sponsors of the museum, to attend today. The writer Johan Cohen, whom she'd met at The Hague Gallery, was here too and was considering a lengthy piece on Vincent.

Gauguin looked as strong and handsome as ever, magnetic and primal. If he was struggling at all, it didn't show. If he was doing well, it hadn't changed the same odd but artful ensemble of clothes. Emile said he was a star with the modern-thinking critics in Paris, but still not selling.

His hair was thick, long, wavy, without any gray. Still wearing wooden shoes, he was the same mélange of ideas, colors, and cultures. Now he appeared even more striking, captivating against the deep green yard, framing him and allowing all his color to stand out.

She felt the pain in her chest, a stab, the wound opening up again, but no prickly feeling of dread washed over her, or a mass of spiders crawling up her neck. She felt the heat of anger flushing her face.

She was on the verge of making Vincent's star rise. That was why he was here. If Gauguin sabotaged her with the museum director, it would be another setback. He was here to hurt her, make her look an idiot in front of her guests and make Vincent into madman.

Perhaps there was a way to fight and not look like a hysterical woman. The guests would be excited to see Paul Gauguin. He was controversial, the top of the avant-garde of Paris, now here, in Holland. A successful luncheon at the Van Gogh Inn, with Paul, would provide the wealthy guests dinner stories for a decade. Or he would succeed in shutting Jo up and making her look a fool, but only if she let him.

"Who is that? Very tall, almost handsome." Fleur was beside her, Andries behind her.

The house was full of prestigious guests, a mix of art professionals and civilians. That had proven the best mix to create excitement over Vincent and sell paintings. With the inn, Vincent was locally known and popular. Unrestricted access to the paintings was a critical factor in selling art. The Dutch, for centuries, had been big collectors. They loved art, and trade professionals, writers, museum administrators, gallery owners were always eager to meet people of means.

"Paul Gauguin, unexpected and perfect timing," Andries said dryly.

"Oh my, so that is the one and only," said Fleur. "Why is he digging up the yard with Willem?"

"It's the moat he's forbidden to dig." Johanna turned to Fleur and examined what she was wearing. "Fleur, can you flirt with him? Maybe wear the blue dress with the lower bodice?"

"Yes, absolutely, I can do that." She flashed her remarkable smile.

"No, you absolutely cannot do that!" Andries rocked back on his heels and stuffed his hands in his pockets. "How is that going to look, my fiancée flirting with that animal?"

Fleur kissed him. "Don't worry your handsome head! You are my one and only forever. I will be discreet. I know his type. They think they are better, above it all. Is he a monster?"

"Yes, he's a monster, and he is a very great artist," Andries said. "Even better, the critics are in love with his work."

"And his suffering is great—that is why he is a great artist," Johanna deadpanned.

"Then we will have to pet and adore him, agree with everything he says and make him feel special. Then he will behave," said Fleur.

"I wonder what he wants," Johanna said.

At lunch in the dining room, Paul held court. Fleur flirted with him, offering him wine, paying endless tributes. Andries was visibly appalled. But Fleur was quick with a squeeze of his leg under the table, and Andries was happy again.

At first it was exciting, interesting to listen to him, how he approached his art, how he looked at life, so very special and unique in the world. And her guests were buying it.

When they get tired of Paul, I will bring it back around to Vincent, Johanna thought. Watching him now, she thought he looked ragged around the edges. Up close he wasn't magnificent, he was seedy. What would Theo look like now?

Johanna snapped herself back to reality. *Bring in the coffee now,* she thought. Gauguin was entertaining with tales of the South Seas, painting, and his primal Incan heritage. "I wish to live in peace and create a simple art, images from my own brain, without the influences of our contaminated culture. I must steep myself in virgin nature, to be one with the savages, to share their life."

Replace "savage" with "peasant" and he sounds like Vincent, Johanna thought, simple people in uncorrupted nature, so spiritual and poor, yet richer than the educated in all true ways. Those ideas were a truth for the artist, and a dream to entice the buyer.

A guest asked what Gauguin thought of Vincent's work.

Johanna shot Paul a warning glare across the table, accompanied by a bright smile. Paul smirked back at her, an expression that said, I am the star blazing bright in your silly little inn.

"There were no ideas behind Vincent's work, no synthesis of thought. No galvanizing of ideas into a movement. He simply painted. You see that in the haphazard strokes, color straight from the tube. We had different approaches. Vincent was impulsive, drew and painted from life. He used impasto, too imprecise, not enough intention, depending on the luck of the stroke to control so much paint at once."

Paul acted out painting as he spoke, like he was conducting an orchestra. He mimed Vincent, his arms swirling about in big awkward movements, his face too close to the canvas, one hand inches from his face, the other holding an imaginary brush.

"Mr. Gauguin, Vincent clearly deviated greatly from the traditionalist, the academic. Isn't that an intention? A choice?" It was the writer Johan Cohen.

"I prefer the abstraction of memory, concentration, and symbolism."

His work is symbolic of his degenerate behavior, Johanna thought.

"I tried to teach Vincent my technique. The Incan blood in my veins—my work flows from the primitive." He waved his arms at the paintings on the walls. "This is elaborate folly. These are just decorative color harmonies, but I will give Vincent his expressive brush strokes. It was his madness that spoke, not talent or ideas."

Jansen went for the jugular immediately. "Are you saying that Vincent's work came from madness?"

Johanna interrupted before Gauguin could answer. "Vincent was a true artist with paint. He wanted his paintings to soothe the soul with color, the rapture of color. His goal was always to share his love of nature, of people. Art is for people, not critics and writers. When I publish his letters, all his ideas are compellingly laid out in a very personal—"

Paul interrupted, "Vincent and Mrs. Van Gogh have more than Theo in common. Mrs. Van Gogh here—she is first a woman. Her biology commits her to emotional ideas. Again, absolutely no artistic training. Luck, a few tricks here and there."

"Oh my," Johanna said. There was no way she was going to let this go by. "Oh dear, an old-fashioned idea from Mr. Gauguin. We are in the twentieth century now, Mr. Gauguin. An avant-garde intellectual like yourself should know better than to speak about women in such an unenlightened way. It must be the uneducated, primitive side of you bubbling to the surface."

She made sure to smile and look at Mrs. Schmidt. She smiled back with twinkling, sly eyes. Yes, he is talented, handsome, and exotic. But I am with you, her eyes said.

"As a matter of fact, my husband, Theo, the noted art collector, used to say the superstitious side of you might get the better of you. Have we reached that point? What will you paint in the tropics? Nudes? Very young girls?" *Maybe Vincent was mad, but he wasn't an exploiter of innocents,* she thought.

Nervous laughter, followed by silence. Paul stared down at Johanna. A laugh from Mr. Schmidt, who had been drinking too much.

"Mr. Gauguin, where in the tropics are you traveling?" Johan Cohen asked.

Fleur poured Gauguin some more wine, standing quite close to him, her lovely velvet-covered breast not even a little discreetly grazing his shoulder.

Paul reflexively turned toward her, and she was waiting with that smile, those eyes. She slowly lowered her eyes down to his chest and admired his elaborately embroidered vest.

Johanna watched. Oh my, she was licking her lips, too.

Debating with humor, no anger—keep it smart, impersonal. This wasn't so hard, Johanna thought. She felt energized from their exchange—a rush of energy, like skating on the canals when she was a child, when she had skated farther than she had ever dreamed and was still ready for more.

Paul blathered on and on but avoided more talk of Vincent. Eventually even the guests grew tired of their role in his performance, the endless nodding and smiling at everything he said.

It was time to end the luncheon—relief with the end of the dessert and get everyone looking at the paintings again.

"Mr. Gauguin, did you know Vincent created over eight hundred paintings? This is remarkable, don't you think?" Johan Cohen asked.

"Many painted in one session. This makes my point, you see. Where are they?" He looked down at Jo.

"Over two hundred alone from his time in the South of France," Johanna said. "Completely intuitive. A unique approach, his alone. A true original, a man obsessed and consoled with light and nature."

Mr. Schmidt, without decorum from too much wine, asked, "What really happened with his ear? That was you, wasn't it?" He mimed the wrapping of a large bandage around his head. His wife grabbed his hand in midair. Silence and a few giggles from the table. "Why did he do that?"

Oh my God, the obsession with *the ear*! Silly Schmidt, he'd been in his cups when he arrived! Jansen shifted in his seat, stifling a laugh in his napkin. Willem came in from the kitchen and climbed on Johanna's lap.

"Yes, he was with me," Paul said. "I am writing about this incident, an article for the *Paris Art Herald*. Cutting off one's ear is proof of madness."

Willem jumped off Johanna's lap and ran to Mr. Gauguin and tugged on his sleeve. Gauguin raised his long arm and placed it around Willem's shoulders in a kind, intimate way.

"Did you see him cut off his ear?" Willem asked.

"Willem, please!" Jo said, maybe a little too sharply.

"Did you see him cut off his ear? Was there blood?"

"I saw blood," Paul said very gravely.

"Did it gush? Was the blood gushing a lot?"

"He would have bled to death if it weren't for me. I saved Vincent 's life that night."

"He cut off his own ear! I'll bet it hurt. Did he scream? Mother, do we have a picture of that? Oh," Willem said, "Oh, I'm sick!"

Fleur stood up with a bottle of port and began walking quickly around the table. "Port? Your glasses, please." Everyone leaned in with their glasses.

The awkward silence at the table was broken by Johan, who held up his glass to Fleur. "This has been a delicious meal. My compliments to the chefs. A lovely day altogether."

"Thank you, Mr. Cohen." What a fool, Jo, say something now!

"Hear, hear! Excellent!" toasted Jansen.

Willem grew pale. "Ugh," he said, rubbing his own ear. His mouth and throat moved on their own, the involuntary gag reflex overwhelming him.

"Are you feeling sick, young man?" Paul laughed and slapped him on the back.

Was he trying to make the child throw up? Andries pried Willem away from Gauguin. Fleur grabbed his other side, and they gently guided him into the kitchen.

Schmidt held his glass in the air to be refilled. "Mrs. Van Gogh, I've heard…heard. Ah, there is a rumor he painted himself like that, with his ear cut off. No bloody stump…but…with a large cloth circling his…" Schmidt ran his hand around his head several times, *again*. "Is it true? I would like to see that."

Jo laughed as though it didn't bother her at all. "Please bring your glasses to the gallery room. Have another viewing. Andries can assist you with questions. I will be with you in a moment. Mr. Gauguin, would you accompany me to my office, and we can conclude our business please?" She tried to gauge the damage, but Jansen's back was to her, following along with the Schmidt's.

Johanna sat on the settee in front of the window, Gauguin in front of her, in the middle of the room.

"So, the rumor is you have resorted to paying for a room at the Museum?"

"Vincent will finally get the respect he is entitled to."

"You should stop. The more you exploit your dead husband's dead brother, the more the living suffer."

"Are you suffering, Paul?"

He shook his head and then abruptly said, "I need money to finance my trip to the South Seas. I was hoping to get money from you, a loan."

"A loan in exchange for paintings?" she asked.

"Good Lord, no! I need money. Theo promised me money, but I didn't realize he had gone mad. But he was always a generous sponsor."

"He was, but he also got the paintings."

"Theo made money on the paintings. You look like you are doing well enough. It's my work that helped paint this house yellow. It is Vincent's fault I cannot sell."

"That's your theory? Vincent has been dead for years. What you mean to say is you cannot sell a painting without Theo. If Theo thought it was good, it was good. People bought just on his word."

"So, you will give me money. I need five thousand francs."

"I would consider it, but you haven't told me what I would get in return." Johanna was doing the math in her head. Andries had several Gauguins. Theo thought Gauguin was a good bet.

She wondered. The subject matter of his paintings upset her—natives, uneducated, exploited as much by Gauguin as by any European invader, she thought.

"I need to know now. The association with Vincent and his madness has hurt my prospects in Paris. He undercuts my reasoning. You should let him die. Let history be the arbiter. I demand you think of me, the living."

"But any association between you and Vincent's madness is ludicrous. You have one of the sunflowers, I will buy it." She kept her voice conversational, light, matter-of-fact.

"Sunflowers are sold already."

"You didn't think to ask me first? The sunflowers are the most—remind me Paul, how did you come to own two Sunflowers?"

"Johanna, why have you run away? Back home to Holland, to create Vincent's legacy here? I know why. No one of any standing in Paris will touch Vincent's work or even consider a meeting with you."

He towered over her, crowding her. This close, she could smell his clothes were not clean. His fingernails were caked with grime.

She looked over her shoulder and out the window behind her. The yard and garden were empty, the guests must still be in the main rooms.

"This is how you ask for money? Let's get some fresh air. Don't forget your walking stick. I will get your cape." She hoped he understood, giving him his cape and stick, he would not be coming back inside, their meeting was over.

He understood and started fuming. He reluctantly followed her, grabbing the cape and coat.

Outside Johanna checked again to ensure they had privacy. She turned to Paul.

"What were you asking?" she said. "Why I am here and not in Paris?"

"Because you would fail in Paris."

"Did I say that? I'm here to support my family, to put food on the table."

"You are like all women. You run away." Paul glared down at her, his face a mask of swollen anger.

"Wait a minute. Let me ask you something. Have your children eaten today, Paul?"

He took a step closer to her, and she instantly took an equal step back.

"Do you know when your children last ate a meal? Do you even know where they are? Are they warm? Are they lonely for their father? When was the last time you gave them anything but misery? You want money, not for them, not for your family, but for yourself.

You concoct an intellectual fantasy about your painting only an esoteric elitist would bother to read, all so you can paint and live with naked women and—"

"You bourgeois woman, how dare you speak to me like this?" he roared. "I will destroy this idiotic yellow house…all of this," he boomed, deep and loud, swiping his arm over the landscape.

"Really, how? With some brooding article about Vincent's madness? Vincent's madness was real and true. Name one thing that's real about you. Wait I know! The sex, the sex with innocents! That is why you want money, so you can have sex with other people's children and call it art!" She was screaming now. "What a ruse. You are just a common pervert."

Paul threw his cape over his shoulder. He glanced toward the house and spit on the path. "You think you are important now, Johanna? A seat at the table? You are nothing!" he screamed at her.

"What's the matter, Paul? Can't bully me like you bullied and destroyed Vincent? Was Vincent so threatening?"

"Vincent failed!" Paul's voice exploded everywhere at once, in the house, in the backyard, in the gazebo. His voice boomed in every corner. The glass rattled. "You are dead to me!" Paul yelled. "You stupid woman, trying to claim space for your dead men, making yourself a fool. Theo and Vincent—their work, not yours! Selling just like a whore, a pimp, an amateur! You blame me for Vincent's breakdown. Me!" he raged, staring at the heavens. "I was the one holding him together. The real trouble began when Theo told him he was going to marry you. That's why he killed himself. You and Theo killed him—your marriage, your money, your future, house, your child. Vincent was a martyr for you. That is the real tragedy. And now you mock him with a house painted yellow!"

"You are old news. Get off my property!" she screamed at the top of her lungs. "Go rot in the tropics, if you can get there!"

Johanna heard her guests on the porch behind her.

Fleur came to stand beside her. They watched Paul storm away, into the green beyond.

"The guests got an earful," Fleur said quietly. Then she let out a big haughty laugh, tossing her gorgeous curls, as though nothing serious had happened. It gave Johanna a few moments to get her composure back.

"Then they got their money's worth!" she said.

Andries joined them. "Well, I guess we didn't buy a Gauguin. He's still a force in Paris." He was beaming his biggest, most handsome smile, putting on a show for the guests.

"Maybe, but nothing will change. No one in Paris helped me before, no one will help me now."

"True, but now they will call you mad too. The writer, Jansen the museum director—they heard everything," Andries said.

Fleur walked back up the path, smiling at the crowd that had gathered. Drunken Schmidt, Johan, Jansen—all stood frozen, but their eyes all glinted like they had discovered gold.

She gave them all her magnetic smile and in a teasing voice said, "Who would have guessed talent is such a burden?" She held the door open with a laugh.

Finally, the guests were leaving. Jansen was first at the door.

"Thank you again, Mrs. Van Gogh," Jansen said, a little sloppy from keeping up with Schmidt. "You know really, an amazing day." She needed a commitment from him, she couldn't let him leave without it.

"You are welcome, Mr. Jansen. I was hoping to conclude our business?" She couldn't gage his intent. Was he appalled and no longer willing to hold a show for a mad painter? Could he still not see the opportunity?

"How did you find Vincent's work? Stirs the emotions, does it not?"

"Amazing work, Mrs. Van Gogh, agreed, unusual in every way, and of course the personality behind the work…so… unique."

"What selections do you think for the show? Thoughts?"

Jansen shifted on his feet, seeing the writer Johan was listening in.

"Excellent question, what to highlight, to showcase? What will attract the favorable crowd?" Jansen gently grabbed her elbow and moved her away from Johan. He whispered in her ear, "In Paris, many say…Vincent was a lunatic, a failure. Durand-Ruel refuses an exhibit, worrying about a backlash."

"Paris doesn't benefit from Vincent."

"A failure would be terrible for me personally, Mrs. Van Gogh. Our sponsors…you can imagine."

"You have the support of the Schmidts, they purchased again today."

"But you cannot guarantee a crowd or positive notices. I could look a fool."

I will bring the crowd.. The self-portraits, Vincent at his most vulnerable, with his head bandaged after the ear 'incident.

"No," Jo said. "You will look like a visionary, the first to present a Dutch modern master, Vincent van Gogh, in a prestigious museum!"

"I will need substantially more money than you may be thinking to justify the risk."

"Substantially more money" rang in her ears. But she smiled and said, "I understand, Mr. Jansen." She let him peck her on the cheek again and wished she had a saber, so she could slice his fleshy ear off.

Johan, the writer, was waiting to say good night. "A wonderful day, Mrs. Van Gogh." He stood so peacefully and didn't seem in any hurry to leave.

"Yes, thank you for coming, Mr. Cohen. I hope you write well of Vincent's work."

"Yes, count on it. You sold today?"

"Yes. What will you write?"

"I am composing my thoughts. I am an admirer of Vincent's paintings, and your efforts on his behalf are extraordinary."

"Well, it doesn't matter. I will publish all the letters, and Vincent's story will speak for itself. All this other business is just nonsense. Everyone has an opinion, no matter how uninformed." *Just leave now please. Can't you see how late it is?*

Her smile was not going to last much longer. Jansen had put her in the foulest of moods. How would she come up with "substantially more money?"

"Publishing the letters is a brilliant idea. You have much genius of your own."

Really? Genius of my own.

"I was beginning to worry I created a bad impression," she said.

"Well, as you said earlier, everyone has an opinion, no matter how uninformed."

"Oh, I didn't mean you, just generally," Jo said. "It's been a long day."

"I do have a few more question about Vincent."

"Alright, for a few moments. Would you like a sherry?"

"I would love one last drink. I might need a room here, though. And a moment alone with you would be grand."

Grand. Johanna poured him a sherry, wondering if he was flirting. Grand. What was that? He hasn't flirted before. Not the first time they met at the gallery in The Hague, though he kept her too long with so many questions, not today during the viewing and luncheon. He usually pushed hard questions without any tact, but no malice either.

She handed him the sherry. They sat in the study, in the dark and quiet, with the door open.

Johan was good-looking, clear skin and eyes, intelligent, obviously creative, but sensible, not overdone, no overt narcissism. Simple clothes, compact body movements.

One thing she noticed for the first time—he walked slowly, a hallmark of a back ailment. There was something Johanna could see but couldn't name. She inventoried in a halfhearted way.

He seemed ten years her junior, too young for her. The age difference and the lack of possibility for a relationship because of this allowed her to relax. And then there were the blisters and rashes to worry about. She didn't have any, thank the heavens, and it had been years.

"I have questions about Vincent's letters," Johan said. "If you can handle more questions tonight?" He looked into her face in a way he hadn't before, smiling, anticipating, and not holding a pencil.

Suddenly, she saw him differently. Before he had been a writer, a reporter, someone she needed to be nice to. Now there was something vulnerable about him, too thin, maybe a little gaunt.

"In the letters does Vincent explain his work?"

"Yes, his letters explain everything. They are a fascinating glimpse into the mind of a genius. He documents his approach in minute detail."

"You *are* tired. That sounds almost like an advertisement."

She thought back on the afternoon. Emile warned me, Paul will poison Paris against Vincent. He is trying to kill us. He has damaged me with Jansen.

This young man is still talking to me. He has a constant expression of raised eyebrows, as if anticipating the next thing and finding everything interesting. The way he smiled peacefully during the scene with Gauguin at the table—he was comfortable with confrontation, wasn't aggressive, but didn't look away, intelligent, edgy without anger. That's unusual, the warm and cool together. So exhilarating, Vincent might have said.

"All the other painters of his era developed a thesis for their vision, with a historic context. What was Vincent's?"

"Painting consoled him," she said. "In the beginning it was a profession he loved, then a love affair with a movement, then a divorce from the community, and at the end, it kept his demons away, for a while. He wanted to create a more consoling, exhilarating nature, he would say, to do with painting what music could do for the soul."

"Poetic. Sentimental."

Johanna stifled a yawn.

"What about the brushstrokes? His strokes are completely unique, his alone—how did he do that?"

"Are you also a painter, Mr. Cohen?"

"Yes, I paint. Please call me Johan."

"What is your approach to painting? Maybe you are intuitive, you find joy in creating as you go? Or some careful planning. You let the paint carry you someplace else?"

"I let myself get carried away."

He moved very close to her and examined her face. Almost inappropriate, Johanna thought, was he flirting?

"I would like to paint you. Would you allow me to create your portrait?"

"Are you flirting with me?"

"Do you mind?"

She took a breath. "Maybe I will pose for you, but how old are you?"

"I'm thirty."

"I'm not thirty."

"You have fooled me."

"Why are you flirting with me?"

"I should just kiss you."

Then he took her in his arms and very, very slowly moved in for a kiss, looking into her eyes all the while.

It was a good kiss. Thoughts of Vincent, theories of painting, the pain of Theo, Jansen's money—all grew dimmer.

He is a talented young man, was the first thought that made its way back in, as he released her from the kiss. Jo heard the small creek on the staircase of Willem's feet. He must have seen the kiss. And then Fleur's feet creaking on the stairs, and she imagined Fleur putting Willem back to bed. Johan kissed her again. Johanna and Johan broke apart and stared into each other's eyes.

"You know, I'm too old for children."

"I'm happy for you that you have your son. With my health, I could never pull it off."

"What's wrong with you?"

"I was a sickly child."

"A writer and a painter, and you're sickly. This is my lucky day."

"Sarcastic, Johanna. Doesn't suit you."

He kissed her again. It was another good kiss.

"Johanna!" She heard Andries call down the dark steep steps, into the basement of the old Bonger offices, now the storage and resting place of the paintings and effects of Vincent van Gogh. It had been a wise decision after closing the business to hold on to the building. Vincent's legacy was cumbersome, to say the least, and there wasn't room at the inn to store everything.

She shouted back at him, but he couldn't hear her, and his footsteps clomping down the stairs echoed in the vast basement. "The shippers are waiting." She winced at his annoyance.

"I'm adding two portraits." The Stedelijk Museum show was days away. She had finally negotiated a price she could live with and was able to get them to agree on a two-month exhibit. The Schmidts had their eye on the *Almond Blossom*, the painting Vincent had given to Willem as his birthday present. She would never sell that painting, even at a premium price. That painting was reserved for the future Van Gogh Museum. Instead, she'd spent everything she had, sold off sentimental family China, crystal, some jewelry. She had borrowed even more from Andries for publicity materials. She was trying hard not to be a burden to him. She never meant to be, but he was such a good soul he just took it all on, over and over.

She must, must bring in a mainstream crowd, not just avant-garde fringe buyers looking for modern bargains. She wouldn't get another chance to secure their legacy. How many more years could she run an inn?

Showing the portraits was a huge risk. Like putting a spotlight on everything that went wrong with Vincent. It could backfire so terribly. Was this really the best way to get attention and quiet the critics, or would it just inflame everyone? Was she once again pushing too far, not understanding her place? This time if she failed, there was nowhere else to go. She was already home.

She carefully considered all her selections for the grand exhibition, no longer relying on the "experts" from Paris, like Roland. She was going through one of the large crates housing the paintings.

"Hurry," Andries shouted. "If this shipment misses the carriage we'll need a second one…another expense. What are you substituting?"

"I'm coming."

Upstairs, Johanna carefully removed the sheets to reveal two self-portraits of Vincent with his head wrapped in bandages, covering his sliced ear. Vincent, morbid and proud, staring out from the canvas, pipe in his teeth, calmly telling us, "*This is not a mortal wound. See, I am painting.*" A surreal likeness, emotion swirling with all the Vincent hallmarks of flamboyant strokes, strong contrasting colors, and always the pain, soothing his agony with paint. Perfect.

"Why display those wretched portraits?" Andries said. "You're just playing into his critics' hands. Vincent as an imaginative lunatic, not an artist?"

"I have a plan," said Jo. At the large, high desk, Johan and Jo packed each painting into cloth-lined wooden packing crates. He put his arms around her and gave her a gentle hug.

"Speaking as a writer, I would kill to be the first to write a review of a show containing those two portraits. The world has morbid curiosity. Definitely it will create press attention."

"Exactly. You know, Andries," said Jo, breaking Johan's embrace, "that wretched Gauguin article," Jo said. "It is very good for us. It creates controversy, free publicity, cuts down on marketing expenses. And now everyone will want to see the portraits, and we will have our crowd!"

Yes, I will need his heartbreak of a story, Jo thought.

Jo needed to practice the speech she would give, introducing Vincent's work. Johanna assembled Andries, Fleur, Johan, and Willem. They sat in front of her in the bay window of the Bonger office, mimicking an audience. Now that she stood before them, she wondered if she was doing the right thing.

Johan sat on the floor with Willem, waiting for Johanna to begin. He was instructing Willem in a drawing lesson.

"I picked the best pieces from the South," Jo said. "I included *The Potato Eaters* to show the contrast of the artist's journey from dark colors to the rapture of the light. I am calling this speech 'The Man from the North, Who Painted the South.'" Was she avoiding it, afraid to speak Vincent's truth? "What do you think?" Their faces said it all, she knew it was horrible. Everyone wanted to hear about the madness of the man. She had already sent the portraits with the ear. Somehow, she had to make Vincent's pain everyone's pain, in a speech in front of, hopefully, hundreds of people and reporters. Still, she was beyond nervous to reveal the risky truth.

She only needed to speak for about fifteen minutes, Jansen, the museum director, had said. Speak from "a woman's point of view," he'd said. "The audience will want to hear from you, the woman in the picture, so to speak, your personal stories." She was a woman. She had lived with Vincent. If she were a man, would she have a different point of view? Fifteen minutes would feel like fifteen hours, she feared.

"Speak from the heart," Johan said.

She needed courage and sat down next to Johan and held his hand.

"Tell about the ear!" said Willem. Andries picked him up and put him on his lap. He immediately squirmed off. "Uncle Andries! I am too old."

"You sent those portraits," Johan said. "You have a compelling argument to go with them, to counter Gauguin. Reporters will ask over and over, until they are satisfied."

"You know, I have a theory," Fleur jumped in. "I think Paul Gauguin cut off Vincent's ear. He's tall, nasty, with all that primitive talk. Imagine trying to cut off your own ear. You would need pressure. How do you apply pressure? Your reflexes would stop you." She demonstrated, grabbing her ear with one hand and miming a knife in the other.

"Your reflexes wouldn't stop you if you were inebriated enough," Johanna said. "Anyway, I don't think Paul cut off Vincent's ear. But he knows more than he's letting on."

"You never told me why he cut off his ear," Willem said.

"The word in Paris is that Paul Gauguin is starving to death in Martinique," Andries said. "No sponsors, few sales. Reporters are fascinated with him. Better plan the answers, Johanna."

"Martinique is an island. How do you starve to death on an island?" asked Fleur.

"Surrounded by fish, why can't he eat them?" Willem piped in.

"That's a good point, young man. Maybe I should buy another of his paintings, it might shut him up," said Andries.

She feared speaking from the heart. Vincent was overpowering, equal amounts of wonder and horror, his pain and love, uncontrollable and inconsolable. Shining the spotlight on his pain, would that change anyone's mind? And what would the world think of her then?

Fleur jumped in, "No matter how you slice it, that business with the ear really sticks in your mind."

"Oh God, enough," Johanna said. "Willem, your uncle Vincent was ill and didn't know what he was doing. It was an accident."

"How do you cut off an ear by accident? You have to be precise to cut off an ear." Fleur just wouldn't let it go.

"All right, I will tell the personal story of Vincent and art—his rapture, so to speak. Get everyone interested in the letters by quoting from them. I want everyone to stop seeing Vincent as a madman, but rather as a brokenhearted man, who dedicated himself to reinventing Dutch painting and became a modern master." Her stomach flipped over just saying the words.

"Excellent, I agree, and you are the only one who can do it," said Johan.

27

Mr. Jansen, the museum director, walked the gallery, his hands clasped behind his back, beaming with pleasure at every painting. Johanna and Andries and Mrs. Van Gogh walked alongside him. Vincent's mother had never seen much of his work. Now she could enjoy the celebration and feel the pride she was entitled to. Jo had hung the paintings by color scheme, the way Vincent had in her Paris apartment with Theo, years ago.

The first solo exhibition of Vincent van Gogh. She had done it.

She remembered Vincent's first showing in Paris, the *Painters of Le Petite Boulevard*. The bohemian café, the boozy patrons, the wealthy, the avant-garde and tourists mingling together—very modern. And the showing in the Paris apartment, every inch covered in van Gogh colors.

Now this. A prestigious museum in a first-class European city. If all went well, this would be the breakthrough, the beginning of making Vincent world famous. Everyone will know the true amazing story of Vincent van Gogh, the brilliant, passionate artist who cut off his ear and gave it to a prostitute. And the tragedy of his suicide. The story would spread like a wildfire, impossible to put out. Just let it burn and get out of the way.

One day, there could be the ultimate achievement, his own museum. If it didn't go well, and she failed to create the dramatic impression she needed there would be no one to pick up his torch. His star would never rise.

"Well done, Mrs. Van Gogh. What a pleasure to see it all come together." Jansen's voice was hollow sounding, echoing around the large room with its enormously high ceilings, no carpets, and no people yet, only Vincent's paintings to absorb the sound.

"I shall open the doors in a few minutes, and then in a half hour or so, depending upon how long it takes to fill the room, I introduce you at the podium, emphasizing your unique perspective as a woman. Then you will make your remarks. Is that good for you, Mrs. Van Gogh?"

"Yes, perfect." Johanna's voice had a trembling echo. She was nervous and trying to stay calm. *What is well done will always remain well done,* and of course the reverse was also true. What is terrible can never be made good.

Johanna gestured with her eyes to Fleur to meet her in the ladies' room.

They strolled into the restroom. Fleur passed a silver flask to Jo.

She tipped it back twice and then sucked on a mint. Fleur did the same. They stood together at the mirror.

"What if I threw a party and no one comes?"

"I would say at least you made the effort!"

Johanna dropped her chin to chest.

"Don't worry," Fleur said. "There are people already waiting to get in. We've got five minutes."

No one could ever have dreamed this. Johanna Bonger, insurance clerk, schoolteacher, translator, wife, and mother. Now what would she be called? Art dealer.

Johanna could feel her nerves getting the better of her. She was taking shallow breaths.

"Just smile," Fleur said. "This is all brilliant. You really don't know how brilliant. Are you nervous?"

"No," Jo replied. Then, "Yes, I am nervous about failing."

"You won't fail, you never fail. You always find another way."

She knows me so well. "I'm nervous, that feels like a failure of confidence."

"Most women would have asked a man to do all of this, but you didn't. Andries was available."

"I did think of it. But then I would have been a double failure." They both giggled a bit, like schoolgirls.

"There's no such thing as failure. By trying you are already a success," Fleur said. "No one expects such determination from a woman." They stood together in front of the mirror.

"No, they don't expect it from a 'nothing' woman." That is what Gauguin had called her—a nothing woman.

"Isn't it grand to be nothing together?" Fleur hugged Jo.

Jo hugged her back. "Don't think about the artists, they won't be here. If they are here, ignore them," said Fleur.

"The preening peacocks scrounging for crumbs."

"I didn't see any peacocks. Only the cream of Dutch society, curious about the paintings. And they have never seen anything like this before! The men will think you're lovely. The women will think you're brave. Smile, Jo, No one is better than you!"

Johanna smiled.

"*Tres bien!,*" Fleur said.

The room was a hazy ocean of beautifully dressed people. Fleur was right, they were mostly the wealthy Dutch, women with lovely upswept hair and gowns with low lacy bodices, men in fashionable black, people with money. Some couples she recognized from their visits to the inn, some from around town. They had all come to see the paintings and hear about their own Dutch modern master, Vincent. They were all smiling, chatting excitedly with one another.

Johanna had tried to listen for the gossip, to get a sense of the crowd's reaction to Vincent's work but could only get snippets with so many people talking at once.

Bizarre work…almost out of focus…crazy…I think he was institutionalized…I've never seen anything like it… I love the colors.

A mixture of responses, good enough, Jo thought. She passed Mrs. Van Gogh, who smiled and dabbed her eyes with a beautiful, crocheted handkerchief.

And more…*The work is anarchy…it is designed to undermine art…society at large you know… anarchy through art, everyone in Europe knows… She had to pay for the room!*

Johanna stood stiffly at the podium in front of a wall of landscapes. She knew if she spoke loudly, it would help disguise the nervous tremor in her voice. She'd placed *The Potato Eaters* in a prominent position flanked by sunflowers. She knew it wasn't the painting everyone wanted to see, but somehow it was still one of her favorites. The lighting was good, the paintings vibrated with color, even from a distance.

She took a deep breath, smiled, and began.

"No matter where I go, everyone I meet, whether it is here or Paris, a museum curator, a writer, or a person interested in art, always sooner or later they ask me the same question. Can you guess? Was Vincent insane?"

The audience was quiet, a few whispers. She let the silence hold.

"I will tell you my answer. But first, what do you think the next question is?" She paused for a moment. "Is it true that Vincent cut off his own ear?" That got a few of them squirming, and a few people looked at their feet.

She looked at Fleur beaming out from the audience, standing with Andries, her bright eyes glistening with tears of pride, her lips holding back her emotion as she smiled brilliantly at Johanna. Andries handed Fleur his breast-pocket silk handkerchief, and she dabbed at her eyes. He put his arm around her shoulders with a soft consoling half hug, pulling her to him.

"I will tell you this. Vincent was not mad. But he was a man who suffered greatly. Especially at the end of his life, when he painted his greatest paintings, and lived in terrible isolation and loneliness. A true illness of the heart. He found little solace in life to ease his suffering. Except for two things. One was his family, his brother Theo, and the second was his painting.

"The personal, in modern painting, becomes universal. We all suffer together. We are all the same. Vincent used colors to soften his life, which was overwhelmed by suffering. His pain was raw, for everyone to see. In painting, he achieved salvation. He was also a wonderful writer and wrote hundreds of letters, enough to fill several books. I have organized them all and soon they will be published, so the world can see his thoughts and feelings and ideas.

"In one letter Vincent writes, 'I have given my heart to painting and lost my mind in the process.' Painting gave him purpose beyond creation, it gave him solace from his suffering and often left him exhilarated and at peace. This is the peace he hoped to bring to all of us. He was a man of deep thought and contradictions. The suffering of others pained him, and the arrogance of others enraged him, swinging his moods beyond what we think of as normal. His dream more than anything was to help ease the suffering of others, and that is what he hoped his painting would bring. Joy, peace, harmony with life and nature. There is nothing 'mad' about any of that."

She continued, "There is nothing intellectual about the future of modern art. Modern is pure emotion and acceptance of that display."

Her hand rested on her breast. Would the crowd understand? Something good would happen now, she could feel it. Then the applause began.

Jansen held out his arm to her as she left the podium. They glided to the center of the room where the reception line had begun.

Look at that long line, Johanna thought. Wealthy patrons, important writers, almost everyone she needed to create the legend of Vincent van Gogh. She had done it without any help from Paris. *His pain reflects everyone's pain.*

Couples stood together, waiting for a moment with her. The room now had a happy air, full and buzzing with noisy energy. Johanna felt it envelop her, a warm flush of energy.

She had done well. Life had changed, the world had moved. This day had been swirling in the universe waiting for her to capture it, for Vincent and Theo. She was the only one who could have put the pieces together.

Jansen had done his job well. There were at least four reporters, pencils and pads ready to go. Roland was talking to them. He was so disappointed she hadn't asked him to speak at this big exhibit, as if he owned any part of the van Gogh legacy.

"Mrs. Van Gogh, I am hoping to have an interview with you," a reporter said, and the three other voices followed. Jansen was herding them, to wait for her.

"Yes, an interview, just a moment," she said and turned to the first couple on the line. *The critics, the reporters will wait for me, let them see this long line of people, to soften them up. Art is for the people, so I will talk to the people first because that is what Vincent would do.*

"We wanted to tell you how much we enjoyed the exhibit. Thank you so much! So exciting for us to see new works in Amsterdam," the man said.

"The colors are amazing, aren't they?" his wife said.

"Vincent used to say, color expresses something in itself," Johanna said.

"Did I hear you say there are over eight hundred paintings?"

"Yes, it is a large collection."

"Is there a dealer in Paris we can correspond with?" the man asked.

"Not in Paris," Johanna replied. She was distracted by

Roland—he was mingling around the reporters. What was he saying about Vincent, Theo, her?

"The dealer, Mrs. Van Gogh?" the man asked again.

"You can speak with me. I represent the collection," Johanna said, snapping back to attention.

"You? How wonderful," said his wife, exchanging glances with her husband. "I loved your presentation, Mrs. Van Gogh. Cutting off his ear—it was a symbol of his pain."

Everyone was intrigued by the madness, Jo realized. But now with an abundance of sympathy.

"Poor Vincent," the woman said. "The pain he must have endured. You and your husband, all you did for him—what a beautiful family." And that was the consensus Jo heard up and down the line.

After three hours, four press interviews, and countless well-wishers, Jansen and the museum's staff urged the last few guests out the door. She was surprised to see Roland was still here. He had kept his distance from her but was making his way over now, as she was finishing with the last reporter. What nasty gossip was he spreading?

"Mrs. Van Gogh, congratulations to you," Roland said. "When I first heard you were going to deliver the opening remarks, I was worried you'd panic. And who wouldn't, with all these people. Bravo!"

Jo smiled and said thank you, then turned away from him. The reporter resumed his questions,

She talked to them all, the reporters and guests, until her voice turned raspy, and Willem repeatedly met her eye and cocked his head toward the door, a gesture he'd picked up from Fleur.

All art will be personal from now on, the personal is universal, in modern art. I have brought them home, and they will live forever.

Paul

The painting *Breton Village in the Snow* sat on the easel by the window, allowing light to flood the canvas in his darkened room. Was it done? Outside, palm and other tropical trees swayed in the steamy breeze and blazing, bright light. His head throbbed and he took a few deep breaths, pausing for a moment to look out the window.

Women in cotton dresses bustled down the street carrying baskets. Men on bikes pedaled and careened around them. Paul looked at the snow-covered house on his easel and remembered the woman he had loved more than any other woman. She had lived in that house in Pont Avon, France. Now she was gone forever, and his whole body ached for her. He would do anything to be with her again.

When he closed his eyes he saw her, Madeline, vibrating against the white snow. He had painted her once, years ago. He longed for that painting, dreamed about her sitting for him, teasing him, and that sly, smart expression she wore, wise beyond her years.

White-looking flakes that weren't white, but grey, yellow, green. The church steeple loomed large behind the houses, a fence in front of them. That was how he remembered it. His breath was short, and it was hard to fill his lungs. He felt lightheaded and thirsty.

He held the palette and brushes in his arm and hand. He was emaciated underneath his billowing white shirt. Streams of sweat poured down his body, drenching his shirt. He must be feverish, causing him to tremble and struggle with his brushstroke.

He lifted his arm for a dab of paint and collapsed on the floor. Eyes open, staring at the ceiling. His palette stuck on his chest, paint covering his torso. Ha, he tried to laugh at the palette on his chest, but he had no breath left. Black dots circled his vision—he could barely see.

Bare feet thudded over to him. A little wail, and two pairs of women's hands dragged him up to the bed. They tried talking to him, his eyes open, unblinking.

One of them ran to the front door and into the street. He laughed one final time as his world turned to black.

A sign in front proclaimed the Martinique Auction House. It was a large colonial-style building on the steamy tropical street surrounded by smaller, brightly colored buildings. A large poster stood in front and read ESTATE AND PAINTINGS OF PAUL GAUGUIN, TODAY ONLY.

Inside the crowded, muggy, buggy, hot hall, an auctioneer held up a sewing machine, claiming it was in perfect condition. There was a lot of interest, many rapid-fire bids from eager native families.

"Sold!" The auctioneer pounded the block. "For eighty-five francs!" A man with a large family in tow took the machine and happily paid up.

"Next, here is Paul Gauguin's final painting!"

It was his, and it sat on the easel upside down. The bidding opened to silence, except for the rustle of fans swatting at the flies, ladies attempting to cool themselves in the oppressive heat.

After another attempt by the auctioneer, an elegantly dressed young European gentleman bid, three francs. More fanning, more silence, then a bang.

"Sold for three francs!"

Another European gentleman, obviously not local, approached the auctioneer. He righted the painting, turning it from upside down to right side up.

"Would you consider an offer for the entire collection of paintings?"

"Wait a moment, I will get you a price," said the auctioneer.

28

Johanna read from the newspaper in a sarcastic voice. It was a piece by Roland himself.

"The van Gogh woman is charming enough, but it irritates me when someone gushes fanatically on a subject she knows nothing about, and although blinded by sentimentality still thinks she is adopting a strictly critical attitude. It is schoolgirlish twaddle, nothing more. The work that Mrs. Van Gogh would like best is the one that was the most bombastic and sentimental, the one that made her shed the most tears. She forgets that her sorrow is turning Vincent into a god."

"What a rat," Fleur said. "Sounds like you struck a nerve with that one."

"It's just because you fired him and stood your ground," Johan added. "More paper for the fire then!"

"Why is he mean to you, Mother?"

"I don't think he meant to be mean, Willem."

"I feel sick, my stomach hurts," Willem said, looking like he might keel over.

Jo felt his forehead. "You don't seem feverish.. This is a great day for us, we have done it!" Jo said.

"There is something going around." Andries said.

"I am so nauseated I can't move," Fleur said. "My head is swimming like a...like a..." She gave up thinking, groaned, and put her head down on the table. Andries stood behind her and rubbed her back. Fleur was paler than cream.

They better get the wedding planned *tout de suite*, before she gets too big for a white dress, thought Jo.

"I can't go to school. I will have to hide when I throw up," Willem said and put his head down on his arms just like Fleur.

"It's just all the excitement has got your stomach upset. Let me get you some breakfast," Johanna said and leaned across the table and passed him the breadbasket and some slices of cheese and fish. "I'm not worried about Roland. All press is good. Remember Vincent used to say, 'The eternal law demands everything must change, but I would rather have a failure than sit and do nothing.'"

"You are a grand success," said Johan.

"Roland is a rat! Let's go find him and cut off his tail!" Fleur said.

"This is about emotion, and I think you captured that very well," said Johan. "What's wrong with turning Vincent into a god? The whole thing is a compliment."

"Willem, what can I make you? Would some tea and dipping toast help your stomach?"

"Yes, I'll try. But I can't go to school."

"Next on your checklist, Jo," Andries said. "Now is the time to hoard the inventory, get the prices up."

She remembered Theo had always said, 'art must live in the world, not just museums.' She should make a list, what to sell, what to hoard. What to share with museums and what to save for the Van Gogh Museum. Now perhaps there would be money. She would like to move to a house in Amsterdam, with a better school for Willem. A house with a large room where all the pictures could hang where she could receive guests…like at Durand-Ruel. She wanted to see New York. She would translate the letters to English and introduce Vincent to the wealthy Americans.

A thousand thoughts blessed her at once, about Vincent, how to sell, who to trust…what to do next. First she would organize shows across the capitals of Europe…Berlin, London—the town that still laughed the loudest at modern art. She would show them all.

Then she felt something click in her brain and a flood of relief—, the realization Willem wasn't sick, and she wasn't either. She hadn't even thought about that horrible fear for weeks, months. They had been spared. She could marry Johan, if she wanted.

"The museum show is a bona fide hit," Johan said. "The crowd was impressive, and reviews were positive. The announcement of the letters is genius. The anticipation for the volume is astonishing. Not everyone can afford a van Gogh, but most can buy a book. Vincent's life is a mystery everyone wants to solve. He will be seen for the great artist he was." Johan waited a beat and then added, "How are the letters going?"

"I can't get the typewriter to work, that is how the letters are going. I should get another." Publication will mean publicity throughout Europe. Museums, collectors—everyone will read them.

"Can I see the typewriter?" Willem said, picking up his head off his arms. "I am going upstairs. Mom, can you bring me the tea and toast in bed?"

"Of course, Willem."

"Everyone will see the genius in all of Vincent's so-called madness," Johan said.

"You can really see how he made lemonade from the lemons he was dealt," Fleur said.

"Lemonade from lemons …you sound like an old schoolteacher, Fleur." And he pushed back from the table.

"Who are you calling *old*, young man?" Fleur swatted at him as he dodged her blow.

Johanna sat in front of the typewriter, with Johan hovering over her. She was elated from the enormous success of the museum exhibit, despite the stab in the back from Roland. The other positive reviews kept rolling through her thoughts, leaving her feeling a combination of astonishment and peaceful relief. She had a stack of telegrams from dealers, customers, requesting a showing and looking to buy, and inquiries about the Letters of Vincent van Gogh from publishers.

She mustn't rest and now redoubled her efforts to get Vincent's letters ready for publication. Translations were necessary, as Vincent often wrote in French. His handwriting sometimes gave her fits. And no dates. Hundreds and hundreds of letters with no dates. She had developed terrible hand strain from all the writing. And this new modern contraption of a typewriter was malfunctioning.

"I see your problem, let me try." Johan started poking around the machine, alternating between looking at the machine and the directions.

"I can't get the ribbon in, and when I do, it pops out immediately, printing half the letters, and I am ruining all my paper!"

Johan was a talented man. He could paint, write, but there was no way he could fix this. After a few minutes, he gave up and picked up his sketch pad.

"Leave it alone. Let me sketch you, here in the light," Johan said. He leaned over her and brushed his hand against her cheek.

"No." She kept fiddling with the typewriter, adjusting the ribbon, typing a key. The letter was half printed. "Ah!"

"Why no sketch, Jo?" he said so softly she could barely hear him.

"I don't have time to sit still, and I don't want to see a sketch of me lying around for the next twenty years."

"Johanna!" Fleur shouted up from the second-floor landing.

"What?" Jo shrieked. God, the typewriter was driving her mad. After a moment, Jo heard her footsteps up the stairs.

Fleur came into the doorway with Willem.

"There you go, prince. I'll bet twenty minutes, and you've got the machine running smoothly."

Jo wiped her ink-stained fingertips and grabbed for Willem. He edged around her and nudged her away from the typewriter. He peered into the front of the machine, studying all the elements, the keys, the ribbon. He grabbed for the directions, lying on the table next to the typewriter, and read the instructions through a magnifying class.

"Jo, we have a full pride of van Gogh pilgrims downstairs. Dries has them, but we are leaving for town. What do you want to do?"

"Do they look like they have money?"

"No, the usual passionate young painters coming to study their master and feel the rapture."

She said her silent prayer, *before she is done, she will have Van Goghs hanging in every major museum in Europe and the United States.*

Vincent van Gogh, the modern master. She would go greet his pilgrims and feel the rapture, too.

EPILOGUE

1914

Willem

Riding the train to France to meet my mother gave me time to let my mind wander. I didn't realize my mother was famous (in a good, not notorious way) until all at once, in a single moment. People thought our family was normal, which then, in my ignorant youth made me feel more comfortable with all the messy chaos surrounding the art world.

One day, friends of my mother came to visit and gave her a poster for a "Women's Socialist Party" organizing event.

"Mrs. Van Gogh, a woman of your stature, your fame, all your achievements, if you would lend your name to the movement, you alone would make a huge difference."

"I am not famous," mother said, laughing and reading through the large poster. "Well, anyway, this is an excellent idea! The Women's Socialist Party. I will certainly put in the window."

Andries came in, saw the flyer and was very against it, thought it terrible for business. But mother, never one to just go along, stood her ground and kept the socialist poster up anyway.

I arrived at my destination, Auvers-sur-Oises, north of Paris, to my uncle Vincent's resting place, come to witness the re-burial of my father here beside his famous brother. The first person I saw was Emile Bernard, talking with a reporter whose notepad and pencil were almost at Emile's chin. The reporter barked out questions, pushing his notepad up and down for emphasis.

"Is it true Paul Gauguin wanted to leave his desert island…to die in Paris?"

"I don't know," Emile said, digging his hands in his pockets, looking around.

"It was reported his sewing machine sold for eighty-five francs and his last painting sold for only three francs. What do you know about it?"

"Nothing. That was news ten years ago."

"Why do you think he painted the Breton village in Martinique? Do you think he wanted to come home? You painted with him in Martinique, didn't you? Do you think he drank himself to death?"

Emile saw me and held his arms out to me to join him, but the last thing I wanted to do was talk to a reporter. I especially didn't want to get into the notorious squabble between Emile and Gauguin which still fascinated the press even after Gauguin's untimely death. The press had a way of hounding me, the nephew of the famous artist, inheritor of the greatest collection of art in modern times.

I tipped my hat to him, and half listened and looked around the cemetery, wondering why I had agreed to come to attend mother's ghastly new publicity event to sell even more copies of Vincent's Letters. I walked away half listening to Emile fending off the badgering reporter.

I moved through the cemetery toward Vincent's grave and saw Mother and Aunt Fleur close together, their bright red woolen coats brushing against each other. They looked as beautiful as ever. They just went together in a special way. Now that I was off at university, I was just realizing how unusual they both were, in their intelligence, humor, their closeness. They dressed so colorfully, especially Fleur. They always stood out in the sea of boring gray, brown, and black clothes around them.

They stood in front of a stone wall, by Vincent's grave with another freshly dug open grave next to it, waiting for its grotesque delivery, my father's casket with his fifteen-year-old remains. I joined them and we all hugged. Aunt Fleur twirled her outrageously-colored umbrella closed, leaned on it like it was a great prop, and threw her head back, tossing all her thick hair.

"Hello there, Mr. Engineer. You look mighty tall and handsome in that uniform!" Ah, she noticed, good. We were neutral in the war shaking the continent, but still I was in the standing army. She looked so lovely. I gave her a kiss on the cheek, and she cooed at me.

"Willem, such a good nephew! Lord, poor Vincent, what would he be thinking?" Fleur said. "His work everyone thought worthless now hanging in museums across Europe, and soon, the United States. Thanks to you, Jo."

The group of men I passed at the entrance to the cemetery were coming our way.

"Johanna, the press," Fleur said, sounding a little ominous to my ear.

"Don't hate me for this, Willem," Mother said.

I was angry with her for this disgusting grave moving event. And used as a publicity stunt! Well, at least she acknowledged my revulsion.

"Theo would be proud of you. Willem needs to grow up," Fleur said, and gave me a wink.

I watched Mother's face flush, pink to red. Tears welled up in her eyes. "Oh, I think I am losing my mind, Willem. You look so handsome, just like your father."

Johan, my stepfather walked up to them, offering Johanna his arm. She took it. He wiped a new tear off her cheek.

He smiled at her. She smiled back.

Mother kissed me on the cheeks, and she touched my face and held me for a moment and then let me go and turned to look at the press.

My cousin Maria, Fleur and Andries's daughter, saw me and squealed with delight. She ran into my arms. A few years ago, I would have picked her up and slung her on my hip. She was like a miniature Fleur. Now, too big for picking up. I missed her, she was an amazing bundle of energy and always put me in a good mood.

Uncle Dries embraced me heartily. "Willem, so good to see you. How is university? Have you learned to build a bridge, a road? I want to hear all about it! Willem, come look over here," he said. "Come with me please." I walked to Uncle Vincent's grave.

"Horrible, gruesome, I would rather be burned than sit in that hole called a grave." Maria pointed to the empty black pit next to Vincent's grave, meant for my father's remains.

He smiled and clapped me on the back. "This is a very smart move and will help sell the letters. We are aiming for the museum, remember. You could design it."

"Moving bodies, I could never imagine such a debacle. Are we having a séance for lunch?" I said under my breath.

"A séance!" laughed Maria. "Good joke, Willem."

"It's public relations," said Mother, joining us and preparing for us to have our picture taken.

"I am going to hide," I said.

"Hang on a minute," Mother said, smiling at me. She gently grabbed my arm. "I'm going to say a few words, please stand beside me. You can do that for me, can't you?"

Then Mother, Johanna van Gogh-Bonger, stood surrounded by a dozen reporters in front of the gravesite. I stood gamely next to her, looking down at the ground while she made her statement.

"I loved Theo van Gogh. He was a brilliant visionary and the first true dealer in modern art. Many artists owe their careers to him. Theo was dedicated to his brother Vincent. Together they made history. I think they knew they would, and it is their tragedy they didn't live to see it. They belong together, here, for eternity."

She took a deep breath.

"People come to visit Vincent's grave, to retrace his steps, his journey. Without Theo, there wouldn't be a Vincent. It wasn't simply financial support. Giving Vincent's letters to the world has been my life's purpose. Vincent said of Theo in the letters, 'You are more than an art dealer. I see your thoughts in my colors, my compositions.' Theo should have fame and not lie unknown, forgotten. And now he won't. He was loved, adored by the modern painters of Paris, by all of us.

"This is a very emotional day for us. For me. When I lost my husband, I thought my world would end." She gestured to me. "If not for my son, Willem, I think I might have died myself. Thank you for coming," she concluded.

A reporter approached me and attempted an interview. "The nephew of Vincent van Gogh! His namesake, is that right?"

"I go by Willem, not Vincent."

"Oh yes. What was it like to grow up with all those van Gogh's hanging around? Growing up in a household surrounded by genius?"

"You know, he was dead when I was growing up."

The reporter responded quizzically. "Yes. Which is your favorite painting?"

"I am studying to be an engineer. I am not schooled in art," I said.

Then Mother intervened. "The *Almond Blossom* is Willem's favorite. Vincent painted it for him when he was born. It hung above his bed his entire childhood. Vincent was dedicated to Theo, Theo to Vincent—the painting is a symbol of their deep connection."

"How many copies of the *Letters of Vincent van Gogh* have you sold" the reporter asked Johanna.

"They are best-sellers in our country. Early next year they will be published throughout the rest of Europe, including France, then translations for England and America. Thank you so much for coming." She took my arm, "Come, we must go to our luncheon."

"Willem, you really will have to work harder with the press. Make a list of the points you need to make, and have it sound like quick chitchat, bite-sized pieces they can write down."

"I could never do anything like this." This was messy, out of control. "Where is the reason in any of this?" I didn't wait for answer, I turned to leave.

"Where are you going? Wait, Willem. Please don't leave. I have something else to tell you."

"Oh no, what?" I sounded like I was whining, a fate worse than death. *Buck up, Will*, I thought to myself.

"I am leaving Amsterdam."

"Another speaking tour? The war…This Great War they call it. Europe is dangerous. Is that such a good idea? Please don't leave. I'll have endless worry."

"No, I'm going to America, to New York City."

"America! Why are you going? A proletariat socialist convention?"

"No."

"New York! Good for you, Mother! Is Uncle Dries having a fit?"

"No, he is fine. I'm translating the letters into English. There's huge demand for them. Your father and I were talking of moving there before he died. He was going to open a gallery there. He was done with Paris."

"You and father in America? I'd never have guessed."

"I know, I'd forgotten myself. Imagine how different everything would have been if your father had lived. I know he would be so proud of you. I am so proud of you. You've built a strong independent life. I'm sorry, I don't know why I'm so morbid today."

I remember I hugged her a long time, she always liked that.

"I would say don't go to America, but I'm guessing there isn't anyone else you would trust with the translation of the letters."

"I would trust you. Your English is flawless. You take after me that way. And I have something more critical to negotiate with you." She took my hand. "You must promise me to protect the work. Even though we are neutral in this war, I worry about bombs, the fighting…"

"I didn't even think of it."

"This is your legacy—the greatest collection of modern work created by a single artist in the shortest period. Your father said once, 'What we did will always remain well done, and in the end, we can say the argument has been won.' So, there is one last argument." She paused locking eyes with me. I had no idea what was coming.

"The museum—with the war delaying all the plans, I won't live to see it. You can do the museum, in Amsterdam. You must do this, there is no choice."

"There is always a choice. I want a practical, private life. I don't want my name in the paper. I don't know anything about art, making speeches. I'll look a fool. Wallowing in all that emotion—it doesn't lead anywhere."

"Emotion leads everywhere. You're smart, and you'll figure it out. The inventory list is in the Bonger office at home. You must protect the work. And one last gift for you. My journal is also at the office. It tells the story of the legacy, how it was put together. It's for you."

"Your own diaries, of how you created the legacy?"

"It's family history."

"I've wondered. Do you think Vincent would have wanted the letters, his most secret thoughts, his anguish, exploited, translated into different languages? Used to sell his paintings to the highest bidder?" I shouldn't have said it, and the moment I blurted out the words I wished I hadn't.

"You might be right. But I did it, and I won't apologize. What

Vincent wanted was to be a successful painter and to have a family. Now he has both for eternity. Beyond your lifetime, and your children's lifetime, Vincent will still be a household name. We will be dust. Take my journals. They should be part of the record. Willem, it's never too late to learn. Promise me."

"I promise."

Fleur joined us. "Jo, you ready for lunch or need more time with Tall-and-Handsome?"

"We are done. Will you join us, Willem?" Mother asked. I nodded yes.

"All right then, let's go to lunch," said Fleur, grabbing us both and squaring her shoulders like she would break anything in her way.

1974

Mother said people are born the way they are. I was a born an engineer. That is what she called me—the Engineer. I like knowing how things work, especially complicated things. I enjoy understanding what everyone else doesn't. I didn't understand art. At the home of my childhood, it was "rapture, rapture" all the time. I perceived it as a kind of sorcery that was not for me.

At the time of his death, Vincent had sold two paintings. He was known locally in Montmartre, by other avant-garde painters and a few critics. When he died his paintings were not in circulation, no galleries or museums owned him. Shortly after his premature death, his brother, my father, died a horrific death of paralysis and dementia due to syphilis. Then all their friends began dying too. Vincent was on his way to obscurity.

Adolphe Monticelli was a brilliant painter my uncle Vincent was greatly influenced by. A few museum types might know his name, but even a regular museum goer couldn't name a Monticelli painting or even know his name. To my mind this was the possible fate unfolding for Vincent were it not for my mother. She was his champion. Everyone knows *Starry Night*, the sunflowers, the self-portraits. There isn't a major museum in Europe or America that doesn't showcase van Goghs.

Dear Theo,

My dear brother, our neurosis comes from an obsession with art and following the ragged, blasted trail of an artist. We must protect our health, to endure all the setbacks headed our way. Death is always in our midst, but we must work with single focus and prevail. A clean way of living will help our fatal obsession. No idling, no women, little drink, cold water, fresh air, and never let oneself go, no matter how much we may want to. Then we will escape the swirl of black and lose ourselves in our compositions and color and grow our productive days. This is the plan, and we must stick to it. Enough already! I have a heavy paint order, quite substantial, and all of it is necessary for me to make progress while the weather, the flowers, and blooms are still strong. Make haste with the shipment, I beg you!

15 Malachite green, double tubes
10 Chrome yellow, citron ditto
10 Cadmium yellow, # 2 double tubes
3 Chrome yellow # 3 ditto
3 Ocher, yellow
3 Vermilion ditto
6 Geranium Lake, small tubes (newly pounded, if they are greasy, I'll send them back)
12 Crimson lake, small tubes
2 Carmine small tubes
4 Prussian Blue, small tubes
4 Cinnabar green, small tubes

2 Orange Lead
6 Emerald Green
10 lead flake white large tubes
Assortment of palette knives, all sizes, please!

With love, ever yours,
Vincent.

"...ever yours, Vincent." And now he was ever mine, and mine alone. Everyone is gone, and in a few short years, I will be gone too.

I am an older gentleman, and it is time for me to make my own contribution. Despite all my previous bluster, I made a promise, and I kept it.

I gave Vincent, Theo, and Johanna, my family, their final due and created the Van Gogh Museum in Amsterdam. It is a wonderful museum. We are all there.

What was well done, will always remain, forever, well done.

The End

AUTHOR'S NOTE

Thank you to Caitlin Alexander, Rebecca Cremonese, and Gina Panettieri for their help, and also to my friends Linda Elkin, Constanza Mallol and Susan Millican.

If there is any doubt it was Johanna who hung Vincent's star, and we haven't made the case, here is an excerpt from Susan Alyson Stein's wonderful book, "Van Gogh, a Retrospective."

The plans Theo initiated in the months that followed to ensure his brothers legacy produced little more in the way of response. The hopes Theo pinned on Durand-Ruel for exhibition space and on potential biographers Aurier and Gachet all came to nothing. Durand-Ruel refused, Aurier died in 1992, and Gachet apparently lost interest. With Theo's own demise just three months after Vincent's in the early 1890's Van Gogh might indeed have been shrouded in utter silence were it not for the efforts of an interested few and for the gumption of Theo's widow, Johanna van Gogh-Bonger.

What is factual and not regarding the large plot elements in the novel, as best I know --

Johanna was fluent in a number of languages and did some translating in London and Amsterdam, at some point and worked as a schoolteacher in Utrecht. Jo was introduced to Theo by her brother, Andries, a close friend of Theo's. Theo proposed quickly, but Jo was skeptical. Over a year later they married and lived in Paris. They had a son, Willem. She traveled to Paris but didn't work at the

Paris Expo. Jo published Vincent's letters and a memoir of Vincent, she ran a boarding house in Bussum, Holland, for a time. There are references from Johanna's diary in the Bullfinch edition. In those brief diary entries, she describes moving to Bussum in 1891, taking in boarders and completing translations while working to hang Vincent's star.

In 1903 she moved to a larger house in Amsterdam. She was the champion of Vincent's legacy and orchestrated his posthumous rise to fame. She did become a founding member of the Women's Socialist Party in Holland and was generally active in the early feminist efforts. Johanna remarried and was widowed at once more. She married Johan Cohen Gosschalk, in 1901, who was several years younger. I also found references to a possible affair she had with the painter Isaac Israels, who painted her portrait in 1925, the year of her death. She moved to New York in 1916 to expand Vincent's paintings' reach into America and translate his letters into English. She returned to Amsterdam in 1919. Jo moved Theo's remains from Holland to France to lie next to Vincent's. As far as I know she never suffered with syphilis, she died when she was 64 of Parkinson's disease. The Van Gogh Museum has Jo's journals and diaries.

Vincent—his life and art—is the subject of countless books. His letters, which are the source of so many insights into his life, are found in several new and old volumes and now online collections, they are ubiquitous throughout all his literature. His innovations in drawing and painting, his love affairs, travels, and thoughts about life and painting are generally taken from those sources listed above. The two love affairs in this book with Clasina and Margot are well documented in the letters. His relationship with Paul Gauguin and Paul's unique character and legacy have been written about extensively. Much of Vincent's dialogue and thoughts are inspired by his letters, which, as previously mentioned, have been extensively reproduced in different volumes, art journals, and online sources. Some phrases are loosely reproduced, others are original and inspired by his thoughts. Some passages blend both fragments of his thoughts with original content. The sources I used were listed above. *The Complete Letters of Vincent van Gogh*, Johanna's original translations by Bullfinch Press, was the catalyst for this novel. Vincent's early reputation as an "insane phenomenon" is well known in history. However, the phrase "insane phenomenon" is from Paul Signac, again found in the Stein retrospective.

It is common understanding that Vincent and Theo were very close. Theo was his champion and was at Vincent's side at his death. Both died within three months of the other, first Vincent's suicide and then Theo from syphilis. It is generally written Vincent felt tremendous guilt over the financial cost he was causing Theo, contributing to his suicide. However, there are more recent theories surrounding Vincent's death. "Loving Vincent," the fabulous, animated feature deals a murder hypothesis. Theo felt tremendous despair and collapsed shortly after the death of Vincent. Theo did attack Jo and the baby, during a delusional fit caused by his advanced syphilis. He died at a syphilis ward in Utrecht.

There are many theories as to Vincent's actual mental health -- manic depression, bipolar, lead poisoning, absinthe alcohol poisoning, alcoholism, epilepsy—there is a long list of theories and potential posthumous diagnoses. *The Yellow House*, by Milton Gaylord, contains a long discussion of the possibilities. However, his jealously toward Johanna is likely fiction. It did appear that Vincent's spiral downward coincided with the break with Gauguin and Theo's marriage to Jo. It appears Vincent and Jo may have met only a few times. There are many written rumors regarding a potential fight Jo and Vincent may have had while he stayed in Paris. Jo never wrote of one. Vincent stayed with Johanna and Theo in Paris toward the end of his life and left the household earlier than expected after what appears to have been a short chaotic visit, killing himself a few months later. Gachet did sketch Vincent and there is the excellent

"Leaving Vincent" by Carol Wallace offers a compelling account of the Gachet-Vincent relationship and suicide.

Theo was a champion of modern art and was well regarded in his time. The Van Gogh family had a generational history in selling art, Uncle Cent was another well-known art dealer. Theo was Gauguin's art dealer, Monet's for a time, and many other famous impressionist and modern painters as well.

The subplot surrounding Johanna, Aline, Mrs. Gauguin, and Gauguin are inventions. Though it is well known Paul left his family for a painting career, traveling extensively. Paul had several children, some he barely saw. He is a large figure in art history both for his contributions and personality.

Willem was at the forefront of the creation of the Van Gogh Museum and lectured and wrote about Vincent, his mother, and became a champion of Van Gogh. He was nick-named The Engineer because he was an engineer.

Emile is inspired by the real-life painter Emile Bernard and close friend and champion of Vincent. Henri Toulouse Lautrec character is again based on art history lore, and he also died tragically young. His mother did open a museum of his work in his hometown in Toulouse, France.

Johanna's brother, Andries, sometimes seen in print as Andre and Dries, was a close friend of Theo's and collected art. He did leave behind an impressive collection of modern art. Johanna had several other siblings I didn't mention.

Although Vincent and Theo had more siblings, Anna is a fictionalized composite. For instance, one of Theo's sisters did stay with Johanna during her later pregnancy.

As for Richard Roland Holst, he was a painter and writer, and did write that piece of nasty about Jo, after working with her on an exhibit. But otherwise, the rest of his portrait is purely fictional and sorry if I offended.

Fleur is fictional.

The discussion of Durand-Ruel, but attributed to Theo in this novel, and their innovations in selling modern and impressionist art is from the book *Inventing Impressionism*.

Liberties were taken with some dates and facts. For instance, Vincent's relationship with Clasina was earlier than 1887. Also regarding Clasina, there are confusing references—either she had one or two children. *The Potato Eaters* was painted in 1885. *And this is a work of fiction.*

SUGGESTED READING

According to Claire Cooperstein, who wrote an extraordinary epistolary novel about Johanna (1995 Scribner "Johanna".) Johanna's diary is in the Van Gogh Museum and is available for research. I recommend the late Ms. Cooperstein's book, and it is quite a different 'take' on Jo, and meticulous in its depiction of turn of the century Holland and customs.

Gaylord, Martin. *The Yellow House*. Houghton Mifflin Company, a Mariner Book.

Heterbrugge, Jorn. *Vincent van Gogh -- 1853–1890*. Parragon.

Hodge, Susan. *Gauguin, His Life and Works in 500 Images*. Lorenz Books, Anness Publishing Ltd.

Homburg, Cornelia, ed. *Van Gogh Up Close*. New Haven, CT -- Yale University Press.

Jullian, Philippe. *Montmartre*. Phaidon.

Kendall, Richard. *Van Gogh's Masterpieces from the Van Gogh Museum*. Amsterdam.

Patry, Sylvie, ed. *Inventing Impressionism -- Paul Durand-Ruel and the Modern Art Market*. National Gallery Company, London, Distributed Yale University Press.

Pfeiffer, Ingrid, and Max Hollein, eds. *Esprit Montmartre -- Bohemian Life in Paris around 1900*. Frankfurt -- Hirmer.

Stein, Susan Alyson, ed. *Van Gogh, a Retrospective*. New York -- Hugh Lauter Levin Assoc., Inc.

Suh, Anna. *Vincent van Gogh, a Self Portrait in Art and Letters* New York -- Dog and Leventhal Publishers.

Thomson, Belinda, ed. *Gauguin -- Maker of Myth*. Princeton -- Princeton University Press.

Welsh-Ovcharov, Bogomila. *Van Gogh in Provence and Auvers*. Beaux Arts Editions.

Van Gogh, Vincent. *The Complete Letters of Vincent van Gogh*. 3 vols. Bulfinch Press Book, Little, Brown and Company.

Van Gogh-Bonger, Jo. *A Memoir of Vincent van Gogh*. Pallas Athene.

Leaving Van Gogh, Carol Wallace

CPSIA information can be obtained
at www.ICGtesting.com
Printed in the USA
LVHW110952130722
723410LV00008B/16/J

9 781665 720359